THE BURNABY EXPERIMENTS

STEPHEN GILBERT was born in Newcastle, Co. Down in 1912. He was sent to England for boarding school from age 10 to 13 and afterwards to a Scottish public school, which he left without passing any exams or obtaining a leaving certificate. He returned to Belfast, where he worked briefly as a journalist before joining his father's tea and seed business. In 1931, just before his nineteenth birthday, Gilbert met novelist Forrest Reid, by that time in his mid-fifties. Reid's numerous novels reflect his lifelong fascination with teenage boys, and he was quickly drawn to Gilbert; the two commenced a sometimes turbulent friendship that lasted until Reid's death in 1947. Reid acted as mentor to Gilbert, who had literary aspirations, and ultimately depicted an idealized version of their relationship in the novel *Brian Westby* (1934).

Gilbert's first novel, *The Landslide* (1943), a fantasy involving prehistoric creatures which appear in a remote part of Ireland after being uncovered by a landslide, appeared to generally positive reviews and was dedicated to Reid. A realistic novel, *Bombardier* (1944), followed, based on Gilbert's experiences in the Second World War. Gilbert's third novel, *Monkeyface* (1948), concerns what seems to be an ape, called "Bimbo," discovered in South America and brought back to Belfast, where it learns to talk. *The Burnaby Experiments* appeared in 1952, five years after Reid's death, and is a thinly disguised portrayal of their relationship from Gilbert's point of view and a belated response to *Brian Westby*. His final novel, *Ratman's Notebooks* (1968), the story of a loner who learns he can train rats to kill, would become his most famous, being twice filmed as *Willard* (1971; 2003).

Gilbert married his wife Kathleen Stevenson in 1945; the two had four children, and Gilbert devoted most of his time from the 1950s onward to family life and his seed business. He died in Northern Ireland in 2010 at age 97.

BERTHOLD WOLPE (1905-1989) designed the jacket cover for *The Burnaby Experiments*. Wolpe was one of the best-known book designers of the twentieth century and was responsible for a number of typefaces, including Albertus, and designed more than 1,500 dust jackets and book covers for Faber and Faber between 1941 and 1975, many of which are considered classics.

Other books by Stephen Gilbert

The Landslide
Bombardier
Monkeyface
Ratman's Notebooks

Also available from Valancourt Books

The Garden God
by Forrest Reid

The Tom Barber Trilogy
by Forrest Reid

An Air that Kills
by Francis King

The Book of Life
by C. H. B. Kitchin

THE

BURNABY EXPERIMENTS

an account of the life and work
of John Burnaby and Marcus Brownlow

by

STEPHEN GILBERT

With a new preface by Patricia Craig

𝕶𝖆𝖓𝖘𝖆𝖘 𝕮𝖎𝖙𝖞:
VALANCOURT BOOKS
2012

PREFACE

The Burnaby Experiments, Stephen Gilbert's fourth novel, was published in 1952. It is in itself something of an experiment, dealing as it does with the difficult subject of psychic translocation, but presenting it, with all its presumptions and technicalities, in an immensely readable and engaging way. It makes for an unforgettable narrative.

The book has a framing device. Gilbert's central character is called Marcus Brownlow, and *The Burnaby Experiments* is written, as it were, by Marcus's (unnamed) literary executor and inheritor of his papers. The main part of the story—which the "editor" has changed from a first-person to a third-person account—concerns Marcus's somewhat fraught association with a strange and redoubtable old gentleman called Mr. Burnaby. Before the two get together, though, a couple of episodes from Marcus's schooldays come into the picture. At his minor public school in England, the otherwise undistinguished Irish boy exhibits one startling and not altogether auspicious trait, an ability to predict the future in some of his dreams. This untoward ability, with accompanying contretemps, sets the scene for much of what's to follow.

Once his schooldays are over, Marcus finds himself at something of a loose end back home in 1930s suburban Belfast, in Northern Ireland. From his state of vocational uncertainty he is plucked by millionaire Burnaby, a fellow precognition specialist, and installed in a large old house in County Donegal with a martello tower at one end of it. Here the "experiments" of the title are carried out, under Mr. Burnaby's direction. It is largely a matter of concentration. "'It's like learning to swim, or like the children learning to fly in Peter Pan,'" Marcus's instructor tells him. "'First you'll have to learn to move about the room without your body. . . .'"

A tall order, perhaps; but Marcus is an enthusiastic participant, at least to begin with. Gradually he comes to resent his mentor's demand for total commitment on his protégé's part. And once the prospect of a happy and unremarkable life—marriage, a family, the ordinary entertainments of youth—is held out to Marcus, it becomes clear that a dangerous clash of loyalties is impending.

In this novel, autobiography and invention converge, to exhilarating effect. Stephen Gilbert has taken an aspect of his own life, his sometimes difficult friendship with the much older Northern Irish writer Forrest Reid, and subjected all its vexations and complexities to the transforming power of fiction. John Burnaby is Forrest Reid magnified, with many of Reid's characteristics transferred intact to the page, down to his abruptness, his taste in literature (Henry James, Arthur Machen), and other emphatic opinions. Most of the details of Burnaby's background—"He belonged to a North of Ireland commercial family"—are identical with Forrest Reid's.

If it's not altogether an affectionate portrayal, it is none the less very striking. There is also a slight element of tit-for-tat about it. Forrest Reid famously inserted the real-life Stephen Gilbert into a central position in his own novel of 1934, *Brian Westby*. Gilbert suffered a good deal of unease on account of this fictional version of himself, though the strong friendship between the two authors survived the ensuing friction. Gilbert held off with his retaliation— if that's what it was—until after Forrest Reid's death in 1947. He knew how much he owed to the older writer, but at the same time there were things he simply had to get out of his system, including his annoyance at Reid's incessant attempts to impose his own ideas on his younger fellow author. If, however, in this particular instance, resentment or exasperation drove Stephen Gilbert's literary impulse, we should be grateful for its outlet in the wonderfully original and intriguing *Burnaby Experiments*.

All Stephen Gilbert's novels are concerned to some degree with the enlargement of life by fantasy: even the most realistic of them, *Bombardier* (1944), achieves a kind of surreal quality with its deadpan approach to the exigencies of active service in wartime. But *The Burnaby Experiments* is perhaps the most vividly realized. It is also very funny, before an elemental darkness enters in. Take

Marcus's first journey from Belfast to Donegal, in the company (as he supposes) of an old school friend named Caldwell. Marcus's increasing bewilderment at Caldwell's mad and mystifying antics along the way is conveyed with aplomb. ". . . [T]he crowds seemed to confuse Caldwell. Everyone walked straight at him, and to avoid collisions he kept skipping backwards and forwards in the most extraordinary fashion."

Extraordinary indeed. "It took them ten minutes to reach Donegall Square", the passage goes on—an excessive amount of time only if you're familiar with the route they're following. Among the incidental pleasures of this novel is its naming of local places and landmarks—Gibson's Corner, the Albert Clock, the flower sellers outside Mullan's bookshop—as its author goes about evoking a bygone, inter-war Belfast, with its whirring trams and buses, its constant faint smell of the Lough. And then he does the same for Donegal, all heathery hills and grey outcrops of rock, and the yellow glow of oil-lamps shining in cottage windows. Along with his other assets, Stephen Gilbert is endowed with a vibrant descriptive gift. And along with his other activities—as a businessman, CND activist and *pater familias*—he produced a small but distinctive body of work, highly individual in its concerns and techniques, and embodying a unique voice.

PATRICIA CRAIG
November 21, 2012

A leading literary critic and anthologist, Patricia Craig regularly contributes to the *Independent*, *London Review of Books*, *Times Literary Supplement*, *Irish Times* and *New Statesman*, and has appeared on various television and radio programmes.

She is the author of *Brian Moore: A Biography* (Bloomsbury, 2002) and has edited many anthologies, including *The Oxford Book of Ireland* (Oxford University Press, 1998), *The Rattle of the North* (Blackstaff, 1992), *The Belfast Anthology* (Blackstaff, 1999) and *The Ulster Anthology* (Blackstaff, 2006).

THE BURNABY EXPERIMENTS

ACKNOWLEDGEMENTS

My thanks are due to the following:

Messrs. Molyneux & Wright, Solicitors, Dublin;

George Baker, Esq., M.A., Headmaster of Gidley Grammar School, formerly assistant master at Cranlow School;

Dr. R. A. Slade, M.A., D.Litt. (Hon.), Headmaster of Cranlow School; and above all to

Mr. and Mrs. Conway, Malin, Malone Road, Belfast, and to Miss Conway, without whose assistance this book could not have been written.

INTRODUCTION

I was at school with a boy called Marcus Brownlow. His nick-name was Screwey. We were never exactly friends, though for a period, when we were both in the lower school, I saw a good deal of him. Later on I lost touch with him. He was one of those boys who never really succeed at school. No one notices when they leave. Like old soldiers in the song they simply fade away.

I never noticed when Marcus Brownlow left. It was only when I came to write this book that I discovered he had left two terms before me, at Easter 1928. Yet, in the interval, I had often thought of him. I used to wonder vaguely what had happened to him; but I made no inquiries.

Then, in December 1937, I received a letter from a firm of solici-tors in Dublin, informing me that he was dead, and that he had left me ten thousand pounds on condition that I agreed to act as his literary executor. They added, however, that the will in which this and several other bequests had been made was invalid—not having been witnessed, but that the "heirs at law" had "decided to honour what were without doubt the wishes of the deceased". The letter added that so far as the solicitors were aware the late Mr. Brown-low's literary activities had not been extensive.

I accepted the appointment. At that moment I would have done a good deal for *one* thousand pounds let alone ten. I went to Dublin and called on the solicitors, Messrs. Toole, Delaney & Fitzgerald. I had a long interview with Mr. Delaney, the head of the firm. He said that so far they had come across no literary remains whatever, but that if they did they would immediately send them to me. He wanted to know what Screwey had been like at school and I found I could remember a good deal more than I would have thought. In return for my information Mr. Delaney told me all he could about Screwey's life, from the time he left school till the time of his death.

It appeared that for some years Screwey had been a sort of sec-retary-companion to an eccentric millionaire called John Burnaby.

Actually I had heard of John Burnaby. My father and other men of his generation would speak of him sometimes with a sort of envious admiration. I knew that he had made a fortune on the stock exchange in the early nineteen-hundreds, though I had never been quite clear as to how it had been done.

Mr. Delaney didn't know how it had been done either. He said that it hadn't been until after his retirement that Mr. Burnaby had become a client of theirs. He had retired quite early in life and for many years had lived alone, except for a few servants, in a sort of castle in one of the wildest parts of Donegal. From 1929 until Mr. Burnaby's death in 1935 Screwey had lived there with him, and he had continued to live there by himself for all that remained of his own life.

To me it sounded as if Screwey had had a very uninteresting time, but I wasn't quite certain. At Shellborough he had been obscure, unimportant, a dud at both games and work: yet I could remember one week when he had been the most talked-of boy in the school: something quite inexplicable happened and he was at the centre of it, was the cause of it indeed, if such a thing could be said to have a cause. One or two of the facts Mr. Delaney gave me about him also seemed quite inexplicable—as if under all the dullness there had been going on an exciting, secret life.

I left Dublin a good deal puzzled. There were several ways in which Screwey might have got to know that I was writing. What I couldn't understand was why he had appointed a literary executor if he had never done any writing himself.

I had been at home about a week when I received a flat square parcel, of a shape very familiar to unsuccessful authors. By the same post came a somewhat apologetic letter from Mr. Delaney. "I am afraid your position of literary executor is going to prove less of a sinecure than we had anticipated," he wrote. "Under separate cover I am posting you a manuscript which we discovered yesterday. Whether it was intended or is suitable for publication you will no doubt be able to inform us when you have read the work. We shall be glad if you will give the matter your attention."

I immediately jumped to the conclusion that the book was a novel. It was handwritten, and somehow I thought that I would find it tedious reading. Obviously, however, I had to read it: so I began at once. I had read three or four pages before I realized that the book was not a novel told in the first person, but Screwey's autobiography.

This aroused my interest. I found too that his writing was perfectly legible. Except for meals I read straight through the book till I reached the end. It was a long book—about two hundred thousand words I should say—and I found it enormously interesting. It was completely unsophisticated: it gave the impression of having been written by a child. I couldn't imagine any publisher accepting it. Yet who, after all, was I to talk? None of *my* books had been accepted.

Mistrusting my own judgement, I therefore decided to give the book a trial as it was. I went over the manuscript again, correcting spelling mistakes and obvious slips. Then I had it typed and sent it to a large firm of publishers in London.

After two months it came back, with the following letter:

Dear Sir,

After careful consideration, we have decided not to make an offer to publish your book. We return your manuscript herewith.

Yours faithfully,

––––––––––

I always gave my own books three chances and I felt it only fair to do the same with Screwey's. But it was no good: the other two publishers whom I tried also rejected it.

At first I didn't know what to do. I felt that as I was taking the legacy I was obliged to do everything in my power to get the book published. I could of course have paid for its publication; but I thought that a book brought out at the expense of the author, or of the author's executor, would have little chance of success. Somehow or other I had to get it accepted in the ordinary way by a reputable publisher.

I decided to edit it and rewrite it. In the meantime several other manuscripts had come to light and been posted on to me by Mr. Delaney. These consisted of a journal written by Mr. Burnaby, and a mass of notes, some in Screwey's handwriting, some in Mr.

Burnaby's. They had been found in an old oak chest in an attic room in the house in Donegal. I worked at them for over a year. I visited Belfast and Donegal, and interviewed everyone I could find who had known Screwey or Mr. Burnaby. Eventually I produced a book of about a hundred thousand words which was a sort of digest of the notes and of the two journals. In the summer of 1939 I sent it to a publisher. After two months it was returned—rejected. As before I tried two more publishers: the result was exactly the same. By this time the war had broken out and after the third rejection I put the manuscript away.

For nearly nine years I did nothing about it. Occasionally I remembered it and felt vaguely guilty. Early in 1948 I got it out again and re-read it. It struck me that the reason I hadn't been able to get it published was that publishers simply didn't believe it, and were not prepared to put forward as a serious work something which they regarded as no more than fantasy. One course only remained open to me, to rewrite the book as a novel and send it out once more.

Well, here it is. I have changed the names of all the characters. I would only add that none of those characters is fictitious, that all bear as lively a resemblance as I can give them to living persons, or to persons who were living during the period covered by the book.

CHAPTER I

MARCUS awoke very gradually. He was hardly conscious of wakening. He passed from one dream state to another, from night dreams to day dreams. The night dreams seemed real, but in the day dreams he could see a more ordinary world in the background—a tall mahogany wardrobe, faces in the wall-paper, the spray of flowers painted across the top left-hand corner of the mirror on the dressing-table. All these and the battered brass knobs on the big iron bed were only half familiar. For this was the spare room; he had been moved in here temporarily while the night nursery was being papered and painted.

In the morning the nursery was brighter than this, with the early sun glowing warmly on the yellowish brown blinds. There were blinds in the spare room too, but it was on the opposite side of the house and did not get the sun until the evening.

Marcus had soft, black, lustreless hair: it looked rather long and tousled on the white pillow. His cheeks were pale and fat. His eyes were a very dark blue. He had long black eyelashes and very black eyebrows. He was six.

His eyes wandered round the room from the wardrobe to the marble-topped wash-stand, along the mantelpiece to the dressing-table and the windows. Was it nearly time to get up, he wondered. He had been told not to get up till Daddy called him. He listened; the house was silent.

What if Grannie came now? No one would hear the bell: no one would go to the door. Grannie would wait a little. Then she would think they were all on their summer holidays and she would tell the cabman to drive away again.

The more Marcus thought of this the more anxious he became. He thought of Grannie's disappointment, and of how disappointed Mammy would be. Gradually he forgot the injunction about not getting up: the picture of Grannie on the doorstep became more and more vivid.

He slipped out of bed, and without thinking of his dressing-gown or bedroom slippers opened the door on to the landing. On the landing it was much darker than in the bedroom, though not too dark to see. He glanced at the closed doors, the stairs leading up, the stairs leading down. . . . Everything had a hushed air. He tiptoed out and sticking his head through the banisters looked down at the hall. The carpet felt soft and pleasant to his bare feet. He could see only the back part of the hall with the step down to the kitchen door. He remembered the terrible scene last week, when Maggie, the house-parlourmaid, had tripped over the step and spilled the whole tray of breakfast things across the hall. Most of the china had been broken. Mammy had been very angry and Maggie had fainted. Marcus had seen it all from here by putting his head between the banisters just as he was doing now.

Seeing it all over again made him forget Grannie for a little, but soon he remembered her and listened for the bell: it didn't ring. He waited for a minute or two—for ages it seemed: perhaps the bell had gone out of order again. He stole down the stairs feeling a little frightened of the dark corners and of the quietness.

In the hall he hesitated. The sun was pouring through the panes in the top part of the front door, but they were of frosted glass, and anyhow he wasn't tall enough to be able to see through them. He was about to go into the drawing-room to look out from there when he remembered the letter-box, and skipping across to it he lifted up the flap. There was nobody there; the sun shone down through the trees on the glistening, dewy lawn. A solitary thrush tugged at a recalcitrant worm.

Marcus watched till the worm had lost its battle. Then he let the flap down again and started back towards the stairs. In the first patch of sunlight he stopped to let the warmth soak up through the soles of his feet. When the first patch no longer felt warm he stepped to another. After he had stood for a little on all the patches of sunlight he began to feel cold and decided to return to bed.

On the landing he ran straight into Cook. Cook wasn't usually a tidy person. She was fat, with red hair, and big, coarse, freckled hands; but Marcus had never seen her like this. Her hair was down and her feet were bare. Her apron and her stockings hung over her left arm: in one hand were her shoes: in the other was the kitchen alarm clock, looking as if it had suffered a good deal from ingratitude. Cook was sleepy and cross: it was her morning for doing the range. She hated that range: she'd broken it once and she'd a good mind to break it again.

"Mind where you're going," she said grumpily; and then, "Where've you bin? Ye're cold as ice."

"I went to see if Grannie was there," Marcus explained.

"Yer Grannie?" Cook looked surprised. "Sure isn't yer Grannie in Newcastle where she always is?"

"She's coming up today," Marcus informed her.

"Comin' up today, is she?" Cook repeated angrily. "They could 'a' told me, couldn't they?—and I'd 'a' had somethin' for her. That's the way: they never tell Cook anything, so they don't."

A door opened and Daddy came out. He was sleepy-looking too. He had on a hairy dressing-gown and hairy bedroom slippers. "What's all this about?" he demanded.

Cook reddened. "It's me corns, sir," she answered. "They're that throublesome in the mornin' it's murther to draw on me shoes."

"And what are *you* doing, Marcus?"

"I went to see if Grannie was here yet."

"Grannie!"

Mr. Brownlow knew as little about Grannie's coming as Cook. However he didn't ask many questions. He wished Cook "Good morning" and hustled Marcus back to bed. "Now stay there," he ordered, "and don't get up till I tell you."

Daddy returned to his room. Mrs. Brownlow had fallen asleep again, but in climbing into bed he managed to awaken her. "You didn't tell me your mother was coming," he grumbled.

"She's not," Mrs. Brownlow replied. "At least it's the first I've heard of it, and I didn't ask her."

"Marcus seems to know all about it," Mr. Brownlow said.

Mrs. Brownlow yawned. "The child's full of notions. He dreamt it, I suppose."

Mr. Brownlow felt a little aggrieved, particularly as he wasn't certain if he had anything to be aggrieved at. He pulled the sheet over his head and wondered if he would be able to get to sleep again before it was time to get up.

Marcus of course *had* dreamt it. Nevertheless he was right about Grannie. She was just in time for dinner.

CHAPTER II

WHEN Marcus was nine he was sent to a preparatory school in Cheshire. He was probably as happy as most small boys at boarding-schools, but at times he was extremely homesick.

During his first term he slept in what was called "The Kids' Dorm" with four other boys of about the same age as himself. They went to bed at half-past six and at seven Matron turned out the lights. Talking after lights-out was forbidden, but as soon as the sound of Matron's footsteps had died away in the passage conversation would break out as if no one had had a chance to say anything all day. Usually after this burst of conversation had subsided someone would tell a story. At first they took it in turns, but soon Marcus became the recognized storyteller of the dormitory. One by one the others would fall asleep. Then Marcus would stop, and lying quite still with his eyes shut he would pretend he was back in his own bed at home.

But sometimes this pretence would be unsuccessful. Sounds from the real world would force themselves upon him and destroy the illusion he was trying to build up: he would hear a bus roaring along the Chester road, or the scraping of a tree against the window-panes, or the stamping feet of the twelve-year-olds as they clattered upstairs to bed. . . .

One night, after all these things had happened, he gave up trying. He had had an unsatisfactory day: in the afternoon he had had a row with Leather minor, and he had received two "Impots" for talking in class. He couldn't even think of home, though he particularly wanted to. He opened his eyes and listened. All the others were asleep, he thought. In a low voice he called their names, "Compton? Dawson? Parsons? Frame? Is anyone awake?" Nobody was, nobody else in the dormitory. He turned over on his other side and huddled close to the wall.

For a moment he lay there, sorry for himself, homesick. . . . The next moment he was floating in the air with the school far below him. He saw the lights of Liverpool in the distance and went to them: he followed the Mersey to its mouth and crossed the dark friendly sea. He came home. It was home as it always was, with his own room and his own bed just where they always were. His bed was not ready for him. The sheets had disappeared and the pillowcase. The mattress was there and some blankets. He nestled down among them and put his head on the naked striped pillow. It was his own, his own bed, his own old bed at home. . . .

In the hurry of the next morning he remembered nothing of this excursion, but that night when he was in bed once more, it all came back to him. It had been a dream, he realized, and at once he wanted to go to sleep in the same way, and dream the same dream. Surely that had been far better than just pretending: it had been the same as going home in a way: perhaps, even, he had really *been* home.

Suddenly, just at the very instant he was wishing for it to happen, it did begin again. He found himself above the school. He floated towards the city, down the course of the river, and across the sea. . . . But this time he didn't go home: he was carried on, past home, past Belfast, towards Derry and the Foyle: and there was somebody with him, somebody he couldn't see, somebody who like himself had left his body behind.

They didn't stop at Derry. They went on over mountains, and lonely lakes and bogs. At last Marcus saw the sea again, a dim, empty sea battering on a rocky shore. Near the shore was a big house with a tower like a castle. Some of the windows were dark, from others came a yellow glow of lamplight. Outside everything was indistinct, the sea, the black, smudgy mountains, the white line of foam where the waves were breaking against the rocks. . . .

Marcus and his companion entered the house. The porch was square and nearly as big as the drawing-room at home. From this they came into a huge hall, dimly lit by a smouldering turf fire, and an oil lamp turned low. The lamp was on an oval oak table near the fire. The far end of the hall was in darkness, so that Marcus received only a vague impression of its extent. A large, grey dog rose from in front of the fire wagging its stumpy tail. It was like an old English sheepdog, with silvery grey hair covering its eyes; but it was a mongrel.

*   *   *

The rest of the dream Marcus could never afterwards remember very clearly. Indeed it was only in scraps that it came back to him at all. In the days that followed he had half-memories of stone-paved corridors, stone stairs and whitewashed walls. . . . He knew that they belonged to his dream, but he couldn't fit them together and remember what he had done after the first few moments in the hall.

He knew that it was real, this house by the sea—real in the sense that if he came back to it in another dream everything would be exactly the same: the porch and the hall would be the same size and the same shape: there would be the same passages, the same tower and the same worn, winding stairs. But he didn't know if the house existed outside his dream. He wasn't even sure if he wanted it to. He felt that he had come in for a secret inheritance and only for so long as it remained locked up in his mind would it be impregnable.

It was very much in his mind. He would have liked to go there every night as soon as he shut his eyes, and remain there till he was summoned back to school by the first bell in the morning. Often he suspected that he did return to it: yet morning after morning he awoke without any certain knowledge that he had actually been there. For a long time he could only be sure of his first visit. That *had* taken place, he knew, but if there were further visits, by morning they had always been buried by a mass of subsequent dreams. In spite of this Marcus found that he was getting to know more and more about the house, the shape of the rooms, the pictures in the hall and the library.

At last, one morning at the beginning of the summer term, Marcus awoke with the whole scene fresh before his eyes, and the sound of waves in his ears. This time he had not actually been in the house itself, but outside in the grounds. He had been standing on a stretch of rough grass near the hall door, slowly scratching an old, grey donkey on the head. He had been looking at the house, white and sleepy in the morning light. For a moment it was all quite clear, the sad, patient donkey, the dew on the buttercups and grass, the house itself. . . .

The voice that awoke him was shrill, startling, and unwelcome. "Get up, you fool, get up. You'll make *me* late too. The others have all gone—we're the last. Come on for goodness' sake." It was Compton, who slept in the next bed. For a moment Marcus gazed at him stupidly. He still saw the dark mountains behind the house, the clear, bright sky above them. . . .

A moment later he was out of bed, searching frantically for his towel. Mr. Cartwright had promised to take them all for a bathe before breakfast. The others would be in the water before him. It might even be time to get out before he arrived. He and Compton tore down the stairs and out across the playing-fields after Mr. Cartwright and the rest of "The Kids' Dorm". They overtook them just at the entrance to the baths.

"I couldn't wake him up, sir," Compton panted. "He was like what do you call him—Rip Van Winkle."

Marcus blinked at them sleepily. Half of him was still in Donegal. If Compton hadn't wakened him, he might never have known. It didn't prove that he went there every night, but it showed that he very likely did—and it had seemed familiar, as if he were accustomed to being there all the time.

As he stood naked on the edge of the pool poised for his dive another memory of it came back to him. He saw for an instant the sun shining with a reddish glow on the sea far out.

Then he dived. He was first in after all. It was cool, delicious and exciting. "It's boiling," he yelled to Compton. "It's boiling hot, I tell you."

CHAPTER III

AFTER this Marcus took more interest in his dreams than ever. He became slightly odd, but many small boys *are* odd, and Marcus's idiosyncrasies did not make him unpopular. He spent four reasonably happy years at his preparatory school: then he went on to Shellborough.

He had come to collect dreams almost as some boys collected stamps, or cigarette cards, or autographs: they were his hobby. He pondered over them when he should have been doing other things, and tried to complete those which he had nearly forgotten. Every day there was a new supply, and the more he thought about them the more he was able to remember.

After he went to Shellborough he formed the habit of waking ten minutes or so before the getting-up bell was due to ring so that he might lie in bed and try to recall the dreams of the past night. He discovered that if he worked backwards, taking them one by one, he could often disinter buried dreams which otherwise he would have forgotten completely. But it was only occasionally that he was able to recollect dreams about the white house with the tower. When he did he would feel that something important had happened and think about that dream for the rest of the day. The other boys called him Screwey: it was not an unfriendly nickname and he didn't dislike it.

One morning early in the Christmas term at the beginning of his second year at Shellborough, Marcus awoke as usual before the bell had rung. The two dreams which he remembered first didn't interest him very much: the third did.

He was sitting in a classroom at Shellborough: in front of him was a blackboard, on which, written in white chalk, were a number of questions. Marcus recognized the handwriting as that of Mr. Butcher, the junior "Maths" master. These were the questions:

(1) What is the compound interest on:

    (a) £186 17s. od. in 9 years at 2½ per cent.

    (b) £167 18s. od. in 14 years at 4½ per cent?

(2) The population of a town is 22,491. Two years ago it was 20,400. Assuming the same annual rate of increase, find the population of the town three years hence.

(3) Find what sums of money invested at compound interest will provide:

    (a) £525 in 12 years at 3½ per cent.

    (b) £5,200 in 7 years at 3 per cent.

(4) In how many years will a sum of money double itself if invested at 5 per cent compound interest?

(5) At what rate per cent will £5,240 amount to £6,430 in 5 years?

Marcus went through them carefully. He didn't know how to do compound interest sums and he wondered why these had come to him. Had his mind made them up all on its own, or had he seen them somewhere and remembered them unconsciously? Perhaps Mr. Butcher had set them for one of the higher forms and left them on his blackboard after the period had ended. Marcus might have come in in the interval and read them over before his own class began. This seemed the most likely explanation, but another idea occurred to Marcus, and though it could hardly be called an explanation, it appealed to him very much. It would be funny, he thought, if these were questions which had never yet been set— the questions for Mr. Butcher's next test, for example.

Marcus didn't believe this—not really—but there had been cases where people had had dreams of the future—like Joseph in the Bible, for instance. Yet he hoped this wasn't one of them. For if this were Mr. Butcher's next test paper there was a catastrophe in store for him—unless of course someone would show him how to do the questions in the meantime. By an effort he again reproduced the scene. He fixed his eyes on the blackboard and began to learn the questions off by heart. Eventually he was sure of them, and then a curious thing happened. A hand, covered with black hair, came up and with a duster wiped out the writing. Marcus recognized the hand. It belonged to Mr. Butcher. The first bell began to ring. The hand and the blackboard vanished. Marcus realized that he had been asleep and had dreamed his dream a second time.

At the first sound of the bell Lewis, the new boy, had jumped up, and before it stopped he was out of the room on his way along the passage to the bathroom. Marcus, by virtue of a year's seniority, could lie on for another five minutes. He snuggled down and luxuriated in the cosiness and warmth of the bed.

The five minutes passed quickly. Marcus got up and shuffled into his bedroom slippers. He wasn't a fat little boy any more. His pyjama trousers didn't reach his ankles. His face had got longer. He looked enviously at Williamson and Ramsay, the two senior boys in the room. Neither of them showed any sign of being awake yet: but he knew they *were* awake. Williamson would get up at ten past seven and Ramsay, the head of the room, at fourteen minutes past. Everyone had to be in the bathroom by a quarter past. That was a school rule which only prefects could disobey.

Marcus went out and shut the door behind him. There were two steps leading down to a dimly lit passage. Coming along this passage towards him was Caldwell. Caldwell was good at maths: perhaps *he* would be able to do the sums. Marcus stood quite still and waited for him: but he didn't look at him. He stared beyond him, seeing once more the blackboard and the questions in Mr. Butcher's writing.

"Hello, Screwey," Caldwell said. "What's happened to you? Have you got stuck there?"

"No," Marcus responded slowly, "I was just wondering something."

They went to the bathroom without further conversation and it was not till they were both together in the Upper Shell classroom after breakfast that Marcus spoke to Caldwell again. "Caldwell," he began in a low voice, "I know what Gory's next paper's going to be." Gory was Mr. Butcher.

Caldwell was sitting on a bench at the back of the room reading the *Daily Mail*. No one else was near him. He looked up unbelievingly. "*How* do you know?" he demanded.

But Marcus wouldn't tell him. "Just I do," was all he would say.

Caldwell went on reading for a little, but presently he looked up.

"Did you see the answers too?" he inquired.

"I didn't *really* see the questions," Marcus replied.

"You mean somebody told you."

Marcus hesitated. "No, I kind of saw them. Look, I'll tell them to you. I haven't got them written down," and he repeated word for word what had been written on the blackboard in his dream.

Caldwell was puzzled. "Are you sure those are right?" he asked. "How did you get seeing them, and how do you remember them so well?"

But now Marcus felt doubts. "Promise you won't laugh," he demanded.

Caldwell was a conscientious boy. "I'll promise not to laugh on purpose."

"And promise you won't tell anyone else—not unless I give you leave."

Caldwell promised.

Marcus looked round hastily. "I dreamed them," he confessed in a whisper. "I dreamed them all in Gory's writing—on a blackboard."

"But people often dream things," Caldwell objected. "It doesn't always mean that what you dream is going to happen. In fact it hardly ever does. Lots of people have dreams. Some people say dreams go by opposites. It's funny all the same that they're about compound interest."

"Why?" Marcus said. "I can't do compound interest."

"It's the next chapter in the book. I read it the other night in prep. I'd like to try those sums. I think *I* might do them."

Marcus was not good at arithmetic. "You mean you taught yourself?" he asked, "—just by reading the book?"

Caldwell ignored this question. "Go and get your writing pad and write them down," he told Marcus. "I want to have a go at them."

The following morning he produced his results and insisted on explaining to Marcus exactly how he had got them. In so doing he taught Marcus almost against his will how to work out problems in compound interest.

"Now," he said when he had finished, "let's put the questions and answers in an envelope and stick it and see what happens. I feel we are going to get that paper after all."

CHAPTER IV

TEN days later Mr. Butcher announced that he was going to teach the Upper Shell "a method of calculating compound interest by means of logarithms."

Marcus would have liked to look round at Caldwell and catch his eye, but he didn't dare. Like every other boy in the junior school he was terrified of Mr. Butcher. When Mr. Butcher said, as he just *had* said, in that soft, slow voice of his, "Pay attention", he expected absolute concentration on every word that he spoke, on every figure he put on the blackboard. No one, not even the dreamiest of boys, ever failed to pay attention to Mr. Butcher. Mr. Butcher caned a great many boys. Most frequently he caned his favourites. His favourites were always boys who were clever at mathematics. He preferred to cane them in white shorts. White shorts were thin and sometimes, with only four strokes of his thin whippy cane, he could draw blood.

He had been wounded in 1916 and when he was in a hurry walked with a thump, thump, thump, which you could hear a long way off. If he was not in a hurry he could move about quite silently. When he was taking "prep", or when his class was doing written work he had a habit of walking between the desks and peering over the shoulder of each boy in turn. On these occasions it was impossible to tell, without looking up, whereabouts in the room he was; and no one ever dared to look up.

He had an ear for prose rhythms and delighted in reading aloud. He could read beautifully. On the few occasions when he took evening prayers he nearly always read the thirty-fifth chapter of Isaiah.

It was said that he hated women.

Outside school his manner towards the boys was friendly, even affectionate. He was popular, and the Upper Shell, whose formmaster he was, was devoted to him. It was in the Upper Shell too that most of his favourites were to be found.

For three weeks they all hammered away at compound interest. Then, one Friday, Mr. Butcher announced that he would give a test the following Monday morning. As a rule, such knowledge would have been quite enough to spoil Marcus's week-end, but on this occasion he was too interested to be frightened.

Monday was a dark, gloomy day, with the rain pouring down. Maths was the second period—just after morning prayers—and the Upper Shell awaited Mr. Butcher's arrival with some apprehension. This did not mean that they were idle. Mr. Butcher always set a certain amount of work in advance. Every boy had started to work the instant the period began.

They had been working for perhaps fifteen seconds when the door swung open and Mr. Butcher stumped up the room. When he was half-way to his desk the door slammed behind him. No one looked up: no one said, "Good morning, sir". To do either was against Mr. Butcher's rules.

For perhaps a minute there was no sound from inside the classroom. Marcus heard the rain splashing outside. Someone ran past the windows. Then there was a sudden sharp crack from the hot pipes as if they were going to burst. From the left came a slight rustle. The senior boy in the class was distributing sheets of blank paper. Mr. Butcher picked up the blackboard which had been propped against the wall and put it on the easel. Marcus didn't see this, but he heard the easel rattle and knew what was going on. Mr. Butcher always wrote out his questions beforehand, and left the blackboard against the wall with the blank side outwards.

"Shut all your books, except your log tables.

"Answer the questions on the board using the paper provided.

"Write your name on every piece of paper you use.

"You may begin."

Mr. Butcher spoke very slowly, leaving a long deliberate pause between each sentence.

Marcus glanced at the board with a little thrill of anticipation. They *were* his questions he saw immediately, and in spite of his fear of Mr. Butcher, he couldn't help smiling. It was wonderful. Suddenly he noticed that Mr. Butcher was looking at him and his smile vanished.

At any rate, he thought, he had forgotten how Caldwell had done them. So whatever happened his conscience could be clear. If he did get the sums right it would be by his own efforts. He looked at the first question: it seemed very difficult. It would be awful if he wasn't able to do it after all. But in an instant he knew how to do it. Slowly he began to put down the figures. It was the same with the next question, and the next. He worked steadily and confidently. He hardly noticed the time passing, and the ringing of the bell took him by surprise. He was sorry to have to stop, for he was in the middle of the second last question and in another two or three minutes could have finished it. He had never got on so well in a maths paper before.

Outside the rain was over and he found Caldwell waiting for him. "I say," Caldwell exclaimed, "that was *funny*, wasn't it? I suppose you got them *all* right."

Marcus felt slightly uncomfortable. "I didn't remember how to do them," he said.

"You mean, you couldn't do them?"

"I couldn't at first," Marcus replied. "I mean I had to think. I mean I didn't remember how you'd done them before. I worked out how to do them myself."

"Bilge," Caldwell retorted. "You had to think before you remembered how *I'd* done them—that was all."

Marcus didn't like this idea. He hadn't felt as if he were remembering when he was doing the paper. He had felt as if he were working everything out himself. He had been; he was sure. "It wasn't cribbing," he declared defensively.

"Oh no," Caldwell responded immediately, "it wasn't *cribbing*."

They looked at each other uneasily.

"All the same," Caldwell began again, "it gave us a sort of advantage. I could have done them all of course—after all I did them before—but I couldn't have done them so quickly. I did them all and I'm sure I got them *all* right."

"I did four," Marcus said. "I don't know if I got them right or not. I began the fifth, but I hadn't time to finish it."

"I bet you got the third one wrong."

"Why? Did you have it wrong last time?"

"Yes—oh goodness! There'll be a row now all right."

"What?" Marcus demanded.

Caldwell looked at him for a moment without replying. Then he smiled dismally. "I made the same mistake this time and corrected it."

"Maybe I got it right," Marcus suggested hopefully.

Caldwell laughed. "Maybe you did."

The bell started to ring once more. The break was over. The next period was Latin.

They met again in the long interval at the end of the morning. During the last hour a breeze had got up and the ground seemed reasonably dry. They managed to get hold of a rugby ball and took it to one of the far-away pitches to practise place-kicking. They stood at opposite sides of a pair of goal posts and kicked the ball backwards and forwards. Every now and then however one would come towards the other and a little conference would take place.

"Do you think Gory'll notice?" Marcus inquired the first time.

"Sure to. He always notices everything."

They separated.

On the next occasion it was Caldwell who approached Marcus. "Bet you miss it," he said.

"Bet you I don't."

Marcus placed the ball carefully. He walked back a few paces, turned round, took a short run and kicked. The ball rose nicely, and passed between the posts just scraping the cross-bar on the way. Marcus was pleased.

"Fluke," Caldwell shouted, but though it was now his turn he didn't go after the ball.

"It wasn't a fluke," Marcus retorted, "and the ball's as heavy as lead."

Caldwell paid no attention. "I say, Screwey. What if we went to Gory and told him what had happened?"

"Who'd tell him?"

"We'd both go. You'd better do the telling as it was your dream."

Marcus thought it over. "I'd be funky," he confessed.

Caldwell began to go after the ball. "Maybe we'd better just see what happens," he decided. "After all we can always tell him if he *does* ask us."

CHAPTER V

SEVERAL days passed before Mr. Butcher made any announce-ment about the results of the test paper. Each morning the Upper Shell entered his classroom in a state of nervous expectation. Each morning he stumped up to his desk in exactly the same manner and sat staring straight in front of him for up to five minutes without uttering a word.

But on the Friday morning he spoke as soon as he reached his desk. "Pay attention. I have now corrected the papers which you did for me on Monday last. The results are interesting, though not altogether satisfactory." He paused and looked round slowly. There was dead silence. Even Wheezy Whitaker, who was asthmatic, seemed to have stopped breathing temporarily.

"Some of you, I regret to say," Mr. Butcher went on, "have failed to do yourselves justice. One or two have done very badly indeed. There are two exceptions. First comes Caldwell with ninety-five marks out of a hundred; and second we find our old friend Brownlow with sixty-three. Brownlow, I found your paper most interesting, so interesting that I would like to discuss it with you further. You will stay behind at the end of the period and we will talk it over together."

So he went on through the other boys in the class. Six were instructed to go to his study after dinner, four of them being ordered to change into white shorts for the interview. Only Marcus, however, was to stay behind at the end of the lesson.

The rest of the period was spent in going over the questions and demonstrating how they should have been done. This did not give anyone a chance for dreaming or absent-mindedness. Mr. Butcher stood in front of the blackboard and made different boys tell him what to put down. Most of the questions were done by boys who had got those same questions wrong in the test. They were made to prove that they needn't have got them wrong, that it was simply through carelessness that they had failed.

There was one question which only Caldwell and Marcus had

got right. It was the fourth. When he came to this Mr. Butcher called Marcus to the front. "Do it," he said, and handed Marcus the chalk.

Marcus was scared. He wasn't a bit sure that he *could* do it, with Mr. Butcher peering over his shoulder and everyone staring at him.

Suddenly Mr. Butcher addressed the others. "Go on with the work I set you yesterday," he told them. He turned to Marcus. "Well, Brownlow, I have never eaten a boy yet, though I have caned a good many. Let me see you work out this little problem."

Then Marcus was able to think. He remembered how he had done the question previously. He set to work and very soon had the right answer once again.

"Thank you," Mr. Butcher said when he had finished. "You may go to your place."

"Now," he called to the rest of the class, "look at the board. This is how the fourth question should have been done. Yet only two boys succeeded in doing it—Caldwell and Brownlow. Macdonald, we will see if you can follow their example." He rubbed out Marcus's figures and began to go through the problem line by line.

For once Marcus did not pay complete attention. He tried to *look* attentive, but all the time he was thinking about his coming interview with Mr. Butcher. What would Mr. Butcher ask him? Would he believe the truth if he heard it? But, Marcus reflected miserably, he couldn't really tell the truth, not the whole truth, without implicating Caldwell also.

At last the bell began to ring and a minute or so later Mr. Butcher let the class go. Marcus sat on at his desk. He listened to the others shuffling out. He even envied the six who were to be caned after dinner. Very likely he would be caned too—and he was afraid of being caned, but what frightened him even more was the thought of being cross-examined by Mr. Butcher. Could he conceal from Mr. Butcher that he had seen the questions over a month ago, and that Caldwell had worked them out then and shown him the results?

As the last boy reached the door Marcus got up and walked slowly towards Mr. Butcher's desk. Mr. Butcher was gathering together his papers and putting some of them in a portfolio. He looked up as Marcus drew near. "Ah yes, Brownlow," he greeted him in a soft, friendly voice, "I wanted to have a little talk with you."

His voice was kind and encouraging. He was sympathetic, and Marcus longed to unfold to that sympathy, but he knew that he mustn't. "Yes, sir," he answered warily.

Mr. Butcher smiled slightly. He recognized the guarded tone. His suspicions were justified: there was something to conceal. "Brownlow," Mr. Butcher said, "I may as well tell you at once why I asked you to stay behind. I suspect you of cribbing. In the test last Monday you worked out every question in exactly the same way as Caldwell. In the third you even made the same mistake as he had made. He however corrected his mistake before handing his paper in. You did not. Now, I want a straight answer. Did you crib in that test we went over this morning, or did you not?"

Marcus had been expecting some such question: nevertheless he was horrified. He had never cribbed. He had never even been suspected of cribbing, either here at Shellborough, or at his preparatory school, or even at the kindergarten school he had attended in Belfast. Yet he paused before answering and remembered Caldwell's assurance, "Oh no, it wasn't *cribbing*." "No, sir," he mumbled at last, but he kept his eyes on the ground and avoided Mr. Butcher's glance.

There was a pause. Mr. Butcher was quite evidently not convinced. Yet he was too experienced a schoolmaster to regard guilty looks as certain proofs of guilt. He gazed at Marcus intently for almost a minute. He was puzzled. "How do you account for this sudden access of genius?" he asked.

Two of the prefects passed the window outside. They saw Mr. Butcher and they saw Marcus. They knew how interviews with Mr. Butcher usually terminated and they grinned. "I don't know, sir," Marcus replied dismally.

"You see," Mr. Butcher explained, "I would not have been surprised if you had found the paper difficult. I would not have been disappointed if you had got all your answers wrong. I might not even have found it necessary to cane you, provided of course that I was satisfied that you had done your best and that you had not made any careless mistakes. I never looked on you as a clever boy, Brownlow, but I did think you were honest."

He paused and gazed at Marcus searchingly, so that Marcus put in a "Yes, sir," out of sheer nervousness.

From outside came the sound of footballs being kicked backwards and forwards. One came bouncing up the passage between Mr. Butcher's classroom and the carpenter's shop. Someone came running after it. Marcus knew that the sun was shining, though it didn't shine through the windows of Mr. Butcher's classroom, which were in a north wall.

Mr. Butcher gazed at Marcus thoughtfully. He had strong, almost black eyes. To Marcus they seemed very penetrating eyes: he felt that if he were to look up and meet them Mr. Butcher would know all that was in his mind. And if he had really been dishonest, he thought, with a sad feeling of virtue, he had only to point out that he didn't sit anywhere near Caldwell, that he had had no opportunity to crib. Probably it was only the fact that he didn't say that that kept Mr. Butcher from letting him go—and perhaps believing him. But if he were to be believed he would have to say this soon. All the same he didn't say it.

"Would it surprise you very much," Mr. Butcher went on at last, "to know that all your working was identical with Caldwell's, except that you didn't correct your mistake in the third question and that you didn't finish?"

Marcus hesitated. "I don't know, sir," he responded feebly.

Mr. Butcher looked as if he thought he were getting slightly nearer a solution. "Shall I put it this way?" he demanded. "Did you get any help from Caldwell—or," he added as an afterthought, "from anyone else?"

Marcus didn't know what to tell him. If he told the truth Mr. Butcher most probably wouldn't believe it, and besides to do so would implicate Caldwell. Yet he would have to answer something. "Not . . . not during the test," he stammered.

"Oh!" It was a very round Oh and Mr. Butcher lingered on it and smiled. But his smile gave Marcus no comfort whatever. "You had help beforehand then? You had seen the questions beforehand?"

Marcus felt very miserable. If only he could explain. But what was the good of confessing if you weren't going to be believed—and how could Mr. Butcher believe him? "In a sort of way," he answered.

"In a sort of way," Mr. Butcher repeated rather contemptuously. "That means you *had* seen them. This is most strange, very strange indeed." He stared over Marcus at the dreary, empty room. A football rattled against the wire guard of one of the windows and he frowned angrily. "And when did you first see the questions in a sort of way?" he inquired.

Marcus considered. "About a month ago, sir. No, it must have been more: it was before we began to do compound interest."

"My dear child!" Mr. Butcher exclaimed—and for a moment his voice was quite kindly. "The questions didn't exist a month ago. You are now talking nonsense."

"No, sir," Marcus protested confusedly. "I mean I know, sir. I know it sounds like nonsense, but you see, sir, what happened was I dreamed the questions, sir."

There was no doubt that Mr. Butcher was startled. "Really, Brownlow," he said, "you amaze me." But in a moment he recovered his inquisitorial manner. "And did you dream the answers too, may I ask?"

"No, sir."

"Some other fortunate youth dreamed the answers?"

"No, sir."

For a moment there had been a playful expression on his face, but it vanished. "Who provided the answers?" he asked peremptorily.

Marcus shook his head.

"Was it Caldwell?"

"No, sir."

Marcus hadn't meant to say "No, sir," or rather as soon as he had done so he wished that he had said instead, "I can't tell you who it was, sir." But to correct himself would have been as good as admitting that it had been Caldwell: so he said no more.

"I think this is a matter for the Headmaster," Mr. Butcher decided. "You may go, Brownlow."

CHAPTER VI

MARCUS spent a very miserable day. He thought he had never been so unhappy. He didn't know if Mr. Butcher believed part of his story or none of it. He felt as if he were about to stand his trial on a charge of cribbing. He was frightened and ashamed. Every moment he expected to be summoned to the Head's study. He walked about with his eyes on the ground and held furtive conferences with Caldwell.

Caldwell was almost equally dejected. He wanted to go to Mr. Butcher and tell him about his part in the affair. Marcus had great difficulty in preventing him. "Oh no, don't," he pleaded. "It'll only make it worse for me. You see I told him it wasn't you, an' he'd say I was telling lies."

There was a run that afternoon for the third and fourth games, and Marcus and Caldwell went together. As they jogged along they discussed the situation once more. Caldwell still had the envelope with the questions and answers in it; and he thought that this should be shown to Mr. Butcher at the earliest possible moment. It had never been opened. "That'll be proof," he declared. "We'll tell him we stuck it up the day after you told me your dream and that it hasn't been opened since."

"But he mayn't believe us," Marcus objected. "How'll he know we haven't just stuck it up today—or this week since he gave us the paper."

"The ink will be blacker," Caldwell suggested.

"Ink gets black in a day or two," Marcus retorted, "and anyhow we might have held it in front of the fire."

Besides, he thought, supposing Mr. Butcher and the Head did believe them, they might still consider him guilty of cribbing. After all he had passed off what was really Caldwell's work as his own and gained an unfair advantage over the rest of the class—and if Mr. Butcher hadn't cross-examined him nothing would ever have come out.

Schoolboys are peculiar: often they are extremely cruel to each

26

other. Sometimes they make life nearly unbearable for some boy among them whom they do not even dislike. Yet if any boy is in serious trouble with the masters the others tend to leave him alone. This happened to Marcus. He had told no one but Caldwell about his interview with Mr. Butcher, but by the evening he realized that practically every boy with whom he came in contact knew he was in trouble.

In the dormitory there was usually a good deal of ragging in the half-hour between prayers and lights-out. The boys wrestled with each other or played an adaptation of rugby football called "room-rugger". Usually Ramsay, the head of the room, insisted on everyone joining in. But on this night there was no ragging: the boys lay on their beds talking, or reading books. Marcus had a book propped in front of him, but actually he didn't read much, he stared at the book and moped. If he had been made to rag he might have forgotten his troubles for a little. All the same he was grateful to Ramsay. He had asked no questions and would not have heard the real facts; yet there was a certain extra kindliness in his manner which assured Marcus of his sympathy.

The next morning Marcus was told he had to see the Head in his study that evening at half-past seven, in the interval between first and second "prep". So at twenty-five past seven he went through the green baize-covered door which led to the private part of School House. In the hall, just opposite the study door, was a grandfather clock. For five minutes Marcus stood watching this clock. The second hand jumped a second at a time, the minute hand a minute at a time. When the minute hand had made five jumps and the second hand three hundred jumps Marcus knocked at the door.

He had knocked very quietly and at first he thought he hadn't been heard. He was wondering if he should knock again when the Head opened the door and looked out. "Just wait five minutes, Brownlow," he said. "I've someone else here, who'll be finished in a minute or two." He smiled in a friendly, reassuring way, and closed the door.

Now, with the interview almost upon him, Marcus was more nervous than ever, and the Head's smile puzzled him. Did it mean that everything was going to be all right or had he smiled through absence of mind? He might have been talking to Martin, the Head Boy, about the rugby team and just have forgotten to change his expression. But the Head wasn't absent-minded: perhaps the smile was intended for Marcus after all.

Five minutes went by very slowly, ten minutes . . . fifteen—nine hundred deliberate ticks from the grandfather clock. Then Marcus got the surprise of his life. The study door opened and Caldwell came out.

Caldwell grinned at Marcus and winked, but Marcus was too astonished to say anything, or even to wink back: at the same moment the Head called out loudly, "Come along in, Brownlow. I want to see you." Marcus went in quickly, so as not to keep him waiting.

"Cheer up, Screwey," Caldwell whispered as they passed. "You're not going to get whacked after all."

There was a screen inside the door, and it was not till he got round this that Marcus saw the Head. He was a big man—well over six feet—and the first thing Marcus noticed was that he still looked cheerful and friendly. The fire was blazing.

"Come along in," the Head repeated as Marcus paused at the edge of the screen. "I want to get a good look at you. I've never met a prophet before."

"I'm not exactly a prophet, sir," Marcus responded. "It was just an accident."

"On the contrary," the Head replied, "a prophet is exactly what you are—unless you've got some new tale to tell me. Sit down there. I want to hear all about it from the beginning—just the plain facts. Tell me in the first place, what actually did you dream?"

There was a large leather armchair on each side of the fire. The Head sat in one of these: Marcus sat in the other, and rather haltingly began his story.

"But how did you know they were real questions?" the Head interrupted presently. "I mean questions Mr. Butcher was going to set your class?"

Marcus hadn't known, but the Head's assumption that he had was convincing, and he did not pause to consider it. "I just thought they were," he answered.

The Head accepted this, and Marcus went on. "After breakfast I told someone else who's very good at maths and they . . . . ."

"Caldwell says that you told *him*," the Head broke in again, "and that *he* worked out the answers. Is that correct?"

"Yes, sir."

"You needn't worry about *telling*, or sneaking," the Head put in kindly. "No one is going to get punished. Caldwell has told me all his part in the affair, and now, naturally, I want to hear your side of it."

So Marcus concealed nothing. He even explained how he had come to have the third question wrong when Caldwell had it right.

"Do you have many dreams like that?" the Head inquired when Marcus had finished. "I mean prophetic dreams."

"No, sir."

"Did you ever have one before?"

"No, sir." Then he remembered the dream he had had about his grandmother coming, when he was very small. "Not since I was a kid, sir," he corrected himself—and the Head had to hear all about that too.

"You think a lot about your dreams?" he asked next.

"A good deal, sir—about some of them."

"What sort of dreams?"

"It's just about one dream really, sir—a special dream I have sometimes."

"A recurring dream," the Head said. "I'd like to hear what it's about."

But Marcus had no intention of telling him. "I'd rather not, sir. It's a sort of secret."

The Head seemed to be considering. "Oh well," he assented at last, "I won't press you if it's a secret. But I wouldn't think too much about your dreams. After all, it's *this* world you're in, and presumably you've been sent here for a purpose. If I were you I would try to concentrate on whatever you may have to do in *this* world."

"Yes, sir."

"And now," he concluded, "one word of warning. You've had an unusual experience: no one but a fool would try to pretend that the whole thing was a mere coincidence. You may never have such an experience again: or you may have several such experiences in the course of your life: they may even occur quite frequently.

Whatever you do don't try to exploit them: if you do, they will let you down one way or another." He saw Marcus didn't understand, and continued, "I mean don't try to make money by it; no, nor even a reputation. People who go in for that sort of thing . . . . Well, they find the gift deserts them when they need it most. And then, they don't like disappointing people—or can't afford to disappoint them: they become fakes, charlatans. If you do have supernatural gifts you're better to keep them to yourself.

"There is just one thing more. I imagine you have not had a very happy week since you did the paper on Monday. Is that so?"

"Yes, sir," Marcus agreed. "It's been rotten," he added fervently.

"Well," the Head told him, "I said no one was going to get into a row, but that doesn't prevent me pointing out the error of your ways. You found yourself in an awkward situation: in the first place it was through no fault of your own. You could have got out of it by the exercise of a little moral courage, by telling the truth straight away, as you say Caldwell wanted you to do. But you funked it and the natural result was that before long you became involved in an actual lie—when you denied to Mr. Butcher that you had had any help from Caldwell. The moral is, Tell the Truth straight away. However difficult it appears it will practically always prove less difficult in the long run. And a good general rule for making truth-telling easy is, Never land yourself in situations where you will need to tell a lie."

He stood up and held out his hand. "Good night, Brownlow, and if you happen to have any further dreams about exam papers or anything of that kind, please tell the master concerned, or if you'd rather, tell me. But don't wait till the paper's been given: tell us beforehand."

CHAPTER VII

MARCUS and Caldwell were boxing. They were in the gymnasium at school. There weren't very many people there, but all of them were watching. Marcus knew that the games master was there, and the gym sergeant and six or eight boys who were waiting their turn to box. Probably they were taking part in the school boxing competitions at the end of the Easter term; but it could only have been one of the earlier rounds; otherwise there would have been a bigger audience.

Marcus watched Caldwell's face. It was flushed and pugnacious: his lips were slightly parted and his dark hair fell forward over his forehead. Marcus tried to hit Caldwell's face and as he did so he felt a tremendous affection for Caldwell rising up inside him.

Marcus and Caldwell sat on a bench beside the ring, with a number of other boys. Their own fight was over; another was in progress: everyone was watching it intently. The two boys in the ring wore white gym vests, white shorts, and white gym shoes: their legs were bare. Marcus and Caldwell and all the boys sitting on the bench were dressed in exactly the same way. It was a long bench and there were a good many boys crowded onto it. Marcus was very glad to be sitting next to Caldwell, and Caldwell was glad to be sitting next to Marcus. Between them there was a feeling of tenderness, of affection. . . .

They were all in the ante-room just outside the gym. Marcus was terrified that he would lose Caldwell. Suddenly he began to go. Marcus tried desperately to keep him. It was no use. Caldwell said, "Meet me at Gibson's corner."

*   *   *

Marcus awoke with Caldwell's voice still echoing in his ears: but Caldwell had gone. Marcus had a sense of desolation and tragedy. It was as if he had strayed into heaven, by some back entrance, and after a moment been cast out for ever. He felt miserable and without hope. In his dream everything had been infinitely better, infinitely more real than in the world to which he had awakened. In ordinary life he had not experienced an emotion so deep as the emotion which had pervaded his dream—and it had been a happy emotion. He could feel it in his mind, in his chest, in his stomach. He cherished it, but it melted like dew from a window-pane on a summer morning. It was sad: yet even this sadness was dear to him; he hugged it, and squeezed it to him; but it grew fainter and faded away.

Presently Marcus began to think. He was at home. He was eighteen—nearly nineteen—and he had left school over a year ago. The Caldwell he had seen was a boy of fourteen or fifteen, and he himself had been about the same age.

"Meet me at Gibson's Corner." The words still sounded quite clearly in his ears. It was hard to believe that they had not been actually spoken. Marcus wished that they had been spoken, and that he could return again to that schoolboy world. How carefree and happy it had seemed. But his boyhood had gone: like water it had run through his fingers. He felt old and troubled: he was a man and he still wanted to be a boy.

Yet boyhood was not so very far away. It might just be possible to get back. If he could meet Caldwell at Gibson's Corner, then he would get back. Caldwell had mentioned no time, but all at once Marcus knew that he had to be there at eleven o'clock on that very day.

Immediately he became excited and confused. He'd go. No; it was silly. It was only a dream. All the same he'd go, just to see. And anyhow, it wasn't really silly at all. Why shouldn't this dream come true—like the maths questions at school, and the dream about Grannie long ago?

It was queer about Caldwell. He couldn't be like that now. But Marcus hadn't seen him since he *was* like that. For when Caldwell was fifteen his father had gone bankrupt, and he had been taken away from school.

Another queer thing was that at Shellborough, boys didn't wear gym vests. In competitions they boxed in football jerseys, and at other times in cricket shirts and sweaters. Marcus didn't think he'd ever seen boys wearing gym vests. It was funny that his mind should have invented such a scene.

And with that he thought of the year which had passed since he had left school. So far he had been unable to get a job and to put in time he had been taking classes at a crammer's at Belfast. This, however, was Saturday, and a holiday. If he said he was going into town this morning the rest of the family would ask questions.

Marcus opened his eyes and looked round to see what sort of morning it was. His room was on the west side of the house—not the old house they had lived in when he was small, but a much nicer house into which the family had moved when he was eleven. Marcus propped himself on his elbow, so that he could see into the garden.

It was a lovely, warm May morning with the sun shining. Marcus noticed the pink and white apple blossom, and the dewdrops sparkling everywhere, on cobwebs and leaves, and on the strip of grass below his window.

Beyond the garden was a field, and at the far side of this field was a line of trees. Every morning now before he got up, Marcus would look out at these trees, and at one tree in particular—the tree nearest the left-hand corner of the field. It might have been a beech or a hornbeam or an alder—he didn't know. He had only discovered it recently and it had never occurred to him to examine it more closely. He had never even said to himself "That tree is very beautiful". Yet it was its beauty which made him stare at it. He would stare at it unwinkingly for long periods, half-sitting up in bed. Then he would find that he was cold, and that his right arm had gone to sleep and that his eyes were sore. It wasn't a bushy tree: it was tall, slender and graceful. He could see the buds beginning to open, the first small leaves on its branches—and he envied it. Every year it was young again: it was born again, a child again, a boy again. . . .While he. . . . Every year he was older, and staler, and drier. Every year he was one, quite appreciable step nearer the grave. It made him sad. For years he had been young, young and fresh and innocent—and it had all been wasted. He had never even realized the ephemeral, youthful glory through which he was passing. He had even wanted to be grown up so that he could be free—free and independent. Now he *was* grown up, grown up, dis-illusioned, jobless.

And only a few minutes ago he had been back, in that earlier, brighter world. It was tantalizing, saddening, to think that it had been just a dream, a chance dream which might never be repeated. Very willingly he would have sacrificed all the present, and all his future life as well, to have been allowed to remain in that dream. And it wasn't just that he had been back at school: he hadn't been so fond of school as *that*, after all. Of course it hadn't really been school: it was some other place: the school gymnasium had just been a piece of borrowed furniture in a world where there were no calendars, and no clocks, no summer, no autumn, no winter. . . . A world where it was always spring.

Should he go to Gibson's Corner? He couldn't make up his mind. It would be silly to go. How could he expect to meet Caldwell, and find him just as he had been four years ago? He too must have grown up. He would be the same age as Marcus, or about the same age. And suppose he did appear, either grown up, or as he had been in the dream, what would happen? They had been friendly at school, but it had been quite a casual friendship. After Caldwell had left they had both written once or twice, but very soon the cor-respondence had ceased. Marcus remembered that it was he who was responsible for this: Caldwell had written last—and he had never bothered to reply. Very soon, indeed, he had quite forgotten about Caldwell, and for years he hadn't thought of him at all—till this morning. He didn't imagine that Caldwell had thought much about him either. At any rate there had been nothing emotional about their friendship. Why then had the dream been emotional? Why then did he feel that it was so important?

Mr. Brownlow came in and said that if Marcus didn't get up soon he would be late for breakfast; but Marcus had heard him coming and pretended to be asleep. Mr. Brownlow hesitated for a few moments and presently went out, closing the door softly behind him.

CHAPTER VIII

AS soon as his father had gone Marcus realized that he didn't want to stay in bed a moment longer. His father actually had almost kept him back. He threw off the bedclothes and jumped on to the floor. It was ridiculous the way Mr. Brownlow had behaved—practically ordering him to get up, as if he were still about ten. You couldn't give into that sort of thing, but it was best to resist it diplomatically, and not to hurt anyone's feelings.

Marcus felt full of life and energy, and rather pleased with himself. He snatched up his dressing-gown and without waiting to put it on set off at full speed for the bathroom. On the way he burst into the Shellborough football song, yelling the words at the top of his voice with almost no attention to the tune. He turned on the water for his cold bath and, running hot water into the basin, began to wash.

It was not until after he had had his bath and was drying himself that he remembered that it was his morning for shaving. He examined his face in the mirror, and discovered two or three hairs on his chin and a faint growth on his upper lip. This pleased him. He filled the basin with hot water and got out his shaving kit. He sponged and soaped his face carefully, spending a good deal of time working up a thick, creamy lather. Yet in spite of the hairs he had discovered in the mirror, his razor, when he came to use it, met with disappointingly little resistance. He would have liked to hear a crisp, crackling noise—the sound of a blade mowing through tough, stubbly bristles.

When he had scraped both cheeks, his upper lip, and his chin, he took his razor to pieces, and examined the soap which had gathered on the edge of the blade. It was quite white: there was no sign of hair. Marcus was annoyed. Sometimes he did need to shave every week—and sometimes his beard would hardly grow at all: it was most unreliable. He fitted his razor together again, and peering into the mirror shaved off a little hair from each side of his head just in front of his ears. The soap on the blade was black now all right, but he didn't really feel satisfied. He knew he had cheated.

While he was dressing he thought again about his dream. It was the prospect of meeting Caldwell which had made him get up so suddenly, but really he hadn't quite made up his mind to go to Gibson's Corner. He tied his tie, brushed his hair, put on his jacket, and stood in front of the dressing-table, thinking. In the top left-hand drawer was his Post Office Savings book. He got it out and looked at it. It showed a credit of nine pounds, three shillings and fourpence. The last entry was the withdrawal of two pounds, when he was eleven. It had been used for the purchase of a second-hand bicycle. Since then he had deposited nothing, and withdrawn nothing. He put the book in his pocket. The rest of his money was in a purse. He counted it. There were two shillings and four pennies, a ten-shilling note, and a pound note. He wondered if he would need any money and if what he had would be enough.

He reached the dining-room at a quarter to nine and found that he was last. His father and mother and Margaret, his elder sister, had all evidently been down for some time. His mother and Margaret both said "Good morning," but Mr. Brownlow said, "You're late, Marcus. I don't see why you can't come down at the same time as the rest of us. You'll have to get up when I call you in future."

"I did," Marcus told him. "I had to shave."

"What were you shaving for?" Margaret asked, with a slight emphasis on the word "shaving".

"Because I *had* to," Marcus retorted crossly. "You needn't think *you're* the only one that has a razor."

Margaret wasn't pleased, and for a moment Marcus thought he was going to get into a row. They'd say he was indelicate— or something. He saw his father frown, and Mrs. Brownlow exclaimed, "Marcus!" But that was the end of it. And just as well too, Marcus thought. If they'd made a fuss he would have said that she did shave, and where. It was only her legs and under her arms of course, but he knew very well they wouldn't have liked him to talk about it. Actually it was Margaret's own fault. She'd told him about her shaving a few weeks ago. She'd been in one of her confiding, sisterly moods. He hated her when she was sisterly: she was so sentimental about it.

Breakfast continued. Marcus was aware that he was in disfavour, and he ate his porridge without speaking. He realized, however, that he'd have to speak. If he went into town without telling anyone they'd wonder what had happened to him, and make a fuss when he got back. As it was they'd want to know why he was going into town. They were a beastly inquisitive family. Surely he was old enough by now to be able to go into town without being cross-examined by everyone.

He began his bacon, and then, pausing between two mouthfuls, made his announcement as casually as he could. "I think I'll take a little run into town this morning—there are one or two things I want to do."

Even to Marcus himself the remark sounded wrong—though he didn't know why it was wrong—but the effect on the others was extraordinary. Mr. Brownlow stopped reading the paper and they all stared at him.

"What are you going to do in town, dear?" Mrs. Brownlow inquired.

"I thought I might drop into the library for a little," Marcus replied, in a tone that was meant to keep Margaret quiet, but didn't.

"What do you want to go to the library for?" she demanded. "You got three books there yesterday and you can't possibly have read them all."

This made Marcus indignant. "People don't just go to the library to borrow books," he pointed out scornfully. "They go to consult books, and read papers, and journals, and quarterlies, and things. You want to know everything, Margaret. I don't see why you can't mind your own business."

This outburst left Margaret quite unruffled. "I'm only trying to be helpful," she asserted. "What is it you want to find out? Maybe I could tell you."

Marcus determined to be crushing. He'd be sarcastic. He'd say he didn't know why people ever bothered about the *Encyclopædia Britannica* when *she* was about. But all at once he remembered something which the others probably *would* be able to tell him. "Where's Gibson's Corner?" he asked.

"Why do you want . . . ?" Margaret was beginning when Mrs. Brownlow stopped her.

"I don't see why you can't answer an ordinary question," she said quite sharply. "Gibson's Corner is at the Junction, on your left as you turn into Donegall Place from Castle Place. There used to be a jeweller called Gibson there, but it's something else now."

Mr. Brownlow looked up from his paper. "You could go in on your bicycle," he suggested. "It's a nice morning for cycling, and you could leave it in the office."

This struck Marcus as a good idea. He would start immediately after breakfast and avoid any further questions about his real reason for going into town: for he was quite sure that none of them regarded the visit to the library as anything more than an excuse. If he rode quickly he would get to the office before his father. It was just possible that his father intended to waylay him there and ask further questions. He was really just as inquisitive as Margaret.

So Marcus gulped down the rest of his breakfast and slipped out through the kitchen, while Mr. Brownlow was putting on his boots in the hall. His bicycle was in the garage, and in less than a minute after leaving the house, he was out on the road, and sailing downhill towards town.

The cool morning air swept round him. He could feel it rippling through his shirt and chilling the warm skin on his chest and belly. All the leaves seemed bright and fresh: the sun shone: the birds were singing: the sky looked like a pale blue mist. There were only a few small clouds, and they were wispy and ethereal. It was in fact a perfect early summer morning.

Marcus had the feeling that he was setting out on an adventure; but he wasn't quite convinced of it. "When will I see this road again?" he asked himself. Immediately it struck him that he was being silly, and he answered out loud, "About lunch-time, or a bit before it if you're hungry."

This produced a thoroughly practical state of mind. He wondered why he was going into town, and decided that he didn't really expect to see Caldwell. He was going just in case—and because he knew that if he didn't keep the appointment he was sure to regret it ever after. Still, he hoped to see Caldwell and felt that there was a chance that he might. And if he did . . . . Why then, all sorts of things might happen. He felt indeed that if Caldwell *were* there he would be able to open some sort of door, which would lead right out of the present disappointing, ageing world to another world where everything was green and bright and complete and satisfactory. He felt that Caldwell—if the dream Caldwell did turn up—would take him straight back into the world of his dream. He knew too that if he got the chance he would go back there without a moment's hesitation, though it should mean abandoning his family and friends and everything else in his present life.

Marcus had started off at a great pace, but gradually, as he became absorbed in his thoughts, he rode more and more slowly. It was five to ten when he reached his father's office, and he knew that his father might arrive at any minute. He threw his bicycle into the yard at the back and hurried out, hardly pausing to answer the various members of the staff who wished him "Good morning". And it was just as well that he did hurry, for before he reached the other side of the street he caught sight of his father coming round the corner from the station. Mr. Brownlow waved at him with his umbrella, but Marcus pretended not to see and dived down a side street.

After that he went to the library—partly because he had nothing else to do till eleven, partly to justify what he had said at breakfast.

CHAPTER IX

FOR the first half-hour Marcus was bored. He glanced at the papers, but they didn't interest him. Even the pictures in *Punch*, which in the ordinary way hardly ever failed to amuse him, did fail this time.

It occurred to him that a story might hold his attention and make the time pass more quickly. So he went to the next floor and taking the *Strand* from the rack settled down with it in a leather-covered armchair under one of the windows. In the *Strand* was a new Professor Challenger story by Conan Doyle. Marcus began to read it and almost immediately he became enthralled. It was the sort of story he liked—fantastic and exciting. Stories like that made him feel that his eyes couldn't travel fast enough as they moved backwards and forwards across the page. He found that now: his eyes seemed almost to drag. He *knew* there wasn't time to finish the story, but he couldn't bear to put it down and he went on and on, not daring to look at the clock. But gradually a consciousness of guilt began to trouble him and spoil his enjoyment. He stood up and turned round so that he could see the clock on the top of the Scottish Provident building at the opposite side of the street. It was five to eleven. For an instant he hesitated. Conan Doyle's fantasy had somehow made his own fantasy seem more improbable. It was all nonsense. He knew there'd be nobody there. . . .

Next instant he had dropped the *Strand* and was clattering down the stairs. He jumped the last seven steps and burst out through the swing doors into the street. He turned to the left. The pavement was crowded and nearly everyone seemed to be coming towards him. It took him quite a time to reach the near end of Donegall Place. When he turned the corner he caught sight of the clock above the Bank. It was two and a half minutes to eleven. Immediately he got into a panic. The dream was right. Caldwell was going to be there, was probably there now, and he would miss him through sheer slackness. All the rest of his life he'd regret it—and he'd never really know.

Well, he wasn't going to let that happen. He got off the pavement on to the road and ran at full speed down the whole length of Donegall Place. He imagined that he was attracting attention, that people were stopping to stare after him. He didn't mind: he liked it, liked to feel sensational.

He reached the Junction, and there, standing at the corner waiting for him, was Caldwell. He was exactly as he had been in the dream except that he was not dressed in gym togs. He was wearing a grey suit with short trousers, but he was the same age as in the dream and his face was just the same. For an instant Marcus saw him as a little boy and was conscious that he himself had grown up—but it was only for an instant. After that he was ready for whatever Caldwell might suggest.

"Hullo, Caldy," he said a little nervously. "I'm just on time."

Caldwell looked at him with rather hot, dark eyes. "Hallo, Screwey," he answered slowly. "I was afraid you weren't going to come. It would have been an awful pity if you hadn't."

They had both spoken casually, just as if they'd still been at school, and had met an hour or two before: now, suddenly, Marcus was overwhelmed with a tremendous feeling of relief. "Oh, Caldy," he exclaimed. "I *am* glad you're here."

To this Caldwell said nothing at first. He looked at Marcus very seriously, and rather strangely too. "Are you willing to go on with it?" he asked, in a husky voice that was like a grown-up man's.

"Oh yes," Marcus responded eagerly. "I wouldn't go back now, not for anything." What "going on with it" meant he didn't really know. At the very least he expected to have to run away from home, but running away in the ordinary physical sense might not be necessary. It might be something more mysterious than that. He might even have to lead two lives—one secret and glorious, the very thought of which would fill his ordinary life with joy. He might have to give up his present life altogether. He waited for Caldwell to tell him what to do. He was elated. Anything might happen. He felt that the whole, dull, ordinary world which he knew every day might suddenly fall apart and disappear, and that he would find himself with Caldwell in some sort of youthful paradise, bright and green and fresh. This morning, setting out on his bicycle, he had had a glimpse of it, but Caldwell would make him part of it, like the small leaves on the trees and the opening flowers.

Caldwell regarded his enthusiasm rather soberly. "You don't really know what you're in for," he pointed out. "When you do know you'll maybe find you don't like it at all. It'll be very different from what you think."

Marcus couldn't believe this. "I want to go on with it anyhow," he declared impetuously. "I don't care what it's like."

"Very well," Caldwell agreed. "You can give it a trial next week-end." He sounded unexpectedly staid and self-possessed.

"Why not *this* week-end?" Marcus demanded. "I'm ready to go. I've got money with me, and my Post Office book: so we can get more if we need it."

"What about your people?" Caldwell inquired. "Do they know you're going away? What'll they think if you suddenly disappear?"

Marcus hadn't considered his people. Caldwell's question made him a little ashamed. "I don't know," he said. "I suppose they'd wonder what had happened to me. Maybe I'd better wait till next week after all."

"I think you had," Caldwell replied. His manner was grave and slightly avuncular. It made the whole experience seem for the moment less of an adventure, less dream-like, less enchanting.

Marcus was chilled: he felt that the ordinary world was closing in round him. "But, but. . . ." he began. "I mean if I'm going away they wouldn't like it anyhow—or d'you mean I won't. . . ." He broke off. After all Caldwell hadn't asked him to come away anywhere permanently: that had been just his own idea.

"You'll have to decide for yourself," Caldwell told him. "If you want to you'll be able to stay with me, and I think we can manage it in such a way as not to offend your parents."

"I'll want to stay all right," Marcus repeated. "I know that."

"Very well then," Caldwell answered. "Don't say anything about this when you go home. Don't even mention that you saw me."

Marcus looked round uneasily. "How do you know no one's seen us?" he objected. "It's just the sort of thing that would happen. I'll probably meet someone in church tomorrow and they'll say they saw me talking to you."

Caldwell smiled very slightly. "No one has seen me talking to you."

"You mean no one I know."

"No one you know." He paused and it struck Marcus that there was a hidden meaning about his answer, but he couldn't imagine what it was, and Caldwell went on speaking. "I'll write to you— you'll get my letter on Monday or Tuesday—and say I'd like to see you again. I'll say I'm at my uncle's house in Donegal, and I'll ask you to come and stay for a few days at the week-end."

"Maybe they won't want to let me go," Marcus said. It occurred to him that his people were more difficult than other people's people. You never could tell what they'd object to next.

"Oh I don't think they'll stand in your way," Caldwell replied easily. "You can show them my letter."

His assurance annoyed Marcus. "Maybe they won't think such a fat lot of your letter," he remarked.

"Oh yes, they will," Caldwell returned good-naturedly. "Just wait till you get it and see what sort of letter I can write. In any case you're surely old enough to insist on going if you really want to—and in that case they've no excuse for worrying.

"Now I'll meet you here again next Saturday, but an hour later, twelve o'clock instead of eleven—unless there's someone with you. If they see you off I'll meet you on the train after it's started." His expression altered. "Oh look!" he exclaimed, and flung out his hand in the direction of the City Hall.

Marcus looked, but could see nothing unusual. "Look at what?" he demanded. When he turned round again, however, Caldwell had vanished completely.

CHAPTER X

MARCUS looked this way and that: he couldn't see Caldwell anywhere. Once or twice he turned round sharply in case Caldwell should be hiding behind him. But after an hour, spent in searching the streets round about, he gave up hope completely and drifted back to his father's office for his bicycle.

He felt as if he had suddenly become quite different from other people: it wouldn't have surprised him very much if he had discovered that other people couldn't see him. He rode home slowly and dreamily.

"Hallo, Moony!" Margaret greeted him as he came in the front door. "Did you find out what you wanted to know?"

"What I wanted to know?" Marcus repeated blankly.

"Yes," she said sharply, "what you went into the library to look up."

"Oh yes," he answered. "I found what I went to look for." As he spoke he smiled, but the meaning of the smile was a secret. He knew what nobody else knew, that there was another way of living, perhaps another world to live in. He hoped that Caldwell would teach him to appear and disappear, and introduce him to that other, hidden world. He wished it was Tuesday and that the letter had come. He wished it was next Saturday and that he was with Caldwell once again.

The letter did come. It said:

c/o J. K. Burnaby, Esq.,
The Garrison,
Portmallagh P.O.,
Co. Donegal.

Dear Screwey,

I am staying here with my uncle. Like you he's a bit weak in the top story, but it's good enough fun. Could you come next weekend and stay a few days? Uncle John would be delighted to have you. There's bathing and tennis and we could go out in the boat.

I've looked up the trains for you. If you catch the 1.25 from Belfast on Saturday and change at Letterkenny you should get into Portmallagh about eight if the train doesn't break down. We'll meet you there and run you across.

Please do come.

FRANK CALDWELL.

Marcus didn't think it seemed such a wonderful letter after all. It was just the sort of letter he would have expected Caldwell to write. He handed it across the breakfast table to his mother. "I've got an invitation," he announced. "Caldwell wants me to go and stay."

Mrs. Brownlow read the letter. "Who *are* these Burnabys?" she inquired.

Mr. Brownlow lowered his paper. "Burnaby?" he repeated interrogatively.

Mrs. Brownlow handed him the letter. "Yes, dear. They want Marcus to go and stay."

Mr. Brownlow read the letter. "That's very interesting," he remarked, and it was quite clear that he had found something in the letter that had not been noticed by either Mrs. Brownlow or Marcus.

"What *is* it?" Margaret demanded. "Let *me* see it."

"No, you can't," Marcus told her. "It's a private letter of mine."

"Pig!" she retorted. "Mummy, pass it to me."

"It's Marcus's letter," Mrs. Brownlow said calmly, "and it's for him to say who's to read it, though what objection he can have . . . ."

Marcus gave in ungracefully. "Oh, all right," he muttered. "Let her read it if she wants to."

"I think it must be him," Mr. Brownlow went on. "You know the famous John Burnaby . . . ."

"What's he famous for?" Margaret asked.

"He's a millionaire," Mr. Brownlow replied, "and a very peculiar one. He made all his money—and it's said to be at least three million—on the stock exchange in less than five years. Then he retired completely and for the last ten years he's been shut up in that house in Donegal. He's supposed to be a bit odd. I didn't know he'd any relations and from all that's said about him you wouldn't think he'd have a nephew staying with him—or allow that nephew to ask friends. All the same, Marcus, I think I'd go if I were you. It'll be an interesting experience for you."

"I don't know that I like the sound of it much," Marcus responded with considerable cunning.

Mr. Brownlow looked up and frowned. "Really, Marcus," he exclaimed, "you're most unenterprising. When I was your age I'd have jumped at an invitation like that."

"Oh, I'll go all right," Marcus said, "so long as you don't mind my missing my classes."

Mr. Brownlow had forgotten about Marcus's classes. "Oh well," he answered, "if you are back on Monday evening you'll only miss one day and I suppose you'll be able to make it up." In the meanwhile Margaret had read through the letter more than once. Obviously she thought there was something queer about it. Marcus noticed her looking at him and guessed that she suspected him of something.

"When did you last see Caldwell?" she inquired.

"We were in the same form at school," Marcus replied. "He left at the end of his second year. His people lost all their money." He felt that he had been rather adroit in appearing to answer her question without actually doing so. At the same time he knew she was still suspicious. He didn't like the way she was watching him.

"Funny having to leave school like that when you've a millionaire uncle," she observed.

"I never heard of his uncle before," Marcus said. "Maybe his people had fallen out with the uncle and now Caldwell's staying with him to make it all up."

"And they want you to go and stay."

"Yes, why not?"

Margaret considered. Then without any warning and for no reason at all she asked, "It wasn't to meet Caldwell, by any chance, that you went into town last Saturday?"

Marcus was furious with her. How on earth had she guessed? He hated being made to lie. "No," he growled. "Of course I didn't. How do you think I'd see him?"

"Are you sure you didn't see him all the same?"

"Of course I didn't," Marcus repeated angrily. "How was I going to see him?" But he knew that she knew he was lying.

"Really, Margaret," their mother said, "you do get some extraordinary ideas into your head; and I do think you might believe Marcus when he gives a straight answer to your question."

CHAPTER XI

MARCUS packed immediately after breakfast on Saturday morning and caught the eleven o'clock bus into Belfast. He went first to the Great Northern station, where he left his bag, and then to Gibson's Corner. Though he was seven minutes early, he was disappointed not to find Caldwell waiting for him. He had expected everything to happen in exactly the same way as last week. Caldwell's absence undermined his confidence. Had he really seen him at all? Or had the whole encounter been imaginary? He put his hand into his pocket and felt for the letter: it was still there. He pulled it out and read it. The letter at any rate was not imaginary. Yet he couldn't feel that it quite belonged to the ordinary reality about him—it was like part of a miracle.

Marcus was at one of the busiest points in Belfast. He was a stationary object in the middle of a bustling throng. Above the noise of trams and buses and cars, the noise of people's feet, the noise of people talking, he could hear the raucous, almost lamenting, cry of an old man selling newspapers. "Skatchameah! Skatchameah!" For a moment he watched the flower-sellers in front of Mullans'. He wondered what he should do if Caldwell didn't come. He couldn't go home and tell the whole story. He'd have to catch the train and if Caldwell wasn't on it, hope that at any rate he would abide by the arrangement in the letter and meet him at the other end. He pictured himself arriving at Portmallagh. He didn't know Portmallagh, but he imagined himself standing alone on the platform of a Donegal railway station, with no one to meet him and nowhere to go. He looked up Castle Place. From the direction of High Street came a puff of wind, with a faint smell of the Lough. The Albert clock began to strike.

"Hello, Screwey," Caldwell said.

The voice came from behind and Marcus turned round quickly. Caldwell had the air of having been present for some time, but of course he had just arrived. He was a little breathless and his expression was peculiar—cocky, but slightly uncertain, as if he were not quite sure of himself and of his welcome—as if he were unsure, almost, whether he had arrived at all or not.

But Marcus was delighted. He stared at Caldwell without saying anything, without being able to say anything. It was just like last week, just . . . . just as he had wanted it to be. Caldwell was still young, still, except for his clothes, exactly as he had been in the dream. Marcus was immensely relieved. "I was afraid you wouldn't be here," he confessed. "I couldn't believe it would work out right."

"It hasn't worked out yet," Caldwell replied shortly. "Come on. Let's go to the station and make sure about your ticket."

"What about yours?" Marcus asked. "Won't you need one too?"

"I've a return."

They started up Donegall Place side by side, but the crowds seemed to confuse Caldwell. Everyone walked straight at him, and to avoid collisions he kept skipping backwards and forwards in the most extraordinary fashion. It took them ten minutes to reach Donegall Square. "I wish you'd stay in one place," Marcus complained. "It's the way you keep hopping about gets you into people's way. They can't see where you're going."

Caldwell laughed. "I don't think they can."

"You'd better walk behind me," Marcus said, and after that they got along a little more quickly. Nevertheless it was another ten minutes before they reached the station.

Marcus paused outside the booking office. "What class did you come?" he inquired, a little embarrassed at having to put such a question.

Caldwell didn't answer immediately. He didn't seem to understand the question.

"Your ticket," Marcus reminded him. "You told me you'd a return ticket. What class is it?"

"Oh yes. I forgot. My ticket . . . it . . . it's second class."

But he spoke as if he didn't really know, and Marcus wasn't certain whether to believe him or not. "You'd better look and make sure," he said. "I want to book the same class."

"It's second all right," Caldwell repeated. "I remember."

Marcus was annoyed. "You jolly well ought to. It'd be funny if you didn't."

He joined the queue at the ticket hatch, and while he was waiting his turn, watched Caldwell who was standing a few yards away. A man carrying a suitcase was coming towards the booking office. Caldwell was directly in his path. As the man approached, Caldwell began to fidget. Suddenly he stepped to one side. The man, intent on his own affairs, went past without appearing to see him. Marcus thought it over. He tried to remember if, when he was Caldwell's size, people had ignored *him* like that. But he couldn't recall any incident of the kind. There was undoubtedly something funny about Caldwell. It was funny that he had never grown up—yet at times he was very grown-up, far more grown-up than Marcus himself. Yet he didn't look grown-up. At the moment indeed he looked rather like an orphan, a particularly nervous orphan. Though he had put himself in Caldwell's hands, and intended to obey his instructions implicitly, Marcus felt that Caldwell was weak and defenceless. He would need to be protected and taken care of.

Marcus bought his ticket. The next thing was lunch.

A porter had come up and was standing beside Caldwell. He had taken off his cap and was scratching a bald patch on his head. There were several of these bald patches, bare and shiny. Round them grew tufts of long chestnut hair. He had alopecia. Marcus found his appearance slightly disgusting. Caldwell edged away. Marcus put his ticket in his pocket and went over to them. "Come on, Caldy," he said.

Caldwell's expression altered instantly. "Quick," he exclaimed. "You'll have to run." He darted away towards the other side of the station.

Marcus gaped. He was about to follow, but before he could move he felt a hard grip on his arm. "Here! Who are ye callin' Scaldy?"

It was the porter. His face was furious. For a moment Marcus was completely puzzled. Then he remembered what he had said. "It's my friend," he explained nervously. "I mean I didn't call any-one 'Scaldy'. I was speaking to my friend, that chap I was with. I called him 'Caldy'. That's his nickname."

"What chap?" the porter demanded. "I didn't see no one."

"That chap over there," Marcus answered more confidently. "He was just beside you a moment ago." He pointed to where Caldwell was standing just in front of the entrance to the lavatories.

The porter was not satisfied. "Just you watch yer manners," he said. "If we was somewhere else I'd teach ye. If I see ye round here again I'll knock yer bloody block off." He spoke slowly and heavily, but his voice had a sort of mounting forcefulness that was fright-ening.

"But I wasn't speaking to *you*," Marcus protested. "I was talking to my friend"—he wasn't quite sure how to describe Caldwell—"to my friend, that boy over there."

The porter released him grudgingly. "I tell you I don't see no boy. You just watch yerself. That's all. You just watch yerself."

Marcus drew back a step or two. He had been scared, but now that he was safe he wanted to pretend that he had felt quite cool all along. He tried to look grown-up and dignified. "I assure you you are making a mistake," he said. "You're suffering under a—er—misapprehension. If you go on like that you'll probably land yourself in serious trouble."

"G'on," the porter told him contemptuously. "Your mouth's too big. That's what's wrong wi' ye, ye gawky gasbag."

Marcus was baffled. He turned away and walked slowly towards Caldwell. The word nonchalant occurred to him. He hoped that he appeared nonchalant.

All the same he was angry with Caldwell. "What did you run away for?" he demanded. "Were you afraid of getting hurt?"

But Caldwell didn't look as if he had been afraid. The accusa-tion didn't even in the least provoke him. "I ran away because I wanted you to come too. I didn't want a row."

"Well you managed to keep yourself out of it all right," Marcus retorted. "It didn't matter about *me* of course."

"I'm sorry about you," Caldwell said, but he was obviously trying not to laugh. Marcus felt that he had every right to be offended, though really he wasn't any more: and when Caldwell *didn't* laugh he forgave him. "Look here, Screwey," Caldwell went on. "It's all right. I'm going to have to do a lot of things today that'll seem queer. Tomorrow you'll understand, but I can't explain now." He dropped his voice. "Maybe you won't like it so much when you do understand."

Marcus made a last effort to be cross. It was unsuccessful. His sullenness was swept away and he found himself smiling. "If it's only till tomorrow . . . ."

"Only till tomorrow," Caldwell assured him. "Listen, I'll tell you a secret—I'm in disguise."

"No one would ever guess." Marcus looked at him. "What are you like when you're not in disguise?"

At this Caldwell did laugh and Marcus laughed too. He liked laughing and he let himself go. But all of a sudden Caldwell became grave.

"Stop that!" he whispered. "Everyone's looking at you."

"Looking at *me*," Marcus exclaimed. "Why *me*?"

"Come on," Caldwell told him. "If you stay here you'll only get into trouble again."

He walked away quickly and Marcus had to follow him. Caldwell went out of the station and ran across the road into Amelia Street. In Amelia Street he allowed Marcus to catch up with him. "Look here," he said. "You'll have to be careful. I don't know if you saw, but the station constable was watching you. In another minute he'd have been over."

"What could the station constable do?" Marcus inquired suspiciously.

"He could have arrested you."

"You can't arrest people for laughing—and why me any more than you?"

Caldwell ignored the question. "You can arrest people for being mad. . . ."

"But I'm not mad," Marcus expostulated.

"I know you're not, but he probably thought you were. Now don't argue. I've told you I'll explain everything tomorrow, perhaps even tonight. In the meantime you'll just have to take my word for it. You've had a *very narrow* escape."

"You'd think *you* were invisible the way you talk."

Caldwell smiled faintly. "All right, *we've* had a very narrow escape. It was my fault of course, but you simply mustn't be seen talking to me any more. Listen to what I say, but don't answer unless there's no one about—and if you meet anyone you know don't introduce me. Pretend you don't know me." He raised his hand as if to put it on Marcus's arm, but didn't quite touch him. "Do please," he begged. "Remember I promise to explain everything tomorrow."

"All right," Marcus agreed doubtfully, but this time he didn't return Caldwell's smile. A strange idea was in his mind. If Caldwell *were* invisible it would explain everything. Of course such an idea was too silly. He mustn't let his imagination run away with him altogether.

In Wellington Place they stopped and looked about uncertainly. In the excitement Marcus had forgotten about lunch, but now the name of a restaurant caught his eye.

"I say," he exclaimed, "what about something to eat? We might as well go in here. There's not so much time till the train goes and it sounds all right—four-course luncheon two bob."

Caldwell looked troubled. "I don't think I want any," he said. "You go on. I'll wait for you outside."

"I'm not going to have lunch unless you do," Marcus told him flatly. Caldwell was queer in so many different ways. Was this something else that would be explained tomorrow? Then he remembered why Caldwell had left school. Perhaps he had no money to buy lunch. Probably the whole family was as poor as anything. Most likely the millionaire uncle didn't help them at all—he'd have them to stay, but never give them a bean. Rich people were like that—mean as Moses. "Have lunch with *me*," he suggested. "I mean, you're having me for the week-end. It's only fair to let *me* stand lunch." He had tried to be tactful, but he didn't think he was very good at tact. He watched Caldwell a little anxiously.

And though Caldwell refused he didn't look offended. It was

even possible that the invitation had pleased him. "No thanks," he answered. "I've got sandwiches with me as a matter of fact. If you got some too we could eat them in the gardens." He pointed towards the gardens round the City Hall. It sounded almost as if he had invented the sandwiches on the spur of the moment; but that of course was another silly idea.

So when Marcus had bought sandwiches they went into the City Hall grounds and sat down together on a seat on the west side of the building. Caldwell was fidgety and Marcus himself did not much like the idea of eating outside in such a public place. He was surprised, however, and hurt, when Caldwell moved away from him to the far end of the seat. For a moment he was inclined to give up the whole expedition, but instead of saying anything, he opened his packet of sandwiches and took an angry bite at the first one. His mouth was dry and he felt what he was eating rather than tasted it. The action of chewing, however, calmed him: presently he felt more philosophical. Caldwell's oddness just had to be accepted. There was no sense in being annoyed by it. He glanced along the seat and said, "What about sharing? You try some of mine and I'll try one of yours."

Caldwell flushed and shook his head. "No. You wouldn't like mine. We'll each eat our own." He smiled and added, "That's another of the queer things to be explained tomorrow," and Marcus, who'd really meant to be huffed this time, smiled back rather grudgingly instead.

For a little they both munched away without speaking. Marcus had bought only ham sandwiches, and he had bought too many. He began to feel thirsty. "I'm sick of these," he exclaimed. "I wish someone would finish them for me."

"There's a dog," Caldwell pointed out. "He'll finish them for you. The poor thing's starving."

Marcus whistled and the dog came up timidly, but he was too frightened to take the sandwiches from Marcus's hand. When Marcus threw them to him he started back, though eventually he gained courage and gulped them down hungrily, never raising his tail from between his legs. "You give him yours too," Marcus said, when the last of his own had disappeared. "You can't want them all."

"I'm afraid I've finished mine," Caldwell answered apologetically. Sure enough, they'd all gone. Yet Marcus could have sworn that a moment before he'd had at least three left.

"You must have bolted them," he pronounced severely. "You'll have a pain in the train." He broke off, listening to his own words. "I say, did you hear that?

> *You'll have a pain*
> *In the train.*

It was quite by accident. I didn't. . . ."

But Caldwell wasn't much impressed. "Buck up," he urged. "It's time we were away."

They stood up and Marcus brushed the crumbs from his clothes. He noticed that there were no crumbs on Caldwell's clothes. He saw too by the clock on Robinson and Cleaver's that there was no need to hurry. The train didn't leave for another fifteen minutes.

"When we get to the station," Caldwell instructed him, "you walk straight through. I don't want you to have any more trouble with that porter or the station constable."

"But what about *you?*" Marcus said indignantly. "Aren't they just as likely to make trouble with *you?*"

"I told you I was in disguise. I *am.* I'm like the spy in *The Thirty-nine Steps.* I just alter my expression and you wouldn't recognize me any more. Look!"

Marcus looked—and there, for a flash, was an old man with a stern, bony face. The next second—before he could even blink—Caldwell was there again with the sternness all gone and instead a half-confiding, half-impudent expression. "What d'you say to that?" he inquired.

But Marcus didn't say anything, for he felt that something had happened which he didn't like. He was shocked. Caldwell saw the effect he had produced and tried to remove it. "Cheer up, Screwey," he called out. "Remember I promised to explain everything tomorrow. It's not *black* magic anyhow." Marcus noticed the slight emphasis on the word "black".

It struck him that there was a good deal to be explained tomorrow, and he wasn't quite sure that he was looking forward to the explanation. He suddenly realized very strongly that he was taking a definite and rather dreadful step. He was going out beyond the edge of the world he knew into another world. This other world bordered his own world and in places the two might overlap. He didn't really know. He couldn't know yet. But he realized that if his mother and father had any idea of what he was doing they would be horrified and would drag him back with all their might. They *had* no idea. They imagined he was spending an ordinary week-end at the seaside. Of course he expected to return. Caldwell had said this was only a trial run. Yet Marcus knew that after this adventure he would never be quite the same again.

They reached the station with seven minutes to spare. Marcus went through the barrier and Caldwell followed closely behind him. They went up the train till they found an empty, second-class carriage. They got in and sat down in the two corner seats on the side next to the platform. Just as the train was about to start they were joined by a red-faced man who sat down in one of the corner seats at the far side of the compartment.

CHAPTER XII

THE journey was one of the dullest Marcus had ever experienced. He had nothing to read, and every time he began a conversation Caldwell stopped him with a warning glance towards their travelling companion.

At Strabane they changed trains and for the rest of the journey they had a compartment to themselves. They had been in this second train for an hour or so, and Marcus was beginning to look forward to a substantial meal when Caldwell said, "I'm afraid Portmallagh isn't quite the end of the journey after all. The address is Portmallagh, but actually the house is four or five miles from the station. I hope you don't mind a bit of a walk."

"Oh no," Marcus responded, though he minded a good deal. He immediately felt much more hungry, and wished it hadn't been so late. He was surprised too that no arrangement had been made to meet them. "Couldn't we hire a car at the station?" he suggested presently.

Caldwell frowned: it was clear that he didn't want to hire a car, though at first he didn't seem able to think of a legitimate objection. Marcus wondered if it was again a question of expense, but Caldwell didn't enlighten him. "*I'm* going to walk," he declared. "*You* can do whatever you like."

"I'll do whatever you do," Marcus answered, but he was annoyed. He was tired and hungry—and now there were five miles to walk—Irish miles very likely, and *they* were nearly twice as long as English ones. He felt exasperated with Caldwell. "And what about my suitcase?" he demanded. "Have I to lug it for five miles across country?"

"You'd better leave it in the station," Caldwell advised. "You won't need it. You'll find everything you need in your bedroom." He thought for a moment, and then went on, "D'you remember what I said about not talking when there was anyone else about?"

Marcus nodded.

"Well. You're not very good at it. I mean you might forget again and start talking to me in the street."

"What if I did?" Marcus inquired. "Does it matter such an awful lot?"

"It would matter," Caldwell said. "In fact I don't think we'd better walk together—not till we're clear of the town that is. We'll go out of the station as if we don't know each other. I'll walk fifteen or twenty yards in front. As soon as I think it's safe I'll tell you—in fact I'll wait for you."

"Safe!" Marcus echoed. "You mean it'd be dangerous to talk?"

"Oh not dangerous exactly," Caldwell returned impatiently. "Dangerous to our plans I mean. It might spoil them."

But the use of the word *dangerous* had reminded Marcus that he was engaged in an adventure. The long dreary railway journey had made him forget it. He suddenly remembered how it had begun—the dream appointment, all his excitement and hope. "I'll do whatever you say," he promised. "It seems very funny now, but I do want to do it right."

It was after eight when they reached Portmallagh. They went straight through the town, and it was not until they were some two hundred yards past the last house that Caldwell let Marcus overtake him. They were on an empty, narrow, badly-made road which wound upwards towards the hills. On either side of them were small fields, enclosed by low walls of uncut stones piled loosely together. The sky was covered with thick grey clouds, and though it was not yet time for sunset, the sun was invisible, and the light had begun to fade. A chilly breeze was coming down from the hills and it looked as if there might be rain.

Marcus didn't feel cheerful. He wondered where they were really going, and in what sort of place he would have to spend the night. He thought of the warmth of home, and of the comfortable dinner he would just have finished, had he stayed there.

"They *are* expecting us, aren't they?" he asked. "I mean they know, don't they, that we're coming off this train—because I'm jolly hungry."

While he was speaking these last few words Marcus had been looking back over the town. Now, not receiving an immediate reply, he turned towards the spot where Caldwell had been standing a moment before. He wasn't there—there was nothing but the grassy bank at the roadside and the grey stone wall on top of it. Marcus stared.

Caldwell's voice came faintly from behind him. "I'm here," he said.

Marcus looked. Was he there? For a moment it seemed not quite certain. Everything was grey—the road, the hills, the distant sea.

Yes, Caldwell was there all right. It was as if a shadow had taken substance. Marcus stared at him for a moment. "It must be the light," he decided. "There's something funny about it."

"We'll have to hurry," Caldwell urged. "There's not much time left."

Marcus was a little puzzled, but he was tired, and not inclined to think very much. "I'm not keeping you," he said. "I suppose you're getting hungry yourself now."

"No, I'm not hungry yet," Caldwell responded in a queer, faraway kind of voice. He seemed to make an effort, to pull himself, almost visibly, together. "That's the road," he pointed out. "You have to go over the top. Once you get over the top it'll seem much quicker." Marcus looked. The road wound on up into the hills like a pale grey tape. They went on again, plodding along side by side without speaking.

Soon they passed the last of the fields, and the stone walls bordering the road ceased. On either side of them were heather-covered slopes, broken here and there by patches of gravel, and grey outcrops of rock. There were a good many turf-cuttings too, reached by narrow tracks, some short, some long—winding away into the heather for a mile or more. Each of these tracks seemed to take something from the road, so that it became always rougher and poorer. From time to time they passed turf stacks, and where these were the road was covered with a thick black mould, and was soft underfoot. Elsewhere it was a browny-grey colour and in one or two places it had been mended with sods and loose stones thrown into the worst of the pot-holes.

The whole country was oozing with water and presently the road dipped down to a desolate-looking lake, where dark waves were lapping among the reeds and against the grey, stony shores. Near the centre of the lake was a little island with the dead stump of a tree, leaning out over the water.

After the lake the road rose once more, and Marcus thought that they were on the last upward slope. He was glad for he had a stitch. Very soon, however, he saw that he had been mistaken: there was still another stretch of hill before them. "What about resting for a little?" he suggested, breaking a silence that had lasted since they first came together outside the town. "Are you not a bit tired too?"

"No," Caldwell answered in the same half-dreamy voice as before. "At least not that way. We'll rest for a little if you like, but not for long. It's not . . . ."

"Not safe," Marcus could have sworn he was going to finish. His manner had changed since the morning. Now he seemed not younger than he could be, but older, far, far older. He was still a boy of course, but he didn't speak like a boy any more, and he was no longer enjoying the adventure: he was anxious. Marcus became anxious too. It was wild, lonely country. During the troubles there had probably been murders here—here or hereabouts: perhaps even now it might be dangerous after dark. Was that why Caldwell's manner had changed? Was that what he was thinking about? Marcus didn't like to ask for fear of being accused of cowardice himself.

They sat down on the crumbling stone parapet of a bridge. Below them was a narrow stream running in a bed of smooth, grey rock. Neither of them spoke. Marcus was tired and hungry and Caldwell seemed troubled. He was fidgety too, and before long he jumped up again. "You've surely rested enough," he said. "The sooner we get there, the sooner you'll have something to eat—after that you'd better go straight to bed."

"I don't want to go to bed," Marcus responded a little indignantly. "I'm not *sleepy* tired." Caldwell at times had a very elderly way of speaking which Marcus resented. You'd have thought that it was he who was grown-up, and that Marcus was a child.

For the next half-mile or so they walked more quickly. Marcus was trying to set a pace that Caldwell would find too strenuous. But he couldn't: besides he still had a stitch. It hurt him more and more. Surreptitiously he pressed his hand against his right side— and he tried holding his breath. Presently Caldwell noticed. "That's no good," he said. "Touch your toes. Do it three or four times."

Marcus obeyed, not because he expected it to work, but because he was glad of any excuse to stop. Caldwell's cure did work all the same. At any rate the stitch became a great deal less painful, though it didn't disappear completely. "It's quite a good thing," he admitted rather grudgingly.

"You'll be all right when we get over the top," Caldwell told him. "We're nearly there now."

The last stretch before the crest was steeper than ever. The road was like the dried-up bed of a river and the cart track zigzagged back and forwards across it. Marcus was sick of looking at the ruts and the stones, and at the dark, gloomy heather which surrounded them.

Then they came to the top. He felt a fresh breeze against his forehead and saw a new view stretching out in front of him. To the right the ground still sloped upwards to a peak where there was a small cairn of loose stones. Straight before them was the sea, grey like everything else, but a luminous, pearly grey. Part of the coast-line was hidden from them by the hill, but on the left was a green, triangular plain, widening out towards the south, where a sea lough cut into it. Beyond the lough a range of mountains ran out into the sea, ending abruptly in a high cliff which dropped straight down to the water. At the head of the lough were more mountains.

Low, rambling walls divided the plain into hundreds of tiny fields. The cottages too were small—little patches of white in a grey and green landscape. A considerable distance away, near the entrance to the lough, was a larger building, like a barracks or a coastguard station: it had a slated roof and at one end of it was a martello tower.

During the last part of the ascent Marcus had felt too worn-out to care much about what was going to happen. Now, revived by the breeze, he began to enjoy the adventure again—at least a little. He felt more hungry than ever.

"If you're in a hurry I don't mind running a bit," he told Caldwell, "—till we get to the bottom of the hill at any rate."

Caldwell immediately agreed. He ran very lightly, very quietly, keeping always exactly abreast with Marcus. Marcus himself ran a little awkwardly, partly because he was tired, partly because he was naturally rather clumsy. His feet slipped and skidded on the bad surface and small loose stones went shooting and bounding down the hill ahead of him.

At first, by sudden spurts, he endeavoured to get slightly ahead, but Caldwell skimmed along, without any apparent effort, keeping his position exactly. This annoyed Marcus, and he ran more and more recklessly.

"You'll fall," Caldwell warned him; and indeed Marcus had already stumbled more than once.

Nevertheless he ignored the advice. "Fall yourself," he retorted breathlessly, and with the words hardly out of his mouth he tripped, and shot headlong into the ditch.

He wasn't hurt, he discovered, after the first shock, but he was very much shaken. He was lying in a little patch of grass and rushes: and for a moment or two he didn't move. Cold water oozed through the knees of his trousers and the sleeves of his jacket. He scrambled up indignantly. "You might have helped me," he complained. "You'd just let me lie there." He tried to brush the turf-mould from his clothes, but it clung damply to the knees of his trousers and the elbows of his jacket.

"I'm sorry," Caldwell said. "We were going too fast."

At this conciliatory answer Marcus was suddenly ashamed of himself. Caldwell's behaviour had irritated him all day, and ever since they left the railway station he had been conscious of his own resentment as a barrier between them. The adventure was turning out so differently from what he had looked forward to. Now he felt a sudden gush of friendliness and affection. He liked Caldwell in the way he wanted to like him: the relationship that had been there in the dream seemed to be re-establishing itself.

For a little they walked along quietly, very content with each other's company: then, simultaneously, without either of them having suggested it, they began to run once more. This time they ran more slowly and more carefully. Marcus remembered Saturday afternoons at school in the winter, when they had jogged along together just like this, coming back from a run in the twilight, with the relaxation of the week-end before them. He was still tired, but it was in a different way. Supper, and a fire, and bed seemed pleasantly near, and he expected a happy tomorrow.

For another mile or so they trotted along silently with the breeze in their faces. They were down on the level now, among the fields, and not far in front of them Marcus could see a cluster of cottages. They came to a fork in the road. "We go to the left," Caldwell directed. "There's another bit of uphill, but I don't want you to be seen in the village."

The road they took curved round the back of the village. They could see firelight in some of the cottage windows and from two of them shone the yellow glow of oil-lamps. Through a gap in the houses they saw the quay, a darker grey against the paleness of the water. There was a group of figures at the seaward end of the quay and Marcus could see the masts of three boats.

"They're waiting for the tide," Caldwell said. "They'll be going out about midnight."

They passed a Roman Catholic church and a graveyard: then a solid stone house painted yellow—the priest's house, Caldwell said. After that the road sloped downhill again to rejoin the road through the village.

At the bottom of the hill the sea was hidden from them by a high demesne wall: on the other side of the road were small fields, and occasional narrow lanes, leading up to white-washed cottages.

When they had gone on for a little with the wall on their right, Marcus heard horse's hooves on the road behind them. Presently he looked round and saw that they were being overtaken by a man driving an outside car. The man wore a paddy hat. As the car drew nearer Marcus turned to watch it more and more frequently. "Will he give us a lift?" he inquired hopefully.

Caldwell didn't reply at once: he seemed to be considering. "All right," he said at last. "I'm sure he will if you ask him, but you must do exactly as I tell you. I'll run on a little. You wait for him. When he catches up say you'd like a lift to Mr. Burnaby's. He won't mind, and you can give him a bob when we get there. I'll wait further along the road and hop up on the other side when you pass. Don't take any notice, don't even speak to me—just the same as before."

He ran on and everything happened as he had arranged. "To Mr. Burnaby's is it?" the driver inquired. "Sure it's on my way. I'll go through the demean and out the back gate."

Marcus climbed into the seat on the opposite side to the driver and the horse started again of its own accord. A moment later they passed Caldwell, waiting in the shadow of a tree at the side of the road. Caldwell sprang up behind the driver, but so lightly, and quietly, and cleverly, that Marcus wouldn't have noticed if he hadn't been on the look-out. The driver did not seem to see him at all.

They went on in silence, the car swaying from side to side on the uneven road. In spite of occasional bumps, and the fact that he had to hold on tight to avoid being thrown off, Marcus dropped into a pleasant, dreamy state. It was soothing going along like this in the summer twilight, watching the dim, old horse, and wondering a little how much of an effort he found it to pull them all on the soft, sandy road.

In the train, and at Portmallagh, and coming over the hill, he had felt that he was in a strange country: but it didn't feel like that now. Everything was sleepily familiar and when they came to the top of a small rise, and began to go downhill again, it was more familiar still. He supposed he had been somewhere very like this before, though he couldn't remember where. He remembered that a master at school had told them once that there was a scientific explanation for experiences like this—something about forgetting and remembering, and forgetting you had known before.

They came to a gateway in the wall, with tall, rusty, iron gates which looked as if they hadn't been shut for years. They turned in, and away from the shadow of the wall, or because of the reflected light of the sea, it was not so dark. For the sea was in view again. It had turned to a deep, purplish grey and looked very smooth. The drive curved towards it, getting further and further from the wall. The wall grew more and more vague, gradually fading into the atmosphere, till at last it was hidden entirely by some intervening high ground.

The short, seaside turf on either side of the drive was covered with rabbits. Hundreds of them were nibbling the grass. As the outside car came towards them they hopped away a little from the drive, and a few, more nervous than the rest, darted back towards their burrows with thudding feet and white scuts flashing.

The shore was out of sight, but Marcus could hear the sound of waves breaking, softly, sleepily. . . . Then the drive dipped, and they came to the edge of a small, sandy bay. There were rocks at either end of it jutting out into deep water, and Marcus thought it would be a good place for bathing.

After that he must have dropped asleep for a few moments, for the next thing he knew was that the driver was shaking him. "Ye'd have fallen off if I hadn't caught ye," he said, "but I seen the way of it an' got me han' on ye. Ye're wore out, but no matter—here ye are."

Marcus opened his eyes, and recognized the large, whitewashed building he had seen from the hill-top. Though the sun had set a good while ago now there was still a faint, reflected pink in the sky and this, more faintly still, was reflected again in the white of the house. The tower was massive, a real piece of fortification, built from huge blocks of dressed stone. In front of the house the drive widened, but there was no sign of a garden—and the drive itself was neglected and almost without gravel. Everything was strangely familiar. His mind fumbled sleepily for the explanation, but it eluded him.

Caldwell had hopped down and was walking towards the front door. Marcus, with a sudden fear of being left behind, jumped down quickly too. He fumbled in his pockets and found a shilling. "Good night," he said putting it into the driver's hand.

The man thanked him, wished him "Good evenin'," and flicking his horse with the whip, drove on. Caldwell was standing between Marcus and the door. With the house behind him, he looked very small—hardly noticeable, Marcus thought. It was strange. The house had a queer, blank look, and no one had come out to welcome them.

"Where do we go now?" he asked.

"We go in."

Marcus gazed round slowly. He was stupid with sleepiness. Something was puzzling him and he couldn't even make out what it was.

Caldwell had become very excited. He rushed to the closed door and stood before it. "Come on," he shouted. "Push it open—*you* push it open."

Marcus followed him slowly. "Why don't you push it open yourself?" he demanded suspiciously. "Is there something funny about it?"

"No, no," Caldwell answered. "Of course there's not. Oh you'll see in a minute. It's just that I can't, I can't. Please do hurry. It's been too long already, much too long—you don't want to spoil it *now*, do you?"

All at once Marcus felt very sorry for him. He saw that the excitement was not a happy excitement. Caldwell seemed to be in a sort of agony.

Marcus ran to him and gave the door a push. It swung open and Caldwell darted through. "Come on, come on," he cried.

Marcus followed, nervously and cautiously. Why was there no one about? Surely there were servants. Of course it was Saturday: perhaps they all went out together on Saturday nights—and Mr. Burnaby might be in his study.

They passed through a large, round porch, which was as big as a room in itself, into a huge hall with a high, vaulted roof. "Why, it's like the chapel at school," Marcus exclaimed.

Caldwell paid no attention. He had hurried away to the left and now stood at the foot of a short flight of broad, stone steps. At the top of the steps was a stone archway across which hung dark curtains of velvet. "Come on, for goodness sake," Caldwell shouted, and leaping up the steps, he vanished through the archway without even seeming to stir the curtain.

The anxiety in his voice, more than the urgency of his words, made Marcus hurry. He ran towards the doorway, gathering in the gloom only the vaguest impression of the hall. The walls were white-washed like the outside of the house. The windows were high in the walls, and narrow. Close to the steps up which Caldwell had gone was one of the biggest fireplaces Marcus had ever seen.

Beyond the curtain was a stone-flagged landing, and on the right of this, the beginning of a spiral stone staircase. Caldwell was waiting a few stairs up, but as soon as Marcus appeared he ran on. On the outside the stairs were broad, though on the inside they narrowed away to nothing. The white-washed walls made the most of what light there was. Marcus could see enough not to stumble. Soon they came to another landing with several doors opening off it. Caldwell raced across this and up a further flight of stairs. Marcus followed, but Caldwell went on faster than before, and in a moment he was out of sight. Marcus kept on, pounding up and up, as fast as he could go.

He reached a third landing. It was empty. It was shaped like the second, but it led to no further stairs. There was a choice of three closed doors. Though he hadn't quite seen him Marcus knew that Caldwell had gone through the door in the centre. He opened this door and went in also.

He found himself in a large room with a stone floor and big windows facing towards the West. It was still quite bright. The stone walls were bare and white-washed. There was rope matting on the floor, an oval table of some dark wood, a few wooden chairs, a few books. Marcus could see no sign of Caldwell, but he saw someone else.

There was an old man sitting in a wooden armchair near the fireplace. He was sitting perfectly still with his back to the windows. He was clean-shaven. Marcus noticed that his eyes were shut, and that his head was tilted back rather oddly over the back of the chair. The top of his head was bald, and the hair at the sides and back was grey. His face was an uneven, yellow colour.

Marcus couldn't take his eyes from the old man's face. A horrible suspicion began to steal into his mind. If only the old man would move—but he didn't move.

Marcus felt that he was in a trap, some ghastly, ghostly trap.

He knew now that there had been no Caldwell, that Caldwell had been an illusion: this was real. He was terrified. He stood without moving hand or foot. He was afraid to move.

CHAPTER XIII

FOR perhaps a minute Marcus was too terrified to be able to think. He was terrified of the stairs behind him, of the two closed doors on the landing, and of the body. . . . He strained his ears to hear footsteps, heavy, deliberate steps beginning far below and gradually coming up and up, and nearer and nearer. He listened for the stealthy creak of an opening door. At the same time he watched the old man's face, expecting every moment to see it turn slowly towards him.

But the place was completely still: not a clock ticked, not a board creaked. Marcus had never known such silence in a house before—and this was an old house, an old, old house: only his own breath made a whistling noise in his nostrils. He began to breathe through his mouth, gently, carefully. He remembered that soon it would be completely dark.

Gradually Marcus got over the first shock of his discovery. The outside edge of his mind began to thaw. He was able to think a little. He wished he was at home. He might so easily have been at home, sitting with the others, round the morning-room fire. Last night after dinner he and Margaret had played tennis on the lawn in front of the house. They had gone on till it was nearly dark, too dark to see the balls properly. It had been pleasant and safe and homely. If only he could get back: if only he could think that this was a dream: if only it could be morning—even here—with the sun shining through the windows.

He wished he had sufficient courage to run down the stairs and out into the open. He would run and run—but perhaps the whole demesne was haunted, the village and the road, all the land between the sea and the mountains. . . . Perhaps he wouldn't be able to get back: perhaps he had stepped across a line into another world and was now whirling on a different orbit, an orbit which would never again coincide with the orbit of the old world with which he was familiar.

A black cat which Marcus hadn't noticed before crossed the room from its basket near the window and jumped on to the old man's knee. It turned round once or twice, sinking its claws into his trouser-legs and pulling them out again. Its tail brushed the end of his nose. The old man sneezed, startling Marcus and the cat almost equally. Marcus jumped and the cat hopped down quickly to the floor: from there it looked up inquiringly, and then it was back again, purring and rubbing itself against the old man.

Marcus felt slightly relieved. It struck him that he ought to have found out if the occupant of the chair were really dead or not, that he ought to have tried in some way to restore him to life. Yet still he didn't do anything: he was too frightened. He knew now that the old man was going to become completely conscious, was going to open his eyes and discover his visitor. Marcus felt a new dread: how was he going to explain his intrusion into this wizard's lair?

The cat curled up and went to sleep on the old man's knees.

And at last the old man did open his eyes: he opened them slowly, without any other movement of his face or body. "Light the fire," he said, in a low, husky voice.

Marcus saw at once that the fire was laid and that there was a box of matches on the edge of the fender. He hurried over to the hearth and kneeling down struck a match and put it to the paper. The fire started easily. Marcus remained on his knees, watching the sticks catch, then the turf. He was no longer really frightened. He was only nervous, because he didn't know what to do, and because he didn't know how to explain his presence.

"Put on more turf," the old man said, "a lot more. Now sit up in that chair and look at me—and for goodness sake don't get into another panic."

Marcus made no reply, but he began to understand. He felt ashamed and rather hostile. He sat down in the chair at the opposite side of the hearth, but he looked into the fire.

"Do you know who I am?" the old man asked.

"Caldwell," Marcus whispered, without raising his eyes.

"Yes, Caldwell," he agreed, "but only the Caldwell of today, and last week—the Caldwell of your dream. I have nothing to do with your school friend Caldwell. Where *he* is I don't know. I am also John Burnaby."

"I suppose . . . ." Marcus began. He was going to say that he supposed the real Caldwell was grown up, but suddenly he felt that Mr. Burnaby wasn't interested in the real Caldwell, that he didn't want to talk any more. His eyelids had begun to droop, for a moment they flickered as if he were making an effort to keep awake: then they closed completely.

Marcus watched him and knew that he would wake again presently. His manner had been slightly cross, but he was kind-looking. Marcus felt more at ease. After all he knew the old man already—he was the boy with whom he had spent the day, and that strange fact was more reassuring than frightening—but how he wished it had really been a boy, not this queer, wrinkled old man. At any rate it would not be he who would have to do the explaining. Caldwell had promised to explain everything, and no doubt the old man would fulfil that promise. Of course a great deal was explained already—the peculiar incidents of the journey, why Caldwell hadn't been able to open doors, why everyone had ignored him: but the whole existence of the illusory Caldwell was still a mystery. Would the old man explain that?

Marcus studied the face of the sleeper calmly. With eyes shut and head tilted back Mr. Burnaby's expression was slightly saturnine. He had a wide mouth, which though it was closed now in an almost straight line, turned down a little at the corners. His lips were thin. The nose was very broad and snub: the cheeks were almost chubby. Marcus had only seen his eyes open for a few moments, but he thought that they were grey. Caldwell's eyes, he remembered, had been nearly black.

The cat was still on Mr. Burnaby's knee, and his hands rested on it lightly. The cat was not asleep. With one half-open, green eye it watched Marcus. Mr. Burnaby's hands were unusual, narrow and small-boned with long, delicate fingers. Marcus had read of people having aristocratic hands, and this he imagined was the shape aristocratic hands should be. But they were not attractive hands: the skin on the backs was coarse and red and hairy—and somehow a little toad-like. Marcus's eyes strayed on down and fixed on the

black-socked feet—very small feet with high insteps—surely more
like a woman's than a man's.

"They've been asleep," the old man said, "—very much asleep.
I'd no idea pins and needles could be so unpleasant."

Marcus was a little startled: how long had Mr. Burnaby been
watching him? He gave the impression of knowing everything that
Marcus thought. Marcus was guiltily aware that his thoughts had
not been all that they should have been. "Could I do anything?" he
offered awkwardly.

Mr. Burnaby gave him a hard look. "Yes. Rub them: rub my
hands and feet."

Marcus rubbed first one foot and then the other, but he didn't
like doing it, didn't like touching the old man at all. He had thought
at first that Mr. Burnaby was a corpse and this idea still lingered in
his mind. Old people were like corpses: their skin had withered
and dried up, and their flesh had shrivelled away. Though they
were still alive, death was already creeping in on them from the
outside. They were fires which were nearly burnt out, little heaps
of grey ashes glowing only at the centre. Mr. Burnaby's feet were
hard. It was as if there were only the bones of a skeleton inside the
thick woollen socks.

Marcus kept his head lowered. He felt that if Mr. Burnaby saw
his eyes he would guess his thoughts. But Mr. Burnaby did not
guess, for his voice, when he spoke, sounded grateful and pleased.
"That's better," he said. "Now put on the kettle. I always drink a
glass of hot whiskey after these adventures: it helps to bring me to
life again."

Marcus's parents were both strict teetotallers. For a moment he
was surprised and a little shocked at Mr. Burnaby's request. Then
he remembered that it was only wrong to use alcohol for pleasure.
It could sometimes be used beneficially for medicinal purposes. No
doubt Mr. Burnaby required the whiskey for medicinal reasons.

There was a black iron kettle beside the hearth. Marcus found
that it was already filled, and he made a bed for it in the fire. When
he had put it on and was sure that it was quite steady he looked up
at Mr. Burnaby. Mr. Burnaby's expression had changed: it was no
longer saturnine: instead he was watching Marcus with a broad,
benevolent smile. Marcus was embarrassed: he lowered his eyes

quickly and fixed them on the kettle. Mr. Burnaby was pleased, pleased to have Marcus there, pleased at the success of his scheme: but Marcus didn't share this feeling: he felt almost that he had been cheated. He didn't exactly wish that the adventure had never begun, but he wasn't sure that he hadn't had almost enough of it. He was on his guard.

When the kettle boiled Mr. Burnaby pointed to a cupboard beside the fireplace. There Marcus found a bottle of whiskey, a bowl of sugar, and some glasses. "What about you?" Mr. Burnaby asked. "Will you join me?" His tone was slightly jocular and it grated on Marcus.

"I'm a teetotaller," he answered disapprovingly.

"And a very good thing too," Mr. Burnaby responded with a sort of weak gaiety. "Publicans, you know, like their barmen to be teetotallers; then they don't get drunk themselves, or help themselves to the stock."

Marcus didn't like being compared with a barman, but Mr. Burnaby seemed to have no idea that he had offended. He was painfully feeble. It cost him a considerable effort to talk at all, but he was trying to put Marcus at his ease. "And I'd like a dessertspoonful of sugar in the bottom of the tumbler," he directed. "Now fill it half-full with whiskey—go on till I tell you to stop. That's all right, that'll do. Now put in hot water almost to the top and give it a bit of a stir."

Marcus, being careful not to give Mr. Burnaby a drop more whiskey than he demanded, carried out these instructions correctly. He handed the glass to Mr. Burnaby. Mr. Burnaby, however, was at first unable to grip it, and Marcus, feeling suddenly a little ashamed of his own stiffness, had to hold it to his lips.

After two or three mouthfuls Mr. Burnaby was a great deal steadier and when the glass was half-empty he was able to take it himself. "I'm not usually quite so decrepit as this," he said apologetically. "You'll see a great change tomorrow."

"Would you not like a doctor?" Marcus suggested: "I could go to the village . . . ."

"There's no doctor there," Mr. Burnaby replied, "and I don't want a doctor. There's not a thing wrong with me. A doctor forsooth!" All the same he didn't look displeased.

He finished the glass of whiskey slowly, and demanded another. While he was drinking it, he began to talk. "This one's just for pleasure," he explained, tapping the glass, and unconsciously re-awakening all Marcus's prejudices. "The first really *was* medicine." After a pause he went on, "What puzzles me is that you didn't tumble to it much sooner and surely you must have recognized the house—or haven't you realized that even yet?"

"I did think on the road . . . ." Marcus began and stopped. A wave of understanding flooded into his mind. "Oh yes," he gasped. "I didn't. . . . I didn't think before. Oh yes. This is where I came in my dream." It was overwhelming and very, very strange.

Mr. Burnaby watched him gravely.

"I liked it in my dream," Marcus muttered to himself. "I always wanted to get back."

"And now you're not so sure?" Mr. Burnaby's voice was kind, but he sounded disappointed, and perhaps a little bitter.

"It's taken me by surprise," Marcus stammered. "I didn't know it was real. It was like a place I could go to—only sometimes I couldn't go—and it's a long time. It stopped when I was at school."

"You can stay now," Mr. Burnaby said, "if you want to, that is."

Marcus put his face between his hands, and stared into the fire.

"I don't know that I've done everything in the best way," Mr. Burnaby confessed, "but it was difficult. I could have explained everything to you at the beginning; but would you have come if I had? I could have told you this morning that I was invisible to everyone but you; but again I was afraid to. As it was I gave you hints. It gave me a sort of mischievous pleasure. You see when I was Caldwell I felt like a small boy. You have no idea what fun it is to an older person to be young again, even if only for a short time. It's a sort of holiday.

"And you see I've wanted you for so long. I needed you for very special work—nobody else would do. I've known about you since you were quite small."

"When I was ten?"

"I suppose so. You had just gone to your preparatory school. There was no one else wandering about like that . . . . just you and I: and *you* didn't understand."

"I don't think I understand yet." Marcus spoke coldly. He

wanted time to think. Till he had thought, calmly and alone, he didn't want even to hear the plans which he knew Mr. Burnaby must have made for him.

"I've work for you," Mr. Burnaby said, "hard work, work I can't complete myself. It's more important than anything else in the world."

"Oh." Marcus was determined not to commit himself, determined not to give Mr. Burnaby any encouragement. He knew that if he showed the slightest enthusiasm Mr. Burnaby would tell him what the work was: but he didn't feel enthusiastic. He had set out in the morning in search of youth, and joy, and light; and he was offered important work. He might accept the offer: he might do the work: but it couldn't fail to be a disappointment. Besides, he was hungry and tired: the most exciting adventure in the world could not interest him just at present.

Suddenly Mr. Burnaby realized this. He had begun to feel angry, and to look it. Now his expression altered. "You must be famished," he exclaimed, putting down the cat and getting rather unsteadily to his feet. "I should have thought of that before." He crossed to a table in the corner where there were two candlesticks. He picked up one of them and lit the candle by thrusting it into the fire. From this he lit the other which he gave to Marcus. "What would you like?" he inquired.

"I don't mind much," Marcus replied. "Whatever's easiest."

They went out on to the landing and holding their candles above their heads, began a slow descent of the winding stairs. On the lower landing Mr. Burnaby paused and turned half round. "Do you like cheese?" he enquired.

"I could eat anything," Marcus answered.

"That's good", Mr. Burnaby returned, "—if there *is* anything." He was half joking of course, but it was not very encouraging. Marcus felt that Mr. Burnaby didn't really know whether there was any food in the house or not, and apparently he was not hungry himself.

They went on down, the old man, and the cat, and the youth, with the shadows leaping around them, with the darkness melting before them and closing in again as they passed. Marcus watched Mr. Burnaby's slow progress, and remembered how quickly, as Caldwell, he had come up those same stairs a short time before.

When they reached the bottom they crossed the great hall and passed through a door at the far end into a stone-flagged passage. This brought them to a big, white-washed kitchen, with black rafters in the ceiling. There was cold ham in the larder and plenty of bread and butter, but as the fire in the range was out Marcus had to do without tea which he would have liked—for it didn't seem worth while to go all the way up to the tower, and refill the black kettle and boil it again, and bring it down. The ham was nicely cured and mild, and Marcus ate four slices of it and two rounds of bread and butter. Mr. Burnaby ate practically nothing: obviously he was only keeping Marcus company.

When he had finished, Mr. Burnaby, with the cat twining in and out round his feet, took Marcus back to the tower, to show him the bedroom where he was to sleep. "There you are," he said, opening a door on the second landing and standing aside. "I hope you'll find all you need. The door opposite is the bathroom, though I'm afraid the water'll be cold now. If you want a bath you'll have to wait till the morning. The water'll be hot any time after eight. I usually have breakfast at nine."

They wished each other good night. Marcus shut his door and stood quite still, listening. After an interval of perhaps thirty seconds he heard Mr. Burnaby's footsteps go slowly up the stairs. Very cautiously and quietly Marcus turned the key in the lock. Then he looked round his room.

It was a big room, with two straight sides and a curved one. At the far end was an iron bed, painted white: it was broad and low, and looked very inviting to the sleepy Marcus. Like most of the rest of the house this bedroom had white-washed walls. The floor was of dark polished oak. There was no carpet, but there were a good many thick rugs, and an easy chair. On the right was a window, set half-way through the wall, which was evidently at least six feet thick. Spread out on a wash-stand below the window were wash-things and shaving things. They were all new and arranged so that Marcus could not fail to see them. At the opposite side of the room there was a wardrobe and a dressing-table, with a pair of hairbrushes and a comb.

The bed-clothes had been turned back, and a suit of pyjamas

was laid out on top of them. On the bedside table was a small clock, a carafe of water, and an electric torch.

Marcus put the candle on the bedside table and undressed quickly. The pyjamas were summer ones made of some light, dark-blue material. Marcus got into bed without even washing his teeth. He found two hot-water bottles and threw them onto the floor. He wondered who had put them in: they were still slightly warm. Even without them, he found the bed too hot: so he pushed off the down quilt. The bed was comfortable. He blew out the candle and within a few minutes was sound asleep.

CHAPTER XIV

WHEN Marcus awoke it was exactly eight by the clock on his bedside table—and he could hear the sea. He remembered at once where he was and what had happened the previous day. At first he had a feeling of strangeness, almost of nakedness, as if he had wakened up in a crowded picture-house with only his pyjamas on. But when he looked round at the comfortably furnished bedroom, and remembered that the door was locked, his self-confidence returned. He was rested and refreshed, and he began to have a pleasant sense of excitement. He had no longer the slightest wish to go home.

He had always liked staying at the seaside, chiefly because he was fond of bathing, fonder of it, almost, than of anything else in life. It occurred to him that if he hurried there might just be time for a bathe before breakfast. So he hopped out of bed, and ran to the window to see what sort of morning it was. He found that the sun was shining brightly—rather too brightly, he thought: it would probably rain later.

The window faced south-west and the sea was quite close. When he opened the window wide and leaned out the sound of the breaking waves became clearer—a soft, inviting sound. Just below his window was the rabbit warren. The rabbits were still there, still feeding. They must have stayed up all night—or perhaps they were different rabbits, and last night's rabbits were in bed now. That would be called working in shifts. This idea tickled Marcus and he laughed.

His eyes wandered out over the sea, the Atlantic. The word *Atlantic* had always made a special appeal to him, emotional and half-mystical. He liked to think that he was gazing at the huge free ocean, thousands of miles wide, miles deep—not just some narrow sea. On the left across the inlet he could see the mountains with a bright fringe of foam at the foot of the cliffs, where the waves were breaking. The sky was a lightish blue with a good many large white clouds drifting in over the mountains. The colouring of the sea was patchy—purple and blue and green. Marcus stared at it unthinkingly, with a sort of dreamy delight.

Presently he shivered. Standing barefoot on the stone floor had made him cold. He no longer wanted to bathe. He turned and looked at the clock. It was twenty past eight. There would hardly be time now, and in any case he would have to seek out Mr. Burnaby and explain where he was going. He noticed a pair of bedroom slippers under the bed, and a dressing-gown on a hook behind the door. He put them on and taking a sponge, a tooth-brush, and a tube of tooth-paste from the wash-stand, unlocked the door and stepped out on to the landing.

There he stopped to listen. Not a sound—the house might have been empty: it was in fact just that sort of silence. The landing itself was completely bare, with no pictures on the white-washed walls and no mats on the grey, stone floor. The floor was uneven, worn away in the centre and to a lesser extent before the various doors. At either end of the landing were the stairs up which Marcus had come the night before. They gave Marcus a curious impression—as if the landing were perched midway in space, and they ascended and descended, winding on and on, up to illimitable heights, and down to infinite depths. He crossed the landing and opened the bathroom door.

It was the biggest bathroom Marcus had ever seen: it was far too big. Obviously it had only quite recently been made into a bathroom. Everything about it was modern—the black and white tiled floor, the chromium fittings, the pedestal basin, the shower in the corner, the telephone-like hand-spray on its rests between the taps. Next door was the W.C.—another fairly large room, with the lavatory pan looking lonely and ridiculous at the far end from the door.

Marcus had been brought up, both at school and at home, to take a cold bath every morning. He had always boasted that he liked cold baths, and of how fit they made him feel. This morning, however, he decided to have a hot bath for a change. It was partly because the water was hot—as Mr. Burnaby had said it would be—partly because a hot bath in the morning always gave him a sensation of luxury. While the bath was filling he brushed his teeth: then he hung his towel on the heated towel rail, slipped off his pyjamas, and stepped in.

He washed his hands and arms, and as much of his legs and body as could be conveniently soaped without standing up. After that he lay still, with the sponge as a cushion at the back of his head, and thought over the events of the previous day. How long he lay steeping he had no idea, but presently he was jolted into guilty consciousness by a knock at the door. A voice said, "I'm going down. Breakfast's in the hall you came through last night."

Marcus was so startled that he didn't reply at once. It was Mr. Burnaby, of course, but his voice sounded a great deal more vigorous. Marcus felt that he had been caught dawdling. "Thank you," he called back awkwardly. "I'll be down in a few minutes." He lay tensely motionless until he heard Mr. Burnaby's footsteps cross the landing and start down the stairs. After that he hurried. Not much more than ten minutes later he came down himself, and pushing through the velvet curtain entered the hall.

He was wearing rubber-soled shoes, and Mr. Burnaby, who was looking out through one of the windows at the far end of the room did not at first hear him. Marcus cleared his throat. Immediately Mr. Burnaby turned round. "Oh! You've arrived, have you?" he said rather coldly.

In the daylight he appeared much younger. He still looked old, of course, but there was nothing doddering about him. His face was firm and healthy and sunburned. Last night it had seemed yellow: this morning it was an even, red-brick colour. He was cross: it showed in his expression, in the way he rang the bell and returned instantly to gazing out of the window. Marcus wondered what was the matter. Was it his own unpunctuality? Or was there something else wrong? He stood a little behind Mr. Burnaby and looked out over his shoulder into a small, walled-in garden. There was a lawn surrounded by a broad flower border: against the walls were pear trees and apple trees: the apple trees were in blossom. The black cat was sitting on the wall washing herself.

Marcus had imagined that the bell would bring a manservant, dark, suave, and a little mysterious—for if there were any ordinary servants, where had they been last night? A genie would hardly have surprised him. But the breakfast was brought in by a maid. She had a round West-of-Ireland face, with wide-apart blue eyes, high cheek-bones, and protruding teeth. She smiled cheerfully and wished them good morning.

Mr. Burnaby introduced Marcus. "Kate, this is Mr. Brownlow who has come on a visit."

Kate smiled again. "Ye're welcome."

"Thank you very much," Marcus said.

She began to unload her tray, and as she did so she gave Marcus instructions about his breakfast. "There's a plate of porridge for you to begin with," she told him, "and there's bacon an' eggs in the silver dish here. It's one of them patent dishes as keeps them warm: so you needn't be hurrying too much over your porridge. The Master, he only takes porridge and toast: so the rest's all for yourself."

She departed, and with her all cheerfulness disappeared from the room. Mr. Burnaby looked at the table, gloomily. "Well! I suppose we'd better eat it," he remarked, and pulled back his chair. So began a very silent meal. Mr. Burnaby offered Marcus tea and marmalade. Marcus passed the toast. But they didn't look at each other: they didn't even discuss the weather.

Marcus didn't try to talk: he was afraid to. He didn't know what was wrong. Perhaps Mr. Burnaby just *was* like that in the mornings and would gradually become more pleasant. He was taken completely by surprise when Mr. Burnaby put down his teacup with a bang and said roughly, "I suppose you want to go home. I won't hinder you. You can be home tonight if you want to."

At first Marcus was too startled to answer. For a moment he thought that Mr. Burnaby really wished to get rid of him. Then he saw that this downright rudeness probably meant exactly the opposite. "I'd rather stay if I can," he responded hesitantly.

Mr. Burnaby looked at him very searchingly and rather grimly. "You'd rather I was Caldwell, wouldn't you—the little schoolboy, I mean, not whatever the real Caldwell's grown into now?"

"No," Marcus answered firmly.

Mr. Burnaby threw him a half-hostile, half-troubled look. "It would be very strange if that were the truth," he said suspiciously.

"It is the truth," Marcus declared, but he didn't really know whether it was or not.

In any case Mr. Burnaby didn't believe him, and his disbelief showed in his expression. He stared at Marcus, and Marcus felt extremely uncomfortable. He would certainly rather have had Caldwell than this.

"I can always tell whether a person's speaking the truth or not," Mr. Burnaby observed: and Marcus was convinced of his own falseness and its futility. He took a very small bite of toast and tried to eat it without making a crunching sound.

Mr. Burnaby pondered.

"Whether it's the truth or not doesn't matter very much," he pronounced at last. "If you're willing to do the work—and *can* do it—nothing else is of great importance. You'd better come to my study again and I'll tell you more about it."

He got up and started across the room, and Marcus, after a moment's indecision, began rather reluctantly to push back his chair. Mr. Burnaby turned, and immediately noticed Marcus's half-finished piece of toast and marmalade, his untouched cup of tea. He apologized, and coming back sat down again at the table. "Living alone makes one very bad-mannered," he explained. "Have some more toast."

But Marcus, though he had a healthy appetite and if left alone could have managed another two or three pieces of toast, found great difficulty in finishing the piece on his plate. He ate it hurriedly, swallowing each bite almost as soon as it was in his mouth. "That's the way to give yourself indigestion," Mr. Burnaby pointed out. "When I was young I was taught to chew my food properly." He produced a pipe and blew through it once or twice. Marcus heard a whistling sound, and a faint bubbling. " 'nation!" Mr. Burnaby exclaimed. He took the pipe apart and shook it. One or two drops of nicotine sparked on to the floor. A small strand of dark wet tobacco hung from the vulcanite end of the shank. Mr. Burnaby brushed it off and wiped his fingers and the mouthpiece on his socks. He filled the pipe and lit it.

After this he looked more amiable. He pressed Marcus again to have more toast, another cup of tea: but Marcus assured him that he had had all he wanted.

So they got up and went back through the velvet curtain into the tower, and up the stairs to the room where Marcus had first seen Mr. Burnaby the previous evening. In the daylight the room looked very pleasant and clean. It had been dusted and the empty whiskey glass and the black kettle had gone. The windows were open and there was a fresh coal fire on the hearth. They sat down in wooden armchairs on either side of it.

"Now," Mr. Burnaby began in a very business-like voice. "I may as well tell you the worst to begin with. You needn't make any decision yet. You needn't give me one for a month, if you don't like—and even then it needn't be final. You'll always be free to give everything up if you want to. Of course I'll be disappointed if you do—especially if it's after some time."

He paused and Marcus felt that a remark was expected of him. "I understand," he said.

"It would be strange if you didn't," Mr. Burnaby replied. "There's been nothing very difficult so far."

"Except you," Marcus thought, determining not to utter another word unless he was asked to. Mr. Burnaby did not appear to realize that he had been rude, and presently he went on as if Marcus had never spoken. "As you have no doubt gathered by this time, I have the power of projecting myself out of my body and going not wherever I please exactly, but wherever I please within certain limits. What those limits are you will hear later. Of course I am invisible on these expeditions, but on a mind like yours it was relatively easy for me to produce a false impression of the boy Caldwell. This Caldwell, by the way, I took from your own mind in the first place. As I told you last night, I have been watching you off and on for a long time, and recently I have been on the look-out for just such an opportunity as this dream of yours gave me. You began the dream. I stepped in at the end and made the appointment. I couldn't be sure of course that you would keep it, but once you

did the most difficult part was over. The Caldwell you expected
to see was already present in your mind: all I had to do was to fit
myself into that ready-made image and bring it to life. I imperson-
ated not Caldwell precisely, but a rather mischievous small boy of
my own imagining. It was like a difficult and risky game, and the
more risky it became the more I enjoyed it. It was largely a matter
of sustained concentration and it was that that nearly defeated me
in the end. By the time we left Portmallagh last night my own old
body was telegraphing wildly for me, and if you hadn't been so
sleepy there were one or two occasions when you would almost
certainly have found me out.

"Caldwell appeared to sit down and get up, to walk, to stand, to
run. You thought you heard him talk, but no sound actually passed
his lips." He looked up almost as if he expected Marcus to dispute
this, but Marcus, having accepted the fact that Caldwell was an illusion had no intention of arguing about what kind of an illusion he
might be. Nor did he want to risk so soon another display of Mr.
Burnaby's irritability.

"Of course all that is fairly plain sailing," Mr. Burnaby continued. "I'll be able to teach you to do just as much yourself. It will
take a long time, and a great deal of patience at the beginning—
and a great deal of concentration."

"All my school reports used to say 'Lacks concentration'," Marcus put in, forgetting for an instant his determination to be silent.
He didn't quite know why he had to say this—it came out with a
sort of defiance. He was willing to go either way, to give up life
or to embrace it again—just as the novice in the monastery must
hesitate, fascinated on the one side by the beauties of a holy life
and drawn on the other to the toils, and troubles, and rewards of
the world without.

"No doubt you do lack concentration," Mr. Burnaby agreed,
and, though his voice had still a touch of its previous sharpness,
he spoke more kindly than before. "But at any rate you'll be able
to do this if you try. It's like learning to swim, or like the children learning to fly in Peter Pan. First you'll have to learn to move
about the room without your body. You'll have to begin by sitting in your chair, say here, and getting up to that corner of the
ceiling on the right of the fireplace. When you're able to do that

completely you'll have advanced a long way. It may take you weeks or months—I hope it won't take you longer than a year. You'll have to spend hours at it every day, as many hours as you can stand. At the start you'll have no success at all: then you'll feel a faint link growing up between you and the place you're aiming at—like the sucker of an octopus, touching and letting go and finally fixing. At first only very little of you will be in the corner: but gradually there will be more and more. At first you will be mostly in your body: in the end there will be only the faintest thread connecting your body with the real you—wherever you may have gone. Yet that is only the beginning."

"What's the end?" Marcus couldn't help asking, forgetting again his decision not to speak.

Mr. Burnaby, however, seemed no longer to mind interruptions. "Ah! that's what we don't know," he responded. "I can tell you about the second stage, and something of the third stage: after that I don't know: I can hardly even guess." He stopped there and seemed to reflect. Suddenly he added, "It's for after that I want you. Together we may find out what has baffled me alone—or perhaps you may succeed where I have failed."

There was another pause: then Mr. Burnaby explained what he meant by the second stage. "After you have learned to get completely out of your body, it's not very difficult to learn to move about the room—and from that you gradually learn to extend your range. Presently you are able to travel as far away from your body as you wish—as far as your time and strength will permit. It's not just a case of wishing and finding yourself wherever you choose. You do definitely travel through the intervening space—and once more it's like flying, for taking off and landing again are the most difficult parts. Perhaps now you are visualizing something like a magic carpet on which you rest at ease on these journeys. That too is wrong: every step of your journeys will cost you intense effort, intense concentration.

"The fact that all this can be done is of interest: scientifically, I suppose, it is more important than the discovery of wireless. But after all it is not completely satisfactory. It is only another means of communication between man and man—a means which could be much improved, but which, nevertheless, has been going on, though perhaps only in a very rudimentary way, since the beginning of things. Yet there is very little you will learn by such a means that you won't by that time know already."

There he stopped. As he talked he had been filling his pipes with tobacco, putting each as it was filled into a rack by his side. Now he knocked out the pipe he had been smoking and put it on the mantelpiece. He took one of the filled pipes from the rack and lit it. It was clear that he had come to the most difficult part of his explanation.

Marcus was listening with something of the enthusiasm of a convert at a revival meeting. His mouth was half open; his eyes shone. What Mr. Burnaby wanted him to do, he didn't know. It was something great, something demanding self-sacrifice, something that only he could accomplish. Marcus was ready to do anything, to endure anything, to sacrifice everything. Whatever Mr. Burnaby asked he would say "Yes", however great the dangers and difficulties.

But Mr. Burnaby didn't ask anything. "The third stage is to find out what happens to the human soul after death."

As soon as Marcus heard this he knew that it was what he had been expecting. "But how?" he demanded. "How are you going to find out?"

"I don't know," Mr. Burnaby answered, with a disappointing effect of flatness, "but I think that we both have a power, or powers, which if we learn to use them properly might bring us near to the solution. At present we are both able to project ourselves in two different ways—in space and in time. With you both these forms of projection are entirely uncontrolled by your waking mind. I have learned to control almost completely my power of projecting myself in space. So far as time is concerned I can project myself when I like; but only into the future, and a very small part of the future—that part where there is knowledge of the financial news. It is almost ludicrous. What I hope is to train you, first to project yourself as I do in space, with the idea that you may then learn to project yourself in time or perhaps into space in, in," he hesitated, "in, shall I say, a non-dimensional direction. Souls, when the body dies, seem to go somewhere. I want you to be able to go with them and return, or to go into the future of your own soul and discover its experiences after the death of your body. I am almost convinced that one or other of these things may be possible. After all the spirits of the dead do sometimes come back; why should the spirits of the living not go forward?

"In my lifetime I have made a good deal of progress, but it seems to me I have got as far as I will ever get alone. Through lack of guidance when I was young I did not use all my powers in the best way: now some of those powers have weakened, or left me. You have similar powers, and you are still young. With my guidance you should be able to make better use of them than I did. You can begin almost where I leave off: you can avoid my mistakes.

"And then, when you have been trained, there is one particular experiment that we should eventually be able to make together. It is an experiment which might be decisive. It will need both of us, but my part, from the nature of it, can only be performed by the same individual once. For that reason, before attempting it, I would like to know something of its chances of success. It is really a sort of desperate last throw. With your help we may attain the knowledge we require by other methods.

"One thing more, whatever we do, whether we succeed or fail, it is most important to keep notes—to put down everything we do every day. If anything should happen to me my notes are in the cupboard there ready for you to use. There is also a duplicate typed set, going up to the end of last year, in my bank in Dublin. I hope the time will come when your notes may be useful to someone else, or rather to a great many other people.

"I am asking you to make this work your career: therefore I owe you certain assurances. You have very likely heard that I am rich. I have been told that I have become a sort of legend on the stock-exchange. Well, I am even richer than people think. I have so arranged things that little short of world-wide revolution could interfere with my work. I have a hundred and fifty thousand pounds, or the equivalent in local currencies, invested in Japan; New Zealand and Australia; Canada; the U.S.A.; Argentina; South Africa; Egypt; Italy; Switzerland; Portugal; Norway and Sweden; Great Britain, and the Free State here. That is to say I have treated Australia and New Zealand as one, Great Britain and the Irish Free State as one, Norway and Sweden as one. That is twelve different blocks of one hundred and fifty thousand—a total of very nearly two million.

"If you accept my offer my total estate will pass to you. Death duties I suppose will account for about half of it. Even so you will have far more than enough to live on with all the comfort and seclusion you can need if any one of those countries preserves the capitalist system of society.

"My affairs are now in the hands of very able solicitors and accountants. Whatever happens don't concern yourself with them in the slightest. If you see your money lost in country after country, don't think about it. At the first sign of trouble here, or wherever you may have settled, go away. Go to wherever conditions appear most stable. Find a secluded place to live and carry on your work with complete disregard for the outside world.

"I hope you are neither avaricious nor a spendthrift. A fortune is only valuable in so far as it enables you to give up thinking about money. I believe more human thought is wasted through concern about money than from any other cause.

"Now go out and think it over. I don't expect your permanent decision. What I want you to tell me as soon as possible is whether you're prepared to work with me for a trial period of one month— at the end of that month you can tell me if you're prepared to go on for a further six months. After that I shall expect a definite decision. Of course you'll always be able to give up at any time. I can't bind you—but if you did give up later I'd feel that you'd let me down. Try not to let the fact that you have the chance of inheriting a fortune influence you in any way."

He stood up, a rather small man with a big head. Marcus stood up too and they looked at each other a little shyly. Marcus noticed Mr. Burnaby's grey eyes—very steady, yet very alive, kind eyes glowing with enthusiasm. He was holding an unlit pipe tightly in his right hand, and pressing it against his chest. His left hand hung by his side. Marcus felt embarrassed: he tried to think of something to say. He caught sight of the windows with sheets of rain streaming down them, and of the grey sky beyond. "It's pouring," he remarked. "I just thought it would rain when I got up. It was too bright to begin with."

Mr. Burnaby smiled. "I never know what it's going to do next," he said. "It's a detestable climate. I don't know what induces me to live here—except that I like the scenic results. I wish all the same they could be obtained in some other way."

"It'd be all right with a raincoat," Marcus told him, though without a great deal of enthusiasm. Then he remembered. "Oh blow!" he exclaimed. "I left it at the station."

"Of course you did," Mr. Burnaby said. "You left everything at the station, but it doesn't matter. I got another for you before you came, and in any case you can't go out in that—at least you'd be very silly if you did. I didn't mean, necessarily, that you should go out into the open air—or if I did I didn't realize that it was raining. I'll get them to light a fire for you in the library. You can amuse yourself there and think about it all till lunch-time. I have lunch at half-past one as a rule, if that suits you."

Of course Marcus said that it would suit him, and they set off for the library.

CHAPTER XV

THE library was a long upper room in the same wing as the kitchen. There were bookshelves on three sides, from floor to ceiling; on the fourth side, looking out towards the sea, was a big, square bay-window, with a wide, deeply cushioned window-seat.

Marcus was impressed with the seriousness of the occasion. He paced two or three times slowly up and down the whole length of the room. "This is one of the most important decisions of my career," he told himself. "My whole future depends on it. What am I going to do?"

But he knew quite well what he was going to do. He didn't want a month's trial—or to wait six months before he gave Mr. Burnaby a definite answer. He was ready to commit himself irrevocably, now. He sat down on the window-seat and put his feet up. He supposed that he must have the gift of making quick decisions.

As he looked out at the rain he remembered again his own success as a weather prophet. He was good at the weather: at least he usually knew when it was going to rain—or was very often right anyhow.

A red sky in the morning
Is the sailor's warning:
A red sky at night
Is the shepherd's delight.

It was a jolly good thing that—jolly reliable. Some people made them both shepherds, and some people made them both sailors: but his way was right.

He liked sitting here looking out at the sea. You could look at the sea for ages, just doing nothing, specially when you hadn't seen it for a while. It was funny how its colour always changed with the weather, and with the colour of the sky and the position of the sun. It was quite different in autumn and in summer. Supposing you didn't know, it would almost be possible to tell by looking at the sea what season of the year it was. Now the sea was a sort of battleship grey, spattered with streaks of dirty white where the choppy waves were breaking. Sheets of rain swept across it like ghosts of ancient bishops. Bits of the mountains behind kept being hidden and revealed again. They too had turned grey: they were fuzzy looking and mixed up with the watery sky.

Marcus thought that it would be nice if Mr. Burnaby were to give him this room as his study. He liked Mr. Burnaby, though he was queer. He wasn't like a millionaire—or at least not like any rich people Marcus had met, not so distant, not so grown-up in a way. Marcus was glad he was going to work for him, going to work *with* him.

He was glad too to have settled the problem of his career. During the last few months his future had become rather a worry. All his life he had meant to do something big and important, but it had seemed terribly difficult to begin. He had applied for jobs of various kinds, but no one had seemed to want him—and now he was getting this, which was far more important than any of the *great* things he had imagined—and something that practically no one else *could* do. They ought to be pleased at home when he told them.

He frowned a little. What was he going to tell them? It was queer, but if he told them the truth about what had happened last night they simply wouldn't believe him: and if he told them the work he was going to do with Mr. Burnaby they wouldn't like it. He'd have to say that Mr. Burnaby wanted him to be his secretary, and then, if the salary was all right, his father would probably be quite pleased.

What would the salary be, he wondered. He knew that in his father's business people started with very small salaries. Apprentices were paid a hundred pounds for four years' work. Of course public school men usually got better jobs than that. He'd heard of chaps from school who'd started with two hundred a year. Marcus knew that he wasn't expected to do quite so brilliantly. His father would probably be satisfied if he began with fifty pounds a year, provided of course the job was suitable—a job with prospects.

All the same Marcus thought Mr. Burnaby would give him more than that—probably a hundred a year—and then he'd be living in this house: so he'd be able to save most of it. If he saved ten shillings a week, that would be twenty-six pounds a year. By this time next year he'd be able to buy a motor-bike. He'd always wanted a motor-bike, but perhaps Mr. Burnaby didn't approve of motor-bikes.

Marcus spent the rest of the morning looking out of the window and dreaming pleasant dreams. He felt a little shy at first, when Mr. Burnaby came back, but he stood up and made his announcement immediately. "I've been thinking," he said nervously. "I mean I think I'd like to give it a bit of a trial to see how I like it."

It was much less than he meant. Natural caution, or diffidence, or a little of both, held him back, against his will almost, from expressing the full and enthusiastic assent that he felt.

Mr. Burnaby, however, was pleased. "Good," he exclaimed. "I thought you would." His face shone with smiles. He stood, with his pipe in his hand, beaming at Marcus.

Lunch was a very different meal from breakfast. Mr. Burnaby talked all the time. First he told Marcus that he intended to pay him £300 a year—"as my secretary you know. You won't need that, but it should please your people, convince them that you've got a really good job—and it can be increased from time to time to show you are getting on."

"It's an awful lot," Marcus said. "I mean no one would think of paying me that for anything else."

"Oh, I don't know," Mr. Burnaby answered. "The main thing is to make it enough to satisfy your people. I want them to feel you've got a really good job."

But Marcus was doubtful. "I think they'll think it queer," he explained. "I mean anyone wanting to give *me* three hundred a year. My father'd think it queer. I don't think he thinks I'm very good at things—and I didn't do very well at school. If I'd been brilliant or something it would have been different. I don't think he'll be keen on it anyhow, and with such a big salary he'll think there's something funny about it."

Mr. Burnaby brushed these difficulties aside without appearing to give them very serious consideration. "Your father's a business man," he pointed out, "and from what I've seen of Northern Ireland business men, I feel sure that if he's satisfied about the money side of it nothing else will matter very much."

This annoyed Marcus. He was fond of his father. He didn't like hearing him classified in such an offhand manner as "a Northern Ireland business-man". His father was a great deal more than that. He flushed ever so slightly. "You don't know my father," he said.

"I know the type," Mr. Burnaby retorted, with a shrug that was more vocal than physical. "They're all the same, and in any case, if I set my heart on anything I always get it in the end. I always have. You'll find that whatever difficulties arise will be overcome."

Marcus did not answer. He realized that without ever having seen him, without knowing anything about him, Mr. Burnaby was jealous of his father. He had determined that he himself was to be the main influence in Marcus's future life. Marcus was prepared to let him be, but that did not mean that he would see his faults as virtues or ignore them. He was hurt, but he didn't want to show it now. Some time Mr. Burnaby would meet his father. Then Marcus would demand a retraction of this opinion, and an apology. With that he put the matter aside, and listened while Mr. Burnaby described his way of life and the workings of his household.

None of the servants slept in the house. Mrs. Mullan, the cook, was the mother of the two maids, Kate and Teresa. There was also an odd-job man, named Black, who turned into a chauffeur whenever the car was needed. Black was a Northerner and a Protestant. He lived over the stables. The Mullans were natives of the place and Catholics. Mrs. Mullan had a cottage in the grounds.

"Whenever I'm going on one of my expeditions I give them a holiday," Mr. Burnaby explained. "They were off all day yesterday, and that means they're not allowed near the place. Mrs. Mullan doesn't like holidays, but the two girls are always delighted. They went to Sligo yesterday and had no end of a time."

"You wouldn't know they were in the house," Marcus said. "I haven't seen them once, except Kate bringing in the meals, and I didn't hear a sound this morning before breakfast."

"They're only allowed into the tower when I'm not there," Mr. Burnaby told him. "They have to do the study and make my bed while I'm at breakfast. The three of them do that together. Black pumps the water and lights the boiler at half-past seven every morning. The boiler-room's under the tower. It takes half an hour to get the water hot enough for a bath . . . ." He broke off. "What about this afternoon?" he asked. "What shall we do? I got Black to mark the tennis court on Friday. The rain's over and the ground dries up in no time. Would you like to play?"

CHAPTER XVI

GOING home in the train Marcus tried to decide how to announce his new job to his family. Should he burst out with the news as soon as he arrived, as if he felt quite certain that they would be pleased to hear it? or should he call first at the office and tell his father? If Mr. Brownlow once agreed to let him accept the position he would probably abide by his decision even if Mrs. Brownlow disapproved—and Marcus expected that she *would* disapprove. She was shrewder than his father. She expected more of him than his father did: at the same time she had a lower opinion of his present abilities. When she heard how much Mr. Burnaby was going to pay him she would be convinced that there was something wrong about the job. His father on the other hand might be persuaded that getting the job was an extraordinary piece of good luck—or even an opportunity cleverly seized. Once he was convinced of that it would be difficult to change his mind—for he was obstinate.

So Marcus decided to go first to his father, and when the train reached Belfast he hurried immediately to Mr. Brownlow's office. Mr. Brownlow, however, was engaged. For nearly an hour Marcus hung about, hoping for an opportunity of speaking to him. At last he appeared, but before Marcus had time to utter more than a word or two of greeting Mr. Brownlow was called to the telephone. A long conversation followed, and when that was over there was someone waiting to see him.

Marcus's courage ebbed. He was a little frightened of his father, almost too frightened to be able to tell his story without encouragement. He knew that his father was fond of him, and that he was kind; but—and particularly in the office—he had a brusque manner, which made him difficult to approach.

At last Marcus lost heart and went home. Mrs. Brownlow and Margaret were not busy. They had plenty of time for an interview. They began at once to ask Marcus questions about his visit.

"What did you do all the time?"

"Oh, nothing in particular."

"Did you bathe?"

"Yes." He had bathed once.

"Did Caldwell bathe?"

"No."

"Why not?" Margaret was surprised. "I thought you wouldn't be friends with anyone who wasn't keen on bathing."

"He just didn't want to," Marcus retorted. "Why should he if he didn't want to?"

"Oh I don't know," Margaret responded. "It seems funny not wanting to in weather like this."

"What's Mr. Burnaby like?" Mrs. Brownlow inquired. "Is he nice?"

"He's all right," Marcus replied. He hesitated, blushed and found that they were looking at him expectantly. "He asked me to be his secretary," he said.

"Oh!" Mrs. Brownlow exclaimed, and then, "Well, I think you might have told us sooner."

"His secretary! You!" Margaret repeated in tones of amazement.

Marcus bristled. "And why not, I'd like to know?" he demanded defiantly. "And how could I tell you sooner? Amn't I just in?"

"It sounds more like a job for a girl," Margaret observed nastily. "You wouldn't think of becoming a male nurse instead?"

"Margaret, don't be objectionable," Mrs. Brownlow reproved her sharply. "Important men nearly always have men for secretaries—members of Parliament for instance. It might be quite a good opening. Disraeli's secretary was made a lord."

"Do you think Marcus will be made a lord?"

Marcus glared at her furiously and Mrs. Brownlow frowned. "Does your father know?" she asked.

Marcus shook his head. "I called at the office, but he was busy and couldn't talk to me."

"Oh dear," Mrs. Brownlow sighed. "I'm afraid he's working too hard. You know we always hoped he'd be able to retire at sixty-five—but trade's so bad. It's a pity you couldn't go into the office and take some of the weight off his shoulders."

Marcus sighed too. He didn't want to go into the firm and his father wasn't particularly anxious to have him. The prospects in the wholesale tea trade were bad. Cheap packet teas were capturing the market. The older type of trade, where grocers bought tea by the chest, was dwindling. Marcus said nothing: it had all been discussed before, time after time.

When dinner was over Mr. and Mrs. Brownlow went into the drawing-room and the door was shut.

"Cabinet meeting," Margaret commented, leading the way to the morning-room where they all usually sat. She dropped into a chair and picked up *Good Housekeeping*. Marcus sat down on the window seat with his feet up and a cushion on his knee. He had hidden the *Daily Mail* here before dinner and now he fished it out.

Margaret looked up. "Cunning," she remarked.

Marcus paid no attention.

He read *Looking at Life* and an article on tennis by Stanley Doust. After that he stopped reading and gazed out at the garden. It had been raining and would probably rain again during the night. Meanwhile it was fine, though the sun was not shining. Everything looked fresh, and from time to time a bird sang. It sang very tenderly, very sweetly, and Marcus was moved. He remembered how he had always hated going away to school at the end of the holidays, how he had always longed to come back to just this, the peaceful garden, the quiet house, his own bed upstairs . . . .

Presently Mrs. Brownlow came in. "Daddy would like to talk to you," she told Marcus. "He's in the drawing-room."

As Marcus got up she smiled at him. Marcus smiled back rather doubtfully. She might mean, "I've told Daddy to let you go if you really want to," but he rather thought it was, "I know I can trust you to be a good boy and listen to reason."

He went along the passage, crossed the hall, and opened the drawing-room door. His father was standing in a bay window on the right of the room looking out at the garden. He turned round when Marcus came in, and smiled, though not quite in the same way as Mrs. Brownlow. He looked old and tired. His smile was either an apology for these things, or an effort to conquer them. At any rate it aroused Marcus's sympathy. He wanted to please his father, to be kind to him. "Well," Mr. Brownlow said, "your mother tells me you've been offered a job."

"Yes," Marcus answered, and immediately his awe of his father returned. He was suddenly on his guard. He remembered he had a battle to fight.

"And what *is* the job?" Mr. Brownlow asked. "I'd like to know a little about it."

"He wants me to be his secretary." Marcus knew that Mr. Brownlow was already aware of this. What he wanted was to find out what Marcus's work would consist of, what his prospects would be, what salary he was offered. Marcus could only answer the last of these questions. About the others he was determined to be as uncommunicative as possible. His expression became sullen and slightly hostile.

Mr. Brownlow gave a little sigh. He sat down at one end of the sofa. Marcus sat down at the opposite end. Neither of them leaned back. Their attitudes were identical. They were the same height: they had the same eyes. The father was slightly potbellied, but his knees showed bonily through his trousers and the veins on the backs of his hands were blue. The son was slighter, but his limbs were rounded and his face was plump. An onlooker might have fancied that he was seeing the same person in youth and in age.

"Have you any idea what sort of work you'll be expected to do?"

Marcus stared at the carpet. He knew that his father was looking at him kindly and expectantly. He didn't want to tell a lie. He felt angry with Mr. Burnaby, resentful of the way he had spoken—as if salary were the only thing his father would think about. Why, so far it hadn't even been mentioned. Marcus's gaze shifted to his shoes: they were brown and rather dusty. Half-unconsciously he rubbed first one and then the other on the carpet. Then he pulled up his socks which had dropped down round his ankles. He scratched his right leg and pulled out one or two hairs. He rolled them between his finger and thumb and dropped them one after the other on the floor. A carpet was made up of a lot of little hairs, he reflected. Most of them were quite loose: you could pull them out quite easily.

"Did he give you no idea of what your work would be—what you would actually have to do?" Mr. Brownlow persisted patiently.

"He just said he wanted me to be his secretary," Marcus answered. "I suppose I'd have to do secretarial work."

Mr. Brownlow began to pick at the skin round the nail of one of the fingers of his right hand. The movement made a faint click-clicking, like the thripping of a grasshopper in slow motion. From outside came the sound of raindrops, spattering on the leaves of the bushes in the shrubbery.

"Has he a secretary now?" Mr. Brownlow demanded at last. "Or, has he had a secretary till recently?"

"He didn't say." Marcus looked up. He was pleased that to this question at any rate he could give a candid and straightforward response. "There wasn't a secretary there," he added.

"The reason I'm asking these questions is that we know very little about him," Mr. Brownlow explained. "We've heard of him of course, but I'd like to know more about him before letting you accept this offer. What is his offer, by the way? I suppose you did find that out."

Marcus smiled. "Three hundred a year to begin with," he announced, trying to sound as matter-of-fact as possible.

"Oh!" Mr. Brownlow exclaimed, making no attempt to hide *his* feelings. "That's a very large sum for a boy of your age." He gazed at his son, trying perhaps to discover virtues which had hitherto escaped him. "Three hundred a year!"

"He said it would be increased from time to time," Marcus went on with a certain smugness, "as, as. . . ."—he searched for the right phrase—"as I got more valuable you know."

Mr. Brownlow could only repeat his "Oh!" in a tone of slightly increased astonishment.

And Marcus, now that he had reached what seemed, for the moment at least, to be safer ground, felt more communicative. "I don't think he understands much about money," he volunteered. "I mean perhaps he doesn't realize the value of it. I mean the chauffeur and the maids all looked very content."

Mr. Brownlow laughed and scratched his head. "If they're paid on the same scale I suppose they *would* be satisfied," he agreed. "It's most unusual—I mean that sort of generosity in a million-aire—but I think you can take it that anyone who has made a for-tune like that knows the value of money better than you or I. It would be a pity to start off with a false impression. We'll just have to take it that for some reason he's set his heart on getting you to do the job." Mr. Brownlow's smile vanished and a frown took its place. "The trouble is that a man who makes an offer like that is very often capricious. He won't make allowances for inexperi-ence. In six months' time he may want to dismiss you and in the interval you might have a somewhat unpleasant time. However, six months isn't very long. I don't suppose you'd come to any harm and the experience might be useful to you."

"He said I could come on a month's trial," Marcus suddenly re-membered, and felt that the battle was nearly won.

"Oh did he?" Mr. Brownlow responded. "Well perhaps we might let you do that. You should be able to get an idea in a month. We'll see."

"You mean I can go?" Marcus said. "I can write and say I'm coming?"

"I think *I'd* better write," Mr. Brownlow told him. "There are one or two things I'd like to know before we agree to anything definite. After all you *are* our only son, and we'd like to make sure you get a good start in life. We knew, of course, that you would very likely leave home some day, but we didn't expect that it would be quite as soon as this." He reflected for a little, leaning forward with his hands on his knees. "Do you know if he offered the job to Caldwell?"

Marcus's gaze returned suddenly to the carpet. "I don't think he did."

"That would have seemed more natural," Mr. Brownlow continued slowly. "I can't help feeling that there's something about this I don't understand. It's partly your manner, I'm afraid. I think you are quite open and quite truthful, but you have a habit of looking at the ground when you're answering questions. It's a bad habit and you should try to get out of it. Little things like that count for a great deal in life. When you're speaking to people look straight at them, and speak straight out. Don't mumble."

"Yes, Daddy," Marcus said, still looking at the ground, and mumbling more than ever. Then he looked up. "Yes, Daddy," he repeated more loudly.

"That's better," Mr. Brownlow commented encouragingly. "I said", he went on, "that I thought it would have been more natural if he had offered the job to Caldwell. Caldwell, I suppose, is his heir or one of his heirs. He might easily have wanted him to learn how he managed his affairs so that they would be properly attended to after his death. However, I know these rich men do very often have secretaries. The trouble is I don't see what prospects the job offers."

There was a moment's silence. Then Mr. Brownlow stood up and Marcus knew that the interview was over. He was afraid to ask what decision his father had made. "Would you go and tell your Mother that I'm writing a letter and will be along in half an hour or so." He went over to his desk in the corner and switched on the electric light which hung over it.

Marcus did not see the letter which he wrote at the time, but years later he did see it. This is a copy of it:

Dear Mr. Burnaby,

I have just heard from my son of the very kind and generous offer which you have made to him. Before advising him to accept it or refuse it, however, I feel it my duty to make certain enquiries.

The salary you have suggested seems completely satisfactory, much higher indeed than I should have expected to be paid to a boy of his age. Unfortunately Marcus seems to have no idea of the kind of work he will be expected to do.

I am afraid that in some ways he is very unformed and rather young for his age. This, of course, is a fault which time will cure, but both his mother and I had hoped that he would remain at home for a few years longer, until his character had matured a little and he was more fit to go out into the world on his own account. At present he is rather too impressionable, and before agreeing to let him go, we should like to be sure that his future surroundings and the influences with which he will come in contact will be beneficial both mentally and *morally*. I should therefore esteem it a favour if you could grant me an interview either here in Belfast, or in Dublin, or if necessary I could travel to Portmallagh and see you either there, or at your own house. I should be only too glad to make whatever arrangements are most suitable to you.

I hope you will not consider this an impertinent letter, but you can no doubt understand the feelings of a mother and of a father. Marcus is our only son and his welfare is of very great importance to us.

Yours truly,

T. M. BROWNLOW.

This letter was written in the most perfect copper plate—every down stroke heavy, every upstroke light. Mrs. Brownlow read it over that night and in the morning it was posted.

CHAPTER XVII

MR. Burnaby's reply arrived by the first post on Friday. He said that he was coming to Belfast at the end of the following week and would call at Mr. Brownlow's office on the Thursday morning.

"We'll have to have him out for lunch," Mrs. Brownlow declared, when she heard this news. A thoughtful expression came over her face. "Let me see now. I suppose tomato soup would do to begin with. Nearly everybody likes tomato soup and Nancy makes it very nicely."

"He mightn't want to come to lunch," Marcus put in uncomfortably.

The others looked at him suspiciously, and he blushed. "What that means, I suppose," Mrs. Brownlow observed, "is that *you* don't want him to come."

This was exactly what it did mean, but Marcus was afraid to admit it. His motives were confused and he would not have ventured to try to explain them.

"It's just I thought he mightn't want to," he repeated lamely. "I mean being a millionaire and all that. I mean I expect he's frightfully busy seeing people and all that sort of thing."

"I believe even millionaires have to eat," Mrs. Brownlow returned drily, "but perhaps you're afraid we wouldn't be grand enough for him."

"Oh no, it's not that," Marcus said hurriedly. "He doesn't live grandly at all himself."

"Well, what is it then?" Mrs. Brownlow asked.

"It's just I thought he mightn't want to," Marcus mumbled for the third time.

"Tch!" Mr. Brownlow made a clicking noise with his tongue. He disliked evasive answers.

"He can easily say, 'No thank you,' if he doesn't want to come," Margaret pointed out brightly.

Marcus looked at her. He remembered Burnett at school saying how lucky he was to have a sister. Burnett had no sisters himself of course.

He tried to decide why he didn't want Mr. Burnaby to be asked to lunch. It wasn't that he was afraid of whatever impression his family might make on Mr. Burnaby. Rather he was afraid of what his mother might find out *from* Mr. Burnaby. It would never do for him to be lured into telling her the real nature of the work which he and Marcus were going to do. If once that came out Marcus would certainly not be permitted to go and he didn't think he would have sufficient courage or ruthlessness to defy his parents and go without permission. In any case he was not of age.

Nevertheless, he couldn't prevent the invitation being sent, and in due course it was accepted. Then Marcus decided to write a letter to Mr. Burnaby on his own account. He wrote it on Monday morning in the Linenhall Library while he was waiting to go to his classes.

Linenhall Library.
Monday.

Secret.

Dear Mr. Burnaby,

I hear you are coming to lunch with us on Friday. I expect Mother will try and get out of you what exactly our work will be. Please don't tell her, whatever happens—or Daddy either—because if you do they won't let me go. They don't approve of spiritualism or spirits or anything like that. They think it's the Devil. So please be careful.

Don't reply to this letter. I don't get many letters and they might want to know what it was.

Yours sincerely,
M. BROWNLOW.

On the envelope he put the words "Strictly Private" and underlined them twice.

When Friday came Marcus was in an extremely unsettled state. In the morning he went to his classes as usual: but he got off early and was at home when his father and Mr. Burnaby arrived for lunch. They came in Mr. Burnaby's car, and Marcus, who had been looking out for them, was pleased to see that they both seemed to be in good spirits. He had intended to meet them as they got out of the car, but a momentary attack of shyness made him hold back. It was not till they were in the hall that he came forward to shake hands.

"Well," his father said as he caught sight of him, "here's the secretary," and from this, and something in Mr. Burnaby's manner, Marcus knew that all had gone well, so far at any rate. When he had hung up his hat and coat Mr. Burnaby was taken into the drawing-room, where Mrs. Brownlow and Margaret were waiting to receive him. He was introduced and a few minutes later they all went in to lunch.

At first they talked about Mr. Burnaby's drive to Belfast—for he had come by car—but soon Mr. Brownlow brought the conversation round to the subject of stocks and shares. Though he didn't put the question in so many words it was clear that he wanted to hear how Mr. Burnaby's fortune had been made. And up to a point Mr. Burnaby seemed quite willing to tell him. He spoke with surprising candour of his early speculations, of how he had bought shares with borrowed capital and sold them again at a profit: but he didn't tell them how he knew which shares to buy.

Mrs. Brownlow was probably not very much interested in the share market, or in gossip about old stock-exchange sensations. What she did want to know, as she had announced more than once since Marcus's return, was whether or not Mr. Burnaby was related to the three old Miss Burnabys who had lived in Mount Pleasant when she was a girl.

Mr. Burnaby said that he was their nephew, and this started an exchange of reminiscences that went on till the end of lunch. It turned out that Mr. Burnaby's brother Charles and Mr. Brownlow's brother Henry had both at one time been members of a football club called Albion which had since gone out of existence; that he had once been at a party which Mrs. Brownlow had been prevented from attending by an attack of mumps.

"And I was so disappointed," Mrs. Brownlow said, with a sigh. "I can remember to this day the dress I was going to wear. It came from Brands'—the old Brands' you know—when they were on the other side of Donegall Place."

Marcus listened with a sort of benevolent superiority. If they went on like this, he thought, everything would be all right. But when lunch was over and they were sitting in deck chairs in the garden Mrs. Brownlow changed the subject abruptly. "I hope you'll give Marcus plenty to do," she remarked almost aggressively.

"I'll do my best," Mr. Burnaby responded good humouredly.

"I'm sure you will," Mrs. Brownlow said, "but I'm afraid it's that that's been rather puzzling us. So far as we can gather from Marcus you haven't employed a secretary up to now—and we rather wondered in that case why you suddenly wanted one." She coloured slightly and added, "I hope you won't think I'm rude or inquisitive, but I don't want Marcus to be idle, or grow into idle habits."

Mr. Burnaby lit a fresh pipe. "Do you think Marcus is inclined to idleness?" he enquired.

"No I don't," Mrs. Brownlow returned briskly, "but I think it's bad for any young man to be left without sufficient to do. It's enough to ruin the strongest character."

"I quite agree," Mr. Burnaby said. There was a pause. Evidently he regarded the subject as closed, for his next remark was quite irrelevant. "I love the scent of wallflowers," he announced. "I got a sudden whiff of them there—it's such a warm, clean scent. It always reminds me of a house where I used to stay when I was a boy."

Marcus sniffed sympathetically, but the wallflowers eluded him. The acrid odour of Mr. Burnaby's pipe seemed to pervade everything. He wondered if Mr. Burnaby thought he'd got off with it— for he hadn't: Mrs. Brownlow was quite visibly preparing to renew her attack. "I was wondering how you managed before," she said. "If you need a secretary now you must have had a great deal too much to do before."

"Yes indeed," Mr. Burnaby told her. "That's just it. I *have* too much to do, far more than I want. What I intend is to teach Marcus to do it all. The harder he works the better pleased I'll be—and I'll make him work."

"But what *is* the work?" Mrs. Brownlow was driven to demand.

"The work," Mr. Burnaby repeated thoughtfully. "Well, you know, property requires a certain amount of management, and one way and another I've a good deal of property. If you don't look after it things begin to go wrong, and before you know where you are, you're in no end of a mess. I'm reaching the time of life when one wants to take things more easily. One loses interest in business after a time. Twenty years ago I couldn't have enough of it, but lately I've begun to wonder what was the use of it all, following the markets day after day, trying to make more and more money. . . ."

Mr. Brownlow sighed. He too was sick of it all—and he was an older man than John Burnaby. He too had been trying year after year to make more and more money, but recently it had seemed that he could only make less and less: indeed the nature of the struggle had changed: it was now a matter of seeing how little he could lose.

Mr. Burnaby went on talking rather slowly in a sort of sing-song voice. Somehow he built up a picture for them of Marcus at work, Marcus in a big study sitting at a leather-topped desk strewn with papers, Marcus answering the telephone, Marcus giving instructions, asking for advice occasionally perhaps, but on the whole a model of discretion and efficiency, a prop on whom his chief would come to depend more and more as the years went on.

Mr. Brownlow saw a Marcus who might return eventually to take the weight off *his* shoulders. Even Mrs. Brownlow was impressed, and to Margaret it all seemed wonderful. She felt jealous of Marcus. Why should all this happen to *him*? She could learn to do it far more quickly, and far better she was sure—and she would have loved to meet the sort of people Mr. Burnaby no doubt knew—other millionaires, all sorts of important people who would come to stay. They wouldn't *all* be old and some of them were sure to have sons. There was bound to be lots of time off: there was bound to be bathing and tennis. She was quite sure Mr. Burnaby didn't live in Donegal all the year round. In winter the whole household would move to London, with perhaps a spell on the Riviera. She wondered if there was a steam yacht and decided immediately that there was bound to be. Marcus had boasted a bit, talked of houses all over the place, though Margaret wasn't quite clear as to their whereabouts.

While Mr. Burnaby was actually speaking Marcus had been more impressed than any of them. He had seen the same picture as they had seen, but when Mr. Burnaby stopped he began to feel confused. It wasn't that he disliked the idea of looking after Mr. Burnaby's affairs: being important in *any* way appealed to him. It was just that he wondered exactly what he *would* have to do. All the same he was filled with confidence: he would be able to do whatever was wanted. He knew too that the matter was now decided, and when presently Mr. and Mrs. Brownlow went into the house for a private talk with Mr. Burnaby, he felt no anxiety as to the result, only a pleasant excitement.

By the time Mr. Burnaby's car appeared they were all together once more, having afternoon tea in the drawing-room. Everything had been settled. Marcus was to start work on the fifteenth of June.

CHAPTER XVIII

MARCUS felt very shy when he arrived again at Mr. Burnaby's. He had travelled from Belfast by the afternoon train and been met at Portmallagh by Black with Mr. Burnaby's car. Black had been in his chauffeur's uniform and the car was a Minerva. It all looked very grand. Marcus could only think of himself as the new private secretary—green, and probably inefficient. The adventure with Caldwell seemed more remote than a dream.

Mr. Burnaby had been on the look-out for him, and met him at the hall-door; but somehow it was not the Mr. Burnaby of his previous visit. It was Mr. Burnaby the millionaire, the successful business man, the personality who had made such an impression on Mrs. Brownlow and Margaret. Marcus noticed his English accent. He was quite accustomed to English accents—in England. In Ireland, an English accent always sounded rather domineering and harsh. Marcus responded automatically. His own public school accent, which had been fading during the last year at home, returned in full strength. Listening to them, only an Englishman would have known that they were both Irish.

This tension, or lack of ease, lasted all through dinner, but once they were alone together in Mr. Burnaby's study it began to disappear. "Well," Mr. Burnaby remarked, lighting a pipe and settling himself in his chair, "everything seems to have gone very well so far. Are you ready to begin work in the morning?"

"Oh yes," Marcus replied, but both question and answer had a double meaning for him. He had come prepared to do two kinds of work. Ever since Mr. Burnaby's visit he had been getting new clothes. He had even a new watch and a new fountain-pen—parting gifts from his parents—the old ones being relics of school, battered and unreliable. All this preparation to be a millionaire's secretary had pushed the true nature of the work into the background of his mind. Now, as if curtains had been drawn back, and a brilliantly lit stage revealed, he had a sudden vision of what his real work was to be. The room, the fire, Mr. Burnaby. . . . everything was almost the same as it had been that first night after his journey with Caldwell. Marcus felt a surge of enthusiasm. "Why not begin tonight?" he suggested. "I'll begin tonight, if you like."

Mr. Burnaby smiled. "I think it'll be time enough in the morning," he advised. "You're tired tonight and I don't want you going to sleep over it—which you might quite easily do."

"I'm not tired at all," Marcus assured him. "I won't be sleepy at all. Travelling doesn't make me sleepy. I mean, you're just sitting there resting."

"All the same," Mr. Burnaby answered, "I think we'd better leave it till the morning."

Breakfast the next morning was at half-past eight. Marcus was a minute or two early, but he found Mr. Burnaby waiting for him. Immediately the bell was rung and Kate brought in the porridge. During the meal they didn't talk much. Mr. Burnaby was a quick eater, and as before he finished first. He pushed back his chair and took a pipe from his pocket. As he filled it he watched Marcus with an expression that was friendly, slightly amused, and at the same time completely reassuring. It was clear that he had something to say, but he waited till his pipe was lit and burning to his satisfaction. Marcus in the meantime tucked into toast and marmalade.

"Now," Mr. Burnaby began at last, "we're going to start at ten prompt. That's exactly an hour from now. We'll work till twelve at least, perhaps till one, and during that time I don't want there to be any interruptions of any kind. During every minute of that time I want you to be able to give yourself completely to your work. There must be no wandering of your attention. We won't be interrupted from outside, and I don't want you to have to go out for any purpose whatever. Do you understand?"

Of course Marcus did understand. As soon as he had finished eating he compared his watch with Mr. Burnaby's and immediately retired to the W.C. Next he went to his room and refilled his fountain-pen, though it wasn't actually empty—just in case there should be any notes to take. Afterwards he walked up and down the drive in the sunshine, and back and forwards across the grass between the house and the shore. At five to ten he returned to the house, and with a pleasant feeling of excitement, climbed the tower stairs. On the landing at the top he hesitated for a moment; just as he was about to knock, he heard Mr. Burnaby's voice calling to him to come in.

He saw immediately that the room had been altered since the night before. All the pictures had been taken down and most of the furniture had disappeared. Two wooden chairs, the table, and a large wooden chest were all that remained. On top of the chest was a thick tartan motoring rug. "You can wrap that round you if you're cold," Mr. Burnaby told him. Marcus saw that the fire had not been lit.

"Oh I won't be cold," he declared. "I'm quite warm really."

The table was close to the door and one of the chairs was behind it. "Sit down there," Mr. Burnaby ordered. He himself was standing in the middle of the room like the Captain of a cricket team placing his field. He looked hot, and his scanty, grey hair was standing out sideways. His feet seemed to be just touching the ground rather than resting on it.

He went to the chest and took out a framed picture, measuring perhaps thirty inches by eighteen. Keeping the back to Marcus, so that the picture itself was hidden, he carried it to the far end of the room. There he turned it round, so that it could be seen, and hung it from a nail on the wall. "Try to get there," he said.

The picture was an oil-painting. It showed a ploughboy with two farm horses, a white horse and a black horse. The boy was mounted on the white horse and held the black horse by a rope halter. The horses were standing at the edge of a small pond, with their heads drooping down towards the water. In the background was a row of dark trees. There was a gap in the trees, with a glimpse of open country beyond. The sky was a twilight grey.

"Get into it?" Marcus asked.

"No. Get *to* it."

Mr. Burnaby left the picture and went to the corner on Marcus's left, where the other chair was. Marcus put his elbows on the table, with his chin between his hands, and looked at the picture. He thought at first that it was a very plain sort of a picture, quite nice, but rather dull. Then he began to get interested in a queer, dreamy kind of way. There was a suggestion that the country beyond the dark trees was filled with life and light and beauty. Marcus gazed at it. He imagined himself riding the black horse. Slowly the horses would begin to move, there would be a few splashes, a squelch, squelch of their feet in the mud at the edge of the pond, and they would find themselves going slowly towards the gap in the trees, and beyond . . . .

"Well?" Mr. Burnaby said suddenly.

Marcus was startled. "Yes?" he answered questioningly.

"Where were you?" Mr. Burnaby asked. "What did you see?"

"We were riding on horses' bare backs. We were just coming up to the gap in the trees: they're old, gnarled, hawthorn trees. The leaves are dark on them. The blossom is over and the berries are formed, but they're green still, not. . . ."

"No good." Mr. Burnaby stopped him, making an impatient movement with his hand. "No good at all: you're just day-dreaming, imagining things. It's quite pleasant: anyone can do it. I don't want you to imagine things in your mind. I want you to project your mind itself. We'll try something else."

He returned the first picture to the chest and took out another. It was a picture of an old mill with a big, wooden water-wheel. The mill was on the right of the picture in the foreground: on the left, level with the lower part of the water-wheel was a piece of dark grass with some small figures standing on it. In the background were tall trees: no sky was visible: the trees were a deep, bluish green—almost black.

Mr. Burnaby hung this picture on the wall where the first had been, and Marcus looked at it. There was dead silence in the room: the outer world was cut off in sound, in sight, in smell. Marcus began to hear his own breathing, though he couldn't hear Mr. Burnaby's. He gazed and gazed—but nothing happened. His eyes wandered from the picture to the frame, and round the frame. It was an old gilt frame with studs on it: there was dust on the studs and in the crevices of the frame. He noticed the texture of the canvas in a place where the paint was thin: he could see the marks the brush had made on the paint: in one place a small piece of hair from the brush was embedded in the paint. Marcus looked at the figures on the strip of grass: they weren't really all there: their faces were just blobs, and when you looked closely you could see that their arms didn't fit properly.

What exactly had Mr. Burnaby expected him to find, he won-dered. What did he mean him to do? He couldn't quite remember the instructions. He was to look at the picture *for* something. His eyes remained fixed obediently on the picture, but he could see Mr. Burnaby gazing at him intently from his chair in the corner. He realized that he was no longer really looking at the picture. He had lost interest in it. He couldn't concentrate on it any more. He was really watching himself and Mr. Burnaby. He would have to tell Mr. Burnaby, and hope he wouldn't be annoyed. "I'm afraid it's no good," Marcus said. His voice startled him. It seemed to begin outside of him, as though it was someone else who was speaking, but the sentence ended quite naturally. He blinked.

Mr. Burnaby was surprised. He didn't look annoyed or disap-pointed. "I thought you'd managed it that time," he remarked. "However, I suppose you'd better have a shot at something else."

They tried eight pictures altogether, but by the end of the morn-ing they seemed no further on than when they had started. Marcus began to think that the pictures were a hindrance instead of a help. "Would it not be better if I tried to get up into the ceiling, the way you talked about before?" he suggested at last. "The pictures seem to kind of put me off."

"I don't think so," Mr. Burnaby replied. "I don't know why they should: besides, I have a particular reason for wanting to use them. In any case there's no hurry. We'll try again tomorrow." He looked at his watch. "It's a quarter past twelve. We'll make a note of what we've done and then it'll be time for lunch." He handed Marcus a large, stiff-backed exercise book. "I want you to make notes of ev-erything you do. Never leave them till the next day. If you possibly can—there may later be some occasions when you can't—make notes of what you have done each day the moment you have fin-ished your experiments. *I* always do—at least I always have, since I gave up business and devoted myself to this work."

He sat down at the opposite side of the table and taking out a fountain-pen opened a book exactly similar to the one he had given Marcus. He turned over a good many pages already covered with small, round handwriting, till he came to a blank page. At the top of this he put the date and after that Marcus thought—though it was difficult to read upside-down—"First Experiments with Marcus Brownlow."

Marcus wrote the date at the top of his page, and below it, "First Experiments with Mr. Burnaby."

Mr. Burnaby looked up. "Mind you, I shall want to read your notes," he said. "It doesn't matter much how you write them, but be sure you put in everything."

In the afternoon Mr. Burnaby took Marcus for a walk in the grounds. These were roughly the shape of a triangle, narrowest near the village and broadening out to a width of about three-quarters of a mile: at the base of the triangle was a line of sand-hills and beyond the sandhills the shore at the mouth of the lough. With the exception of the walled garden behind the house, the land was probably almost valueless. None of it was farmed: it was simply a rabbit-warren.

The house had originally been a military barracks: then a coast-guard station. In 1905 the Government had sold it and it had been used as a private house ever since. Mr. Burnaby had bought it in 1918.

"Of course it's inconvenient from the modern point of view. I've often thought of putting in a plant to make electric light, but somehow I never have. I know the lamps are a nuisance to the servants, but I think they suit the place better—and after all if I did have all the up-to-date gadgets I'd need fewer servants—and that would bring Father Donaghy down on me for causing unemployment."

"Who's Father Donaghy?" Marcus asked.

"The parish priest. I should think I owe it to him that I wasn't burned out in The Troubles—like the Temples and the Jerrolds. I expect he pointed out that I paid satisfactory wages, and had no rents to collect—and that my land was of no value to anyone except myself."

In the evening they played tennis again, and again Marcus was beaten. It annoyed him that Mr. Burnaby didn't exert himself very much, while *he* had to spend the whole time running backwards and forwards across the court at full speed.

It was nearly dark when they stopped. Afterwards, sitting in the library, Mr. Burnaby taught Marcus how to play double dummy auction bridge: they went on playing till bed-time.

The next day was spent in much the same manner. For three hours in the morning Marcus looked at pictures which Mr. Burnaby hung up for him. In the afternoon they played tennis once more. Marcus played worse than ever, and when, in the third set, he found himself beginning to win he accused Mr. Burnaby of not trying.

Mr. Burnaby denied this, but Marcus wasn't convinced and they stopped playing. Marcus was glad to stop in any case. He was tired and hot. He suggested to Mr. Burnaby that they should go and bathe: but Mr. Burnaby said he hadn't bathed for twenty years and wouldn't start again now. "All the same," he added, "I'll come with you and show you the best place to go in."

Marcus remembered that Caldwell—the real Caldwell at school—had been a very keen bather. A bathe would have done Mr. Burnaby good, he thought. Marcus, who had a sensitive nose, could smell him slightly. It was a peculiar smell, rather herbal than animal. Marcus knew that different people had different kinds of smells when they were hot. He had noticed it at school. He remembered a boy who had been very keen on physical culture. Every night in the dormitory he had gone in for the most strenuous exercises. Before these were over he would be flowing with sweat, and the stench from that sweat had been overpowering—bitter and repellent. As however he was on the school boxing team no one had ever dared to complain, except behind his back. And there were other boys, Marcus recalled curiously, who when they were hot, had a rather pleasant, friendly smell. This smell that came from Mr. Burnaby reminded him of something. Was it aniseed, perhaps?

Marcus went into the house for his bathing things and they walked across the grass to the rocks. Marcus undressed and dived into the deep, cool water. The sea was very calm, and clear, and not so cold as Marcus had expected. When he came up from his dive he floated on his back and shouted at Mr. Burnaby. Mr. Burnaby had found a comfortable place to sit, and was leaning against a rock, with a pipe in his mouth, and his eyes half-closed.

"I suppose we get the Gulf Stream here," Marcus said.

"I expect so."

Marcus turned over, and doing a surface dive, swam for a little way under water. He discovered that when he got down a few feet the water was much colder. He came up again, and yelled once more at Mr. Burnaby. "I don't think it *can* be the Gulf Stream."

Mr. Burnaby nodded his head and smiled; but he didn't speak.

Marcus felt slightly irritated. "It's only the top that's hot," he explained, raising his voice almost to a scream.

Still Mr. Burnaby didn't answer. He nodded again and re-lit his pipe.

Marcus determined to give him a fright—make him wake up and take a bit of interest. He would swim out for a long way, perhaps a quarter of a mile, perhaps even half a mile. He began with a slow, steady breast-stroke: after thirty yards or so he changed to side-stroke, and then to a slow over-arm that was supposed to be trudgeon. He had once swum a mile in the baths at school. He hadn't enjoyed it much, but at least he had been able to count the lengths to see how he was getting on. He knew that if necessary he could swim more than a mile, but in the baths there had always been the knowledge that at any moment he could stop and get out, the assurance that if he suddenly got cramp in the deep end the swimming instructor would jump in and rescue him. Out here there was no such feeling of safety and comfort. If anything went wrong he would drown. It would be well to take it easy. It wasn't even as if he were fresh. He had felt quite tired after the tennis. He stopped and lay on his back to rest. He spread out his arms and closed his eyes. The sun felt warm on his face, on his chest and his stomach. But the back of his head was cold, an unpleasant, prickly cold, which seemed to eat into his skull. He thought of the deep water below him, full of fish and crabs and lobsters. He imagined some monstrous creature stretching up a black arm and dragging him down to the dark sea-weed at the bottom. He was a little frightened.

He began to swim again. He swam breast-stroke at first, but his neck was getting stiff and he changed to side-stroke. Then, quietly, and without any warning whatever, something happened, which was very like the horrors he had imagined.

About eight yards to his left a large, triangular fin rose above the smooth surface of the water. It was only there for a moment, but when it disappeared it left behind a little swirl in the place where it had been: in another moment the swirl too had disappeared.

Marcus had never seen a shark before, but he had not the slightest doubt that there was one quite close to him now—perhaps gliding up towards him at this very instant with its jaws open, ready to crunch its teeth into his leg. He did not exactly panic. He was extremely frightened, but he acted exactly as he would have done if he had had plenty of time to think. He knew from the adventure stories he had read that sharks were supposed to be frightened of splashing and noise. He knew too, that the faster he swam the more noise and the more splashes he made. All this passed through his mind in an instant. He began immediately to swim back towards the shore, kicking his feet violently and making the strongest and quickest strokes with his arms that he could manage. He had never swum so fast before, and he had never swum fast for so long a distance.

He was completely exhausted when he reached the rocks. He pulled himself out and half hung, half squatted on a narrow ledge just above the level of the water. The rock dug into his flesh and pressed against his ribs, but, panting with relief, he hardly felt the discomfort. He was done in, too weak at first even to climb up to where Mr. Burnaby was sitting, drawing peacefully at his pipe. He had done the crawl—or an approximation to the crawl all the way back. He gasped and gaped like a stranded fish.

Mr. Burnaby peered over the edge of the rocks and looked at him. "You're a clumsy swimmer," he observed. "You shouldn't splash so much." Marcus made no response and he went on, "You should try to learn the side-stroke. It's much the nicest stroke to watch. You fling your arms about too much: it's very ugly looking. I'm sure you could learn it if you tried. I used to do it. I'm sure I could teach you to do it."

Marcus was enraged. After all he had swum for his house in the last swimming sports before he left school—and he'd improved since then: if he'd stayed another term he'd probably have been in the school team. He forgot that he ought to be polite to Mr. Burnaby. "Anyone can swim side-stroke," he growled. "It's too slow."

Mr. Burnaby was offended. "Of course if you're going to take up that attitude", he retorted, "you'll never learn to do anything. As for saying the side-stroke's slow, it's what's always used in races. It's much faster than the breast-stroke, and so much more graceful."

But Marcus too was offended. Swimming was his one athletic accomplishment. Side-stroke indeed! Graceful! "It may have been the thing fifty years ago," he said rudely, "but no one but a dud would swim side-stroke in a race now."

"The over-arm side-stroke I mean," Mr. Burnaby persisted. "It took the place of the old side-stroke. I don't suppose you've ever seen a really good swimmer."

Marcus unfortunately never *had* seen an adult swimming competition. While he dressed he explained that he had been at a school which specialised in swimming and that he knew a great deal more about it than Mr. Burnaby. He talked about the crawl and the trudgeon-crawl, the best method of breathing and the scissor-beat.

When he felt that Mr. Burnaby was convinced he told him about the shark. Mr. Burnaby, however, refused to believe in the shark. "It was probably a porpoise," he said. "They're quite harmless."

CHAPTER XIX

THAT evening at dinner Mr. Burnaby asked Marcus who were his favourite authors.

"John Buchan and Ian Hay," Marcus rejoined promptly.

Mr. Burnaby was horrified. "Ian Hay!" he exclaimed in a tone of the deepest disgust. "But he's so dreadfully vulgar!"

Marcus blushed. He and Margaret had once had a nurse, who on certain occasions was in the habit of demanding, "Who's been vulgar?" If neither confessed they would both be sent to the W.C. Ever since, he had connected the word with the improper, the slightly indecent. "How do you mean, vulgar?" he enquired.

"Cheap," Mr. Burnaby explained. "He writes for the gallery—sentimental in the worst possible way."

Marcus thought of *Pip*, his favourite novel. It had been lent to him when he had 'flu, during his second term at Shellborough. The following holidays he had given a copy of it as a birthday present to his father, and ever since he had re-read it at least three times a year. He had indeed made a habit for a while of giving novels by Ian Hay to the family at Christmas and birthdays, and borrowing them afterwards at intervals to read himself. Margaret had eventually pointed out the meanness of this practice and he had had to abandon it—though by that time the house was provided with cheap editions of *The Safety Match*, *The Right Stuff*, *A Man's Man*, *A Knight on Wheels*, *The Willing Horse* and *Happy-Go-Lucky*.

"Have you ever read *Pip*?" Marcus asked, his mind returning to his favourite. Surely *Pip* was irresistible.

"*Pip, A Romance of Youth*." The very tone in which Mr. Burnaby quoted the title in full was a condemnation. "I tried to read it. It nearly made me sick. You don't mean to tell me you liked it?"

"But I do like it," Marcus declared.

Mr. Burnaby refused to be convinced. "I don't see how you can," he said. "Probably you haven't read it for a good while. You wouldn't like it now."

"I read it at Easter," Marcus told him, beginning to feel a little ashamed of his taste.

"This Easter!" It was hard to believe. "You only think you like it," Mr. Burnaby decided at last. "In a year or two you'll see through it. You won't be able to understand how you could ever stomach the stuff."

Marcus considered that this would be a sad state of affairs, but he thought it wiser to change the subject. He mentioned Buchan, his other favourite. Surely Buchan was safe. At school even the Head had read Buchan—books like *Prester John* and *Salute to Adventurers* weren't just ordinary novels, bits of them were quite stiff reading. It was almost history really.

"Oh Buchan's not bad," Mr. Burnaby replied, without any enthusiasm. "He can write thrillers—*The Thirty-nine Steps* was quite a good yarn, but when he tries anything more serious he gets out of his depth."

"What about *Witchwood*?" Marcus asked. It wasn't one of his own favourites, but for that reason it might be more likely to appeal to Mr. Burnaby.

Rather to his surprise Mr. Burnaby had read it. "I saw a review of it," he said. "The subject interested me: so I sent for it. It's no good. He can't do that sort of thing. He can't bring it off. Very few writers can. The trouble is they don't quite know what they *want* to bring off. Arthur Machen can do it—evolve a sense of the presence of evil—and of course, Henry James did it in *The Turn of the Screw*—but then that man could do anything. The trouble with John Buchan is that he knows nothing about what he's trying to describe."

"Maybe he's better not to know anything about evil," Marcus ventured.

"Certainly," Mr. Burnaby agreed, "and better still not to try and write about it."

This conversation had begun between mouthfuls of soup and continued while Mr. Burnaby carved a roast chicken. Now there was silence for ten minutes or so while the chicken was eaten. Marcus was glad of the respite. He determined that if the inquisition were renewed he would stick to the classics. After all he *did* like Dickens and Scott and Thackeray. *The Pickwick Papers* had made him roar with laughter, he remembered with a certain satisfaction, while *Bleak House* had plunged him into gloom.

He stole a glance at Mr. Burnaby and saw that he was smiling to himself as if something were amusing him. It might just be, of course, that he was enjoying the chicken, for he *was* fond of his food, but it might mean that he had something funny to say. Marcus smiled too, partly in sympathy, partly in anticipation. As soon as he had finished his chicken he glanced up hopefully, ready to laugh if Mr. Burnaby should have a funny story to tell. On the previous evening Mr. Burnaby had kept him in fits of laughter with reminiscences about dogs and cats, and a pet monkey he had once had.

Mr. Burnaby, however, was looking serious again. He rang the bell, and remarked, "You're going to have a lot of time on your hands, I'm afraid. For the present I don't want you to work—I mean do our special work—except in the mornings; but there's no reason why you shouldn't do other work—learn French, for instance."

"I did French at school," Marcus answered. He didn't like

French. When he left school he had felt that he had finished with French, as well as maths and physics, compulsory games and the Officers' Training Corps.

"Can you read a French novel as easily as an English one?" Mr. Burnaby persisted.

"I've never tried."

Mr. Burnaby took this to mean that Marcus couldn't read French at all. "It's wonderful how easy it is to learn," he said, "and yet at school, I suppose, they were so busy teaching you French grammar and making you practise trick sentences, that it never occurred to them that you might want to read the language. The academic mind is a dreadful thing. It's a pity. It has always seemed to me that reading novels should be one of the principal parts of one's education, and I suppose there are more good novels in French than in any other language. I have read most of them—most of the good ones I mean—and it would be a pity if you were never able to do the same.

"Oh well," he went on, glancing at Marcus's unenthusiastic face. "We'll let you off French meantime. All the same I think it would be a good idea for us to read some book together in the evenings. Would you rather have fiction, or something like Jowett's Plato, say—or perhaps you *did* Plato at school?"

"I didn't do Greek at all," Marcus informed him. "I was on the modern side."

Kate had come in with a dish of stewed pears. Mr. Burnaby helped Marcus and himself. "I leave it to you," he said. "You choose a book."

"Oh no, you choose," Marcus responded hastily, feeling that it would be dangerous to show a liking for any author without first hearing Mr. Burnaby's opinion of his work.

But Mr. Burnaby was determined to be magnanimous. "No, we'll let *you* choose this time," he insisted.

Marcus frowned. He didn't want to read Plato, or Julius Caesar, or Livy, even in translations. He might as well have been back at school—and didn't he get any time off? Was he never going to be allowed to amuse himself? Hardly noticing what he was eating, he got the stringy piece of a pear into his mouth and wondered what he should do with it. Should he put it out or swallow it? He swallowed it.

Dickens, Scott, Thackeray. They at any rate must be safe from disapproval. He repeated the names over and over again to himself—Dickens, Thackeray, Scott. . . . At last, because he had to say something, he made his choice. "What about Scott?" he asked.

"Scott!" Mr. Burnaby repeated in surprise. "Do you really *like* him? I always found him the most utter bore—those dreadful descriptions. . . ."

And then somehow he drifted on to the subject of Henry James—the texture of his style, his first manner, his second manner—the extraordinary elaboration of his last manner. Marcus had read one short story by Henry James—*The Great Good Place*. He had come across it in a collection of ghost stories and it had seemed to him the dullest thing in the book. Yet listening to Mr. Burnaby he forgot all about this. He became gradually convinced that a wonderful new experience was in store for him. The only question to be decided was, where should he start Henry James. "To have it all in front of you," Mr. Burnaby remarked, with a half-envious sigh. "I'm not sure that it wouldn't be best to start at the very beginning—I've got the old *Atlantic Monthlies* with the stories he never reprinted. You could study the gradual development of his style—and it was *so* gradual. You'd hardly believe it was the same man—that they really were by Henry James. But there it is, 'Henry James junior'."

Then a doubt crossed his mind. "Of course the early ones aren't nearly so good," he explained. "You mightn't like them. They give no idea of what was to come."

By this time dinner was over and they were in the library. Mr. Burnaby voyaged up and down the shelves with a lamp in his hand. He pulled out *Roderick Hudson* and put it back. He hesitated between *The American* and *The Awkward Age*, but in the end it was *The Spoils of Poynton* he selected, and this Marcus chose as the book that they should read aloud together.

It was a cool evening and the fire had been lit. They had lingered over their coffee and when Mr. Burnaby began to read it was getting dusk. He sat in an armchair on the window side of the fire with the lamp on a table behind him so that its light should fall on the book. Marcus was sprawled in another armchair, deep and comfortable, on the opposite side of the fire. He was in the shadow gazing at the butterfly flame of the lamp and through the window at the bluish grey clouds of the evening sky.

" 'Mrs. Gereth had said she would go with the rest to church, but suddenly it seemed to her she shouldn't be able to wait even till church-time for relief: breakfast was at Waterbath a punctual meal and she had still nearly an hour on her hands. Knowing the church to be near she prepared in her room for the little rural walk, and on her way down again, passing through the corridors and observing the imbecilities of decoration, the aesthetic misery of the big commodious house, she felt a return of the tide of last night's irritation, a renewal of everything she could secretly suffer from ugliness and stupidity. Why did she consent to such contacts? Why did she so rashly expose herself? . . . "

Mr. Burnaby read slowly, his voice rising and falling, giving full emphasis to the cadences of the style. Marcus listened, but almost from the first he found it difficult to grasp the meaning of the sentences. What contacts, he wondered; and how was she so rashly exposing herself? It was like listening to a song: the meaning was drowned by the music. He missed a sentence or two and found himself in a fog. He watched Mr. Burnaby's head moving slowly to and fro in time with his reading.

" '. . . . There were advantages enough it clearly didn't possess. It was hard for her to believe a woman could look presentable who had been kept awake for hours by the wall-paper in her room; . . .' "

Mr. Burnaby paused for slightly longer than the semi-colon warranted to see if this gentle gem had been appreciated, but being rewarded only by a look of dull puzzlement on Marcus's face he went on hurriedly.

" '. . . . yet none the less as she rustled in her fresh widow's weeds across the hall, she was sustained by the consciousness, which always added to the unction of her social Sundays, that she was, as usual, the only person in the house incapable of wearing in her preparation the horrible stamp of the same exceptional smartness that would be conspicuous in a grocer's wife. She would rather have perished than have looked endimanchée.'

"In her Sunday best, so to speak," Mr. Burnaby interpolated softly.

Very soon Marcus gave up trying to understand completely the longer and more involved sentences. He grasped the main outline of the story, and it didn't get on very fast. Staring straight into the light his eyes began to get tired and gradually he let his eyelids close. He could listen just as well that way, there was nothing any longer to distract him. Mr. Burnaby's voice rose and fell, rose and fell. . . . It was like something impersonal, the wind in the trees, or the rush of a waterfall, or a tune being played far away. It was a pleasant, lulling sound. Marcus went to sleep.

What made him wake up he didn't know. It might have been the flick of a turning page or a slight shuffle from the fire as the burning turves fell in upon themselves. At any rate Marcus was startled. For a moment or two he was wide awake and alert. He glanced anxiously at Mr. Burnaby. Had he noticed? But Mr. Burnaby hadn't: he was wrapped in the story. He read on steadily enjoying the sound of his voice, the perfection of Henry James at his best.

Marcus listened intently.

"'. . . . "Things" were of course, the sum of the world; only, for Mrs. Gereth, the sum of the world was rare French furniture and oriental china. She could at a stretch imagine people's not "having", but she couldn't imagine their not wanting and not missing.'"

Marcus heaved a little, subdued sigh of relief. At least they were more or less in the same place—still gassing away about her *old* furniture, and her *old* house. It was a relief at any rate that nothing important seemed to have happened. But Marcus couldn't feel relieved for long, or comfortable, for the desire to go to sleep began again to grow upon him. He had been outside all afternoon, and bathing always made him sleepy. It was the strong sea air, something to do with the salt in it and the iodine. Besides it was very cosy in the library. How delicious it would have been if he could only have relaxed and let himself go to sleep quite openly.

For another chapter and a half he battled against sleep; first with the tip of his forefinger against the flesh behind his chin, so that every time his head drooped forward he was jabbed uncomfortably by his finger-nail. Then he tried sitting bolt upright and gripping the arms of the chair tightly with both hands. 'Fleda Vetch!' There was something stuffy about the very name, and the way she and

Mrs. Gereth were always falling sympathetically into each other's arms.

"Well," Mr. Burnaby demanded looking up with an air of kindly triumph, an air of having brought a quite unexpected treat out of the hat. "Do you like it?"

Marcus gave himself a slight shake to drive back the drowsiness which encircled him on every side like a warm blanket. He didn't dare to say what he really thought. He wasn't sufficiently dishonest to pretend that he had enjoyed the reading as much as Mr. Burnaby seemed to expect. "I suppose it'll get more interesting later on," he answered haltingly. "I mean we're just at the beginning, aren't we? He's just sort of setting the scene, isn't he? I think nearly all good books begin that kind of way. . . ."

"But it's so beautifully *done*," Mr. Burnaby broke in. "The touch is so light, so delicate." He made a little gesture with his right hand. "It's like painting a picture—every brush stroke matters, is something added.

"You must be missing it all," he went on, "and there's so much *to* miss—the style, the manner, the way the sound is made to help in evoking the exact shade of meaning he wants to convey."

"Yes," Marcus said.

Mr. Burnaby looked at him. "I suppose you're sleepy," he decided. "It's quite late. Maybe it's time we went to bed."

The queer thing was that when Marcus got to his room he felt quite wide awake again. He had bought, to read in the train coming down, a copy of *The Strand Magazine* and *The Gangs Come to London* by Edgar Wallace. He wasn't as a rule very fond of Edgar Wallace thrillers, though he liked his African stories, but the idea of American gangsters working in London appealed to his imagination. However, there had been enough short stories in *The Strand* to keep him amused on the train, and he hadn't started the book. He had put it in a drawer of the dressing-table with his handkerchiefs and collars. Now he thought he would have a look at it.

He undressed quickly and propped on his elbow began to read by the light of the candle beside his bed. It was a thrilling story. He had only intended to read a page or two, but he read on and on, chapter after chapter. Presently he became conscious that his right arm had gone to sleep, and at the same time he began to feel guilty. At page seventy he stopped abruptly. He felt that Mr. Burnaby was standing behind him, watching him. In his hurry to start reading he must for the first time have forgotten to lock the door. He was horrified. For two or three minutes he didn't dare to move. At last he decided that he would roll out of bed suddenly on the opposite side to Mr. Burnaby. He took a deep breath and did it. He landed on the floor in a crouching position and scrambled round on his knees so that he could see across the bed. No one was there.

He examined the room carefully and tried the door. He *had* locked it. He looked on each side of every bit of furniture, and opened the wardrobe. He peered under the bed. Yet he wasn't satisfied. The impression of someone there—of Mr. Burnaby in fact—had been too strong. In an old house like this there might even be a secret door in the wall and a passage leading to Mr. Burnaby's room.

For a while he sat up in bed, glancing first at one part of the room, then another. He remembered a ghost story in which the candles one after another had gone out of their own accord. He took the electric torch from his bedside table and tried it. It was working all right and he kept it in his hand. He had more faith in it than in any candle.

Suddenly he was very sleepy again. He didn't want to go to sleep, but he realized he would have to go to sleep sometime. His sleepiness was making him gradually less fearful. He lay down, and at last, when he knew he could keep awake no longer, he blew out the candle and put the torch under his pillow where he could grab it in a moment. He had a vague idea that it was dangerous to let a candle burn out, that it might set the house on fire. He went to sleep.

Slowly and silently a door in the wall was swinging open. Marcus could see it clearly, though everything else in the room was dim. Behind the door was a black space. Marcus grabbed for his torch but it had gone: it had been slipped away from under his pillow while he was asleep. He wanted to get the matches and light the candle, but now he was paralyzed in every limb. He lay still and in terror.

Next moment he awoke, *really* woke up this time. The torch was there all right. He switched it on, and shone a shaky beam round the room. Everything was as before. There was no sign of a secret door and the candle was still on the table beside his bed. He lit it and kept awake for another half-hour.

CHAPTER XX

IN the morning Marcus was very sleepy. He was late for breakfast, and afterwards, sitting with Mr. Burnaby in the tower-room, he could hardly keep his eyes open. At first Mr. Burnaby made no comment, though it was obvious from his manner that he wasn't pleased. But after he had put the fourth picture in position he turned round suddenly and caught Marcus in the middle of a jaw-cracking yawn. Marcus forced his mouth shut, his eyes watering with the effort. He blinked and saw Mr. Burnaby's face turn white with anger. "What's the good of this?" he exclaimed. "How d'you expect to work when you're half asleep?"

"I'm afraid I *am* a bit sleepy," Marcus admitted.

"Of course you're sleepy," Mr. Burnaby returned. "How could you be anything else—sitting up half the night reading penny dreadfuls?"

For a moment Marcus didn't take in the full implication of this. He began by apologizing: "I didn't mean to go on for so long. It was so exciting and I didn't think about it making a difference." Then, seeing Mr. Burnaby's uncompromising face, he suddenly became angry himself. "All the same," he added, "I don't like people spying on me."

"That's an extremely unpleasant remark to make," Mr. Burnaby said. His voice trembled. He had almost lost control of it. "As a matter of fact I looked in for perfectly friendly reasons. I expected to see you asleep after your supposed tiredness. I had no idea it was just an excuse to get reading your Edgar Wallace."

"I *was* sleepy," Marcus retorted indignantly. "I could hardly keep my eyes open."

Mr. Burnaby shrugged his shoulders, and walking over to the window stood with his back to the room, looking out: "A strange sort of sleepiness", he commented, "——disappears at sight of an Edgar Wallace. If you'd been reading something decent I mightn't have minded so much."

Marcus, with his head between his hands, and his elbows on the table, stared at Mr. Burnaby. He hated rows and scenes. He knew he shouldn't have gone on reading for so long, but really he hadn't meant to—and he hadn't thought about it making him sleepy this morning. In any case it was only one morning and they'd lots of mornings before them. Mr. Burnaby was just as wrong as he was . . . . coming into the room to watch him. Surely he was entitled to *some* privacy, *some*times. All the same, he supposed, he'd better repeat his apology. One of them had to apologize, or the row would go on for ever—and Mr. Burnaby didn't look in the least as if *he* would. "I'm sorry," Marcus mumbled. "I didn't mean to spoil the work."

He waited hopefully, but there was no response from Mr. Burnaby. He was like God, Marcus thought, with a fresh wave of dislike. Everything you did, he knew about—and he was always right. It would be impossible to get away from him, even if he were to give up and go home. Whatever he did he would have the feeling that Mr. Burnaby might be watching him, might even be influencing his thoughts. He wished that he was an ordinary person, that his mind had never wandered out when he was asleep and attracted Mr. Burnaby's attention.

Presently Mr. Burnaby turned round. "Would you *like* to go?" he asked. "Give all this up and go home? If you would, you can— now's your chance. I'd promise to leave you alone, let you live your life in peace—never trouble you again." Marcus hesitated and Mr. Burnaby went on slowly: "Think of what a good time you'd have. No doubt you'd go into your father's office. Think of the interesting people you'd meet there, and of course, seeing who you were, they'd all be very nice to you. After a year or two you'd 'go out on the road' and meet more interesting people of the same kind. 'Commercials,' they're called—that's short for 'Commercial Gents'. You'd congregate in the evenings in the bars of *Commercial* Hotels, and you'd hear the latest dirty stories and be advised that so-and-so was a bit shaky and that somebody else was taking longer credit. And later on, I suppose, *being* who you are, you would 'come in off the road' again and take your father's place. How satisfactory that would be, to know that you were leading just the same life as your father had led—and perhaps your grandfather too, following in their footsteps, carrying on the grand old traditions. . . . But of course, the real attraction would be to know that you were completely ordinary and respectable, a business man among business men, a useful member of society, one among millions and millions, all useful members of society. You might even become a Mason.

"I wonder why they're called useful members of society," Mr. Burnaby reflected. "What use *are* they? Do their lives make the slightest difference? They leave everything as they found it. It wouldn't make a pick of difference if any one of them hadn't been born."

"But it would if none of them had been born," Marcus pointed out, brightening up a little, and feeling that the crisis had passed.

"Yes," Mr. Burnaby replied. "There'd be fewer people in the world."

Marcus was silent. For a minute or two he had been tempted to accept Mr. Burnaby's offer. The description he had heard of commercial life had even appealed to him a little. If only he could do just as Mr. Burnaby said—follow in his father's footsteps and feel satisfied with his position, feel that he was one of the great commercial community, a brother among brothers, feel that he *was* a useful member of Society. But he knew he couldn't. He would always feel spurious, that he was only acting a part. Besides he would never forget that he had had the choice and had chosen the lower rather than the higher. All his life he would be conscious of being a traitor. However miserable he was going to be, living his life to Mr. Burnaby's rules, he felt that it was better to be miserable and *matter*, than happy in that sort of way. And anyhow it wasn't as if, now, he *could* be happy that sort of way. There was no choice for him.

"Well," Mr. Burnaby asked quite kindly, "do you want to go?"

"No, I'll stay," Marcus said. "I think it must be horrible." Mr. Burnaby's point of view had suddenly become his own.

"It's wonderful how cheerfully they all put up with it," Mr. Burnaby commented, with the ghost of a smile, "though I suppose the only thing is to be cheerful, or religious, or to drink. However

I'll make a promise. I oughtn't to have spied on you last night—
though I didn't intend it to be spying—it was only the fact that you
were doing something you shouldn't have been doing that made it
spying, in an objectionable sense. But I won't do it again. I can see
that it would make it impossible for you—to have no privacy—but
you will be a good boy after this, won't you? It's a pity to waste
even one morning. It means that you're a whole day further back
just for the sake of an hour or two—and I don't suppose that you
really enjoyed that hour or two. You had an uneasy feeling all the
time, hadn't you?"

"I'm not a boy," Marcus said. "I'm grown-up."

All the same the row was over.

For the rest of the summer everything went fairly smoothly. It
was good enough fun playing tennis and bathing in the afternoon,
though Marcus would rather have played with someone a little
younger than Mr. Burnaby and bathed with someone who bathed
too, instead of sitting on the rocks wrapped in contemplation.
He was happiest when he was alone with a book: but he found it
a bore listening to Mr. Burnaby reading Henry James in the evenings. He wasn't interested in style, or second methods.

One thing only troubled him seriously. He was making no progress at all with his work: so far he hadn't been able to project himself a single inch. He did want to succeed at that. It was partly because of the work itself, partly because he would be ashamed to go
home as a failure, partly too because he didn't want to disappoint
Mr. Burnaby. Not that Mr. Burnaby showed any signs of being
disappointed. Marcus thought he was very kind about it, and very
patient. Time and again he told Marcus not to worry, that they
might have to wait six months, or even longer before they got any
positive results. He was quite sure that Marcus would get results
eventually. He *knew* Marcus had the power to do what he wanted:
it was just a question of learning how to utilize that power.

Marcus on the other hand would occasionally lose faith altogether. He would wonder if the whole thing were not a fraud, if
even Mr. Burnaby himself could do what he said he could do. He
would have to remind himself of what he knew Mr. Burnaby *had*
done—particularly of his two appearances as Caldwell.

Towards the beginning of August it got very hot. *The Spoils of Poynton* was finished and Mr. Burnaby was reading aloud *The Return of the Native*. Hardy was not a conscious artist like Henry James, he had explained to Marcus, but there was a lyrical quality in his work unlike anything which could be found in the work of other prose writers. He had also something in common with the ancient Greeks—a sense of inevitable tragedy. When Mr. Burnaby's voice was tired Marcus would be made to read a chapter or two: but he was bad at reading aloud: it made him yawn, and that always annoyed Mr. Burnaby.

One morning, at about eleven o'clock, they were in the tower room as usual. Mr. Burnaby had already put up two pictures without Marcus having been able to report any success. Marcus was in a dull, lethargic mood. To keep cool he had taken off his jacket and rolled up his shirt-sleeves, but his bare arms were inclined to stick to the table. He had heard Mr. Burnaby say that the picture before them was by some French artist, though the artist's name had gone out of his head. Already, too, he had forgotten if Mr. Burnaby had described the picture as an example of the impressionist or the post-impressionist school. He had seen so many pictures now, and nearly all of them seemed to be examples of some school or other. As soon as the picture was removed the general impression of it became blurred in Marcus's mind. There were a lot of faces in it: it was a painting of a cafe or a bar, or perhaps it was a scene in a park.

And then, just as Mr. Burnaby was about to hang up the next picture, Marcus suddenly saw the former one again. "That was a funny picture, that last one," he remarked inconsequently.

Mr. Burnaby paused and looked round. "Yes," he said quietly. "Why do you think so?"

"Well, you see," Marcus responded, "it's all right when you look at it from here, but when you go up close it sort of disappears: it's just a lot of blobs of paint, put on rather thick. . . ."

"Did you go up close?" Mr. Burnaby asked in the same even tone of voice.

"Oh yes," Marcus replied without hesitation.

"That's strange. I never saw you leave your chair." There was a pleased gleam in his eyes, and Marcus suddenly realized that he had at last succeeded in doing what Mr. Burnaby wanted.

"But I've been looking at them close all along," he exclaimed as the light suddenly flooded into his mind. "Why even the first day I did it—only I didn't understand. . . ."

"I knew you would," Mr. Burnaby told him. "Now we'll have to get on with the next step."

CHAPTER XXI

MR. Burnaby was very pleased indeed at Marcus's success. He explained that nearly all the pictures he had used had been chosen because their appearance altered when looked at from close range. He had been careful not to let Marcus handle the pictures himself or come close to them physically. He had wanted to make sure that his proof, when he got it, was quite definite.

"Of course," he pointed out, "if you had been noting every-thing—as you should have been—in a proper scientific manner, we'd have realized long ago; but scientific note-taking needs train-ing just like everything else."

Now that his patience had been rewarded he was delighted, and several times during the rest of the morning, and during lunch, Marcus found himself being gazed at with beaming approval. He too was very happy. He felt that he had no more need to worry about failure. He knew that Mr. Burnaby had a fresh confidence in him. Till today he had been a pupil: henceforth he would be a disciple: in time he would become a collaborator.

That afternoon they strolled along the shore to the point. They had brought tea with them in thermos flasks, and small packets of sandwiches. Marcus bathed, and they sat on the rocks in the sunshine, talking. It was hot and at intervals Marcus would dive into the sea and swim about for a little to get cool. When he came out he would pull on his shirt and trousers, but until it got late he didn't find it worth while to dress completely. As for Mr. Burna-by he couldn't have too much heat. All through the summer his colour had been getting gradually darker till he had become as brown as an Indian.

He talked of the experiments they would be able to do together when Marcus was capable of projecting himself at will, of the discoveries Marcus might make on his own, surpassing eventually the work of his master. Marcus listened lazily, and with a certain amount of self-satisfaction. Occasionally he threw pieces of seaweed into the water to find out if there were any currents, and to try and decide whether the tide was still going out or just beginning to come in.

"You know you're very lucky," Mr. Burnaby remarked, as Marcus pulled on his clothes finally, preparatory to starting for home. "When I was your age I was working in an office all day and swotting at Latin and Greek in the evenings—that is if I didn't have to work late in the office."

After the discovery that he could project himself to the pictures Marcus thought that most of his difficulties were over. Very soon he found out that there were further and greater difficulties ahead of him: to overcome them would require all the patience he possessed. He hated being patient: it went on for such a long time. He sometimes wondered at Mr. Burnaby who must have faced every difficulty alone without any encouragement but his own enthusiasm.

The first set-back to his optimism was the discovery that he was actually projecting much less of himself than he had imagined. All he was doing in fact was to stretch out a sort of invisible, exploring tentacle: the rest of him remained firmly embedded in his body.

Looking back at it much later, however, it seemed to him that he had gone forward in a series of definite steps. The first has already been described: the second was when he was able to send out his tentacle, as it were, at will, instead of merely putting himself into the necessary trance-like state and waiting for something to happen.

He had from the very beginning been able to see Mr. Burnaby's body if he looked back from the picture—and he saw his own body in the same way—two people, an old man and a youth, sitting very still in their chairs, staring in front of them with a peculiar intentness. But he hadn't been able to do this—see himself and Mr. Burnaby—voluntarily. For months, he found that the moment he became conscious of having projected himself the projection

ceased—as if the tentacle he put forth had touched something hot
and curled back into itself again. He had good days and bad days:
there were days when he could get no further than the pictures;
but by the end of November he was always able to go to *them*, or
at least to most of them.

By the beginning of the second summer, after he had been living for a full year with Mr. Burnaby, his control over his spirit had
become much stronger. His spirit, when outside his body, could
move about freely within a limited area: he no longer had to project himself to a fixed point and remain there throughout the period of his trance. One day, when he was looking at Mr. Burnaby
from a point somewhere above the mantelpiece, he realized that
what he was looking at was not Mr. Burnaby at all, but only his
body. At the same time he was conscious that Mr. Burnaby was
still in the room. He didn't know where precisely, but he knew that
he was close to him and that he was helping him.

This was what Marcus afterwards considered to be his third step,
and both he and Mr. Burnaby felt it to be a very important one. It
meant that he was now able to perceive Mr. Burnaby, the spirit of
Mr. Burnaby, without Mr. Burnaby having to produce any visual
image on his mind. It was almost another year before this percep-
tion became exact. Gradually Marcus became able to know where
exactly in the room Mr. Burnaby was, the *real* Mr. Burnaby—not
just his body. At first it was like seeing an object through a white
mist—in one place the mist is darkened a little: then gradually a
shape emerges. But at first Marcus didn't know there *was* a mist: if
one had lived in a mist all one's life, one wouldn't know that that
mist was hiding anything—and of course Marcus wasn't actually
seeing Mr. Burnaby's spirit—not with his eyes.

While he was learning to perceive in this way Marcus was becoming able to get more and more of himself out of his body,
and to move about the room more and more freely. At first his
movements were affected to a considerable extent not only by the
position of his body, but by the point on which his eyes were fixed.
Eventually both these circumstances ceased to matter. In fact he
made a habit of shutting his eyes before trying to project himself.

When Mr. Burnaby had first talked to Marcus about projecting
himself out of his body Marcus had thought it sounded interesting

and exciting work. Instead it proved to be slow, boring, and on the whole very disappointing. Day after day he would go on trying to repeat his last small success, till what had seemed to happen almost by chance, came completely under the power of his will. Only then could he attempt something further. The whole business was like learning to work a set of muscles which he had never used, like learning to move the skin on his scalp, or to lift his eyebrows independently.

I have passed over the work of two years here suddenly in a few paragraphs. I realize that perhaps I should make more effort to convey to the reader the passage of time. But I do not quite see how to do this without being wearisome. In my first draft I summarized the work of these two years in four chapters. When I came to re-read my manuscript I found them dull—accounts of the same experiments repeated over and over, with only the slightest variations. I reduced the four chapters to two, but they were still tedious. So I cut them out altogether. I am willing to let any reader who has the patience examine the notes for himself. I can safely say, however, that most readers will find them heavy going. Marcus's private diary which tells of his relations with Mr. Burnaby, and describes his own private feelings, is to me much more interesting. From it I have taken most of the material for the following chapters.

CHAPTER XXII

THE first Summer and Autumn Marcus spent at Mr. Burnaby's had been exceptionally fine, but at the beginning of November the weather broke, and from then on they were both much less out of doors. As a rule they went for a short walk after lunch and until the end of the month Marcus bathed nearly every day before tea. When tea was over there was nothing in particular to do and he was usually able to occupy himself as he pleased till dinner time. Generally he contrived to be by himself during this period. If he knew Mr. Burnaby was going to the study, he went to the library. If he didn't know where Mr. Burnaby would be he went to his own room and lay on his bed with a book. Occasionally he slipped out quietly and went to sit in some sheltered place on the rocks, where he knew Mr. Burnaby would not find him. It was not that Mr. Burnaby bored him—though he did bore him sometimes when he talked about Greek ideas of love, or morality, or the identity of beauty and goodness: but Marcus was seeing too much of Mr. Burnaby. He felt often as if Mr. Burnaby were devouring him mentally, trying to destroy his individuality, and convert him into a reflection of himself. In many ways he had already succeeded: Marcus was determined not to let him succeed altogether.

Alone on the rocks, on grey winter afternoons, he would bring out his own battered individuality, like some cherished relic from a cupboard. Then he was very conscious of being himself, conscious that here he was free to think his own thoughts, to criticise Mr. Burnaby if he wished, sometimes even to hate him.

Mr. Burnaby was jealous of all of Marcus's solitude. He would suggest that instead of Marcus reading alone, they should sit together and read aloud whatever book Marcus had chosen to read to himself. On this point, however, Marcus would never give in. If he were very hard pressed he would declare that he had letters to write, and on those afternoons he *would* write letters—to his father or mother or Margaret, or to anyone else he could think of.

His period of solitude was the happiest part of his day. He dreaded the evenings in the library, when Mr. Burnaby read from his favourite authors. Mr. Burnaby enjoyed these readings very much, and Marcus, while he might object to particular books, never expressed a dislike for the readings as a whole.

The Spoils of Poynton and *The Return of the Native* were followed by *Imaginary Portraits* and *Heart of Darkness*. Marcus found them all almost equally dull. Why couldn't they get on with it he wondered.

Not long afterwards he read *Tess of the d'Urbervilles* and *Lord Jim* to himself, and immediately he developed a tremendous enthusiasm for Hardy and Conrad. Buchan and Ian Hay were quite banished from favour, and though Ian Hay eventually regained a small place in his affections, he never again had much feeling for Buchan. In spite of this he could not like *Heart of Darkness*, which Mr. Burnaby declared to be the essence of Conrad, and he always retained a prejudice against *The Return of the Native*. It was very long, too, before he came to appreciate the work of Henry James, and of Pater.

Mr. Burnaby's way of reading may have been to blame. In his fondness for accenting a good prose rhythm he was inclined to turn a book almost into a piece of music. Marcus wasn't musical, but the sound of Mr. Burnaby's voice affected him as a lullaby affects a baby. It was always only with the greatest difficulty that he was able to remain awake.

Mr. Burnaby was in despair. He loved reading aloud, but he intended his readings to be an entertainment for both of them: he *wanted* Marcus to enjoy himself. He was driven to try lighter literature—school stories, thrillers, and above all P. G. Wodehouse. These, partly because they had plenty of action, partly, perhaps, because they had no noticeable prose rhythm, Marcus enjoyed well enough. Nevertheless, privately, he was quite convinced that he would have liked them even better if he had read them to himself in the ordinary way.

Actually Mr. Burnaby didn't do all the reading. Every night he made Marcus read for a little, while he himself smoked a pipe and criticised. "Don't go so fast," he would say. "Don't gobble your words. Pay attention to the punctuation. Here! Give the book to me"—and he would read a passage over again, showing Marcus how it should have been done, after which Marcus would have to have another try. He would begin again more slowly, and for a little all would go well: but very soon he would start to yawn: every other sentence would be interrupted by a yawn. He could never decide whether he yawned through boredom or self-consciousness, or because of some fault in his method of voice production. Finally he would get hoarse and complain of a sore throat. Then Mr. Burnaby would knock out his pipe and take the book back.

During the second half of November and the first week of December they got through the whole of the Jeeves series. Marcus wanted to go on to the Mulliner stories, but Mr. Burnaby insisted that they should try something more serious.

"P. G.'s all very well," he declared, "but you want to form your taste, not ruin it. If you form a good taste early in life it will stand to you in the long run, while if you go on reading this sort of stuff you'll end by being able to read nothing else."

He proposed Plato again in Jowett's translation, but Marcus thought he would rather have a novel. Mr. Burnaby considered this for a little. They were in the library, and he wandered round the shelves, gazing up at the titles. "You should try some of the Russians," he remarked, stopping, and pulling down a volume from one of the higher shelves. "What about *Anna Karenina*? The rest of my Tolstoys are in French. You'll find it quite different from anything else you've ever read."

But Marcus still hankered after P. G. Wodehouse. "I don't care for foreign books," he objected. "They never seem real to me somehow."

Mr. Burnaby returned the book to its place. For a few minutes there was silence. Marcus realized that Mr. Burnaby wasn't altogether pleased. Suddenly he turned round, and without a word, left the room.

Marcus waited uneasily for him to come back. Had he gone off in a rage, he wondered. However when Mr. Burnaby returned at the end of five minutes or so he looked quite unperturbed. He was carrying a slim octavo volume bound in dark green leather. "We'll try this," he said. "It deals with our own subject and it *ought* to interest you."

"What's it called?" Marcus asked.

Mr. Burnaby opened the book, as if he had forgotten, and read out the title slowly—"*Some Suggestions Regarding Extra-Sensory Experience.*"

"And who's it by?"

Mr. Burnaby hesitated for a moment. "It was published anonymously," he replied. He opened the book and began to read.

Marcus thought there was something rather strange in his manner. He listened carefully. The book began with five long quotations from the 'Proceedings of the Society for Psychical Research.' All these dealt with well authenticated cases of revelation of the future. When he had finished them Mr. Burnaby closed the book. "I'm afraid that's all we'll have time for tonight," he said. "What do you think of it?"

"I think it's jolly interesting," Marcus responded sincerely. He was glad that for once he was able to be genuinely enthusiastic.

"Of course we haven't really got into the book itself yet," Mr. Burnaby pointed out. "I mean the author's part. Those were only quotations."

"You've no idea who did write it?" Marcus asked.

"Yes," Mr. Burnaby answered, still in the same slightly unnatural manner. "This copy happens to have been autographed by the author."

He handed the book across to Marcus who opened it and began to turn the pages. It was beautifully, though plainly, bound and printed on thick, hand-made paper. The fly-leaf was blank, but on the title-page, under the title, was the signature *John Burnaby.*

Marcus was embarrassed. He cleared his throat. "You mean, er, you mean you wrote it."

"I wrote it," Mr. Burnaby told him.

Marcus cleared his throat again. "Er, congratulations."

"Thank you," Mr. Burnaby said.

There was an awkward little pause and then Mr. Burnaby went on. "I wrote it five years ago. I didn't send it to a publisher. It was printed privately. I looked after the production myself. I chose the type and arranged the layout and chose the paper—it's hand-made paper. I took a great deal of time and trouble over it—and I must say I enjoyed that part of it, nearly as much as writing it. When I was satisfied—and I took a good deal of satisfying—I made them run off a hundred copies. Then the type was broken up. After that there was the binding. I tried six different bindings before I got one that really pleased me."

"And how did you sell it?" Marcus asked.

"I didn't. I gave away a few copies. The rest I still have. I'll tell you about the copies I gave away some other time. Now it's nearly twelve and we should both be in our beds. Goodnight."

"And how do you like it now?" Mr. Burnaby asked, the following evening at about half-past ten, as he closed his book after reading the fifth chapter. Till this he had put no questions, though he had glanced at Marcus from time to time in attempts to judge by his expression how he was taking it. He had learned nothing. Marcus had appeared to be paying attention, but his expression had revealed no particular signs of pleasure. Did he hear the rhythm of the prose Mr. Burnaby wondered. Did he notice the beautiful clarity of the sentences?

Marcus never lied except in desperation—though with Mr. Burnaby he was often desperate. But he hated lying: his first refuge was always evasive truthfulness. "It's very good," he said.

Mr. Burnaby found a pipe and began to fill it. He hadn't been able to smoke all evening. *Some Suggestions Regarding Extra-Sensory Experience* was too precious to be trusted to Marcus's blundering elocution. He had read it very carefully, very well, and he had been struck with how good it was. The last time he had read it was when the finished book had come to him from the binders. Then he had been just a little tired of it. Sometimes he had wondered since if he shouldn't have kept it longer, given it perhaps one more revision. Coming to it afresh after a lapse of years he was impressed with its quality. There was hardly a sentence that he would have wished to alter. He was surprised that immediately he stopped reading Marcus had not broken out with some expressions of enthusiasm. Though the boy had shown already so much deadness to the finer things of literature, Mr. Burnaby felt that he could not fail to appreciate such an achievement as this. "But what impression does it make on you?" he demanded with a trace of exasperation.

Marcus was troubled. He hardly *knew* what impression the book had made on him, if indeed it *had* made an impression. "It's like things you've said to me," he responded feebly. "It's like hearing you talking," he added with a burst of hopefulness.

"But the style!" Mr. Burnaby exclaimed. "Surely you noticed the style?"

"Oh yes," Marcus agreed immediately. "The style's very good." He was disappointed in himself. He was convinced that the book was good, just as good as Mr. Burnaby thought. The fact that he had found it rather dull was almost a proof of its goodness. He always did find good books dull. Of course he couldn't say that. He tried hard to think of some comment that would please Mr. Burnaby.

He thought for a long time. Then Mr. Burnaby lost his temper. "I don't believe you like it at all," he said. "Why can't you say so, instead of telling a lot of lies about it?"

So far Marcus hadn't lied. Now, not so much in self-defence as in an agitated desire to comfort Mr. Burnaby he proceeded to do so. "I'm not lying," he declared. "I know it's good. I do like it, only it's awfully hard to say anything. I'm not good at saying things."

After half an hour or so Mr. Burnaby consented to be mollified, if not convinced, and shortly after eleven Marcus escaped thankfully to bed.

The next night Mr. Burnaby again enquired what they should read. It was only after considerable argument that Marcus was able to persuade him to go on with his own book. "I don't want to force it down your throat," he said. "I don't like to read it to a hostile audience."

After this Marcus showed a little more cunning. He picked out certain passages which he told Mr. Burnaby that he liked more than others. Nevertheless Mr. Burnaby remained dissatisfied. When at the fourth reading the book was finished there was another scene. Marcus was charged with stupidity and dishonesty. Marcus didn't admit the charges, but he couldn't deny them. Mr. Burnaby's writing was a subject which thereafter was usually avoided between them. Any mention of it there was came from Mr. Burnaby. He adopted a tone of humorous resignation, *Some Suggestions Regarding Extra-Sensory Experience* being referred to as "My despised masterpiece," or with truth perhaps as *"Le chef-d'œuvre inconnu."*

In spite of this attitude it was quite clear he continued to feel hurt by Marcus's failure to appreciate the book. Marcus blamed himself not for the way he had behaved, but for his own lack of good taste. It seemed to him that Mr. Burnaby had every accomplishment, while he had only the beginnings of *one*. He said as much a few evenings after the unfortunate reading had been completed. Mr. Burnaby took him up promptly. "Well, you know, there's not the slightest reason why you shouldn't acquire a few more."

"How d'you mean?" Marcus asked very humbly.

"By hard work—French for instance. If you set yourself to it you could quite easily learn French."

So it was agreed that henceforth two evenings a week were to be devoted to French and three more to a course of solid reading— the books to be chosen by Mr. Burnaby. "If you read a fair amount of good stuff", Mr. Burnaby assured him, "your taste's practically bound to improve. You'll find in time that you don't like reading rubbish."

The remaining two evenings were to be free. They would read books of Marcus's choosing, or play games. The free nights were Saturday and Sunday. Mr. Burnaby sent for a table-tennis set and it became their custom to play this game on Saturday nights. On Sundays they usually read some light novels or played double dummy bridge, of which Mr. Burnaby was very fond.

CHAPTER XXIII

MR. Burnaby never deliberately set out to tell Marcus the story of his life: it came out bit by bit, over a period of years, in scraps of reminiscence and explanation.

He belonged to a North of Ireland commercial family. His grandfather and great-grandfather had been prosperous shipowners in Derry. His father, a younger son, had settled in Liverpool where, for a time, he too had prospered.

"But he was too greedy," Mr. Burnaby would say, when he reached this stage in the story. "Like so many other people he didn't know when he was well off. He put everything he had—staked all his credit too—into financing a silver mine in Peru. I never heard exactly what happened. Perhaps there was no mine, or no silver: perhaps it was just too expensive to operate. At any rate he failed—lost everything. His house, his furniture, his pictures—all had to be sold. He had some quite good pictures too. My mother used to have the catalogue of the sale. Well it was just at this point in our affairs that I came on the scene. They must have been pleased to see me."

Whether this ever came as one uninterrupted speech I don't know. I have taken it from two notes in Marcus's journal, reporting almost identical conversations.

After the smash Mr. Burnaby's father returned to the North of Ireland, where he obtained a position as manager of a small factory in Belfast. For two years he kept his family in reasonable comfort, with a cook, a house-parlour maid, and a nurse for the children.

Then, quite unexpectedly he died of pneumonia. His widow was left to bring up eight children on a hundred pounds a year and the charity of relations.

Mr. Burnaby grew up in genteel poverty, hating the uncles and aunts who helped with gifts of cast-off clothing and with small sums of money doled out grudgingly at irregular intervals. He had never been old enough to know his father, and he was not taught to be proud of his memory. He learned to think of him only as the author of the family misfortunes. For Mrs. Burnaby had never been in love with her husband. She was English, and came of an old, land-owning family who had drifted idly, and with aristocratic extravagance, to distress. She didn't blame them. That they themselves should have entered business she found almost unthinkable. She had married her husband for his money. She considered that she had been cheated, and she resented it. She never said as much, but her youngest son grew up to share her feelings. For *her* relations, whom he never saw, and for their way of life, he felt a nostalgic affection. For his mother herself he had no affection. He was proud of her, proud of her blood, her pride, her good breeding, her obvious superiority to his coarser, prosperous Ulster relatives. All his childish love was reserved for dream companions, and for the memory of an old nurse who had remained with them in their misfortune only leaving through absolute necessity when Mr. Burnaby was four.

In spite of being the youngest in this large family, Mr. Burnaby had had a lonely childhood. He disliked the brother who was next to him in age, and his mother was at pains to break off whatever friendships he formed with the sons of their lower middle-class neighbours. She kept before her children a picture of the way of life and the upbringing to which she considered her birth entitled them.

Mr. Burnaby had accepted this picture. "I ought to have gone to a public school, you know," he would tell Marcus, raising his voice a little, and speaking with a slightly English accent. "It would have suited me down to the ground. All Mother's brothers were at Winchester."

Marcus thought he over-estimated the advantages of which he had been deprived, but these advantages, nevertheless, were very real to Mr. Burnaby. He had grown up to hate poverty, and determined, somehow or other, to give himself the education he felt should have been given *to* him. He had been sent to a secondary school in Belfast, but at sixteen he offended the uncle who was paying his fees, and he was put into business. This was not a great disadvantage, for he was naturally studious. In his spare time he read French and Latin and began to teach himself Greek. But he wanted to make money, and to begin with he didn't know how to set about it. His work as an apprentice was at first to address envelopes, to copy letters and to take letters to the post. Over a period of five years he was paid one hundred pounds, the normal wages for an apprentice in the Belfast wholesale trade at that time.

By his own account he was good at his work, but he made no attempt to hide his dislike and contempt of it. This did not please his employers. He was a dreamy youth, and like Marcus he had occasional dreams of the future, but to begin with he did not attach much importance to them. He knew that he was looked on as a little odd, and that oddness in business was regarded with disfavour. So he kept his knowledge of the future to himself. Besides, the things he did know were not of very great interest to him. He knew that the firm was going to get a new book-keeper before very long, but whether the present book-keeper was going to die, or be dismissed, or retire, he had no idea. In his dream he saw the cash office with the new book-keeper at work. He had a pen behind his ear and was giving the message-boy a penny from the cash drawer to buy milk for the cats. The message-boy was the boy actually employed by the firm at the time the dream occurred, and he looked no older than in everyday life. Six weeks after the dream the old book-keeper *was* dismissed. It had been discovered that he had been systematically defrauding the firm of small amounts over a period of years. He was replaced by the man Mr. Burnaby had seen in his dream. In another dream he saw the furniture being removed from the house next door. This too came to pass, and for two months the house was empty.

"Many people have such dreams," Mr. Burnaby said. "Most of them are forgotten. By some means that I don't yet quite understand I was able to recognize my true dreams—and I didn't forget them."

After Mr. Burnaby had been a year in business the firm engaged another apprentice and Mr. Burnaby was transferred from the 'Post' to the despatch office. The despatch clerk backed horses. Every day at lunch time he visited his book-maker, and every evening the message-boy brought him the *Belfast Telegraph*. Mr. Burnaby got into the habit of looking over the racing results with him. When they were busy Mr. Burnaby read out the results to him. As a rule these were received with groans of dismay.

One night Mr. Burnaby dreamed that he was reading out the results of the day's racing with the despatch clerk beside him, but in the dream instead of groans there were cries of jubilation. He awoke with the voice of the despatch clerk ringing in his ears: "Every one o' them's up. Man dear, we'll make a night o' it."

It was early in the morning of the second of April, 1902. The date on the paper had been the eighteenth of April, 1902. Mr. Burnaby remembered the names of four of the winners. He got out of bed and wrote down on a piece of paper, *Carpet Knight*, *Cogia*, *Ashanti Gold*, *Veles*. Then he returned to bed and went to sleep again.

When he got to the office he showed the piece of paper to the despatch clerk and told him that these four horses would win on April the eighteenth. He was too shy however to say how he had got his information. The despatch clerk was interested, but sceptical. "How much are you puttin' on them yourself?" he demanded.

It had not occurred to Mr. Burnaby to back the horses himself. Judging by the despatch clerk's experience it had never seemed to him that betting was a profitable occupation. To prove his good faith he felt obliged to put a shilling on each of the horses he had dreamed about. It was almost all the money he had. The despatch clerk was convinced. He put ten shillings each on the same four horses.

Mr. Burnaby made one pound, five and ninepence, the despatch clerk twelve pounds, seventeen and six. The despatch clerk said, "Every one o' them's up. Man dear, we'll make a night o' it."

Till then Mr. Burnaby had never tasted whiskey and never been in a public house, but as soon as the office closed the despatch clerk insisted on taking him to one. They fell in with some cronies of the despatch clerk and Mr. Burnaby was introduced as "My

financial adviser." The story of the mysterious bit of paper was
told again and again. Mr. Burnaby kept his secret, but when at last
they let him go home he was drunk.

"I'll never forget it," Mr. Burnaby told Marcus. "The family had
just finished tea when I reached the front door. I couldn't get it
open and Emily, my second sister—she was four years older than
me—came to let me in. She took one look at me and then let out
a shriek: 'Oh Mother, it's Jack, and he's drunk!' I could have mur-
dered her. What a fuss there was. Mother wept, and for at least a
month everyone went about with long faces. They even got the cu-
rate in on Sunday afternoon to pray with me. That's what stopped
me going to church. I told him to mind his own business.

"The only one who showed any sense in the matter was Tom,
my eldest brother. He said I was 'a damned wee fool' to come
home in that state and that if I got drunk again I'd better go somewhere and 'lie up' till I had slept it off."

"And did you?" Marcus enquired.

"Did I what?"

"Did you get drunk again?"

"Occasionally," Mr. Burnaby answered guardedly, "from time
to time. You see I had more money after that—not a lot, but all
I needed. I went on backing horses. I found out that with a little
practice I could induce myself to dream of the future fairly frequently, or perhaps I should say to remember dreams of the future
in which I was looking at racing results. At first, I had a little difficulty with dates. I would get a set of winners but I wouldn't know
on what day or at what meeting they were running. I got over this
by making a habit of always looking at the date on a paper as soon
as I opened it—and very shortly I found myself doing the same
thing in my dreams. But I didn't bet only when I knew the winners.
I didn't want to attract too much attention to myself. So I backed
a certain number of losers as well. Partly on this account, partly
because I didn't feel it was quite fair to the bookies, I didn't stake
very large sums. For the same reasons I spread my bets, particularly when I knew I was backing certainties. I arranged things so
that I made a small profit every week—usually about two pounds,
never more than five.

"I don't want you to think I spent all my spare time knocking about pubs and bookies. I didn't. All I did was to have an occasional night out. Most nights I worked. I had a desire for learning, for its own sake, and I had no idea then that I was going to make a fortune in the way I did. I wanted to get rich largely because I hated being in a position of subservience to people who I felt were my intellectual inferiors—in the office I mean. It was quite by chance that I started to take an interest in the stock-exchange—in fact, I had a dream in which I found myself reading the stock-exchange prices instead of the racing results."

Mr. Burnaby's attitude to these past successes was a curious mixture of pride and shame. At times he liked to talk of them, at others he would brush any references to them aside as if this part of his career had been rather disreputable. He disliked business people as a class, though formerly he appeared to have had a good many friends among them.

"But how did you make yourself dream the future?" Marcus asked him one autumn evening, during his third year at The Garrison, when they were walking along the shore before dinner. A wet July and August had been followed by a lovely September. It was then about the middle of September. Every day the sky was clear and the sea in the sunlight was a pale, golden green.

"It's not that one makes oneself dream of the future," Mr. Burnaby replied. "Probably a great many people dream of the future, but by the time they wake up they've forgotten all about it. We know very little about our own minds, any of us."

He paused reflectively and Marcus seized the opportunity to raise a point about which he had thought a good deal from time to time. "I don't see how you *can* dream the future. I mean I know *you* have, and *I* have, but I don't see how we can, all the same—how it's possible I mean. I don't see how you can get ahead of time, and that's what you do do, isn't it?"

Mr. Burnaby didn't answer at once: presently he said, "I suppose you can understand dreaming of the past."

"That's just remembering," Marcus responded.

"It may be," Mr. Burnaby admitted. "But some people think that time's all there—the past, the present and the future. . . . Like space, we are just conscious of the particular part of it in which we happen to find ourselves." He knocked out his pipe against the heel of his right shoe and felt in his pocket for his tobacco-pouch.

"Space-time," Marcus put in—he had read a magazine article on the subject—"the fourth dimension."

"I don't care much for that term—the fourth dimension," Mr. Burnaby objected, "and now I think they've any number of them, haven't they? If one tries, after all, one can define several new dimensions oneself. My own favourite is through the looking-glass."

Marcus wasn't quite sure whether he was making fun or in earnest. "Through the looking-glass," he repeated doubtfully.

"Yes, the dimension you see when you look in the mirror. Things are turned round in a way they can't be by any physical means we know of—your right hand becomes your left for instance."

Perhaps Marcus had not been paying complete attention. At any rate he didn't take in this theory until Mr. Burnaby had repeated his explanation and enlarged on it a little. Then he returned to space-time. "Do you believe in it?" he demanded.

"I don't disbelieve it," Mr. Burnaby answered, "but I can't say I thoroughly understand it. At times it appears delusively simple, but as soon as I try to make it definite the simplicity vanishes. I can think of another explanation for these visions of the future which seems to me a good deal more plausible and does not involve any monkeying about with time: nor do I think it clashes with what we know about our minds—what you and I know about them—not that we really know very much. We know more than most people, but that isn't saying a great deal."

"What *is* your explanation?" Marcus asked immediately. He was afraid that if he didn't keep him to the point Mr. Burnaby might drift on to something else.

"There's nothing very new about it," Mr. Burnaby responded, "and I don't say I believe in it. It's a theory, a theory capable of a good deal of modification and variation. Can you imagine a universal consciousness to which your mind—and every other mind—is always transmitting every impression it receives, every idea it receives—like a gramophone record of an orchestra?"

Marcus thought he could.

"Well then," Mr. Burnaby went on, "forget about the record: imagine this universal consciousness, or universal mind. Everything that has ever happened would be stored in that mind, everything that happens would go onto it the moment it occurs, everything that is thought the moment it is thought.

"Now each one of us in our everyday waking life is constantly forecasting the future. The farmer ploughs in November and sows his seeds in the springtime because he can foretell the cycle of the seasons. The only reason we cannot foretell the future more largely is that we cannot know all the factors which are contributing to it and could not relate them if we did. But there may be some portion of our unconscious minds, or perhaps I should say *more* conscious minds, which can get in touch with the universal consciousness, assess what it finds there, and present occasional glimpses of the result to our ordinary, waking, everyday minds. Very often these glimpses are in the form of visions or dreams. Because they occur among ordinary dreams, and are remembered with the ordinary dreams, may be why these visions are sometimes distorted to a greater or less degree. There seems to be some sort of a barrier between the two portions of our mind. Like St. Paul 'we see through a glass darkly'—and not only is the glass dark, it is faulty.

"All the same I incline to the theory that the power of assessment is not in the part of the human mind of which we are unconscious, but with the total consciousness, in the universal mind.

"Suppose for a moment that your mind is the universal mind and that each of your fingers is an individual, with at least the illusion that it possesses a mind of its own. Your fingers would be conscious of each other as individuals, but not conscious of your mind nor of what they themselves were going to do. But if they *could* see back into your mind they would not only know, but see, what each finger was likely to do in the immediate future. In your mind after all there is always a moving picture of your intended actions, and the picture is always a little ahead of the actions themselves. The picture is produced by your reasoning powers and projected on what you might call the screen of your imagination. It is a process developed during early childhood. In an adult it is automatic and almost unconscious. Now suppose you and I, and every living thing, while remaining individuals, are fingers belonging to the body of the same universal mind and that somehow we do occasionally see back into it. A few years to it would be like a few seconds to your conscious individual mind."

" 'A thousand ages in Thy sight are like an evening gone,'" Marcus quoted, with a sudden memory of standing in the family pew in church. "You mean we see into God's mind."

"Yes," Mr. Burnaby agreed. "That is if this theory is correct, but as I said it is capable of a good deal of modification and variation. At any rate such a mind would know what it was going to do with all the individuals it controlled for some time ahead—for a very long time by our ideas. When you and I dream of the future all that happens may be that for a moment we become aware of the knowledge or part of the knowledge of the complete mind."

Marcus thought of this for a little and suddenly it seemed to him absurd. "You mean then that God is thinking of horse-racing and stocks and shares."

"Ah no I don't," Mr. Burnaby returned. "But he is aware of these things—just as he is aware of everything else. That is my misfortune, or weakness if you like. I was able more easily than most to remember something of the knowledge of the universal mind and what does my own rotten little mind choose to bring back—next week's winners or the stock exchange news. The trouble is that I got into the habit before I ever considered what might be happening. For years I thought of share prices and of how to make money and of almost nothing else. Even now, though I have gained a great deal of control of my waking thoughts, I still at times find my mind straying to such things, and my uncontrolled mind seems to have been formed in youth, formed in corruption. 'Blessed are the pure in heart: for they shall see God.' Have you ever thought of that text? It's called a beatitude. It's looked upon as a gift with which Christ will reward the pure in heart. But it's nothing of the sort. It's a statement of fact. The pure in heart will see God simply because He will not be hidden from them by other thoughts."

"But you don't only see share prices and racing results," Marcus objected. "I mean in the experiments you are doing with me"— they nearly always referred to them as experiments—"you see everything, whatever you want."

"But they only deal with the present," Mr. Burnaby answered, "——so far at least. In them, probably, it is simply that our own minds are liberated from our bodies without being in touch with the universal mind at all. In that state I can know anything,

anything in the present I want to know, but nothing of the future. You, if you are careful, may be able to know the future, not as a whole perhaps, but in something more than insignificant and sordid details. But I don't know that it is a great thing to know the future of this worldly life. If we can learn the future of one of us, what happens to one of us after death, it will be more important to humanity than to see a vision of the whole human society in a hundred years time.

"If we could only once accompany the spirit of a person who has died we might find out something of what we want. There are great difficulties, the chief of which seems to be that the departing spirit does not want to be accompanied. I have made attempts, but the necessity of keeping in touch with my own body has always been a hindrance, has always made it easier for the spirit of the person who has died to get away from my spirit.

"Of course if the released spirit, the spirit of the dead person, were willing to co-operate the experiment should become much more simple—if for instance it was one of us."

Marcus shivered. He didn't want to die: he didn't want to die and be followed into death by Mr. Burnaby.

"It's all right," Mr. Burnaby said. "It was my own death I was contemplating, not yours. I would like to find out without having to die, to have the satisfaction of *knowing* while I am still in this life. Such an experiment, as I told you once before, would only be a sort of desperate last throw—not that if we already know we may not make it in any case when I do come to die."

Mr. Burnaby and Marcus had many conversations of this sort. Indeed, like most people who are a great deal together, they had what were almost the same conversations again and again. The conclusions might vary slightly, and the strength of Mr. Burnaby's belief in his own theories varied too with his mood. "I don't know," he would say when Marcus appeared unduly optimistic. "There may be some perfectly simple explanation for it all that nobody has ever thought of. We have very little imagination you know—practically no creative imagination. The most we can achieve is a few variations on what we have seen and heard."

Marcus too suffered from moods. At times he would be full of enthusiasm, both for the work and for his part in it. He would rejoice in his unique position and be glad that he had been taken out of the world, as it were. He would feel a contempt for ordinary people, for the very depth of their ordinariness.

But sometimes his feelings were quite different. He would feel that he was missing all the joys of youth, all the pleasures of that inconsequent period when the fetters of childhood have been removed and old age is still too distant a threat to be regarded as anything more than an incitement to make the most of the warm-blooded present. Then he hated Mr. Burnaby. Just how much could Mr. Burnaby do, he wondered. He had been so old when Marcus first came and now he seemed younger. He was a sinister old man, with his disdain for all the ordinary ways of life, all the usages of society. Marcus often suspected him of other curious powers, powers which he had not revealed to his pupil. Living here with his youth slipping away, might it not be that Mr. Burnaby was actually stealing it from him, sucking it up, living it himself. . . .

And there was the horrible knowledge that his every act, his whole mind, was open to Mr. Burnaby's inspection. It was worse than to be always naked before him. It was true that Mr. Burnaby had promised not to spy, but having such powers could anyone be trusted to refrain from using them?

Yet in spite of these discontents and suspicions Marcus progressed steadily with his work and for a great deal of the time he was reasonably happy. Mr. Burnaby was very widely read, and Marcus found him an amusing and entertaining companion. He was interested in all sorts of things—art, cricket, literature, the ballet, heresies in the early Christian Church. . . . He could talk for hours on any of these subjects and of the people connected with them. He liked gossip, but it was usually old gossip, some of it centuries old. He would tell Marcus stories about hermits in the Libyan desert, when Alexandria was the strongest centre of the Christian Church, or about Ranjitsinhji, and Jessop, and Grace, and cricket matches he had never seen. He had a passion for cricket, at least in the abstract, and always read the accounts of the test matches in the papers. Cricket was one of the things of which he felt he had been deprived by the misfortunes of his father. He liked to imagine himself playing in the Eton and Harrow match, or for Oxford against Cambridge. Such conversations were most likely to occur in the summer. They might be brought on by the sight of the smooth, shaven lawn behind the house on a hot afternoon. Just as often, however, he would talk of poetry, or music, or painting. He was fond of the Lake poets, and of the pre-Raphaelites, of describing concerts by Pachmann which he had attended. He collected prints. He was interested in the woodcuts of the eighteen-sixties and seventies, and in various black-and-white artists of the nineties. In time Marcus began to feel as if he himself had met them all, Charles Keene, Aubrey Beardsley, Whistler, Syme, Phil May, as well as the cricketers and the writers.

On the whole Mr. Burnaby's taste in literature was inclined to be highbrow and ninety-ish, but there were a good many exceptions. He bought all P. G. Wodehouse's novels as they came out, and he could read very indifferent school stories with pleasure. His interest in public schools was tremendous and he encouraged Marcus to talk about his life at Shellborough. He liked to hear about the services in chapel, the talking in the dormitories at night, the relations of prefects and fags. Marcus got to know eventually that Mr. Burnaby had created for himself an imaginary public school and that he liked to think of himself as a boy there. The school stories and Marcus's reminiscences provided fresh material for his day-dreams.

CHAPTER XXIV

AFTER he had been four years with Mr. Burnaby Marcus was left alone at The Garrison for the first time. They had both been going to London to meet an Indian mystic with whom Mr. Burnaby had been in correspondence. Marcus had been looking forward to the trip, partly because he had never been to London, partly because the Indian had brought a pupil with him, who was about Marcus's age.

Unfortunately the day before they were due to start Marcus took some kind of gastric chill. He was very sick and very miserable, and Mr. Burnaby was forced to start without him. It was three days before Marcus was able to get up, a week before he felt fit to travel. By that time the meeting with the Indian was over, and Mr.

Burnaby had started on a round of visits. Marcus considered. The more he thought of it the less he wanted to encounter Mr. Burnaby's English friends. One of them, a writer, he had already met. He had visited The Garrison the year before, and he and Mr. Burnaby had done nothing but discuss each other's books. On the two occasions when Marcus and the writer had been left alone together the writer had taken care to impress on Marcus his extraordinary good fortune in being Mr. Burnaby's companion and collaborator. This had irritated Marcus extremely. He wanted to feel that he himself was something in life—something more than just a satellite of Mr. Burnaby. So now he sent a telegram to Mr. Burnaby:

"AM BETTER COULD TRAVEL BUT WOULD PREFER REMAIN HERE MARCUS"

Mr. Burnaby replied:

"AGREE DONT WORK HOLIDAY WILL DO YOU GOOD SUGGESTED READING BUCHAN WODEHOUSE WALLACE AND IF YOU MUST IAN HAY ENJOY YOURSELF BURNABY"

Marcus was grateful, but he determined that even if he did amuse himself most of the time, he would do a little serious reading as well. While he was ill he had been reading Mark Twain and Robert Louis Stevenson. After lunch on the day the telegram arrived he went to the library to look for something which he could read with a feeling of virtue. He spent an hour or so going round the shelves, but none of the serious books that he took down appealed to him. Suddenly it occurred to him that he should try Shakespeare again. He had hated *doing* Shakespeare at school, and never since he left had he read any of the plays. All the same he felt that his dislike of Shakespeare was a weakness. He would try him again, and try to like him. He took down *The Tempest*, which he knew was Mr. Burnaby's favourite play, and glanced at the opening scene. Somehow it didn't appeal to him. He chose instead *Twelfth Night*. He knew nothing about it. He had never *done* it at school, and for fear of being put off he didn't open it till he was outside lying on the short turf in a hollow at the edge of the rocks.

> *If music be the food of love, play on;*
> *Give me excess of it, that surfeiting,*
> *The appetite may sicken and so die—*

That strain again;—it had a dying fall;
O, it came o'er my ear like the sweet south,
That breathes upon a bank of violets,
Stealing and giving odour. . . .

There were small wild violets among the grass, wild pansies, and strawberry flowers. From the south came a light, warm breeze. Marcus read on slowly, pausing every now and then to look up at the sky and think of love. He had never been in love, not really. He remembered two sisters, twins, whom he had met at a party one Christmas holidays, when he was sixteen. He had thought he was in love with both of them all through the following term. He had spent considerable periods imagining situations in which he found himself alone with one or other of them among the most beautiful surroundings: but when he had seen them again in the Easter holidays they had looked different and he had lost interest in them. From time to time he had felt attracted to other girls, girls he had seen in shops or in church, or in a tram or a bus. He had thought of them for a day or two, tried to remember exactly what they looked like. Often he could only remember one detail of a girl's appearance—her expression, when she smiled; or the soft curves of her neck; or her legs, shapely and alluring in silk stockings.

Since he had come to live with Mr. Burnaby he had met very few girls. Peasant girls whom he passed on the road and the maids at The Garrison never attracted him in the slightest degree. There were two or three houses in the village which took in visitors in the summer and among these visitors he occasionally saw girls who looked interesting. However Mr. Burnaby always avoided the summer visitors and Marcus never had a chance to get to know any of them. He sometimes thought that Mr. Burnaby was deliberately keeping him out of temptation.

This idea came back to him and he felt angry with Mr. Burnaby. It was all very well doing special work, but you could only be young once and it wasn't fair for him to be prevented from leading a normal life. Youth glittered before him as something lovely, and brief, and exciting, something at which he could only peer through the iron bars of a hermit's cell. If only he could go to sleep and wake up on the sea coast of Shakespeare's Illyria. With a discontented

jerk he rolled over on his face and immediately caught sight of two
girls who were approaching along the rocks from the direction of
the village. He plucked a stalk of grass and sticking it between his
teeth, propped his chin on his hands, and settled down to watch
them.

At first they were too far away for anything to be distinguishable
about them except that they were girls, but very soon he noticed
that one was able to get over the rocks much more easily than
the other. She would advance ten or twenty yards at a time, slim,
upright and fearless, stepping from rock to rock confidently, and
without hesitation. Then she would pause to wait for her companion, who clambered along slowly using her hands almost as
much as her feet. Marcus had plenty of time to study them as they
approached. He knew he was hidden from them by the bracken;
it was almost as if he were at the pictures and they were part of
the film. But he was excited. Through his clothes he was conscious
of the earth below him, and of the sun beating down on his back.
The second girl was short and uncomfortably fat. She seemed to
be almost bursting out of her clothes, and her round, patient face
was red with exertion and shining with perspiration. But it was the
slim girl's face that Marcus wanted to see. As she came nearer he
grew more and more curious. If she would only look in his direction for a moment! But her face was always towards the sea; or
else she had her back to him as she turned towards the fat girl and
waited for her to catch up. She never even seemed to look where
she was going: she floated along as if her feet had eyes of their
own. Both girls were wearing print frocks: the fat girl had black
shoes; the slim girl an old pair of tennis shoes. They had bare legs,
the fat girl's white and flabby-looking, the slim girl's straight and
smooth and brown and beautiful. Marcus examined her from head
to foot. She had fair hair, or would you call it golden brown? Marcus wasn't sure. It was short and caught back in some way so that
her left ear was visible to Marcus. It was the most beautiful ear he
had ever seen. He had no idea that an ear could be so beautiful.
Her skin was tanned and the one cheek he could see was tinged
with a soft pink. Her dress seemed to be part of her—like the pet-
als on a flower, he thought.

More than ever he wished she would look in his direction. A

faint cynical residue in him reminded him that girls, who from the back were most promising, often turned out to be simply ghastly when seen from in front. He wanted to see this girl's eyes, her nose, her mouth. . . . The slim girl, however, appeared to be more interested in the sea than ever. "What about here?" she enquired unexpectedly. "I think this would do: it *looks* all right, and you could get out quite easily over there."

"I don't care," the fat girl panted back, "so long as we don't have to go any further."

"It doesn't matter where we undress," the slim girl went on. "There's no one about."

"Anywhere'll do me," the fat girl responded. "I'm wringing wet already."

Marcus stood up reluctantly. He would have liked to have gone on watching, but he would have felt mean—and how awful if they had discovered him afterwards. There was nothing for it, but to go away. "I'm afraid *I'm* here," he announced apologetically, "but I can read somewhere else." He brandished *Twelfth Night* to indicate that up till this instant he had been buried in his book.

The two girls gazed at him for a moment without speaking. The fat girl's astonishment was ludicrous: she remained on all fours, peering at him sideways, like some startled animal. Then the slim girl smiled, and suddenly Marcus couldn't see her in detail any more. He was conscious of her as a sort of radiance in the air. Out of this radiance came a voice. "Oh no. You were here first. We'll find somewhere else."

Marcus turned his eyes away. He wanted to stare and stare, but he knew he mustn't—the slim girl wouldn't like him to stare at her. He shifted his eyes first to the fat girl, who glared at him as if he had actually tried to watch them undressing, and then to the ground. What did he mean by it, the fat girl seemed to be thinking. Was there no other spot in the whole of Donegal where he could read his beastly book?

Yet it was not to save the fat girl from toiling reluctantly on round the rocks that Marcus replied: "Oh no. There's nowhere else as good. It's easy to get out here, and there are lots of places to dive from, and there's always plenty of water—and it's warm too. I think it gets the Gulf Stream."

"It sounds perfect," the slim girl responded.

The fat girl's expression relaxed a little. "I don't see why any of us should go away," she remarked. "We can undress behind that rock there, and there's nothing to prevent him from looking the other way."

"Will you promise to look the other way?" the slim girl appealed.

"I can look when you're bathing, can't I?" Marcus begged, feeling that he was being slightly daring and at the same time paying a compliment.

Neither of the girls seemed offended. The fat girl suppressed a giggle: the slim girl directed at her the faintest ghost of a frown. Then she turned to Marcus half grave, half smiling. "All right," she agreed, "if you promise not to look till we tell you you can."

Marcus was dazzled again. His tongue seemed to have grown big and clumsy. "I promise," he brought out at last. He felt the utmost difficulty in speaking at all.

The slim girl was called Hazel, the fat girl Joanna. Marcus picked up their names as they were getting into the water. Hazel dived in cleanly, swam a little with a stylish over-arm action, and scrambled out. She sat on a flat rock with her hands clasped round her knees and glanced across at Marcus. "It's not so hot as all that," she remarked. "I think your old Gulf Stream must have strayed or something."

Joanna backed her up. "It's not hot at all," she declared. "It's icy." She was lowering herself into the water by inches with every appearance of disgust and disapproval.

Marcus didn't answer. He couldn't. He was gazing at Hazel, and if he had spoken he could only have said out loud what he was repeating again and again in to himself: "I think you look lovely, lovely, lovely. . . ."

The glistening black bathing-suit clung tightly to her body: her ears and hair were hidden under a black bathing cap. Her legs and arms gleamed wetly in the sunshine. It was as if he were having a fresh vision of her: she was different and yet the same. She looked up again and smiled at him. "It's an awfully nice place to bathe," she remarked. "I'm glad we didn't go away."

"So am I," Marcus blurted out. He felt that she realized why he had been unable to speak before, and that she liked him. He thought she had the kindest smile he had ever seen.

Joanna grunted and slipped into the water with a splash. Hazel stood up. "I suppose it doesn't matter how deep you dive," she said. "It looks awfully deep."

"There's thirty feet of water," Marcus told her. "It's forty feet to the bottom from the high rock there. That's where I dive from," he added. "We measured it once with a stone on the end of a fishing line—Mr. Burnaby and I—and a big crab came up on the end, holding on to the stone. We had it for supper, but we never got any more."

"Crabs!" The fat girl sounded concerned. "I didn't know there were crabs."

"It's all right," Marcus reassured her. "They can't swim, you know—they're only on the bottom. Besides there was only one."

"A hermit crab," Hazel suggested.

"No an eating one," Marcus informed her. "Hermit crabs are wee small things and this was. . . ." He broke off. They were both smiling at him. He smiled back vaguely and suddenly understood. "Oh yes, I see. It *was* a hermit, I suppose."

Hazel dived. Marcus hoped she didn't think him dull and stupid. He wished he could be bright and witty. He watched her swimming down and down. After a quarter of a minute she came to the surface again, clutching a handful of sand. "I went to the bottom," she announced. "It's frightfully cold down there." She climbed out and stretched herself on the rock. "I'm going to do a bit of sunbathing to get warmed up."

"It's getting out all the time makes you cold," Joanna said. "You should stay in like me. I never get cold." She was swimming round slowly in circles, obviously enjoying herself. She completed another circle and then, as her explanation had been received with rather obvious silence, went on, "I suppose you think it's blubber, but it's not only that."

Marcus thought she was, after all, very pleasant too, in a plain, matter of fact sort of way. "Thin people can never stay in so long," he responded tactfully.

"You think Hazel's too thin," Joanna took him up unexpectedly. "I always tell her she should try and put on a little more weight—for my sake. She'd try if she had a really nice nature."

"Oh no. I don't think she's thin at all," Marcus declared. "I think she's. . . ." He pulled himself up abruptly, with the word 'Perfect' trembling on his lips. "I think she's. . . . I mean I think she's all right the way she is."

Hazel dived in again and began to swim out from the rocks. Marcus watched her. He wished he could swim like that, so easily and cleanly. He knew that his own style, though it got him along fast enough, was horribly clumsy. Suddenly he felt concerned. He stood up. "Don't go too far," he shouted. "There are sometimes sharks."

Hazel turned. "What's that?" she enquired.

"Sharks," Marcus yelled. "There are sometimes sharks."

Hazel swam back slowly. "I'll stay near Joanna," she said. "They'd always take her first."

"Miaow," Joanna retorted. "Puss."

"Well you said I was too thin."

"Miaow all the same."

Hazel got out. "You'll have to turn your back again," she warned Marcus. "I'm going to dress—or you can glue your eyes on Joanna."

Marcus hesitated. He would have been quite happy to turn his back, but he felt it might be rude to Joanna. "I'll, I'll glue my eyes." He had been going to finish "on Joanna," but remembered that they hadn't really been introduced. She might resent such familiarity.

While Hazel dressed Joanna continued to swim round in the same lazy, contented fashion. "How about the octopi?" she asked presently. "Have they been much trouble this year?"

Marcus didn't quite know how to deal with this. If he had been bathing himself he would have been very tempted to duck her. He said so.

"She doesn't duck," Hazel told him, coming out dressed from behind the rock. "I've tried. You just rise out of the water. It's like trying to duck a buoy—the kind that floats in harbours I mean." She was rubbing her hair with a towel. "That beastly cap leaks. I never seem able to get a cap that doesn't."

Marcus liked seeing her hair ruffled, with her face half hidden every other moment, and then peeping out again from the towel.

He tried to decide the exact colour of her eyes—a sort of green-ish blue, he thought, varying with the light. "Does it matter?" he enquired. "Do you mind getting it wet?"

"It makes it all sticky," she complained. "The salt makes it sticky. It makes it so hard to do."

She sat down beside him and they both watched Joanna. Joanna stayed in a full half hour; and when at last she came out and began to dress, Hazel and Marcus walked away a little, along the edge of the rocks, together. "I know who you are now," Hazel said.

Marcus was pleased. It made him feel that he *was* somebody. "Who?" he demanded.

"Marcus Brownlow. I remember Margaret at school," she added. "She was always a form ahead of me all the way up."

"But how did you know about *me*?" Marcus said.

"Oh, we've known about you for a long time," she answered. "You see we come here every summer—we've been coming for years—and this was always a sort of mystery place. We used to call it *The Hermitage* and Mr. Burnaby was *The Abbot*—and then one year we heard about you. Sometimes we saw you in the distance. We used to call you *The Novice*."

"And now I suppose you'll go home and tell the others you've met *The Novice*." The nick-name offended him a little. It empha-sised the element in his situation which he most disliked. He imag-ined her as one of a gay little community—girls and youths on hol-iday, carefree and happy, with a background of comfortably-off, providing parents. He envied the imaginary boys and young men who would have her company every day. They would look on him as an oddity, a prig. He imagined the jokes with which the story would be received on her return. "He'll get into a row for speak-ing to you."—"He'll be put on bread and water for a fortnight."—"He'll be confined to his cell for a month."—"Hazel's got off with *The Monk*." He envied even Joanna.

"I might have said that," she admitted after thinking it over, "but I won't now. I'll just say 'I met Marcus Brownlow.'"

Marcus felt grateful: he was touched. "Thank you very much," he mumbled awkwardly.

There was a hail from Joanna. "Hi, you two. Hi, Hazel. We'll have to get back: it's nearly time for tea."

They turned, and Joanna came to meet them. "You should come and bathe here again," Marcus ventured. "It's far the best place. I'll be bathing tomorrow morning."

"What about the . . . ? What about Mr. Burnaby?"

"The Abbot's away," he answered abruptly. "*The Abbot's* in England."

There was a certain deliberate and vicious brutality in this, and after she had gone he was ashamed. He wandered about for a long time, conscious of guilt and treachery. But if he was unhappy he did not reach the stage of repentance.

CHAPTER XXV

WHETHER to expect her or not Marcus didn't really know, but he hoped and hoped that she would come. During the evening and through the night he repeated her name over and over again to himself. He had never yet addressed her by it, but he determined that he would do so tomorrow. If she didn't come to the bathing place, he would seek her out: somehow he would manage to meet her.

He didn't sleep—not a wink. He didn't try to sleep; he didn't want to. He was quite happy to lie and think of her—Hazel, Hazel, Hazel. . . . It seemed to him a lovely name, suggesting glades in the woods, and sunlit vistas opening on the sea.

Towards five o'clock he began to feel restless. He knew that she wasn't likely to appear before eleven—people on holiday always began the day late. Still, he felt that the time of their meeting, if they *were* to meet, was approaching. In six hours he might be talking to her. He got up and dressed, without washing or shaving.

He still kept his bedroom locked at night as a sort of guard against the big, grey emptiness of the house. In his room there had been a glimmer of light, but the passages were dark, and on the stairs he had to feel his way cautiously, keeping close to the outer wall. He was reminded a little of his first arrival at The Garrison. The possibility occurred to him that even now Mr. Burnaby might be in the tower room; or worse, invisibly following him, or invisibly coming to meet him through the empty hall.

As soon as he got outside that tension relaxed. If Mr. Burnaby were near, Marcus didn't expect to see him any more—or to be seen by him. It was brighter too than it had been in the house. Everything close at hand looked quite clear. There was a kind of stillness in the half-light: it depended not on an absence of sound or movement, for there were rabbits feeding, and he could hear a corn-crake, and the restless, ceaseless sea: it was rather that in the secrecy of the night the sky had come closer to the earth, and wrapped itself about it. Now it was reluctantly rising, uncovering the sandhills and the shore, and drawing white wrappings of cloud up the mountain-sides.

He went first to the bathing place. He lay where Hazel had lain to sun-bathe: he stood on the rock from which she had dived. His rock, her rock, their rock. He had never known anyone else to use it, never seen anyone else bathing there. He was glad now that Mr. Burnaby didn't bathe.

He half hoped that Hazel too could not sleep, that she would give it up, and like himself come out wandering along the shore to look at the place of their meeting. There would be a moment of surprise and embarrassment, then a delicious understanding, a recognition that they were both in love. He went over the whole scene, speaking Hazel's sentences as well as his own, varying the words slightly with each repetition.

But there was no one in sight, and presently Marcus walked away slowly in the direction of the inlet. It had been mean to wish Hazel awake, he thought, and now he tried to imagine her asleep. He found it difficult. Though he knew the colouring of her hair, and of her eyes, and of her skin, he remembered her as a presence rather than a face. Her face had been too bright for him to see it clearly, and it was only the brightness he could visualise. He wondered if he would know her with her eyes closed, with the brightness cut off. There seemed to be something beautiful and tender in the very idea. He pictured her unconscious head on a white pillow, her hair tousled, her eyelashes against her soft cheeks. . . .

After two hours he returned to the house. He undressed and got back into bed. This time he went to sleep immediately. When he awoke Kate was knocking at the door. "It's after nine," she called. "Are ye nearly ready?"

"I'm sorry," Marcus said. "I slept in."

"Me mother says, will ye stay where y'are till ye've had yer breakfast?"

"No thanks," Marcus called back. "Tell her I'll be down in a minute or two. I'll hurry."

All the same he lay on for a few moments. He remembered Hazel in her wet bathing suit, Hazel swimming, Hazel walking along the rocks by his side. Suddenly it occurred to him that she might after all come early. He jumped up and dashed across the passage to the bathroom. He put a new blade in his razor and shaved carefully, but in his anxiety not to let a vestige of bristle remain, he cut himself in three places.

He gobbled his breakfast, and as soon as the last bite was swallowed rushed out. It was ten past ten. Except for two cormorants perched on separate points of rock the shore was deserted. It occurred to him as a horrible possibility that Hazel might have come and gone. It was unlikely; more probably she wouldn't come at all. The sky was cloudy; the sun was out of sight; a light breeze from the mountains blew down upon the sea. But the hollow where he had lain yesterday was sheltered and he settled there once more very comfortably. He had his bathing things with him and *Twelfth Night*. Since he had seen Hazel he hadn't read another line, but he felt an affection for the book on her account. He felt that perhaps it was some hidden magic in the play which had brought her to him, and he hoped that it might be his talisman a second time.

At first he lay on his face, gazing along the coast towards the village. Presently it occurred to him that just having the book with him might not be enough. Perhaps it was necessary that he should actually be reading the play. He opened it and went on from where he had stopped the day before.

When he came to the line,

Poor lady, she were better love a dream,

he paused and sighed. He too might better love a dream. What could come of loving Hazel? For a moment he looked at the problem, but it was black and intricate. To think of it would only make him miserable. He would take this little bit of happiness with his eyes shut to the future. He read on trying to drive all thought of Mr. Burnaby from his mind.

> O mistress mine, where are you roaming?
> O, stay and hear; your true love's coming,
>   That can sing both high and low:
> Trip no farther, pretty sweeting;
> Journeys end in lovers meeting,
>   Every wise man's son doth know.
>
> What is love? 'tis not hereafter;
> Present mirth hath present laughter;
>   What's to come is still unsure:
> In delay there lies no plenty;
> Then come kiss me, sweet and twenty;
>   Youth's a stuff will not endure.

He read the song over three times. It was all so relevant to his own case, and the advice in the second verse seemed as if it had been particularly designed for him. But he hated Sir Toby Belch and Sir Andrew Aguecheek. He couldn't understand why Shakespeare had allowed these horrible, coarse, old men to intrude into his beautiful love story. They bored him. He skimmed over the next few pages and then turned back to reread the Clown's song.

> O mistress mine, where are you roaming?

Where indeed? he reflected wryly. He felt suddenly weary and pushed the book away from him. In a few seconds he was sound asleep.

He awoke to find Hazel staring down at him. She was prodding his ribs with her foot. "You're a one," she remarked. "Don't ever try and tell me how fond of Shakespeare you are. I wondered what it was you were waggling so impressively yesterday. Now I see through you."

"'Enter Viola in man's attire,'" he quoted. The coincidences were extraordinary. Hazel was wearing long, navy-blue trousers, and a navy-blue sweater with a polo neck.

"Do you mean my slacks?" she enquired: "They're not man's attire: they're girl's attire, women's wear if you like."

At that he noticed that they were different from men's trousers in the manner of their buttoning. He blushed. "It makes you like a sailor boy," he said shyly.

The comparison didn't appear to displease her. "It's got so cold," she complained. "I'm not going to bathe."

"But you've got your things," Marcus pointed out.

"I know. I wish I hadn't. I don't know why I brought them."

By this time Marcus was on his feet. He felt not the slightest trace of sleepiness. He remembered his resolution to use her Christian name. He looked at her squarely. "It was nice of you to come, Hazel." He spoke awkwardly, trying to hide the passion in his voice. She was so close to him, so confiding. Would she mind if he kissed her, he wondered.

"It was nice of you too—Marcus." She added his name deliberately, after the slightest of pauses, with a little, knowing, provocative smile.

He took a heavy step towards her, raising his arms: but she darted away from him. He stopped immediately and his face fell. She looked not frightened exactly, but put out. Marcus was ashamed.

She came close to him again and smiled. "Now look," she said, "I like you, but don't let's be silly. It'd only spoil everything."

"I'm sorry." Marcus drooped his head penitently—though evidently it wasn't very bad: she wasn't too much offended.

"It's all right," Hazel told him. "It was my fault as much as yours. I led you on. I didn't mean to, but I didn't know you'd be so inflammable. I should have brought a fire-extinguisher. Will you promise to behave yourself in future—be quiet and tractable."

"I'll be good," Marcus promised, "—quiet as a lamb—easy to lead, but hard to drive." He hoped he sounded light and amusing.

"All right, Lambkin," she responded, "but I want you to do the leading. I'm the explorer, you're the friendly native—not too friendly, of course," she put in hastily. "I've always wanted to come in here, but I never have before. I could never get the family to come. The people in the village always said Mr. Burnaby didn't like trespassers, and that was enough for Daddy—he's frightfully law-abiding. Nobody knows I'm here now except Joanna. I'd an awful job to get her to come yesterday—and she absolutely refused today."

"I'm glad she didn't come," Marcus said.

"So am I in a way. It'll be nice to go back and tell them I faced all the perils alone—like darkest Africa or something."

"But you won't be alone," Marcus said. "Do you not count me?"

"Oh yes," she retorted. "I do—you're one of the perils."

"A peril conquered."

She ignored this and they walked on round the coast, away from the village and the house in the direction of the lough. Marcus wished that it was new to him too, but it was all familiar. He had been over every inch of it with Mr. Burnaby. He would have liked to share her feelings exactly, to think that he also was exploring.

They scrambled over the rocks peering into pools like children. In the small, sandy bays they stopped to skim stones over the water. They talked about themselves incessantly. Marcus noticed how much more pleasant he found this chatter than the many, more profound conversations he had in the past, walking along the same shore with Mr. Burnaby. Hazel told him a good deal about herself and her family. She had a younger sister, who was both a little dear and a perfect horror—also a brother who had stayed in Belfast to look after the business while his father was away. She herself had been doing the housekeeping for the last year, because her mother had been ill and had been ordered to take things easily. Now, however, her mother was better and when they went home was going to take charge again.

"That'll give you more time," Marcus observed.

"Indeed it won't," Hazel responded. "I'm going to Queen's* in the autumn to do first year medical: so I'll have to work."

"And afterwards I suppose you'll marry some doctor," Marcus said gloomily, "and that'll be that."

For the first time he saw her looking really angry. "It's stupid to talk that way," she told him. "Daddy went off on that tack once—but only once. Some men are so conceited and old-fashioned that they think girls spend their lives hanging about waiting for men to propose to them. *I* don't want to get married, let me assure you. I'm going to go abroad and see a bit of the world. I don't know

* Queen's University, Belfast.

how I'll work it yet, but if they have women ships' doctors I'll have a shot at that: if not I'll have to find some other way."

"You mean you're determined never to get married?" Marcus asked.

"No, I don't mean that exactly," she answered, "but I want to *do* something first. I'm not going to get married simply because people do. I won't think of it for years yet—get married and settle down: it's sort of finishing off, isn't it?"

"It might be just beginning."

"The beginning of the end."

Marcus too talked about himself, though not as openly as he would have liked. The shadow of Mr. Burnaby hovered in the background of his mind forbidding candour—and he had not much to be proud of. He told her a little about school and a little about the family at home, but about his present life he said nothing till she pressed him.

"Do you stay here all the year round?" she queried presently, "—winter and summer?"

"Except when I go home on holidays."

She looked at him curiously. "I'm sure I'd get bored," she said. "Do you not feel awfully out of it?"

He imagined that she must think him very odd. For a moment he was tempted to confess how much out of it he did feel, to tell her miserably all that he hated in his life with Mr. Burnaby. Pride, or loyalty, or a fear of appearing contemptible prevented him. He answered instead: "No: it's I who *am in* it. You see my work's frightfully interesting."

"I thought it'd just be business—stocks and shares, and all that sort of thing."

"It's not that at all—that's what everyone thinks it is."

"Well what is it then? What do you do?"

"It's a secret."

"Oh all right!" Yet she didn't look satisfied. He remembered how his mother and Margaret had tried to persuade him to talk about his work.

"You won't tell anyone?" he demanded anxiously.

"How can I, when you haven't told me anything?"

"I mean that it's not stocks and shares."

She regarded him rather coldly and then, when he was almost in despair, her face softened a little. "Not if you don't want me to," she agreed. "All the same I think you're awfully funny."

He walked on moodily for a bit kicking at stones and scowling. He was angry with Mr. Burnaby for putting him in this position. He wanted to pour out everything that was in his mind to Hazel and here he was warning her off, telling her, almost, to mind her own business.

Presently she put her hand on his arm. "It doesn't matter," she said. "If you've promised not to tell of course you can't say anything. I'd love to hear all the same."

"I haven't exactly promised," Marcus confessed. "It's just that I'm trusted."

"That's the same thing."

The sun came out and they bathed in a small bay between two rocky points. It would all have been perfect but for the dark shadow of Mr. Burnaby. Never for more than a few moments could Marcus forget him.

CHAPTER XXVI

THE next morning at ten o'clock Marcus called at the house where Hazel was staying. Hazel had promised to spend the day with him: they were going to climb Slieve Pennion.

When he arrived he was told that Hazel was just getting ready. For five minutes he talked awkwardly to Mr. and Mrs. Morley, Hazel's parents, and to Betty, her younger sister. All three had been in the little front garden of the house when he arrived. Betty was watching her father, who was testing the reel of a trout rod. Mrs. Morley was reading a day-old copy of the *Belfast Newsletter*.

Marcus recognised them as a perfectly ordinary family of Belfast business people. They were the sort of people he had been accustomed to all his life. They seemed friendly and easy-going, and he liked them.

Hazel didn't keep him long. He caught a glimpse of her at an upstairs window. He heard her whistling, and a moment or two later she appeared at the front door, carrying a packet of sandwiches and an orange. She was wearing a short, wide, grey tweed skirt, and the same navy-blue sweater as on the previous day. Her legs were bare except for ankle-length socks which just emerged above the top of her small, black, low-heeled shoes. Marcus gazed at her in admiration and approval. Then it struck him that he was embarrassing her a little, and he turned away quickly. He glanced instead at the rest of the family. He thought of Hazel doing the housekeeping so that her mother could get well again after her illness. Doubtless she did all sorts of things for the others as well. He felt that in possessing her, her whole family must be perpetually happy. Each of them shone a little in the light of her beauty.

"Hello," Hazel greeted him, with a slightly forced over-cheerfulness. "Sorry I'm late. My old watch stopped again—there must be sand in it, or something."

"Oh, you're not too late," Marcus assured her. "I expect I'm a little early." These words came out entirely of their own accord, and without any reference to fact: he knew that he had been neither early nor late. He had taken particular care to arrive on the very stroke of ten.

"Have *you* got a watch?" Mr. Morley enquired, in a dry, business-like voice.

"Oh, yes," Marcus said.

"Does it go?"

"Yes."

"Good."

It seemed to Mrs. Morley that he was being a little unkind. "We don't want you to be late, dear," she told Hazel, "and don't get caught in a mist or anything. All mountains are dangerous if you get lost on them."

"Don't worry. We'll be careful all right," Hazel assured her, and set off down the road with Marcus. It was pleasant for walking, sunny with a light breeze from the sea. Marcus was to look back on it as the happiest day in his life.

Going through the village they didn't talk much, yet Marcus was conscious that for the moment at any rate they were united in feeling. They were sharing the sunshine and the smell of the sea and the brightness of the morning; not quite as two individuals, but almost as one. They were joined by an invisible link: it was spiritual and at the same time physical; for their whole bodies seemed to be in harmony.

They passed one or two fishermen, one or two women and girls coming from the well with pails of water, a small boy leading a donkey which had empty wickerwork panniers slung at its side.

Everyone they met greeted them with friendly smiles and wished them "Good morning," in the soft Donegal brogue.

Hazel knew them all to see. Marcus knew their names. "The wee boy's Micky Flynn," he informed her. "He's going to the bog for turf."

In a few minutes they were out of the village on the lonely track leading up to Slieve Pennion.

> What is love? 'tis not hereafter;
> Present mirth hath present laughter:
> What's to come is still unsure:
> In delay there lies no plenty;
> Then come kiss me, sweet and twenty;
> Youth's a stuff will not endure.

"You're talking to yourself," Hazel said.

"I know. I meant you to hear," he added frankly.

"You should speak a bit louder then. Come on, out with it!"

But to come out with it boldly, without explanation, was a little embarrassing.

"I *was* reading Shakespeare, the other day," he began.

"I know you were: nobody said you weren't."

"I mean it wasn't just show—*Twelfth Night*: I think it's lovely."

"We did it at school once. I was Malvolio: it was rather fun—all that cross-gartered bit, you know."

"You should have been Viola," Marcus told her huskily. "I think you're awfully like Viola."

"I hope not," Hazel responded. "I mean she was pretty soppy, wasn't she? What bit were you quoting? I expect I could carry on."

Marcus repeated the last two lines out loud. "That's the important part," he said, blushing, but determined nevertheless not to be faint-hearted.

Hazel frowned. "I am afraid I can't."

Marcus was surprised. He wasn't prepared for a direct answer. "You're afraid you can't kiss me."

"No, you silly. Of course I can't—or rather I won't. I mean I can't go on—I don't know what comes next. Oh yes I do though, something about the smell of people's breaths—no, that's the line after. Wait a minute. Something about a mellifluous voice. 'A mellifluous voice, as I am true knight' and the other one says 'A contagious breath.' That's it. And anyhow," she added unexpectedly, "I'm only nineteen."

Marcus was puzzled by this last remark. Did it mean that she was relenting—that she might let him kiss her after all? Even if it didn't, it gave him a little thrill to hear her announce her age so candidly. He had wondered how old she was, but had not liked to ask. It touched him to think that she was so young: but, after a pause, he said, "There's not much difference. I mean nineteen's almost twenty."

Hazel disagreed. "There's lots of difference. At twenty you're in your twenties—and twenty-nine's not the same as nineteen: why it's almost thirty." It was a game: she was teasing him, but he didn't mind. They had the whole day before them, and nothing could be more pleasant than to play a game with *her*.

"I mean I want to kiss you all the same—even more perhaps."

"You mean you won't want to kiss me as much when I'm twenty."

"I'll want to kiss you always, just as much, more and more and more."

"But it's so early in the morning," she objected. "You shouldn't be thinking of things like that when it's not half-past-ten yet."

"I'd like to kiss you at any time: it would never be too early or too late. I'd like to kiss you at half-past-six or at half-past-three, or at two or at one."

Suddenly he wondered if he had offended her. Did she think him sensual and disgusting? Maybe she wished she hadn't come. If he wasn't careful she might tell him she was going back. He walked along gloomily for a yard or two and then brought out abruptly. "I'm sorry if you think I'm horrid. I'll stop if you like. I'll do anything you like. Maybe you hate the idea of my even touching you."

Again she put her hand on his arm, just in the same way as she had the day before. There was something extraordinarily gentle about her, and the gesture moved him almost to tears. "But I don't," she assured him. "I quite like touching you. It's only that . . . . that I don't believe in kissing anyone, and that sort of thing, unless you're serious; and I don't want to be serious, not with *any-one*—not yet. People when they're in love get so tied up. They sort of own each other. I don't want anyone to own me—not for years and years—perhaps not ever."

Marcus's spirits soared again, just as quickly as they had fallen. "You did *know* I was in love with you?"

"You shouldn't ask that sort of question." She looked at him crossly for a moment; but suddenly she laughed. "I'd never have guessed in a hundred years. You're so undemonstrative, you know—one of those stern, silent men with an impassive exterior."

"And you're not in love at all?"

"I'm not prepared to be," she declared emphatically and rather reprovingly. "I wouldn't let myself be—and I don't think you should either."

This was fairly definite, but Marcus risked one further enquiry.

"You said you didn't mind touching me. Would you mind if we held hands?"

"Only for practical reasons. But people don't hold hands at half-past ten in the morning. You hold hands when you're 'Roaming in the gloaming.'"

"What are the practical reasons?"

"There are lots of them. In the first place both our hands would get damp, and horrid, and sticky. We'd both want to let go and neither of us would like to say so. In the second place you can't walk very well holding hands. In the third place we've come out to climb Slieve Pennion—not to spoon. If you promise to talk no more nonsense I'll forgive you: if not I'll be angry. Now come on. If we can get to the top by twelve we might be able to do that other mountain behind in the afternoon. I looked it up on the map last night, but the name's gone out of my head."

An hour and a half later they reached the top. They were both very hot. Hazel had taken off her sweater and was carrying it hanging down her back with the arms knotted loosely round her neck. Underneath she was wearing a light, short-sleeved sports shirt, open at the throat. Marcus had removed his jacket and pullover. His pullover was stuffed into his jacket pocket and his jacket was thrown over his left shoulder. He held it in this position with one finger thrust through the hanger.

They each put a stone on the cairn which marked the highest point of the peak and then Hazel flung herself down on a flat slab of rock and gazed out at the country below them—the long, heather-covered slopes broken by black turf cuttings, the white cottages with their thatched roofs, the small, stone-walled fields which made up the narrow strip of cultivated ground between the mountains and the sea.

"How blue the sea is," she remarked. "The higher you get the deeper blue it seems to be."

"It's lovely," Marcus said, "and being with you makes it even better—it makes it just perfect."

She twisted round to look at him. "You're hopeless," she told him. "I thought that climb would have put the nonsense out of you."

"That isn't nonsense," Marcus replied. "I was just stating a fact."

In turning she had accidentally given her shirt a slight upward tug. At her waist just above her right hip a small gap had appeared. Marcus gazed at the little patch of white skin. He was tempted to put his finger into the gap and run it round, pressing it against her body and loosening the shirt altogether. With an effort he took his eyes away. He knew he shouldn't even imagine things like that: yet the next moment, he found himself remembering a story in which a boy and a girl had found themselves alone together in a hay-loft; the girl had invited the boy to put his hand inside her blouse and feel the beating of her heart.

"What are you frowning at?" Hazel demanded. "I know my hair's in a mess. So's yours for that matter—but then it always is. You've a big, damp lock hanging down over your eyes. It makes you look quite distinguished in an arty sort of way."

Marcus pushed back the untidy lock. "It needs cutting," he said. "I meant to get it done if I'd gone to London. I'll have to get it done in Portmallagh; but they half shave you and leave a sort of tonsure on top."

"And what *were* you frowning at?" Hazel persisted.

"I wasn't," Marcus told her, "or if I was, it wasn't at anything to do with you."

"Otherwise, mind your own business."

"Oh no," Marcus was distressed. "I didn't mean that at all. I mean there's nothing wrong with you. I think your hair looks awfully nice like that—the way it is—almost nicer than usual. I was frowning at myself, at something I was thinking."

"And I'm not to know?"

Marcus lay down beside her on the rock. As if by accident his left arm just touched her right elbow. She didn't move her arm away; perhaps she didn't notice, though surely she could hardly help noticing. He felt a little tremor of excitement; perhaps she didn't mind; perhaps she really quite liked to have him touching her, if she could pretend not to know.

"Is it so secret that you won't even tell me whether I'm to know or not?"

"I'll tell you if you promise not to be cross with me."

"That means I ought to be," she responded. "However I want to know. That's the worst of being a girl. You suffer from feminine curiosity. What were you thinking?"

"You promise?"

"How can I promise? If I'm going to feel cross, I'll feel cross, even if I don't say anything. I'll promise not to say anything unless I can't help it. What was it?"

Marcus considered. "Well you see," he began awkwardly. "It's just . . . . . I mean your shirt's coming out a wee bit."

"So's yours," she retorted. "It came out about five times on the way up."

"I know," he admitted, "but I tucked it in again."

"Well," she answered indignantly, "so would I have, if I'd known. If that's what you were frowning about, I must say. . . ."

"It wasn't that," Marcus interrupted. "It was what I was thinking made me frown."

Hazel stood up. "You just keep looking at the view," she ordered sternly. "Now, what *were* you thinking?"

Marcus stared steadily out in front of him, but what he saw was the white shirt on Hazel's back and the small, tantalizing portion of her naked waist. "I wanted to put in my finger and pull it out all round," he blurted out suddenly.

There was a distinct silence. Marcus felt as if a storm were gathering behind him. *"You are a shocker,"* Hazel exclaimed at last. "You'd every right to frown at yourself. You'd better go on frowning and frowning and frowning."

"You promised you wouldn't be cross."

"I said I wouldn't be cross if I could help it. I can't help it. You oughtn't to let yourself think things like that, and if you do think them you oughtn't to say them."

"I can't help thinking them."

"Well you ought to keep them to yourself."

"But you made me tell you," he expostulated.

"I couldn't *make* you."

"You could make me do almost anything."

Hazel sat down clasping her hands round her knees. "Oh, dear," she said, "I wish, I wish. . . ."

"What do you wish?" Marcus asked, "—that I wasn't a nuisance?"

"Or that I wasn't," she responded sadly. "No, it wasn't that exactly. I wish I were a boy in a way, then there'd be no more of this trouble."

"I'm sorry," Marcus said. "I'm afraid I'm spoiling everything for you. I suppose you wish you hadn't come."

She reflected for a moment. "No. I'm glad I came—and you're not really spoiling things. You would be if I didn't like you of course, but that makes it worse in a way. I don't suppose you can help feeling the way you do, though. . . . It's a pity I'm not a boy and we could be friends without anything like this cropping up."

"I'm glad you're not a boy."

"If you were a girl it would come to the same thing. How would you like to be Joanna, now?"

"I don't think I'd like it very much," Marcus confessed, "though I did envy her the other day."

"Envy Joanna!"

"Yes. Being friends with you and going home with you, when I didn't even know if I'd ever see you again."

"Poor Joanna," Hazel said. "I don't know that I'm much of a

friend for her. She'd much rather sit in a deck chair and read, or knit, and I'm always trying to drag her out and make her walk. They're all away to Bundoran in the car. They've gone for the day. Joanna'll sleep all the way there and all the way back. She always sleeps in cars. I think it's very clever of her."

"Is she clever?" Marcus asked. "I mean at other things besides sleeping."

"Joanna," Hazel repeated thoughtfully. "I suppose she is quite: she can be very amusing at times, chiefly personalities of course. She never did anything special at school, but she always did well enough—and she never seemed to work: so I suppose she *is* quite clever. She says she worked for senior—though it was only for the week before the exam—and that she's never going to work again. I think everyone should work, don't you?—I mean girls as well as men, even if they've plenty of money like Joanna and don't need to. Anyhow I don't believe in people having lots of money. What do you think?"

She paused, but Marcus had no answer ready. He thought of Mr. Burnaby and how his own career was planned. "I think it's a good idea for some people to have money," he said slowly. "I mean there are some kinds of work to be done that need money, and don't earn money, and that no one would subscribe money for."

"The work you do, I suppose," she responded. "Couldn't you just give me a teeny idea what it's all about? I'd promise never to tell a single, solitary soul—and I can keep secrets: really I can."

Marcus considered. He believed that, if she promised, she could keep secret anything he told her. After all it was different from telling his people. It wasn't as if she could put her foot down and make him give it up—yet he knew he ought not to tell her. "I'll show you something I can do because of my work, because of the work we've done," he suggested at last. "I can't tell you about my work unless I tell you everything. Even this will look like a trick, but it isn't: it's part of something bigger—and all the same I'm not sure. . . . Maybe I'd better not."

"Oh do," she begged. "Go on. I promise faithfully I'll never tell a soul—unless you say I can, of course."

"All right," Marcus consented doubtfully, "but I say you *can't*:

you must never tell anyone." He looked round. "Have you got a pencil and a piece of paper?"

"No, I'm afraid not."

Marcus took a pencil and an envelope from his jacket pocket. "You can use these. I'll go and sit with my back to you beside that little pool of water over there. You go up to the cairn and write down something on the envelope."

"What shall I write?" she demanded.

"Anything you like, so long as you don't tell me. Just one sentence, not anything long that I won't be able to remember."

"And what are you going to do?"

"I'll tell you what you've written."

She was much less impressed than he had expected. "I saw something like that at the circus once. People wrote down questions on bits of paper and a woman answered them, without seeing the bits of paper. I wrote down something, but she didn't answer. It was supposed to be telepathy, but John—that's my brother you know—said it was faked. Is yours telepathy?"

"No," Marcus answered, "though telepathy's mixed up with it." He wished now he hadn't undertaken the demonstration. For the first time she had irritated him—making comparisons with some woman in a circus indeed!

Hazel got up. "Oh well, here goes," she remarked.

Marcus got up also and walked to the small, black pool he had indicated. It was merely a slight depression in the mountain-top filled with dirty rain-water and bordered by half-withered clumps of heather. He sat down with his back to Hazel. He had a moment's panic when he thought he wasn't going to be able to project himself at all. Then he managed to calm down. He searched for something to fix his eyes on—it was easier that way. He picked on a large, grey boulder about twenty yards in front of him. He would go to that first and then back over his own body to where Hazel was sitting at the cairn.

It was the first experiment he had made since before his illness and it came to him almost like a new experience. How pleasant it was to float away from his body! How free he felt! He drifted out from the mountain like a cloud: for a moment he hung there without any thought of Hazel, and gazed around. Far below him a hawk was hovering, but he didn't want to look at it more closely. He had watched a hawk once before, remained beside it in the air, and followed it unseen and unknown on its swift downwards swoop. The victim on that occasion had been a young rabbit, but he didn't want to see such a spectacle a second time. He turned back towards the mountain and caught sight of Hazel sitting at the foot of the cairn. Immediately he remembered what he had to do and he came close to her. She was staring at his body lying still beside the pool. "Marcus," she called, and then more loudly, "Marcus, are you ready? I've written something down."

He had just time to glance at the envelope before she got up, shouting, "Marcus, what's the matter? Why don't you answer?"

He was back before she reached him, but he did not get up immediately. He had been too completely detached from his body to be able to return to it in an instant. He felt her grip his shoulder and shake him. He looked at her and blinked. "'Marcus is a big silly!'" It was what she had written on the envelope, and now he repeated it aloud to her.

Hazel was cross. "So you are too. Why didn't you answer when I shouted to you?"

"I couldn't," he replied. "You see I wasn't there. I was up where you were, reading your message."

He had expected her to be impressed, but she didn't seem to be. "If that's all you do I think it's stupid," she said. "Just a stupid trick."

"It's not all we do. It's only part of it."

She frowned. "Well it's the sort of thing I don't like."

Marcus was huffed. Mr. Burnaby was right about one thing. Women were conventional. They didn't like things that weren't obvious, things that were unusual.

They went back in silence towards the flat rock where they had lain admiring the view. At first they walked a little further apart than before, but gradually they drew closer again. Marcus was glad that she had been worried when he failed to answer her. Of course she had admitted that she liked him, but he construed her anxiety as a proof that the admission was genuine.

"What do you say?" Hazel asked. "Shall we eat our lunch now, or shall we go on a bit first and have it later?"

Marcus looked at his watch: it was a quarter past twelve. "Let's go on," he said. "If we're going to climb the other mountain we don't need to go right down. There's a sort of saddle in between, and there seems to be a stream in the middle. We could have lunch by the stream."

"Right oh," Hazel responded, and they set off once more.

The stream had not appeared very distant, but it took them an hour to reach it. On the way they had to cross a bog. Whether it was really dangerous or not they didn't know: suddenly they found themselves in it, but they were deluded by the fact that the ground always looked firmer a few paces ahead. Instead it got wetter and wetter. In the worst places they were jumping from one tuft of reeds to another; even so they sank in well above their ankles. They felt that if they were to stop for a moment, they would sink right down and be unable to go on. When at last they came to firm ground Hazel's legs were black, while Marcus's trousers were splashed up to the knees with the dark peat mud.

At the stream they both took off their shoes and socks and washed their feet. They rinsed their socks and spread them out in the sun to dry. After this they sat down and began to undo their parcels of sandwiches. Suddenly Hazel stopped and looked across at Marcus, "I wish you'd give it up," she said.

"Give up what?" he inquired uneasily.

"Give up whatever you're doing—give up Mr. Burnaby."

Marcus didn't answer at once. For the moment there was nothing he would have liked more. He had a vision of going back home, living an ordinary, normal life. He had never spent more than a fraction of his salary. He had plenty of money saved. Perhaps he would go to Queen's like Hazel. He might even take medicine. After all he was still only twenty-three: it was late, but not too late, to start. Of course he'd have to do a lot of swotting first, but he felt certain that if he did decide on such a course Hazel would help, and with her help he felt he could accomplish almost anything. He stared at the idea and it dazzled him. They would go through Queen's together. Year after year they would be companions, comparing notes, taking the same exams, residents in the same hospitals—and perhaps after that. . . . Perhaps when they were both through she might think of marrying him. After all it need not interfere with her career. He imagined a brass plate:

MARCUS BROWNLOW M.B.
HAZEL BROWNLOW M.B.

He had not spoken and Hazel's voice broke in on his daydream. "Could you not, really? Please do. I'm sure it'd be better. I don't know what you do do, but there's something queer about it. I don't like it. I somehow feel it's something not quite right."

Right and Wrong. The dream was shattered. If it was a question of right and wrong, there could be no doubt as to what his duty was. He would have to stay with Mr. Burnaby. He looked at his duty stretching away coldly in front of him like a corridor in a prison. "What do you think matters in life?" he asked presently. "Contributing to the general happiness—the greatest good of the greatest number—or being happy oneself?"

"I never see how you can know what's going to be the greatest good," Hazel responded practically. "We'd a mistress at school who was always talking about it. I think your own happiness counts for a good deal, but I think you're more likely to be happy if you're doing some sort of useful work."

"And if I told you we were doing work that might change the outlook of the whole world—might, if it came off, make everyone in the world more happy?"

Hazel looked completely disbelieving. "Well, of course, I'd have to say go on, though I must say I don't see how telepathy, or whatever it is, is going to make the world so much happier."

Marcus sighed. "I wish I could tell you. Suppose—mind you I'm not telling you—only suppose that I said we might be on the verge of a discovery that might take all the unhappiness out of dying."

"I wouldn't believe you," she told him promptly. "You might think you were, but, but. . . . You know, Marcus, all those things have turned out to be frauds. They don't stand up to the scientific tests—all the big scientists are against them. We're not really anything, you know—just bundles of cells that act and re-act with each other. It's horrid to think of, but it's true."

"Perhaps we might be able to prove that it wasn't true."

"But you can't go against science," she insisted. "I know

spiritualists and people say you can, but it's just a sort of weak-mindedness, shutting your eyes to the facts."

Marcus felt that he had said too much. He had no right to be talking about his work. "I was only saying *if* that was what we *are* doing."

"Oh well," she answered, "when you won't tell me what you're doing I obviously can't say if I think it right or wrong. Not that I've any business coming poking my nose in—just it seems such a pity, such a waste. A waste of *you*, I mean."

Marcus looked at her without speaking. "Oh, I wish, I do wish things were different," he brought forth at last.

"It doesn't seem to have made *you* very happy," she pointed out suddenly, "and they could be different if you liked. Are you sure it's not just a matter of having enough strength of mind to break with this Mr. Burnaby man?"

"I could never be happy if I did," he assured her. "It's to give up everything for the sake of what we're doing, for the one thing that really matters, that takes the strength."

She shrugged her shoulders. "In that case there's nothing more to say. Come on, let's eat our lunch." She glanced at the two packets of sandwiches, both lying open, but still untouched on the rock between them. "I tell you what," she went on more cheerfully, "we'll eat them turn about: first we'll each have one of yours and then one of mine—it'll make it more interesting."

The idea pleased Marcus. There was a queer, almost sensual pleasure in sharing the food with her. He felt that it brought them closer together. They munched away, smiling at each other from time to time, in a friendly picnic spirit. "If only the whole of life was like this," Marcus said. "I'd like to go on like this for ever."

"One long lunch. You'd burst."

"One long picnic," Marcus returned. "Being here with you all the time, and nobody else for miles and miles."

"You'd get bored. So would I too. I don't mean I'm the slightest bit bored now," she added hastily. "I'm not. I'm loving it all, but I know I'd get fed up doing it every day and all the time."

"*I* wouldn't get fed up," Marcus insisted.

When they had finished the sandwiches Hazel peeled the

orange and divided it into two. "No, you should take it all," Marcus protested. "I didn't bring one. It's not fair."

"Don't be silly," she told him. "Do you think I'm going to sit guzzling it all by myself?"

He didn't really want to refuse. The fact that it was hers, that she had been carrying it all morning, that her hands had been touching it a moment before, made it even more pleasant to him than the sandwiches.

Afterwards they lay down on the bank and drank from the stream. "Do you think it's clean?" Marcus enquired.

"I don't care," Hazel answered. "This time next year perhaps . . . . Maybe I'll have all sorts of ideas about germs and things—and liver flukes from sheep. Now I just don't care."

"I wonder where we'll both be, this time next year." Marcus couldn't help sounding a little melancholy. He made an effort to be cheerful. "Ah well! Gideon wouldn't have chosen either of us."

"Gideon? I can't remember who Gideon was."

"He chose his men by the way they drank. He rejected all the ones who knelt or lay down to drink. He only took the ones who lapped the water out of their hands."

They waded across the stream, carrying their shoes and socks. On the other bank they dried their feet on Marcus's handkerchief. Then they began to climb the second mountain. It was called Slieve Gull, Marcus suddenly remembered.

On the way home Hazel asked about The Garrison. She wanted to know what size the rooms were, how they were furnished, was it not very cold and draughty in winter-time? Marcus knew that she hoped for an invitation to see over the house, but he was afraid to give it: at last she made the suggestion herself. "I wish you'd let me see through it. I've always wanted to see inside it and I've never had the chance before."

Marcus tried to put her off. "There's nothing to see. I don't think you'd find it very interesting."

"I love seeing through houses," Hazel replied, "specially old ones."

"It's not really old, not very old, at least. It was built during the Napoleonic wars as a garrison for soldiers."

"I know that," she responded sharply. "Will you take me over tomorrow?"

"I'm afraid Mr. Burnaby wouldn't like me to," Marcus answered reluctantly.

"I think he's a horrible man," Hazel said. "It's not as if I was going to do the place any harm. He hasn't anything to hide, has he?"

"I don't think so." Marcus hesitated. He felt bound in justice to defend Mr. Burnaby. "He never actually said I wasn't to show anyone over."

"Then it's you I think's queer. It's you yourself won't show me over it."

Marcus received this in complete silence. He didn't want to blame Mr. Burnaby. His very refusal was dictated by the fact that he understood Mr. Burnaby: yet he couldn't say, even to himself, why Mr. Burnaby should object to her seeing over the house. He just felt he wouldn't like it. But perhaps he was wrong: perhaps after all Mr. Burnaby wouldn't mind, or wouldn't mind very much: perhaps there would be no harm in doing what Hazel wanted.

"I know what it is," Hazel said. "You're just scared stiff of him—that's it, isn't it?"

"I'm not scared of him at all," Marcus told her gruffly. "What would I be scared of?"

But he knew he didn't sound convincing; Hazel wasn't convinced. "Of course you're scared of him—and that just proves what I say. It can't be good for you, living all the time with someone you're scared of."

Marcus didn't contradict her again. He suddenly realized that he would have been quite willing to show her the house if there had been no possibility of Mr. Burnaby ever suspecting he had done so. It was not then any moral obligation to Mr. Burnaby that was governing his behaviour, but plain funk. Yet he wasn't quite sure. Perhaps he was afraid because he knew he would be in the wrong and could not expect any support from his conscience if he had to meet Mr. Burnaby's accusations. He walked along frowning, staring at the ground and kicking viciously at loose stones on the track.

Hazel was the first to speak. "Don't," she said. "I think you're quite right—and I'm being awful. I should never have asked you.

It was awful cheek in the first place—but it was just that I wanted to see it so much. It seemed like a sort of adventure going over it when the Abbot was away. Of course it would be more of an adventure to go over it secretly when he was there, but I don't think I would have the nerve for that. You see it's always been a sort of mystery house for us—ever since we were children, and I do love mysteries. And I think you're quite right. You'd be wrong to take me through it unless you were quite sure Mr. Burnaby would approve: it's not as if it were your own house."

This decided Marcus. "I'll take you over it," he declared. "Will tomorrow morning do?"

"No don't, I really think you'd better not."

But Marcus now was quite determined. "I will," he said. "I will."

"No; no don't. I don't really want to any more."

"But I will. Do please come. If I can't do that. . . ." 'What is my love worth,' he meant, 'if I can't risk Mr. Burnaby's anger for you?' But he didn't quite like to say as much—or didn't like to annoy her by mentioning the word 'Love' again.

"No, no."

"Please do."

They went over it all once more, but this time each used the arguments the other had used before. In the end Hazel gave in. After all she *did* want to see the house.

CHAPTER XXVII

WHEN Marcus awoke the following morning it was raining heavily. He had arranged to call for Hazel at half-past ten, and for a few moments he wondered if she would want to come out. It might be better to wait till it was fine to show her over The Garrison. Immediately he remembered her remarks about "Roaming in the Gloaming," the half-implied suggestion that at such a time his love-making might be more acceptable. He hoped that it would go on raining all morning. He would try to persuade her to put off her visit till the evening. He would make two meetings out of one. He would see her home in the twilight. Perhaps then she might let him hold her hand for a little; perhaps she might relent even further and let him kiss her. Why shouldn't she after all? She had said that she liked him. Had girls such very different feelings from boys? In any case, whether she let him touch her or not, it would be very sweet to say good-night to her in the dusk—a long, loitering, tender good-night. . . .

But when he woke up more completely, he realized that Hazel was hardly the sort of girl to change her plans merely because it was raining. He'd have to tell her how much better the house looked on a sunny evening, how dismal it seemed on a wet day.

Though Marcus knew exactly how long it took to reach the village he set off shortly after breakfast, and arrived half an hour too soon. He had intended to put in the time wandering about the shore and the harbour, but he couldn't resist walking past the house where the Morleys were staying. Mr. Morley, gazing out at the rain, caught sight of him, and tapping on the window beckoned to him to come in.

In the sitting room he found Mrs. Morley. She was knitting, with a newspaper spread out in front of her on the window-seat. Hazel was again reported to be upstairs and due down in a minute or two.

"Powdering her nose, or something," Mr. Morley observed with a man to man air. "A woman always needs at least half an hour's preparation before she can venture out of doors. You and I just put on our hats and there we are—ready for anything."

"I'm not so sure of that," his wife retorted. "In any case, Hazel and Betty are making the beds at the moment—*your* bed included. One of the maids here has had to go home in a hurry," she explained to Marcus. "So we're all trying to help."

"I'm afraid I'm early again," Marcus said apologetically. "Our clocks are often a bit slow so I thought I'd better come in good time to make sure."

"Oh we're glad to see you," Mr. Morley assured him. "Too early's not a bad fault. Have you looked at the papers this morning?"

"They're not in yet," Marcus told him. "They come in the bus at twelve o'clock."

"I know ours does," Mr. Morley replied. "That one's a day old, but I thought you might have some way of getting them sooner. What did you think of yesterday's news?"

"I'm afraid I didn't read the paper yesterday."

Mr. Morley looked surprised. "Dunlops are down again. I thought you'd be keeping a pretty close eye on things with Mr. Burnaby away—looking after his affairs and so on."

Marcus was taken by surprise. He was inclined to forget his reputation as a stock-exchange expert at second-hand. But the situation was becoming familiar. When he went home his father's friends often questioned him about the prospects of different securities. He had become accustomed to putting them off, and was even, he gathered, acquiring a reputation for being deep and discreet. On this occasion, however, he was off his guard. "Oh no, I don't bother," he responded in some confusion, and added rather lamely, "You see I'm on holiday too. I don't bother with the markets when I'm on holiday."

Mr. Morley, like the rest, merely assumed that he was being evasive. Mr. Morley was accustomed to evasiveness in business. His interest immediately increased. He prepared to cross-examine Marcus. A formidable gleam came into his eyes. Marcus recognized it with apprehension. Luckily Mrs. Morley had not been listening. Quite innocently she came to Marcus's rescue. "It really is a dreadful day!" she exclaimed. "I'm sure you'd both be better to stay in the house this morning. Hazel's got the beginnings of a cold, and if she goes out she's sure to make it worse."

"That's what I was thinking too," Marcus agreed. "I could easily show her over some other time. It'll probably be fine in the evening and the house looks far better when the sun's out."

"Over The Garrison?" Mr. Morley queried.

"Yes. I was going to take her through the house."

"Indeed," Mrs. Morley remarked drily. "She only told us you were going for a walk."

Marcus felt he had made a mistake and he tried to cover it up. "I thought she might like to see over it. Of course, if she doesn't want to, we'll just go for a walk instead."

At this moment Betty appeared. She was a chubby-looking schoolgirl of about fifteen. She had her sister's colouring, and a bouncing, friendly smile. "Hazel's getting ready," she informed

Marcus. "She says she'll be down in a minute. You're early, aren't you?"

Marcus was beginning his explanation again when Mr. Morley interrupted. "Betty," he said, "Run upstairs and tell Hazel not to get ready. She's not to go out this morning."

Betty obeyed, and returned a few minutes later followed by Hazel, looking rather puzzled and rebellious. "Who says I'm not to go out?" she demanded. As no one showed any immediate sign of accepting the responsibility she turned to her father. "Betty says you told her to tell me not to go out."

Mr. Morley cleared his throat, and looked anxiously round for support. "Your mother and I. . . ." he began and paused.

Mrs. Morley went on for him. "We're not stopping you going out dear, but it's such a dreadful morning! We all thought you'd be better to put it off, and Marcus says he'd much rather wait till it's fine."

"Oh *does* he?" She gave Marcus a quick glance, to which he tried to return a smile which should be both explanatory and apologetic; but he was immediately aware that this rather sheepish compromise was a failure.

"You know, dear, you *have* a cold," Mrs. Morley put in mildly.

"I have not," Hazel declared.

"You were sniffing last night, and you know you were sneezing at breakfast."

"I told you at the time that that was the *pepper*. It's because Daddy can't put pepper on his scrambled eggs, without peppering the whole room."

"It made me sneeze too," Betty chimed in loyally.

Marcus felt that here was an opportunity of retrieving his own position a little. "Pepper makes me sneeze like anything," he announced, but the remark sounded fatuous.

Fortunately no one was paying much attention. Hazel and Betty were looking accusingly at their father, who finding himself again under attack, said severely, "Sneezing's very good for you, clears your head—and pepper. . . . Most people don't use pepper half enough."

Mrs. Morley laughed and Marcus told them that *his* father took pepper on strawberries. For a little they discussed pepper and its uses. The atmosphere became quite friendly again and presently Hazel asked, "If we're not going out, what *are* we going to do? We can't just spend the rest of the morning flattening our noses against the window-pane."

"Let's go out to the loft and roll each other in the hay," Betty suggested immediately. "There's a loft full of hay above the stables in the farmyard. Bob and I were up there yesterday evening. There are holes in the floor above the mangers for putting the hay through. We pushed down a whole lot. They got extra rations."

"Don't be silly," Hazel hissed in a low voice.

Betty looked aggrieved. "You didn't seem to think it silly that year at Portballintrae when it was so wet. You remember, with Frank Davidson and the McMasters."

Hazel apparently did remember, but her expression indicated that she was no longer interested in such childish frolics. Everyone indeed smiled at poor Betty in a very grown-up way so that she realized that she had said something foolish. Marcus joined in this smile, looking quite as superior as Hazel, though to tell the truth he had hoped for a fleeting moment that Betty's suggestion would be taken.

"Why not get in Joanna and Bob," Mrs. Morley said, "and play some game in the dining-room."

"I'll get them," Betty volunteered immediately.

"Could *I* not go?" Marcus offered, but Betty was already half out of the room.

"Let her go," Mrs. Morley said.

"She and Bob are very pally," Hazel added. "They're both going to be farmers when they grow up—so they say. Last year it was round-the-world fliers, but they've gone all bucolic. Bob's Joanna's younger brother."

Ten minutes later the hall door burst open and Betty stuck her head into the sitting room. "Come on you two, we're going to play racing patience."

"Who says racing patience?" Hazel demanded immediately.

"We've voted for it," Betty retorted.

"You couldn't vote without us."

"Yes we could. We all voted for racing patience: so it doesn't matter what you say, racing patience it is."

"I'm glad it's not rummy anyhow," Hazel pronounced, as they crossed the hall. "I hate it—the way everyone always tries to play to different rules."

"I don't like rummy either," Marcus agreed, "but I'm afraid I've forgotten racing patience."

"'Demon' you know," Hazel explained, "but Mummy doesn't like calling it that. That's why we always say 'racing patience.'"

They played one round slowly to show Marcus what to do and then the game began in earnest. Each player had a battered pack of cards. "Are we all ready?" Joanna asked.

Everyone was ready.

"Better let him start," Betty said. She hadn't quite decided what she ought to call Marcus.

"We'll have to take it in turn," Bobby insisted.

Marcus thought they all looked very desperate. He began to feel a little desperate himself. "Shall I say it?" he enquired, after an anxious pause, in which he found everyone staring at him.

"Yes, go on," Hazel urged, "and remember, put out your cards as fast as you possibly can."

"Go!" Marcus said. "Of course I *have* played before, you know," but these words were drowned by a frenzied thump, thump, thump, as the others put out their cards.

Marcus began to count out his own, "One, two, three, four, five, six, seven: one, two, three, four, five, six: one, two, three, four, five."

Goodness Betty had all hers out, and so had Bobby—and Hazel. Only Joanna lagged a little. "One, two, three, four: one, two, three." Joanna had started to build. "One, two: one." And now for his bank; thirteen in the bank, that was it. Hands were shooting backwards and forwards across the table. Betty was building on his cards, and Hazel, and Bobby. Was that allowed? He felt almost inclined to protest.

"Out!" shouted Betty.

The flurry ceased.

"I'd three kings in my bank," Bobby grumbled, "—and at the very top. Did you ever see such rotten luck?"

"I'm five," Hazel announced.

"And I'm eight," Joanna sighed.

Bobby had four cards left in his bank, while Marcus had the whole thirteen. He felt slightly ashamed of himself.

"It takes practice," the others reassured him comfortingly. "You'll improve after a hand or two."

It was true. The next time he got two cards out, and the time after three: but he never succeeded in getting his score below nine, while even the lethargic Joanna twice got as low as four. Obviously he would be the first to reach a hundred.

They played on. Presently Marcus dropped out and then Joanna. Marcus was glad to be out. He didn't really enjoy playing, but he liked watching Hazel. *She* was doing better now. Her score was forty, with Betty at thirty-nine and Bobby at forty-four.

It was quite clear they wouldn't have time to finish, and when Bobby had reached fifty-seven a maid came in to lay the table for lunch.

Marcus got up to go, but as he was taking his coat from the stand in the hall Mrs. Morley came out of the room opposite. She whispered something to Hazel and went upstairs. "Mother wants you to stay to lunch," Hazel told him.

After a slight hesitation Marcus refused. He explained that he was expected at The Garrison—he never called it home—and that he had no way of letting them know.

"I wish you *would* stay," Hazel urged. "Could you not send a message; or go up and tell them, and come back?"

"I'm afraid not. They'll have it made, you see, and they mightn't be pleased." He had a feeling that Mr. and Mrs. Morley didn't really want him, even if Hazel did—and he wasn't quite sure of that.

She didn't press him further and he put on his coat. At the door he paused. "You'll come this evening, won't you?" he asked. "I could call for you at half-past seven."

"Thank you very much. All the same I've got a crow to pluck with you, or a bone to pick." She smiled as she spoke; yet he could see that she was a little displeased with him.

"Oh! What have *I* done?" Marcus enquired. He made an effort to sound innocent though he had a good idea what she meant.

"Don't you go arranging what I'm to do and not to do, with Father and Mother when I'm not there. I've forgiven you this time, but I won't forgive you again."

"But there was a reason," Marcus protested. "Give me a chance to explain."

"You don't need to explain. I told you I'd forgiven you—and anyhow I know your reason. I was supposed to have a cold or something."

"It wasn't that at all," Marcus said triumphantly. "It was something quite different—something secret."

"What?"

"I'll maybe tell you this evening."

"I won't come this evening unless you tell me now."

Marcus hesitated. He had thought he was being rather cunning in providing a bait for her curiosity, so that she would look forward to meeting him in the evening and hearing what he had to say. It hadn't occurred to him that she would act so unfairly.

"I can't tell you now," he was beginning, when the dining-room door opened and Betty appeared in the hall.

"Oh, hullo!" she exclaimed. "I thought you'd gone. Sorry."

Hazel looked annoyed. "All right then," she told him. "Keep it till this evening, but it had better be a jolly good explanation."

Marcus went away rather doubtfully. The rain had eased off to a thick, Donegal drizzle. The sea was very smooth, and the harbour and village had a clean, washed look. He was inclined to be happy. As he thought over the morning he felt that he had enjoyed himself a great deal. He recalled the expressions he had seen on Hazel's face—the look of concentration as she dealt out her cards, the little flush of triumph as she called, "I'm out!" No wonder he had played badly. It had been impossible not to watch her—and she had smiled when he was going. She wasn't seriously annoyed with him.

He called for her again at half-past seven. The rain had stopped completely and for the last two hours the sun had been drying up the wet country-side, raising steamy clouds of haze from the puddly road, and the soaking hedges and fields.

Hazel had evidently been looking out for him and came down the short cement path to meet him as he reached the gate. "Quite wrong of course," she announced. "You should have been kept waiting for a little, making polite conversation with Papa and

Mamma. But Pop's gone fishing and Mamma's watching him—
and Betty's down at the harbour with Bobby. So really I've been
awaiting your arrival with impatience. I wish I'd asked you to
come sooner, but of course I didn't know we were going to have
such a lovely evening."

"I wish you had," Marcus replied fervently.

"Oh well—here we are."

Marcus hoped she would enquire why he had wanted to take
her over The Garrison in the evening instead of the morning, but
she seemed to have forgotten all about his promised explanation.
Instead she talked about her father. . . . "I do hope he catches something tonight. He *should*—with any luck. The fishing's been rotten
all summer—it's been so dry: but they should be rising tonight."

She sounded very gay and carefree, and her light-heartedness
infected Marcus. They made silly jokes and laughed a good deal.
The people they passed gave them friendly glances, so that Marcus felt that the whole world was sharing their happiness. "All the
world loves a lover," he remembered, and it pleased him to think
that perhaps, seen together like this, they looked like lovers.

All the same he did wish she would demand again the explanation he had withheld from her in the morning. He wondered if she
was teasing him by pretending to have forgotten about it—or had
she really forgotten?

At last he brought up the subject himself. "Do you not want to
know?" he said.

"Know what?"

"Know why I wanted you to come this evening instead of in the
morning."

"Oh yes. Why?"

Now he knew she was teasing him, but he went on stolidly
like a child eating up its porridge. "It was what you said yesterday
about 'Roaming in the gloaming. . . .'"

"'By the bonny banks of Clyde,'" Hazel sang.

But Marcus was determined not to be put off. "You said people
held hands when they were 'roaming in the gloaming.'"

"Yes, but I wasn't intending to do any 'roaming in the gloaming'—and I *don't* intend to. You're going to show me over The Garrison, and then I'm going home."

"I'll see you home, but—"

"That's very nice of you. As a matter of fact I rather expected you would, but that doesn't imply any roaming. It'll be 'Home James and don't spare the horses.'"

For a moment Marcus was half inclined to be huffy, but he suddenly saw that that would be silly. Why spoil the happiness he had, because he wanted just a little more happiness? He would abandon himself to the pleasure of the moment. And then he wondered if there was any pleasure in the moment, in being with Hazel like this. He loved her. He knew that as an absolute certainty—and each time he saw her it seemed to him that he loved her more. Yet tonight he would only be with her for an hour or two, and this was the most he could ever hope for, this was the culmination of his love. He looked at her, so blithe and carefree; if he had touched her heart it was only with the lightest of fingers. Of course he should be glad of that. If he could not marry her, it was better that she should not be in love with him. All the same he wished that she had been, partly for the sake of his pride, partly because it might have made her more willing to kiss him, partly that he might have had the luxury of feeling that they were miserable together. Perhaps secretly she did love him; perhaps really she too was feeling miserably that time was flying away from them.

"Are you happy?" he said abruptly.

Hazel received the question with suspicion. It was quite clear that she didn't like it. "Yes, thanks, quite happy," she answered coldly.

Marcus felt he ought to explain. "I mean I like being with you, and if only I thought we could go on seeing each other every day and being . . . being . . . being friends, I *would* be happy. You know I like being with you more than anything, but each time it's one time nearer the last, and they're each so short, and there can't be very many."

"Maybe I'll be back next year. Maybe I'll see you when you go home on holiday."

"Maybe you will," he responded heavily.

"I like being with you too, you know—I told you that. If only you'd do what I say and go back home we could see quite a lot of each other. Let him get another secretary."

"You don't know what you're asking," he told her glumly.

"I'm not asking," she retorted. "I'm only making a suggestion for your own good."

"I know you're not asking," he agreed hastily. "I didn't mean that. I know it doesn't matter to you what I do. I wish it did," he added in a lower voice.

"You know quite well it does," she said. "If it didn't I wouldn't be saying all this—and I wouldn't be here with you now. Just look at it from my point of view for a change. Here you are practically telling me that you're miserable, but that you're determined to go on being miserable, to do absolutely nothing about it. If we can't see more of each other, whose fault is it? I've told you I like you, and I don't think I've ever said that to anyone else. I don't mean that I don't like anyone else—that would be stupid. I like lots of people, but I'd like you a lot more if you were more cheerful. I think you're nice, but sometimes you'd almost think you were hypnotised or something—as if you'd no will of your own, just Mr. Burnaby's will. It's you that are making everything temporary. Well it should be a very nice temporary. It's lovely here: we get on very well together, so long as you stay sensible. Let's enjoy it. Give me a start and I'll race you to the house. Count seven and then run."

She began to run herself as she spoke and Marcus after a moment of indecision began to count as she had told him. As he saw the distance between them increasing he counted more quickly and then went after her.

Going about with Mr. Burnaby he had almost forgotten how to run. It took him a moment or two to get up speed, but soon he began to overtake her.

He came abreast of her on the sweep of drive in front of the house. He touched her shoulder with his hand as he passed, and getting to the door before her, put himself in front of her, barring the way. She hurtled into him and for an instant he held her. Her face was flushed: her eyes were sparkling: her hair was slightly dishevelled. She had succeeded in taking him out of his gloom. As they entered the house the knowledge that for the moment he was gay and happy flitted through his mind. He brushed it away from his consciousness: he knew that to go on being happy he must not consider his happiness too closely.

He had told Mrs. Mullan that Hazel was coming, and rather
to his surprise the news had pleased her. "It's about time you had
a bit of company," she declared, and she had wanted Marcus to
ask the whole Morley family to dinner. Marcus, however, had
had scruples about this—and besides, it was only Hazel that he
wanted.

Mrs. Mullan was now waiting for them in the hall and at the
sight of Hazel her good-humoured face became covered with
smiles. "Ach sure I know all about ye," she exclaimed as Marcus
introduced her. "Isn't Mrs. Taggart a friend of me own, and many's
the time I've heard her talkin' of the whole lot of you. It's a pity
your brother's not down this year he'd make a good companion
for Mr. Brownlow. Your father's a fine man by all accounts. Is he
gettin' much fishin' the year?"

"He's out fishing now," Hazel told her.

They stood talking for ten minutes or so. Then Mrs. Mullan
withdrew to the kitchen. "Ye'll have a cup of tea before you go,"
she insisted, "an' then you'll see me two daughters. Teresa—that's
me second youngest—has a notion of goin' to Belfast, an' she'll
want you to tell her about it."

When she had gone Marcus led the way to the library. He was a
little nervous and he felt that if possible he would rather not take
Hazel to the tower. And at first it looked as if she were going to
spend the whole evening in the library. She liked the room and
spent some time admiring it, and kneeling on the window seat
looking out at the view. Then she began to go round the shelves,
taking down a book here and there. They came to the section on
psychology and she noticed, on a top shelf, the works of Freud.
"Oh!" she exclaimed. "Those are books I want to read some day.
I've read *Totem and Taboo* and *The Psychopathology of Everyday Life*.
I've got them in Pelicans."

"Those are in German," Marcus said. "Can you read German?"

"A bit," she answered. "I took it in Senior, not that that means
much."

To Marcus who was bad in languages and bad at exams it
seemed to mean a good deal. The books were out of her reach
and he asked her which she would like him to get down.

"I want to look at them all," she said. So Marcus brought her a small step-ladder and mounting to the top she sat down and pulled out *Die Traumdeutung*.

For a little Marcus stood below watching her. Her untidy hair had fallen over her forehead, and he thought she might have been sitting for a picture of feminine concentration. But she wasn't posing: she had become completely engrossed in the effort of understanding the German.

"Is there a dictionary?" she enquired absently, and Marcus went to fetch one.

"I hope you don't mind," she said as he handed it to her. He assured her he didn't, and it was true. He felt he was seeing a new side of her. He was impressed with her studiousness, and he liked being impressed.

Gradually his eyes drifted away from her face and he found himself, as so often in their short acquaintance, admiring the shape of her legs. Suddenly he realized that the direction of his gaze was tending to become indiscreet. He looked away hastily, with a guilty burning in his cheeks. There was another ladder at the opposite side of the room. He brought it across, and climbing to the top, sat down beside Hazel. She handed him the dictionary.

When Mrs. Mullan came in with tea she burst out laughing. "Well, I declare! Is it birds ye think you are?"

They explained what they were doing. Hazel had been translating out loud. Marcus had been looking up the difficult words.

They had tea sitting side by side on the window-seat with the tea-things on a large oval table, which Mrs. Mullan had pushed over from the middle of the room.

They were very polite in a self-conscious, amused sort of way. Mrs. Mullan had provided fresh pancakes, hot soda buns, and an iced madeira cake. They pressed each other to have more tea, another bun, a little more sugar.

"Goodness!" Hazel said at last. "I *can't* eat any more. I don't usually have such a feed at this time of night. I must say you do yourselves proud."

"It's only because you're here," Marcus explained. "I usually have just a glass of milk and a biscuit at bed-time. Mr. Burnaby sometimes has tea, and sometimes a glass of whiskey; but if it's tea he gets it himself. Mrs. Mullan usually goes straight after dinner."

"You mean she's stayed because of me?"

"I suppose so. I didn't ask her to, and I didn't know she was go-ing to. I think she feels it would be letting the house down if you weren't offered something to eat."

"It's very nice of her anyhow," Hazel said. "I think we'd better go down and see the daughters and I'll give my advice about the allurements and pitfalls of life in Belfast. I feel rather like an official of *The Girl's Friendly Society*."

In the kitchen they were met by three smiling faces. There was no doubt that the Mullan family approved of Hazel. They too had been having tea, and it was quite clear that they had not found it any hardship to stay late. Mrs. Mullan explained Teresa's require-ments. "She'd like to go as a house-parlourmaid. She'd do as a gen-eral of course, for she can cook as well as I can, but I tell her there's no use her killin' herself. Maybe ye'd know of some good place at the Malone end or the Knock—though they say the Malone Road's the best."

"I'll ask Mother," Hazel said. "She might know of somewhere—but won't Mr. Burnaby mind?"

"Not a bit of him," Mrs. Mullan assured them. "Sure it used to be Maggie till she married Willie Trew, and I've Susan comin' on. The Master'll hardly know a bit of difference. Doesn't he call Te-resa Maggie half times as it is?"

So Mrs. Mullan's address was written down on a piece of paper and given to Hazel to keep, and they all said "Good night."

Hazel and Marcus went out, and along the passage to the hall. Marcus felt slightly relieved. He knew that Mrs. Mullan would say nothing of Hazel's visit to Mr. Burnaby. There had been some-thing in her manner that told him as much: it was to be an un-mentioned secret between them. He led the way across the hall towards the porch. He was looking forward to seeing Hazel home. Already he could feel the influence of the warm summer evening, and anticipate an atmosphere of romance in their walk back along the shore, with the sound of the waves coming up to them softly through the dusk.

He had his hand on the door into the porch when Hazel en-quired, "What about the tower? I haven't seen the tower yet."

Marcus's spirits fell. "Oh there's nothing to see," he responded, "just a few bleak rooms and a lot of winding stairs."

"It's that that makes it exciting," Hazel said. "Don't you think there's something rather thrilling about winding stairs—they're stone stairs too, aren't they?"

"Yes, they're stone stairs," Marcus agreed in a flat voice, "but there's nothing interesting."

"I just want a peep," Hazel begged, "just the littlest peep."

They went up the steps to the tower. Marcus held aside the heavy curtain and they passed through the archway and began to climb the winding stairway. "It's very quiet," Hazel said, "very quiet and dark."

Marcus didn't answer. The emptiness was oppressive. He was thinking of the first time he had climbed these stairs. It had been a summer night rather like this. It had been later of course, but tonight it was getting dark early. The state of the light was nearly the same.

"I know the windows are small," Hazel remarked, "but if they were washed and the cobwebs cleared away it would brighten the place up no end. It's not much of a recommendation for Teresa."

"It's not her fault," Marcus said.

"I don't care which of them's responsible; what I mean is it's not much of an advertisement for the family—I'm afraid I'm being rather rude."

"It's not any of their faults. It's Mr. Burnaby. He likes spiders. He won't let Mrs. Mullan dust away their webs. She cleans them away if she thinks he hasn't noticed them, but there's an awful row if he finds out. It's hard luck on the spiders if their webs get bust up," he added. "They put so much work into them."

"And it's hard on the flies if they get caught," Hazel responded. "I must say you've some extraordinary ideas, the two of you."

"Mr. Burnaby doesn't like flies: he hates them. I think that's partly why he's so friendly to the spiders."

They reached the first landing and Marcus showed her his own room and the bathroom. "And what's that?" she asked, pointing to the door of the W.C. He told her and began to lead the way downstairs again.

But Hazel had crossed to the far side of the landing and was staring at the foot of the next flight of stairs. "What's up here?" she demanded. "I want to go to the top."

"There's nothing interesting," Marcus told her, "—just Mr. Burnaby's bedroom and the study—the room where we work."

"But that's what I want to see most of all," she declared. "I want to see the room where you work."

"Oh all right," Marcus agreed reluctantly, and slowly re-crossed the landing.

"I know of course, I'm being very inquisitive," Hazel said, "and if I was nice and polite I'd take the hint, but I'm not. I'm just plain curious. All the same I think you're being very queer. You'd think there was some sort of dreadful bluebeard secret. If you want to stop me the only way is to refuse point-blank to show me any more. I won't ask to see Mr. Burnaby's bedroom, but surely you can show me the room where you work?"

Marcus said nothing, and they climbed the stairs to the top in silence. "This is the study," Marcus announced and opened the door.

Mr. Burnaby was sitting in his usual chair. He looked up when they entered and for a moment the customary, benevolent expression remained on his face. Then it altered. It was replaced by a look of the most terrible anger. His eyes grew dark, and cold, and furious. He gazed at them with the utmost hatred.

"It's a nice big room," Hazel was remarking casually, "but it's very bare. I think if I had it I'd put some sort of cream wash on the walls, something to make it warmer looking. Of course . . . Why, Marcus . . . ?"

Marcus stared at Mr. Burnaby. He couldn't speak or move. His mouth dropped slowly open. "Oh, oh," he muttered. "Oh, oh, I didn't, I didn't know. . . ."

Mr. Burnaby didn't speak. He continued to stare and his face was like the day of judgment. Vaguely and from very far away sounded Hazel's voice, urgent and perplexed, "Marcus! Marcus! What's happened? What's the matter?"

Suddenly Mr. Burnaby was no longer there. Marcus began to hear Hazel's voice. It was as if he were coming to, after having been stunned by a heavy blow. He was shaking all through. He caught her hand and held it tightly. "Come away quickly," he muttered huskily. "Come away."

She was completely puzzled, and only a little frightened. "But what's wrong?" she repeated. She spoke lightly, ready if he chose to turn the incident into a joke. But she didn't snatch her hand from him, and in his grasp there was no emotion but fear. He let go suddenly and pushed her from the room. "Come on," he ordered harshly. "We'll go outside." They hurried down the stairs again slipping and stumbling, but once they were through the front door he could go no further. He sank down on the steps and crouched there, while Hazel gazed at him in bewilderment. He was sick and panting: there was an icy sweat on his forehead and round his eyes.

"But what *is* the matter?" Hazel demanded again and again.

At last he managed to answer. "*He* was there. He was sitting in the chair looking at us."

"You mean he's come back?"

"No. He's gone away now. He went away while we were there."

"But if he was there I'd have seen."

"No, no: you couldn't have seen him: nobody could have seen him but me."

He realized after a time that she thought he was talking nonsense, that she thought he was demented. "But Marcus, he wasn't there," she kept repeating. "You only think you saw him."

He got up and made some attempt to appear more normal. "I'm afraid this is a funny way to see you home," he said apologetically.

"Oh it doesn't matter about seeing me home," she responded impatiently. "It's *you* that's the problem."

"Oh I'm all right," he assured her. "It's just I got rather a shock, and I'm afraid I didn't put up much of a show, but it's not what you think. I'm not suffering from hallucinations or anything. I mean I understand perfectly well what happened. It . . . it's something to do with our work—the work we're doing."

He began to walk down the drive and Hazel walked beside him. He knew he was no longer capable of taking her home by the path along the shore: it was too rough and uneven. They would have to go by the road and that would be difficult enough. He felt desperately in need of something to hold on to. Suddenly he found that he had it. Hazel had given him her hand. He grasped it thankfully as if it had been a rail or a banister. He remembered with a faint and distant amusement that this was what he had wanted to do so much—but this was not what he had imagined. He was like a convalescent being helped on his first, brief walk, by the cool hand of a nurse.

After they had walked in silence for some two or three hundred yards Hazel spoke. "Marcus, you mustn't go back to that house."

"But I've nowhere else to go," he pointed out, admitting, tacitly at least, that for the moment he dreaded the idea of returning.

"Yes, you have," she told him. "You can come to us for tonight. There's a spare room at Mrs. Taggart's—the house where we're staying, you know. It was being kept for John, my brother. He was to come down at week-ends; only he couldn't get away." She was explaining everything, as if to some extent he had lost his memory. "I'll tell Mother that you're not well, and that there's no one at The Garrison to look after you. You could go home in the morning. Daddy would drive you over to Portmallagh in the car. You could catch a train there."

The offer was very attractive. Marcus considered it in silence for so long that Hazel began to wonder if he had heard her. "It would be no good," he answered at last. "It would be worse in the end. I couldn't give up."

"But you must give up," she insisted, "give up Mr. Burnaby, I mean. This just proves everything I've been saying. It's bad for you: he's bad for you. Whatever this work is you're doing, it's bad for you. It's making you queer and mad. You're seeing things that aren't there."

"But he was there," Marcus expostulated sadly. "I saw him just as clearly as I see you, more clearly"—for they had come to a place where the road was overhung by trees and it was nearly dark. "Besides it was quite possible. There was nothing strange about it—if you only understood. At least if it was strange it was something I understand. It's all happened before."

She might have complained that he had given her no chance to understand, but she didn't, not so much from kindness perhaps, as because she didn't really believe he was talking rationally. Instead she went on quietly: "You wouldn't need to go back—ever. You could go to Queen's. I could help you, you know—at least I think I could—with your prelims. and that sort of thing."

It was the plan Marcus himself had thought of, when they were on Slieve Pennion. He tried to consider it clearly, but his brain was too confused to grapple with the problem. If only he could do as Hazel suggested, without ever having to think of Mr. Burnaby again, but if he accepted her offer he knew that he would have no peace. He would be haunted by Mr. Burnaby either as a product of his own conscience, or more positively because Mr. Burnaby would not let him go without a struggle.

"I can't," he repeated dully.

"You *could* perfectly well," she retorted firmly, but not altogether unkindly. "It's just a matter of will-power. Do it, and you *can* do it. The trouble is you've let Mr. Burnaby get control of your will. It's not your own will keeping you back; it's his."

He wasn't sure if this were true or not and he did not contest it. "I just can't," he said.

"At any rate there's no reason why you shouldn't stay with us tonight."

"No, I'll have to go back; and besides," he added feebly, "my pyjamas are there, all my things, my pyjamas and shaving things; all my things are there."

"That's just nonsense." They had been talking very slowly, with long pauses. Now they had reached the beginning of the village and Marcus was walking quite steadily. Outwardly he was completely normal. Hazel withdrew her hand, but when he reached for it she let him take it again.

"Please," he said. "I won't, I won't do anything you wouldn't like."

They passed through the village like this, walking ever so slowly without speaking. There was no one about, but when they came near Mrs. Taggart's they saw Mr. and Mrs. Morley approaching from the opposite direction. Mr. Morley was carrying his rod and Mrs. Morley had a string bag or perhaps a landing net, through the meshes of which could be seen the scaly glint of fish.

"I see your father's had some luck at last," Marcus observed. "He should be pleased."

"Yes, he'll be pleased," she answered.

"I think I'll say good night now," Marcus said. "I'll have to go back."

"But Marcus, won't you even let Daddy run you back in the car? He won't mind a bit."

"No, I'll be all right—thank you very much all the same."

They stopped and he let go her right hand from the grasp of his left hand. Then he took it again with his own right hand. She realized that he was shaking hands. "Goodnight," he said, "and I hope you enjoy the rest of your holiday."

"But, but . . ." she stammered in bewilderment.

"He'll be back, you know," he told her, "not tomorrow I suppose; he wouldn't have time."

"You mean. . . ."

"I mean Mr. Burnaby'll come home at once"—he half laughed—"in the ordinary way, so that anyone will be able to see him." He had difficulty in controlling his voice. He knew it sounded slightly hysterical. "The day after tomorrow, that's when he'll arrive."

"And tomorrow. . . ."

"Tomorrow won't be worth anything. Tomorrow. . . . Goodnight." He gave her hand a shake. "And, and I hope you'll enjoy the rest of your holiday."

"Goodnight." The word came out in a whisper, so that he was only just able to hear it.

He wavered. "And, and Hazel, thank you very much. . . ."

"Goodnight," she repeated. She spoke with determination, but her voice sounded choked. "You'd better go away. The others are coming."

He turned and left her. He didn't look round, but he knew she didn't move till her parents joined her.

Marcus did not return through the village. He took the back road past the chapel. He wanted to avoid meeting anyone who might speak to him. He had deliberately broken his friendship with Hazel but he hoped that it wasn't broken permanently, that somehow, sometime, circumstances would bring them together again. He wasn't quite sure of his own motives. He would have liked to think that he had sacrificed his own happiness for a great cause, Hazel's friendship for the sake of his work. But he didn't know that that was true. It had been an influence no doubt, but there had been other influences—fear of Mr. Burnaby, fear that if he were to accept Hazel's plan he would suffer from a perpetual guilty conscience. For a time he tried to work it out, to attribute his behaviour to one cause or the other. If he had acted through cowardice ought he not to go back on his decision? Tomorrow it would not be too late to do what she had suggested. He could still go into Portmallagh and take the first train home to Belfast. Surely if he did she would forgive him. He had hurt her tonight—tonight when she had been so kind and nice to him. . . . It was hateful to have hurt her, when he loved her so much. He hated Mr. Burnaby. Mr. Burnaby had taken advantage of his youth and inexperience, had forced him into a position which was going to make his whole life a misery. All the same, he reflected, finding an unexpected grain of comfort, she must care for him more than she had admitted; otherwise she wouldn't have been so upset.

He came to the gate in the demesne wall and stopped. He was afraid to go in. He saw the wall as a boundary between two worlds. Outside he might not be safe from Mr. Burnaby, but at least he was free: he could meet him on more or less equal terms. Outside, if he were to explain his case, public opinion would be on *his* side, on Hazel's side. Inside it was different: inside there was only one set of values—Mr. Burnaby's. The very innocence of the dilapidated, wide-open gate was a deception. Once he went in he would be caught, sucked on towards the terrible, dark house. The gate was a sort of valve. He went in, feeling like a solitary Roman adventuring into the country beyond Hadrian's Wall. But he had none of the elation of the adventurer—only the apprehension of the bewitched child in a fairy tale, wandering alone in the land of the enchanter.

As he went up the drive the rabbits made way for him, as they always did, leaving him in a little moving island of loneliness, resuming their quiet, alert nibbling of the grass when he had passed.

He reached the house, and sitting down on the steps before the door, put his head between his hands. He remained like this, hardly thinking. He was conscious of being very tired and very lonely. He remembered his bed at home, safe in the peaceful, sleeping, suburban house. At last he realized that he was stiff and cold. He got up, and walking out a little way onto the grass turned round and looked at The Garrison. In the semi-darkness it was a vague, greyish white. The windows had a blank, empty expression.

He gathered together what little courage was left to him, and returning, pushed open the door as gently as he could. He hated the creaks and squeezed in by the smallest possible aperture. He did not close the door behind him. In the hall he paused to listen. There wasn't a sound anywhere. It was as if the whole building were tense, ready to pounce. Surely such a silence was unnatural: surely, however still a house might be there were usually rustlings, faint, distant, unexplained footfalls, mysterious thumps? Yet any such noise would have thrown him almost into hysterics.

On no account would he venture into the tower. It was the centre of all, whatever it was, that he dreaded, the special place where Mr. Burnaby's power was greatest. He tiptoed up the stairs and along the passage to the library. Mrs. Mullan had left a lamp on the table. He lit it and opened the window. It was not far to the ground. If necessary he could leap through the window and so escape at any rate from the house. He sat down on a corner of the window-seat. Before morning he dozed a little from time to time.

CHAPTER XXVIII

AT seven o'clock Marcus stood up and stretched himself. He was no longer on the verge of panic. Weariness had relaxed the tension of his nerves. He felt dirty and sticky, and he would have liked a bath: but he hadn't the courage to go and take one. He was still afraid to go into the tower, and he was even more afraid of getting into a bath where he would be trapped and naked should Mr. Burnaby appear to him again. He wanted to be able to run away, though there was no refuge he could run to.

He knew, however, that once the Mullan family were in the house he would be less fearful. There was something calming and reassuring about Mrs. Mullan. He felt that when she was present the phantom Mr. Burnaby was not likely to appear. He was dreading the return of the physical Mr. Burnaby, but of the other Mr. Burnaby—the disembodied spirit, the living ghost—he was now blindly terrified. So he went to a window in the passage above the kitchen where he could look out along the back drive and watch for the arrival of the Mullans.

At a quarter to eight he saw them in the distance—Mrs. Mullan in the centre, with Teresa on one side and Kate on the other. He drew back a little, for he did not want them to catch sight of him. He waited till they had almost reached the house and went quickly, almost stealthily, to his own room in the tower. He untidied his bed, rumpled the pillow, and threw back the bed-clothes. Next he went to the bathroom, and without undressing at all, washed his face and hands and shaved. He was careful not to make any noise. He couldn't rid himself of the notion that Mr. Burnaby was in the room above, listening; ready to appear at the slightest sound.

He still needed to go to the W.C.: but he was afraid of being caught in the closed room, with his trousers down—unable to run away, with Mr. Burnaby perhaps between him and the door. He decided to go outside. He met Kate in the hall. "Good morning, Mr. Brownlow," she greeted him. "You're early astir today."

"I didn't sleep too well," he responded. "I want to get a breath of air before breakfast."

"It's a grand morning for it," she told him. "It'd do you good just to see how well everything is after the rain."

It was true, but the damp freshness and the sunshine did not exhilarate Marcus. It was as if he saw it all through a glass, a picture into which he could not enter. He did what he had to do, and walked for a little beside the sea, stopping here and there on the edge of the rocks to gaze down into it. He couldn't regard it as impersonal, or as anything but a kind of God. If by plunging into it he could have become part of it, conscious as he felt it was conscious, he would have done so. Before he returned, he climbed down to a low, sea-weedy ledge, and crouching there filled his hands with water and splashed it over his face and hair.

Mrs. Mullan herself brought in his breakfast. He realized at once that she had done so out of curiosity. "I hear ye had a bad night," she remarked, as she put down a plate of porridge in front of him.

"I didn't sleep too well," Marcus answered shortly. "Must have been the heat or something."

Mrs. Mullan stepped back and regarded him shrewdly, but benevolently. "Ach ye're not too bad," she said reassuringly, "and maybe it wasn't the heat altogether, and maybe ye're not the only one didn't sleep."

"I'm sure I'm not," Marcus replied, refusing to acknowledge any deep meaning in the remark.

Mrs. Mullan withdrew. "Ah well," she concluded, "don't fret yourself. All's for the best in the end."

It was Teresa who brought in the tea and toast. She made no enquiries about his health, but she took a good look at him. It was clear that he was being discussed in the kitchen, that they were each having a peep in turn, and comparing notes. Marcus was slightly irritated, slightly amused. He thought he could imagine pretty well the nature of the conversation.

When he had finished he looked at his watch. It was just a quarter past nine. Well, he could still catch the morning train. It didn't leave Portmallagh till half-past ten. He could get O'Flynn to run him over in his Ford: he only charged ten shillings. There was plenty of time: in any case the afternoon train at half-past three would do just as well. All that was necessary was to make sure he was safely home before Mr. Burnaby arrived tomorrow morning. He had not the slightest doubt that Mr. Burnaby would return at once. If not already on his way, he would at least be preparing to start. In that case there was no danger now of another visitation like last night's. To project himself Mr. Burnaby would need absolute solitude—he had explained that often enough. For the time being therefore the whole place was safe. He could go to his own bedroom in the tower and sleep without the slightest fear of being disturbed. He would just have to tell Mrs. Mullan—and he did want to sleep.

All the same he still had a dread of the tower. He would rather sleep somewhere in the open air. Immediately he knew where he would go—to the hollow where he had been lying on the morning he first met Hazel. Perhaps she would come again and find him there. If she did he would treat it as an omen. He would take back what he had said last night. He would catch the afternoon train to Belfast, and know that somehow everything was going to work out right.

He got a waterproof to lie on, in case the ground should still be damp after yesterday's rain. He set out quite hopefully. It was a relief to have left to Fate the responsibility for his decision. He reached the hollow and found that after all it was quite dry. He lay down and closed his eyes. He would open them to see Hazel standing over him. At once a drowsy feeling of comfort, a satisfying consciousness of the sun, and of the warm air stole over him. In a few minutes he was asleep.

Even before he opened his eyes he knew that Hazel hadn't come. He was hot, and stiff, and uncomfortable. The arm on which he had been lying had gone to sleep. The sun had got too hot: it was the heat which had awakened him. He looked round, blinking at the too bright scene, the hard, glittering sea. It was all so unkind.

He looked at his watch—a quarter to one, nearly time for lunch. He walked back heavily towards the house. He hated the whole, bare countryside, the glaring whiteness of The Garrison itself.

Kate brought him a telegram and he read it—"Expect me about five-thirty Burnaby."

"Tell your mother, Mr. Burnaby'll be back for dinner," he said.

And after that there was nothing to do but wait. He realized horribly that now he couldn't go for the train. He had no longer any will of his own.

In the afternoon he mooned about, trailing from the library to the garden, and back to the library. He hadn't even the energy to bathe, though he knew it was the only thing which might restore his self-possession. His feet dragged wearily, but he couldn't stay in one place. He wondered what Hazel was doing. He felt sure that at least she was less miserable than himself.

Marcus was waiting on the door-step when a black car, which he had never seen before, drove up. Mr. Burnaby got out. No word of greeting passed between them. Mr. Burnaby paid the driver, and calling Mrs. Mullan, instructed her to prepare him a meal. Then he and Marcus went upstairs together to their workroom in the tower. Each sat down in his usual chair. During all this time Mr. Burnaby had never looked at Marcus. His face was as grim as a headland in a storm.

Marcus, in his hopelessness, had almost reached a state of detachment. Presently he found himself putting a question, which did not interest him particularly, but which, nevertheless, had puzzled him from time to time, since the arrival of the telegram. "How did you get here so soon?" he enquired.

"I engaged an aeroplane," Mr. Burnaby replied. "I came from Belfast in the taxi you saw. Black is crossing in the boat tonight with the car. He'll be here tomorrow."

"Oh," Marcus said. "I didn't expect you till tomorrow—not till I got your telegram."

"I thought I had better warn you," Mr. Burnaby replied drily. "Where is she now, if one might enquire?"

His tone was cold and deliberately provoking. Marcus pretended not to understand him. "Where's *who*?" he asked.

"Your girl."

Marcus flushed. "There's no need to speak of her that way," he retorted angrily.

"How would you like me to speak of her? You haven't told me her name. The young person you had here last night, should I say?—your lady friend?"

"I don't know what you should say—and I don't know where she is. She's with her people, I suppose."

"At any rate she's not on the premises. That's very considerate of you."

Marcus was silent. For another long period they sat quite still, without speaking. Mr. Burnaby's eyes remained fixed on the empty fireplace. From time to time Marcus glanced at him, but his glances were not returned. Mr. Burnaby looked old, in a way Marcus had never seen him look before. It was as if he were dead, someone who had been dead a long time, a malignant skeleton determined to revenge himself on the living. Marcus hated him, and at the same time knew that he was very unhappy. He had no wish to make him happy, no wish indeed except that Mr. Burnaby were really dead and gone, so dead as to leave not even a memory alive.

He hardened himself against any feeling of pity. He knew that he had a duty to Mr. Burnaby. He was prepared to carry out that duty. Wasn't it on that account that he had said goodbye as he did to Hazel last night, letting her know that it was a final goodbye, the end of their friendship? But he wasn't prepared to tell Mr. Burnaby about that. Mr. Burnaby would treat it as something trivial. He would scoff at it. He could think what he liked.

What *was* he thinking, Marcus wondered. There was no indication. Mr. Burnaby was unhappy and angry. Let him be unhappy. He would get his way in the end, but he might as well know, that in doing so, he was depriving Marcus of everything that was most pleasant in life. After all, Marcus thought, he had been got hold of in the first place by a sort of trap. He hadn't realized what he was in for; and Mr. Burnaby must have known that he didn't realize. It was all very well for Mr. Burnaby to give up the world. It wasn't as if Mr. Burnaby had been a boy fresh from school. He had had *his* youth. He had experienced life.

Time went on. It was very trying. Mr. Burnaby remained completely still. Perhaps he had died suddenly, Marcus thought, with a momentary flash of hope; but he hadn't. Marcus recalled bitterly how fond Mr. Burnaby was of speaking as if he had only a little longer to live. He would go on living for *years*.

At last there was a knock at the door. Marcus waited for Mr. Burnaby to answer, but he didn't. After a pause the knock came again. Marcus cleared his throat. "There's someone knocking," he said.

"Tell her to go away," Mr. Burnaby said, but when the knock came a third time he heard it, and shouted furiously, "Come in, can't you, and stop that noise."

Mrs. Mullan put her frightened face round the door. "It's only me, Sir. I'm sorry to disturb ye, but the dinner's ready this half hour. It'll be spoilt if I keep it back any longer."

"Haven't I often told you . . . ?" Mr. Burnaby began, but he broke off without finishing his sentence. "All right then. We'll be down directly."

At the beginning of dinner Marcus made one or two attempts at conversation. He didn't want the Mullan family to guess that Mr. Burnaby and he had quarrelled, but Mr. Burnaby's replies were so surly that he was forced to give up. Neither of them ate much, but Marcus soon began to realize, that whatever his own state of misery, Mr. Burnaby's was very much worse. His hands were trembling and whenever he took a drink of water the glass rattled against his teeth. Marcus began to feel nervous about him.

It was not until the coffee was on the table and Kate had finally withdrawn that he looked straight at Marcus for the first time. Suddenly he pushed back his chair. "Well," he said, "I must know what you intend to do. What are your plans?"

Marcus was taken by surprise. "Plans?" he repeated stupidly.

"Yes, *plans*. What do you intend to do? Surely that's simple enough. Can you not even understand words of one syllable?"

"I don't even know what plans you're talking about," Marcus returned. "I don't intend to do anything in particular."

"That's a lie," Mr. Burnaby said flatly. "You know perfectly well what I'm talking about."

"I know you're talking about. . . ." Marcus stopped. Somehow he didn't like to mention Hazel's name to Mr. Burnaby.

"Come on," Mr. Burnaby urged. "Is her name so wonderful that it can't even be spoken?" His manner had altered slightly as if he suddenly saw that the situation might not be so bad as he had imagined.

"She's called Hazel Morley," Marcus told him in a flat, carefully controlled voice.

Mr. Burnaby let the name, as it were, float in the atmosphere for a few moments, while he studied it. "Hardly out of the top drawer, I should imagine," he then commented.

Marcus flushed. "I don't know what drawer she's out of," he retorted angrily. "She's probably out of just as good a drawer as you or I, if it comes to that. You'd think you'd been brought up in a palace or something. You're a snob, that's what's wrong with you."

"It's not a question of where one has been brought up," Mr. Burnaby replied stiffly. "It's a matter of breeding. There's no snobbishness in it. There are such things as heredity and good breeding: there's no sense in shutting one's eyes to facts. My mother for instance would never have given one of her daughters such a name—very pretty no doubt, but. . . . " He shrugged his shoulders.

Marcus glowered. "What were your sisters called?" he enquired derisively, "—Emily, Jane, and Elizabeth. We'd a maid called Emily and another called Jane. Their mother must have come out of the same drawer as yours."

"There's no need to be offensive," Mr. Burnaby said. "That's a cheap remark: besides it has nothing to do with what we're talking about. I want to know your plans. I've a right to know them."

"I told you I hadn't any plans," Marcus answered wearily, "and it's true. I don't know what more you want."

"You must know what you intend to do."

"I don't intend to do anything."

"You mean you're not going to see her any more," Mr. Burnaby's voice became suddenly hopeful, almost congratulatory.

But Marcus, in spite of the nature of his parting with Hazel the night before, had no intention of committing himself to such an extent. He felt that all his troubles were the result of his having bound himself too much to Mr. Burnaby, and he was not going to give any promise that would constitute a fresh bond. "I hope I *will* see her again," he said fervently.

All the light died from Mr. Burnaby's face. It became as cold as ice. "You mean you're going to marry her?"

"I would like to marry her if I could."

"Oh you'll be able to all right," Mr. Burnaby said scornfully. "It's always happening. She may pretend to refuse the first time, but she'll take very good care. . . ."

"You don't know anything about her," Marcus broke in hotly.

"I know enough, and enough about you too, to know what'll happen. You haven't the least strength of will, and you're completely callous. My position doesn't enter your head at all, or if it does you push it aside, because it happens to stand in the way of your sexual desire. You needn't protest", he went on raising his voice to prevent Marcus speaking, "that this is something different, that it's a case of pure love. If you'd slept with her a few times and lived with her for a month you'd be sick to death of her, but then it would be too late. That's what marriage is for, to make it too late when a man comes to his senses. Of course I don't know how things are nowadays with contraception and that sort of thing. Perhaps you can get over it without getting married. . . ."

"Oh shut up," Marcus shouted. "You've a horrible, dirty mind."

Mr. Burnaby stood up. He stared at Marcus with hatred. "Go to her," he said. "I don't want to see you again. I wish I'd never had anything to do with you. You've spoilt the whole work of my life. I'm too old to train someone else—even if I could find the right person. There's no point in my going on. I can't get any further myself, and there's no one else. I'm going out. Leave me alone."

He went to the door, but Marcus remained standing where he was, not following him even with his eyes. The door opened and closed. Marcus was alone.

For a few moments he stood reflecting. Mr. Burnaby had been right to call him callous. He wasn't moved by Mr. Burnaby's distress. He was sorry for him, but he was more sorry for himself. He saw Mr. Burnaby's point of view, but he was determined not to accept it. He was the injured party, and he would maintain that opinion. Meantime he wondered if Mr. Burnaby intended to commit suicide. He had often discussed suicide with Marcus, and Marcus knew that the idea of it at any rate was attractive to him. He knew too, that once, when Mr. Burnaby was a boy, he had tried to poison himself with laudanum, but taking too much had been violently sick instead. If he committed suicide now Marcus would be free. He might be troubled afterwards by feelings of guilt and remorse, but he would probably be able to suppress such feelings.

Having reached the conclusion that he would like Mr. Burnaby to die, Marcus followed him out to make sure that he did not kill himself. He didn't know quite why he did this. He imagined that his behaviour was governed purely by convention. One tried to prevent people committing suicide; he was doing the correct thing.

CHAPTER XXIX

MARCUS overtook Mr. Burnaby on the back drive and fell in beside him. Mr. Burnaby did not look up. They walked slowly towards the gate, and passed through it onto the smooth, sandy road. It was a sultry evening.

A fisherman, wearing a blue jersey, heavy serge trousers and rubber boots was coming towards them. On his head was a worn, grey tweed cap. He had blue eyes and a red, weather-beaten face. He was old, and a little stooped. They both knew him well. He was one of their nearest neighbours, and besides his share in a fishing boat was the owner of a ten-acre farm. As they approached he took a short clay pipe from his mouth. "Nice evenin'," he said, with a friendly smile.

"Yes, isn't it," Marcus responded, but Mr. Burnaby neither looked up, nor spoke.

The fisherman gazed at them with a kind of innocent curiosity, and Marcus, who had an idea how shrewd such innocence could be, made an effort to distract his attention. "It's a great change from yesterday," he remarked.

"Aye," the fisherman agreed, "but the rain was needed. It did a power o' good. We could do with more yet."

They all went on; but when Marcus glanced round a little later he saw that the fisherman had stopped and was staring after them. "Another witness for the inquest," he reflected, and he decided afresh that there must be no inquest.

Presently Mr. Burnaby turned into a narrow cart-track. Marcus knew that it led to a small glen, and came out eventually at a cottage on the lower slopes of Slieve Pennion. They had been there once or twice before, gathering wild-flowers for a collection they had begun two summers before: recently this collection had been neglected. There were plenty of wild-flowers blooming now, Marcus noticed, on the banks at either side of the lane and among the low, wind-bent trees.

Suddenly Mr. Burnaby stepped from the track and Marcus made to follow him. For the first time since they had left the house Mr. Burnaby looked at Marcus. It was not a friendly look but as well as hostility, there was an expression of intolerable anguish in his deep, grey eyes. "Leave me alone, can't you," he ejaculated hoarsely. "I'm going to vomit."

Marcus stopped, and Mr. Burnaby disappeared behind a clump of bushes. Was he really being sick, Marcus wondered, or was this merely a ruse to get by himself? He watched the bushes anxiously, considering the possibility that Mr. Burnaby might at this very moment be killing himself. Yet he didn't think it very likely. So far as Marcus knew, Mr. Burnaby didn't possess either a pistol or a revolver, and it was not probable that he carried poison about with him. He had a penknife of course, but Marcus didn't believe that he had sufficient savage resolution to cut his own throat. All the same Marcus decided to go and see what was happening.

He took a step or two towards the bushes, but was brought up by the sound of Mr. Burnaby clearing his throat and spitting. Mr. Burnaby *had* been sick then: certainly he had looked sick enough, with his face a sort of pale khaki-green and his eyes rolling. Marcus didn't think that he himself could ever be quite so miserable as that.

Mr. Burnaby reappeared, wiping his lips with a coloured silk handkerchief. He seemed slightly better. Marcus felt curious. "*Were* you sick?" he asked. His voice sounded detached and rather brutal.

"No, not actually," Mr. Burnaby retorted angrily. "It passed off."

Marcus wondered if Mr. Burnaby were a little annoyed at this lack of sympathy on the part of his stomach. He was faintly amused, but he didn't smile. He was genuinely sorry for Mr. Burnaby. He was glad he hadn't been sick, because if he had it would have indicated an extra violence of emotion. Not that his emotion was not violent enough, but the failure to vomit in a way set a limit to it, left it perhaps still within the bounds of comprehension.

The walk continued. They went on up the mountain, avoiding the cottage and reaching eventually another track which brought them down again to the road they had left. Marcus was fearful that they might encounter Hazel, that she might have chosen this direction for a walk, either alone, or with Joanna, or with her family. But they met no one at all, and at last, when it was nearly dusk, came back to The Garrison.

Mr. Burnaby went straight through the hall and up the stairs in the tower. Marcus still followed him, on past his own room, right to the very top. On the landing, outside the study, Mr. Burnaby spoke again. "What's the use of going on like this?" he demanded. "I'm sick of you. You're contemptible. I never want to set eyes on you again."

"What do you want me to do then?" Marcus inquired.

Mr. Burnaby regarded him with deliberate loathing. "I don't care what you do—only go away, leave me. Is that not plain enough?"

"All right," Marcus said. "I *will* go away."

"You needn't pretend you care," Mr. Burnaby told him. "You don't care in the slightest. You're completely without feeling in the matter. You want *nothing* but to get your own way, and at the same time to justify yourself to your conscience—or whatever it is does you instead of a conscience. There's no sense in being a hypocrite about it. You can't have it both ways."

All this sounded so like the truth that Marcus found some difficulty in answering. Did he care? It was very hard to know what he felt. Though he pitied Mr. Burnaby, he pitied himself more. He felt that in not taking Mr. Burnaby at his word, in not leaving him, he was doing a great deal. He could do more of course. He could tell Mr. Burnaby that he was prepared to give up Hazel completely, that he was determined never to see her again. Then Mr. Burnaby would be pleased. He would treat the whole affair as a temporary weakness of the flesh. He would be glad that Marcus had come to his senses. He would be very kind about it, and assure Marcus that in a week or two he would have quite got over it all. But Marcus couldn't bear to allow him this smug triumph: he couldn't bear to let his love for Hazel be treated so cheaply—and more than anything he couldn't bear to leave himself without a faint flicker of hope that somewhere, somehow, he might meet Hazel. He had deliberately made such a reunion extremely unlikely. If Providence should bring them together again, he couldn't commit himself to act in the same way a second time. He had to have some hope, some comfort for his imagination. And nothing would have induced him to describe to Mr. Burnaby his parting from Hazel. He imagined the half-tolerant, ironical sympathy with which the description would be received—the superior air of contempt. No: that parting was something for himself alone, for himself and Hazel too perhaps, if she didn't prefer to forget it—a sad, secret memory.

Mr. Burnaby was standing in an attitude of impatience with his hand on the door-handle of his study. He wished to shut himself in there, to sit by himself, and brood. "Go away," he cried querulously. "Leave me. What's the good of hanging round like this? I've told you I don't want to see you again—and *you* don't want to see *me*. Is that not enough? Don't pester me. You're worthless."

"Yes, it is enough," Marcus said slowly, making up his mind at last. "I'll go tomorrow, first thing. I'll get the first train."

"You've got your own way: you ought to be happy," Mr. Burnaby sneered.

"Yes," Marcus agreed. "I ought to be happy." The last words were no more than a whisper: he added out loud, "I am sorry all the same. I'm sorry I've let you down. I'm sorry I've made you unhappy."

He turned, and as he descended the stairs, he heard Mr. Burnaby go into the study and close the door behind him. Well, he *was* happy. He could see a new life ahead of him, a new, bright world. He could forget Mr. Burnaby, or nearly forget him, push him into a dark part of his mind where he would only be troublesome occasionally. Of course he had not done nearly all that he might have done. A saint would have behaved differently: a saint would not have taken his own happiness into account. But he was not a saint, and he had stood a good deal from Mr. Burnaby. He knew he was forsaking a great work: but why should *he*, more than anyone else, give up all that was sweetest in life for the sake of a possible great good, something that might after all turn out to be nothing?

Now that he had reached a decision he felt quiet and relieved. It was as if he had volunteered for a rocket-trip to the moon and been told that after all he wouldn't be needed. Ordinary life was there for him again.

He washed and prepared for bed. He locked his door as usual. Strangely, since the return of the physical Mr. Burnaby, it was only of the physical Mr. Burnaby that he was afraid. He felt that there was a possibility that Mr. Burnaby might try to murder him in the night, but with the door locked he was safe from that.

He got into bed and blew out his candle. He was exhausted and fell asleep immediately.

He awoke in the morning with a delightful feeling of freshness and freedom. He remembered all that had happened and was glad that he was going away. He looked up at the window, and saw the bright, morning sky. He thought of meeting Hazel again. He would write to her when he got home and ask her to meet him as soon as she returned to Belfast.

He looked at his watch: it was almost a quarter to eight. It was unlikely that Mr. Burnaby would come down for breakfast. Marcus might never need to see him again. Mr. Burnaby, quite clearly, did not want to see him, and *he*, certainly, did not want to see

Mr. Burnaby. He was quite justified in slipping away quietly after breakfast—more, it was the best thing to do. He had better get up at once, and pack as much as possible before breakfast. He threw back the clothes and sprang out of bed, as if he were back at school and it was the last day of term.

Two envelopes were lying on the carpet half under the door. They must have been put there at some time during the night. Letters from Mr. Burnaby. Marcus looked at them with a feeling of apprehension. If there had only been one it might have meant that Mr. Burnaby had committed suicide; that would be bad enough, but two. . . . He must want to make it up. For a moment Marcus thought of moving one of the rugs up to the door and leaving the letters on the floor beneath it. Mr. Burnaby would find them after he had gone, and think that Marcus himself had never seen them.

They were both addressed simply 'Marcus', but across the top of one of them was written, 'Second letter. Read the other first.' The first said:

I am completely miserable. I can't go on without you. Forget what I said. Don't go away. We must carry on somehow. I can see your point of view more than you think. I am sorry I behaved as I did. Come and tell me that it is all right.

J.B.

Marcus opened the second note. Like the first it was written in pencil. He read:

Don't think I admit your behaviour is excusable in any way. You have treated me badly and shown that whatever respect I had for you was founded on an illusion. I don't forgive you. When I said I saw your point of view I didn't mean that I accepted it or regarded it as anything but base. Do as you like.

J.B.

Marcus read these letters coldly, and with a feeling of horror. He knew at once what he would have to do, and that all his hopes of freedom were shattered. There was no need now to pack. He saw too, that for the time being at any rate, he would have to treat

Mr. Burnaby almost as if he were sick mentally. He would be tied to him. His imprisonment would be just as rigorous as before, and partly because he saw it now so clearly *as* an imprisonment, infinitely more irksome. He felt inclined to get back into bed and pull the bedclothes over his head. But he didn't. After considering the bleak prospect for a minute or two he crossed the landing to the bathroom. He washed and dressed rather more carefully than usual; then he put on his outdoor shoes and went upstairs to see Mr. Burnaby.

Mr. Burnaby was sitting up in bed, very small and lean and haggard. He was unshaven and the bristles on his face were white. He was looking at the doorway when Marcus came in, but after a glance at Marcus's face, he turned his head away quickly and lay down in the bed. "What do *you* want?" he demanded roughly.

Marcus hardly knew how to reply. "I got your letters," he said at last.

"Did you read the second one?"

"Yes."

"I told you to do what you liked."

"Well, here I am."

There was a pause. "Don't tell me any more lies," Mr. Burnaby warned him. "If we're going to carry on you'd better try to tell the truth in future."

Marcus sighed. "Shall I bring up your breakfast?" he inquired.

"I don't want any breakfast. If you want your own, go and get it."

"It won't be ready yet," Marcus said. "I'll go down when it's time." He walked to the window and looked out at the clear, sunny morning. It was strange that with all this beauty around them they should both be unhappy. He wondered if Hazel was looking out dejectedly at the clear sky and bright, shining sea. He turned back towards the room and found that Mr. Burnaby, with the bedclothes half over his head, was watching him almost furtively. Mr. Burnaby, when he saw that he himself was being watched, averted his eyes. Marcus was embarrassed, but he realized that for the first time since they had known each other he was feeling superior to Mr. Burnaby.

This surprised him a little. It was not that he was sure that he was morally in the right. Very likely he was in the wrong: he couldn't tell any longer. But he hadn't lost his self-control. He was harder than Mr. Burnaby and at the moment less unhappy. As time went on he might be the more miserable of the two: but he would be miserable in secret. There was a part of him which, in spite of all Mr. Burnaby could do, he would keep to himself. Mr. Burnaby at the moment was abject and he was in Marcus's power. Marcus intended to make things as pleasant for him as he could, within certain limits. He knew what those limits were, and that he could make Mr. Burnaby recognise them. Now he wanted to get away from him: Mr. Burnaby was not pleasant company. Marcus felt that he had enough to do in bearing his own misery, without sharing Mr. Burnaby's more than was absolutely necessary. He had done sufficient in the meantime towards getting things started again.

"I think I'll go down and see how they're getting on," he said. Not more than five minutes had gone since he had announced that it was not worthwhile going down yet. It was obvious that he was just making an excuse to go away. Yet Mr. Burnaby did not protest. Marcus left him alone.

CHAPTER XXX

MR. Burnaby stayed in bed for a week. He was undoubtedly ill, though it would have been difficult to say precisely what was the matter with him. At times he had severe headaches, and when he got out of bed he had great difficulty in walking without support of some kind. This weakness annoyed him very much. He knew that he had suddenly fallen into old age, that he would never recover fully his former strength and energy. In the past he had thought a great deal about growing old, but he had never anticipated physical senility. He had imagined that he would grow old without discomfort, that death itself would be like the closing of a book.

He grumbled continually about the state in which he found himself. Sometimes this grumbling was good-humoured enough: he would make little jokes about his condition, and describe to

Marcus what *he* would be like as an old man. At other times he would be depressed and bitter.

Yet he was able to get a certain amount of pleasure out of his weakness. He was fond of making tours round his bedroom leaning heavily on Marcus's arm. He would stand for ten minutes at a time, clinging to Marcus and staring out of the window. Marcus would have preferred him to stay in bed. He had always felt a slight physical aversion to Mr. Burnaby. Since Mr. Burnaby's return this aversion had increased: he disliked having to touch him, or being touched by him. And he knew Mr. Burnaby enjoyed touching him. Once or twice, when Mr. Burnaby unexpectedly put his hand on Marcus's wrist or sleeve, Marcus started back involuntarily. Then there would be a row.

"Can I not even *touch* you?" Mr. Burnaby would demand.

"It's not that," Marcus would answer sheepishly. "It was just you took me by surprise."

They both lied on such occasions. Mr. Burnaby would deny that the touch had been intentional. Marcus would declare that he didn't mind being touched. In the end Mr. Burnaby always accepted Marcus's explanation. He couldn't bear to disbelieve it.

Marcus would have liked to call in a doctor, but Mr. Burnaby declared that if a doctor were brought he would refuse to allow him into the room. "I'm not ill *that* way," he insisted and Marcus gave in, largely because he didn't really expect that a doctor would be able to do a great deal of good.

Mr. Burnaby would not even allow Mrs. Mullan, or Kate, or Teresa to come to his room. So Marcus was kept busy carrying trays up and down the stairs, making Mr. Burnaby's bed, tidying and dusting. . . . Mr. Burnaby liked these attentions, and gradually, as he came to realize that Marcus didn't intend to leave him, he became more cheerful. He drank a good deal of whiskey—four bottles in the week, to be exact; and when he was half-drunk he was extremely good company. Yet Marcus was never entirely at ease. Even when he was roaring with laughter at some story of Mr. Burnaby's youth, he was watchful. Mr. Burnaby's bursts of hilarity were apt to give way, without warning, to moods of the greatest depression.

When he was in these moods Mr. Burnaby's attitude varied

between two extremes. Marcus never knew which side he was going to take. Sometimes he would profess to see Marcus's point of view, and become embarrassingly sympathetic. He would admit that, after all, their experiments might be useless, that so far they had discovered nothing of value, that there might be no such thing as a human soul, or a divine soul with which human beings could get in contact. In that case it would be wise to get the best of this life: all pleasure seekers would be justified.

Yet just as often, instead of being sad and resigned, Mr. Burnaby would attack Marcus for his faithlessness. To such attacks Marcus would listen in silence. He thought they were deserved. He believed in the importance of their work, and recognized his own weakness in wanting to give it up for the sake of Hazel. But he hadn't given it up, he told himself. It was Hazel he had given up. Surely he deserved credit for that, even though he refused to tell Mr. Burnaby what he had done. Nevertheless he would have been furious if Mr. Burnaby had taken it for granted that he had given up Hazel, and whenever Mr. Burnaby tried to find out what his intentions actually were he continued to answer that he hadn't any plans, and to be annoyed when he was pressed to give a more definite answer.

Marcus spent the greater part of every day with Mr. Burnaby, but he couldn't stand the strain of his company for much more than three hours at a stretch. At intervals he would leave him to go and sit in the library, or, if it was a fine day, on a deck-chair in the garden. He did not go to the shore for fear of encountering Hazel. It was not that he no longer wanted to see her, but he had determined to avoid temptation rather than to throw himself in the way of it.

Presently the day came on which he knew the Morley family were due to return to Belfast, and on the following day he learned from Mrs. Mullan that they had indeed gone. From the way in which she gave him the information it was clear that she was anxious to find out what had happened between him and Hazel. Marcus tried to treat the news as if it were only of casual interest, and almost immediately he changed the subject.

He felt, however, as if the last door had now been closed, and he

was thrown once more into the deepest gloom. With Mr. Burnaby
he was morose and almost completely silent; and the fact that Mr.
Burnaby, to begin with at any rate, seemed more cheerful than
usual, made him almost savage. He couldn't bear to stay with him
longer than was absolutely necessary for attending to his wants,
and tidying his room. Mr. Burnaby attempted to keep him, and in
spite of seeing how pathetic these efforts were, and almost sym-
pathizing with them, Marcus had to go. He wondered that Mr.
Burnaby should not prefer solitude to such an uneasy and mutu-
ally irritating companionship. Marcus found relief in being alone:
alone he could think his own thoughts and plunge as it were in a
bath of self-pity and melancholy.

One afternoon, a few days after the Morleys' departure, Marcus
was going out, when Mr. Burnaby asked him to send Mrs. Mullan
up to talk to him. Marcus gave the message, and went for a walk
by himself on the shore. Almost automatically he took what was
Mr. Burnaby's own favourite route—along the edge of the rocks
towards the point. It was a grey day, but Marcus would not have
had it otherwise. Coming home he lingered at the bathing-place,
contrasting the present dullness with the brightness of the morning when he had first met Hazel there. Before returning, though
by now it was quite chilly, he decided to bathe. He ran up and
down once or twice to get some warmth into his body, and undressing quickly, dived in. After the first moment or two, in which
he was almost agonizingly cold, he began to enjoy himself. It was
not that he got warm, but that he reached a state of numbness
in which he was no longer able to feel the cold. He had a curious, wild feeling of association with the sea and the wind, as if he
himself had become a companion element. He didn't care what
happened. He gave himself up to the sea, neither swimming nor
consciously floating, but moving with the choppy waves instead
of battling against them. Why he got out at last he hardly knew;
but when he did, he felt as if in bathing he had performed some
spiritual act: he was different from when he had gone in.

He dried himself with his handkerchief—for he had had neither
towel nor bathing suit. Through being only half-dried, he had difficulty in putting on his clothes, and when he *was* dressed he still had
the same elemental feeling as if his clothes no longer mattered.

He ran back to the house, and hastened reluctantly upstairs to Mr. Burnaby's room. Mrs. Mullan was still there, standing by the door, as if she were on the point of going. Marcus guessed that she had been standing like that, with her hand on the door-handle for a considerable time. Evidently she and Mr. Burnaby had been having a good gossip—or crack, as Mrs. Mullan would have called it. They were both smiling and for a moment Mr. Burnaby hardly noticed Marcus. "And had he really drunk every bottle?" Mr. Burnaby demanded like a small boy, who insists on hearing his favourite story repeated over and over again.

"Every single one," Mrs. Mullan replied, "aye, to the very dregs. Faith that was a sermon. I never heard the like before or since."

Mr. Burnaby was still in bed, but he looked more like himself. His eyes rested on Marcus, first almost as if he didn't see him, but suddenly with keen attention. "Why you're frozen, child!" he exclaimed. "You're quite blue."

"I've b-been b-b-bathing," Marcus told him, through chattering teeth, and the more he tried to talk the more uncontrollably his teeth rattled.

He peered in the mirror to see what his face really looked like, but found that though there were purplish blue patches, the predominant colour was really yellow. Mr. Burnaby wanted him to take a hot bath and go to bed, but Marcus refused. Finally he agreed protestingly to drink a glass of hot whiskey, mixed with sugar and lemon. Mrs. Mullan departed to prepare this beverage, and Marcus stood by the window looking out. "You'd better go and warm yourself by the kitchen fire," Mr. Burnaby told him. "I'm getting up in a minute or two. I'll be down for dinner. Perhaps when you're warmed you'll come back and we'll go down together."

He was better, Marcus saw, though afraid that he might fall on the stairs. He too must have heard that Hazel had gone.

CHAPTER XXXI

THOUGH Mr. Burnaby's health got steadily worse during the next two years he refused absolutely to see a doctor. He appeared to be suffering from some kind of progressive paralysis.

There were curious twitchings in his muscles and he found it more and more difficult to walk.

After a time Marcus started to work again, but Mr. Burnaby took no part in the experiments. Marcus worked harder than before, and gradually he was able to lengthen the period of his excursions, sometimes by a minute or two a day, once or twice by as much as five minutes. This was not a steady progress. He had bad days when his body seemed all along more powerful than his spirit, and he could not leave it for more than half an hour at a time.

Presently he found that the nature of his work was altering. With great difficulty he had learned to detach himself from his body and move about, looking at one scene or another. Now he began to find such movement less necessary. It was as if he were gradually stepping further and further back, so that where before he had only seen fragments he was beginning to recognize a complete picture. As the picture grew, the more serene became his consciousness of it, the more acute his awareness of its details. Always there was something new slipping in, from above and below, from the sides, from behind and before. . . . With every extension of his vision came a cool joy—a secret pride, which he did not completely reveal to Mr. Burnaby.

In the meantime a new relationship slowly grew up between them: in some respects it was not very different from the old, but it was less happy and less open. Marcus had become more reserved, and there was always in the consciousness of both of them the knowledge that there was one subject which must never be discussed, hardly even alluded to.

Marcus didn't go home that summer. He wrote that Mr. Burnaby had been ill and wasn't able to spare him. Both his parents replied to this letter, and, though they told him to do whatever he thought best, it was clear that they were hurt and imagined that he was only using Mr. Burnaby's illness as an excuse to please himself. This of course was wrong. Marcus would have liked very much to go home, if only for the sake of escaping for a little from the strained atmosphere of The Garrison. It was simply a sense of duty which kept him back and he looked forward eagerly to his next holiday at Christmas. At last it came and he set off with every intention of enjoying himself and of pleasing his parents. Yet somehow nothing went as he had intended. The whole holiday was a failure from start to finish. Marcus was less anxious than ever to talk about the life he was leading, and when his family talked about their own affairs he was bored. He found their friends dull, and once he was quite rude to an old acquaintance of his father's, who, like Mr. Morley, wanted to talk to him about stocks and shares. This rudeness was not due to boredom, but to fear: Marcus was afraid that his ignorance might be exposed and his whole relationship with Mr. Burnaby called in question.

It was a relief for all of them when the holiday came to an end and Marcus set off once more for Donegal.

After his return to The Garrison Marcus started a new series of experiments. He attempted more and more to get in touch with the spirits of other living people: he also tried to get in touch with the spirits of people who were on the verge of death, and remain in contact with them after death.

So far as the spirits of the living were concerned his efforts met with some success, but only in cases where the other spirit was itself partially detached from the physical body. He made contact with people who were in very deep sleep, with one or two mediums, with several people who were on the verge of death.

Mr. Burnaby had at one time or another made similar experiments himself, but he had never known for certain whether or not he had succeeded in maintaining contact after death.

"The difficulty", as he pointed out when discussing some of Marcus's experiences, "is to know the exact moment when physical death occurs. At present no one does know for certain if people do die the moment breathing ceases and the heart stops beating. The brain may continue to live on for some time, perhaps for a very considerable time."

After he had carried out a number of these experiments Marcus began to meet with a new phenomenon. He was still doing his ordinary work, what, for the sake of distinction, might be called his contemplative expeditions, when he sought only to detach himself from his body and observe the ordinary, physical world. This phenomenon was a kind of double sight. To begin with it only

troubled him occasionally, but after a month or two it occurred in
nearly every experiment he made, whether he were watching the
dying or the healthy, an empty landscape or a populated scene. I
cannot say if Mr. Burnaby understood the reason for this from the
beginning. If he did, he did not at once tell Marcus, though eventually he led him to the explanation.

As I think I have made clear in the earlier part of this book Marcus had not been particularly happy at school; but certain aspects
of school life retained a nostalgic attraction for him, and one Sunday in spring he felt a sudden wish to be present again at the evening service in Chapel. He arrived just as the boys were filing in,
and though he knew that he could not expect to recognize any
one of them he gazed at each boy as he came up the aisle, hoping
to find a likeness to some of his contemporaries. There *were* such
likenesses, perhaps younger brothers or cousins of boys he had
known, and he pretended to himself that they were the same boys.
He looked only at *them*, and at those of the masters who were really the same, and who had been there in his own time.

The service began and the faces grew blurred: they were part of
the scene: they had lost their individuality. Marcus was back, but
not quite back. The service made the same queer appeal to him as
it had always made, reminding him that Spring was the prelude to
Autumn, and Youth to Death. As a boy there he had seen himself
as an old man, ready like Simeon to leave the world behind him.
The service swam by and through him. He saw nothing clearly;
everything was misty, and warm, and sad.

The singing ceased: the music died away. The Headmaster
stood up to preach. He was the same Head who had been there in
Marcus's time, and from the fact that it was he who was preaching Marcus realized that it must be the end of term; for the Head
only preached twice a term—at the morning service on the first
Sunday, and at the evening service on the last. Marcus found that
the manner of his sermons had not changed. He chose as his text:
"Finally, brethren, whatsoever things are true, whatsoever things
are honest, whatsoever things are just, whatsoever things are pure,
whatsoever things are lovely, whatsoever things are of good report; if there be any virtue, and if there be any praise, think on
these things." It was not a religious sermon: it was sound advice

on how to avoid certain temptations, and a warning of the danger of yielding to them.

For a while Marcus listened to him closely, but presently his mind wandered, and he thought of boys who had given way to the kind of temptation about which the Head was speaking. He remembered watching two of them during just such a sermon as this and wondering what they were thinking—and then he began to feel as if it were he himself who was preaching. He felt himself leaning forward towards the congregation, appealing to them, yearning to fill them with a desire for purity and goodness, to make them want, and be strong enough, to lead straight, upright lives.

The boys he saw now were different from those he had seen when he first came in. One or two of the older ones wore soft, silky moustaches, which they fingered surreptitiously, and self-consciously. It was to one of these in particular that the preacher seemed to be appealing. . . . And suddenly the organ began again before the sermon was finished. Marcus looked at the boys and the masters. For a moment there was that confusion of sight to which he was becoming accustomed, faces looking through faces, like a photograph when two exposures have been made on the same piece of film. In an instant it was all clear again; the faces were those Marcus had seen on his arrival. Everyone was standing up. They began to sing the end of term hymn, 'Lord, dismiss us with thy blessing.'

Marcus went back to Mr. Burnaby and described what had happened.

"You'll have to be more careful now," Mr. Burnaby warned him. "They won't all be good spirits, you know, and it may be some of the worst who will want you to join in their experience."

"I suppose that was some old headmaster," Marcus said. "Their clothes were all different—the boys' clothes I mean—not very much, but they just didn't look the same."

"Perhaps he had used the same text," Mr. Burnaby reflected. "I should think it must be a favourite with headmasters. I suppose the old man hadn't half finished. Your man was brief in accordance with modern practice. At any rate it's a very good text for *you*."

Marcus flushed. "How do you mean?"

"I mean you're going to have a great many of these experiences. Some of them will be unpleasant. You will have to learn which to avoid, which are safe."

"But shouldn't I know everything, and experience everything?" Marcus asked. "Shouldn't I see life whole?"

"To know fire it is not necessary to be burned alive," Mr. Burnaby replied. "If you are wise you will flee from everything that is horrible at first sight: even so you will see enough to give you unpleasant memories: you don't want to be haunted."

"I don't quite understand," Marcus said. "Why am I only going to see things now?"

"Tonight," Mr. Burnaby told him, "you encountered the spirit of a man who died a great many years ago. You didn't see him, but being in the same place as he was, and in something of the same mood, you saw for a time what he saw. Fortunately for you he was a good man. I should think, probably, he was one of those 'great' headmasters of the nineteenth century: Arnold of Rugby is the best-known example. These men devoted themselves, their whole selves, their whole time, to their schools, and it is not surprising to find the spirit of one of them lingering over the scene of his work.

"Most people, I think, when they come to die are ready to leave this world, or at least to leave their old affections and occupations. But there are some, who for one reason or another, are not. They feel that their work is incomplete; or there is someone or something they love, or hate, too strongly to part with. These are what are called ghosts, and in certain extraordinary circumstances they become visible to ordinary people. There are far more ghosts than are ever seen. From now on you will get to know many of them. Places are haunted by ghosts, but to an even greater extent are the ghosts haunted by places, and by scenes that have occurred in those places during their physical lives. Sometimes these scenes are of violence so terrible that they have left too strong an impression on the participants for the act of death to bring forgetfulness or peace. Sometimes the haunting spirit is the victim and sometimes the perpetrator of the wrong. Sometimes there is no wrong but only a memory so clear that it cannot be forgotten. You will learn all this for yourself. I only say to you, be careful. Do not allow yourself to become haunted in your turn."

"But why do we never see it happening?" Marcus asked. "When we try to follow the dead they always go on beyond us, beyond where we can go with them."

"Because they nearly all *do* go on," Mr. Burnaby explained. "At any time you may come on one who doesn't, but it will be a rare chance, and an unlikely one."

"But aren't there other spirits," Marcus said, "spirits who have come back?"

"Yes, I think so," Mr. Burnaby agreed with a touch of impatience. "I don't understand everything, you know. I believe I have an inkling of the way things work, but there are some things I don't completely understand: they may fit in one way or another. It may be that some individuals have work to do after death, work which necessitates the retention of their individualities; or it may be that some individualities are too strong to be quickly absorbed: such individualities might shuttle to and fro, for a time in contact with the mind of the whole, and then for another period with the physical or mortal part—not I suppose that any part is really mortal: there is probably a spiritual fluidity just as there is a physical fluidity—and each of us is a microcosm of both. The individuals you are thinking of may be in touch at the same time with the spiritual whole and with various beings here who are incarnate parts of that whole. It is even possible that complete attributes of the spiritual side of the whole are constantly incarnate—dwelling in the flesh, I mean: it's difficult to find the right words—or that complete attributes may for a time be incarnate in one individual. If that were so, such an individual would appear to have a complete spiritual immortality in himself. The existence of an individual of this kind seems unlikely. No one would understand him; for as he possessed the whole of his quality, nobody else would have even sufficient of that quality to be able to appreciate it in him. What is it Beckford says—'Not an animal comprehends me!', though that of course doesn't mean that there was no one capable of comprehending him.

"As I said before we can't understand—I can't understand—*everything*. I have met the sort of spirits I think you mean—or encountered them rather: one doesn't really meet them in the full sense of the word: one is aware of them, one just gets in touch with them, or with part of them. They appear to know what is going on here; but are they the spirits they seem to be?—or are they something greater? Do they appear to us as they do appear, only because we cannot see them more completely? Are they in fact a portion of the whole on which for a moment we can shine a light? Whatever they know they seem incapable of imparting to us—or more likely we are incapable of taking it in. That's it, you know: we can't conceive of life without smelling, feeling, seeing, hearing, tasting—or without the imagination of these things—life in silent intangible darkness, knowing. Sight, real or imaginary, is the hardest to part with; yet sight is just as much a physical experience as any of them."

"Oh but no," Marcus objected, realizing suddenly that this was something about which he could argue. "You can see without your body. You can see with just your spirit."

"Oh but no," Mr. Burnaby mimicked, "or at least you can't be certain. Your spirit may know what's there and from that imagine seeing it, hearing it. . . . and all the rest: but you can't be sure there's any more than that."

"You could say the same about all our physical sensations," Marcus pointed out, "that we imagine feeling, that we imagine seeing. . . ."

"I know you could," he admitted, "just as no one can prove the existence of anything apart from his own mind—the rest may be imagination."

"All the same," Marcus said, "we all believe there is more than one of us—at least in that way—the other is just a sort of philosophical joke. Anyhow, even our ordinary seeing is partly imagination: we become aware of things through our eyes, but we don't know that what you see and what I see is the same, or what relation it bears to reality. Your red may be my green, or we may each have a different spectrum with not a single colour like anyone else's."

"I hardly think it's likely."

"It's not," Marcus agreed, "but what I mean is that all our seeing, and hearing, and feeling is largely the imaginative interpretation of physical phenomena, and if when we're out of our bodies it's *all* imagination, it's still as much seeing. Colour and sound and smell may be real things—real things of the imagination—and our eyes and ears and noses only the physical means by which we become aware of them. Don't you see, and smell, and feel in dreams?"

This started Mr. Burnaby on a new tack and quite characteristically he immediately forgot about the subject under discussion. "Did you ever wake up crying?" he asked.

Marcus was embarrassed. "I don't remember," he prevaricated. "I mean I'm not sure."

"Well if you haven't," Mr. Burnaby retorted, with a little twitch of his eyebrows, "it's an experience you've missed. I wasn't going to inquire what about."

Marcus had studied the behaviour of Mr. Burnaby's eyebrows. They twitched like that when he was making fun of somebody, or enjoying a semi-private joke. "I maybe have, some time or other," he confessed cautiously.

"Probably a dream of self-pity," Mr. Burnaby commented unkindly. "It's the most sincere form of pity. The point is that one's dream griefs have an intensity, an exquisite purity that far excels any unhappiness one can experience when awake. In dreams all the emotions can be pure—happiness and unhappiness, love and sadness, are all more intense, more tender, but not in every dream, only when the body is quiescent, when there are no physical sensations to distort the vision of the mind."

CHAPTER XXXII

AS a writer I am dissatisfied with the ending of the last chapter. I have to break off through lack of material. I don't know whether Mr. Burnaby went on talking about dreams or whether they both went to bed.

The account of Marcus's visit to the school chapel is taken partly from Mr. Burnaby's notes, partly from the autobiography Marcus wrote after Mr. Burnaby's death. An account of the conversation which followed is also in the autobiography, but it is reported more fully in Marcus's journal.

Since Mr. Burnaby had given up taking part in the work himself, Marcus had stopped taking notes. He described his experiments to Mr. Burnaby, and Mr. Burnaby made notes: he had little else to do. Marcus did however continue to write in his journal. It was his one emotional outlet, and it was only at the very end that he lost interest in it.

The spring and summer of 1934 is very well documented indeed. Mr. Burnaby's notes and journal, and Marcus's journal were all better kept than at any other time. The first to deteriorate at all was Mr. Burnaby's journal. In it he complained increasingly of being tired, of physical weakness, of the uncontrollable twitchings in his muscles. Finally his journal became merely a catalogue of the symptoms of his illness. About Christmas the quality of his notes too began to change. They degenerated from careful descriptions into jottings; shortly after the New Year they ceased.

Why Marcus did not begin taking notes again himself when Mr. Burnaby stopped, I do not know. I imagine that it was due partly to laziness. Certainly there was a streak of laziness in him, and this laziness, more than anything else, affected the course of the rest of his life.

There is another possible reason. By this time Marcus knew exactly when Mr. Burnaby's death would take place. He had told Mr. Burnaby, and Mr. Burnaby had immediately proceeded to discuss the details of 'The Last Experiment,' about which he had talked to Marcus on many occasions. Shortly before the time of Mr. Burnaby's death, Marcus was to lock himself into his bedroom. He was then to project himself and to get into contact with Mr. Burnaby's spirit. Mr. Burnaby undertook that when death occurred he would not try to elude Marcus, but instead would endeavour to communicate to him whatever he might discover. I think it likely that if Marcus knew so much about Mr. Burnaby's death, he may also have known the result of the experiment. Probably he knew a great deal more. Perhaps he wished to keep this knowledge from Mr. Burnaby; perhaps he knew something so dismal that he did not wish to put it down at all. He seems to have been growing indifferent to the implications his work would have for Humanity at large. He was interested in it only for its own sake—or for *his* own sake. He didn't really feel that he *was* a human being any more.

Only when he projected himself out of his body could he be fully alive. Only then can he have felt happy.

In any case there is no further direct record of the experiments Marcus was making, though indirectly it is clear that these experiments were increasingly successful. Marcus achieved, or thought he achieved, periods of complete unity with the universal mind. His journal claims that in this state he had complete knowledge— past, present and future were all open to him, though it would appear that at first he was only able to report to the mind of the physical Marcus Brownlow a small proportion of his knowledge. He brought back a series of snapshots, rather like flashes from a cinema newsreel. Many of them he did not understand. A few of them are identifiable in the light of what has happened since. Some appear completely trivial: one or two are connected with events, which when they actually occurred, received world-wide publicity.

Gradually Marcus must have learned to be able to make a voluntary selection from what he knew in his disembodied state. It was probably done by limiting the degree of his submergence, by preserving his own identity at the same time as it sank into the universal. Whatever the means, it presently became possible for him to choose what he saw, or to choose what he would remember and bring back. So the vision of the future that he obtained, that the embodied Marcus Brownlow obtained, gradually became a vision of his own future. He saw more than he wanted to see. He was oppressed with a sense of the inevitable. His course was set. His every action was determined by a host of other actions. It was useless for him to think of his future, to try to decide anything. Yet he *would* think, and he *would* make decisions, and be conscious that every thought, every decision, was predetermined: he was running on rails; all the points were set; all the signals were down.

Mr. Burnaby grew more feeble. The convulsive twitching of his muscles became more noticeable. It was unpleasant to look at. He ate less. He became thinner and the bones in his face stood out. Like Marcus his life was no more than the colouring of a pattern which was already complete. It was no good trying to eat more, or to husband his strength. He knew the day and the hour.

The tower stairs troubled him. For a while he laboured up them

doggedly three times a day. An armchair was put on the first landing and he would sit in it for a little before starting on the last
flight. Marcus suggested that he should have his bed moved to one
of the rooms over the kitchen and use the library as a study. It was
a useless suggestion. He knew it to be useless. Yet for his own sake
he longed for it to be accepted. If it had been all his knowledge
would have been proved false. He would have had another chance.
He could have looked forward to Mr. Burnaby's death as a release
from his bondage.

Mr. Burnaby refused to move. The tower had become almost a
part of him. He was determined to die there.

Through the spring and early summer Mr. Burnaby grew steadily weaker. Towards the end of July he caught a chill. It began with
attacks of shivering, and soon he developed a cough. Marcus took
his temperature and found it was 103 degrees.

"You'd better get the doctor," Mr. Burnaby said. "He won't do
any good, but unless you get him now there may be trouble about
a death certificate."

So Doctor Sheehan, the dispensary doctor from Portmallagh,
was called in. He examined Mr. Burnaby carefully, but didn't say
very much till he was alone with Marcus. Then he questioned him
about Mr. Burnaby's health during the last few months.

"He's got pneumonia now," he pronounced, "and in *his* state
there's not much chance for him. He'll maybe last seven or eight
days, but he wasn't long for this world in any case, poor gentleman. Perhaps it's just as well it happened this way."

"Why, how do you mean?" Marcus asked uncomfortably, for he
felt that the doctor might have guessed something of his own part
in bringing about Mr. Burnaby's original ill-health.

"He's suffering from a form of paralysis," the Doctor answered,
"—progressive muscular atrophy, I would say. He has very little
power in his legs and arms, and you must have noticed this twitching in his muscles."

"Oh yes," Marcus said, "but he wouldn't let me get you, you
know. Of course, he's been getting weak for a long time."

The doctor shrugged his shoulders. "Oh well, there are a lot of
old people like that—afraid to know what *is* wrong with them—
and it wouldn't have made any difference in the long run."

Mr. Burnaby died on the third of August, 1935 at twenty-nine minutes to three in the afternoon. He was exactly on time. Two days later he was buried in his own grounds half-way between the house and the sea.

CHAPTER XXXIII

THERE is very little about Mr. Burnaby's death in Marcus's journal—just a note of the date and the time. When I first went through Marcus's papers I hoped and expected to come across some fuller account. There was nothing. I was disappointed, because I wanted to know if 'The Last Experiment' had actually taken place, and if so, what had happened. I thought at first that the experiment had not been made. I supposed that in the distress of his last illness Mr. Burnaby had forgotten about it, or that he had been too worn-out and apathetic to care any more. When, however, I came to interview Mrs. Mullan I gathered that Marcus had behaved very strangely at the time of Mr. Burnaby's death. As she was a little incoherent I decided to go and see Dr. Sheehan and verify what she had told me. He did verify it in every particular, but as his account was much more straightforward than hers I will report it exactly.

Dr. Sheehan had left Portmallagh a few months before I arrived, and gone to Dublin, but I had no difficulty in getting his address. A week later I called on him. I had made an appointment and he was waiting for me when I arrived. He was a reddish-faced, vigorous looking man in his early thirties. He was living in a rather shabby terrace house in one of the older Dublin suburbs. I only saw the waiting-room and his consulting-room, where he received me. I got the impression that the house was only half-furnished, and the furniture I did see was well-worn. All the same Dr. Sheehan looked like a man who intended to get on in the world. He spoke with a slight Irish brogue, which I shan't attempt to reproduce.

He looked busy and I explained at once why I had come.

"I've been commissioned to write a book about John Burnaby and Marcus Brownlow. I heard you had attended Mr. Burnaby in his last illness."

"I did," he answered at once. "That was a queer business. They were a queer pair, the two of them—him and the young fellow."

"Why do you say it was queer?" I demanded.

"Because it was," he replied. "The man was in a bad way when I was called in the first place—double pneumonia on the top of progressive muscular atrophy—if you know what that is?"

"I'm afraid I don't," I confessed.

"It's a kind of paralysis," he explained. "It begins in the legs, with weakness in the legs. You can't do anything about it. At first the patient finds it curtails his powers of walking. The muscles get tired: there's a twitching in the muscles, and of course it spreads. After the legs the arms begin to go. It's an unpleasant thing—usually takes about a couple of years."

"And that's what Mr. Burnaby had?"

"Yes, though it wasn't what killed him. He died of pneumonia. That's the way it usually goes. The patient gets something else, and with his resistance gone he can't stand up to it."

"I think I understand," I said, "but what was queer about it?"

He shrugged his shoulders and I thought that perhaps I had annoyed him a little. "Oh, chiefly the young fellow, I suppose. I thought it was strange the way he went on. He was upset, but not quite the way you'd think somehow. I'd have thought there was something fishy if the symptoms hadn't been quite clear. He seemed to be expecting the old man to die. He seemed more frightened of me, than worried about his boss dying—and then, when it got near the end, he wouldn't stay in the room. I don't know if he was frightened of death, or what it was; but half an hour or so before the man died he went away and shut himself up in his bedroom. I wasn't there of course. I'd called in the morning and I knew very well it'd be all over by the time I got back in the evening. So it was too. I ran out at about half-past eight and was met by the housekeeper. She told me that young Brownlow had sent for her at about two o'clock and told her that he was going to his bedroom and must not be disturbed on any account—'Not even if Mr. Burnaby dies,' he told her. Then he left *her* to take charge of the sick-room. And when I came at half-past eight Brownlow was still in his bedroom and not a stir out of him.

"I didn't know what to make of it. The idea of suicide did cross my mind—you never know with these neurotic types—and according to all the rumours they'd both been dabbling in spiritualism, or black magic, or something—though that didn't come out till afterwards, now I come to think of it."

"You thought that Marcus Brownlow might have committed suicide," I put in for the sake of absolute clarity, "not Mr. Burnaby?"

"Oh no. I knew Mr. Burnaby hadn't killed himself, and I didn't really believe the young chap had. I thought he was just skulking as a matter of fact, but I had to make sure. So I went off and knocked on *Master* Brownlow's bedroom door. No reply. I knocked again. Still no reply. Well I wasn't going to be put off as easily as all that. So I started battering on the door with both fists and one foot. At last he opened it and blinked out at me. He looked at me in a dead-and-alive sort of way. He might have been lying low after a booze-up by the look of him.

"'Been asleep?' I asked.

"'Not—not exactly,' he said.

"'Mr. Burnaby's dead,' I told him. 'He's been dead six hours.'

"'I know,' he said. 'He died at twenty-nine minutes to three. What do *you* want?' Funny how the exact words have stuck in my mind.

"Well I thought that pretty cool, and I went off the handle a bit—let him have it hot and strong. Somehow it didn't seem to have much effect. He just went on blinking at me in a dazed sort of way and at the end asked me what he ought to do.

"I told him he ought to be making arrangements—funeral, notifying relations, and so on. Then, out of pure badness, I put in something about withholding the death certificate; an inquest might be necessary—I'd have to make sure there had been no neglect.

"That shook him a bit. He didn't want an inquest. No one ever does; but *he* was scared of one.

"He kept looking over his shoulder all the time as if there was someone else in the room, listening to us. He'd kept the door half-closed. So I gave it another kick to see if there was anyone there, and it flew open: but there wasn't, unless they were hiding in the wardrobe or under the bed.

"By this time he was pretty abject. I had him where I wanted him. I gave the certificate of course—I couldn't do anything else. I'd no real reason for withholding it. If there had been an inquest I couldn't have made anything of it. All the same I wasn't very surprised when I read about his suicide. He was pretty unbalanced."

That was all Dr. Sheehan could tell me, but it was enough to make me feel certain that the last experiment *had* taken place.

What then happened? What did this last experiment amount to? We can only guess: but to me the answer seems almost certain. Mr. Burnaby had instructed Marcus to behave exactly as he did—to go to his room, to put himself in a state of trance, and, in his disembodied state, to return to the sick-room. If Marcus succeeded in carrying out these instructions he must have been in touch with Mr. Burnaby's spirit at the moment the physical Mr. Burnaby died.

Whether or not Marcus noticed the death taking place, at the time it did take place, I don't feel quite certain. His remark to Dr. Sheehan about the time may have been half a question, designed to verify his earlier knowledge. What then was the outcome of the experiment? Simply, I think, that the spiritual Mr. Burnaby did not go away. His spirit remained with Marcus, it remained not only with the spiritual Marcus, when his spirit was disembodied, but with him all the time, or almost all the time, for the rest of his life. My reason for this assumption will appear in the following chapters.

And why did Marcus not record this—almost the most important fact of all—in his autobiography?

I think he couldn't bear to. I think he found it too horrible to write about; or so horrible that he couldn't write about it without describing his horror; he preferred to leave it out. That at any rate is my interpretation. If some reader has a better one I should be glad to know of it.

CHAPTER XXXIV

FROM conjecture I return to fact. After the funeral Marcus went home with his father. He stayed at home just over a month, returning to The Garrison early in September.

Before leaving home he had started to write his autobiography, and at The Garrison he went on with it. He thought it the easiest way to bring his knowledge, or a portion of his knowledge, before the public. He wrote from a sense of duty or because of an acceptance of Mr. Burnaby's sense of duty. He himself did not care a great deal whether his knowledge was passed on or not: and as he didn't like writing, the book advanced very slowly.

He kept the same hours as he had with Mr. Burnaby, and he spent most of his time in the tower. So far as the servants were concerned the routine of the house was exactly as it had been when Mr. Burnaby was alive. As master of the house, Marcus was more reserved, but less troublesome than Mr. Burnaby. The servants thought him queer, but they were accustomed to queerness. Presently they noticed that he had begun to talk to himself.

The first strange thing happened about Christmas 1936—the exact date is uncertain. I can't explain what happened. I have no inside information. At least I have no information that *explains* it: there is information which in a way corroborates it.

As a rule Marcus's lunch consisted of three courses—soup, meat, and pudding, followed by tea. Marcus didn't like coffee. Usually he ate very little, but Mrs. Mullan always insisted that his meals should be served properly. She didn't allow the food to be brought in on the plate from which he was to eat it.

On this day Kate was bringing in the lunch as usual. The table had been laid half an hour before, and almost automatically she carried in a small tureen of soup and a soup-plate. She thought Marcus was sitting at the table. She thought she put down the tureen and plate in front of him. As she was going out it struck her that he had not said, "Thank you very much", as he did invariably, in an unchanging, slightly apologetic tone. With her hand on the door she turned to look at him. But instead of Marcus she saw Mr. Burnaby. She didn't faint: she ran to the kitchen screaming. There she had hysterics: presently she told her mother and Susan what she had seen: Teresa wasn't there. Some months previously she had gone to a place in Belfast.

Mrs. Mullan did not believe Kate's story. Yet she believed enough to be frightened. They discussed it up and down, and Mrs. Mullan and Susan tried to explain it away. When the time came Mrs.

Mullan took in the meat course herself. She felt it to be her duty: besides both Kate and Susan had refused point-blank to leave the kitchen. She found Marcus sitting in his place. He had finished his soup and was crumbling a piece of bread on the table. She thought he looked rather anxious. There was no sign of Mr. Burnaby.

She spoke to him—she does not remember what about—and he replied if not perfectly normally, normally enough. Mrs. Mullan says now that he seemed nervous. I think, however, that this nervousness may have been added as a result of later events. If she did feel something queer, as she says, she had no right to scold Kate—which was what she immediately set about doing on her return to the kitchen. Kate burst into tears and Susan, who was evidently the calmest member of the family, intervened to restore order. This scene, I may say, was described to me by the Mullans themselves, about a year after Marcus's death. I remember particularly how vehemently—and volubly—Mrs. Mullan reproached herself for having doubted Kate's word—"an' her me own daughter!"

Susan took in the third course and the tea. She did not see Mr. Burnaby and to her Marcus looked much as usual. When the tea was being taken in Kate had recovered sufficiently to accompany Susan as far as the dining room door. She peeped in, and was a good deal reassured. She was inclined to think that she might have been rather silly. At the same time she was not convinced. She still *felt* that she had seen Mr. Burnaby, and in the course of the next few days this feeling had a definite effect on the others. They began to believe that something queer *had* occurred. There was an uncomfortable atmosphere in the house. They realized how odd Marcus was becoming.

After this Kate and Susan made a point of doing all their housework together; in particular neither of them would go into the tower alone. Mrs. Mullan confined her activities to the kitchen. While ridiculing her daughters' fears she ran no risks herself.

A month went by without anything further happening to disturb them. Gradually they all grew more confident.

Then one day in January there was a fog. When the Mullans left their cottage it was not very thick, but all through the morning it drifted in from the sea. The house became more and more gloomy. Mrs. Mullan lit the lamp in the kitchen and blazed up the fire. Even so she felt cold. Outside she could see nothing but a greyish, billowy whiteness. She didn't like it: she couldn't get warm. She began to wish for a pink, woollen cardigan she had left hanging behind the kitchen door at home. She was a selfish old woman: she decided to send Susan for the cardigan. But she didn't know where Susan was. Susan was somewhere about the house with Kate, turning out rooms. Mrs. Mullan went into the hall and called. There was no reply, and she felt angry. Those girls! They had probably heard her perfectly well and didn't want to trouble themselves. She'd give them a piece of her mind. She put her head into the outer hall, and then went up the steps and through the black curtain into the tower. In the tower it was very dim. She climbed the stairs slowly, still calling. It occurred to her that if she had behaved like this in Mr. Burnaby's time she would have got into trouble; but Marcus wasn't so particular. Suddenly she realized that someone was coming down the stairs to meet her. For a moment she thought it was Marcus. Then she knew it was Mr. Burnaby. She squeezed herself against the wall. He didn't look at her and he didn't speak.

I won't describe her feelings. She herself has described them fully to a great many people, and I'm sure will continue to do so to the day of her death.

In case however it should seem that I am inclined to give undue credit to the incident I should like to make it clear that I realize the following facts. It was almost completely dark on the tower stairs. Marcus and Mr. Burnaby were within two or three inches of the same height. Mrs. Mullan was, and is, just as superstitious as any other Irish peasant. What concerns this story is what she did.

She spent another five minutes on the stairs in a state of panic. As nothing further happened she gradually gathered sufficient courage to return to the kitchen. She had a pot of stew on the range and a pudding in the oven. She removed them both and put them on the kitchen table. She banked up the fire, closed the dampers, and put on her hat and coat. With a piece of half-burnt coal she wrote on the whitewashed kitchen wall where it would be most easily seen, "Come home at once, Mother." The message was still on the wall in 1939. Probably it is there today. After writing it Mrs. Mullan went back to her cottage. Half an hour later she was joined by Susan and Kate.

What Marcus did about his lunch nobody knows.

Black didn't learn of the Mullans' departure till late in the evening. He didn't believe in ghosts, and he felt very annoyed at Mrs. Mullan's behaviour.

The next morning he encountered Marcus in the garden. He said that his wife would be willing to do the cooking and part of the housework till fresh servants could be found: but Marcus thought he could manage by himself if the Blacks would do his shopping for him.

Black had no wish to give up his job. He liked it and nothing had occurred to frighten him. He was glad to do whatever Marcus required. The only objection he made was when Marcus sent him to the Mullans' cottage with a month's wages for each of them. "They don't deserve a penny piece," he declared.

"But it doesn't make any difference to me," Marcus insisted, "and I'm sure they'll need it."

"Let them work for it," Black retorted. "It's the only way to teach them." Nevertheless he delivered the money, though, as he informed Marcus afterwards, he had taken the opportunity of telling Mrs. Mullan what he thought of her.

Black urged Marcus to get new servants. Even if he did not turn the Mullans out of their cottage, which belonged to The Garrison, there was plenty of room in the house itself for a housekeeper and two or three maids. Marcus, however, realized that it would be difficult to persuade servants to come to a house which was reputed to be haunted. Besides, if he knew all that was to happen to him, he must have foreseen quite clearly that there weren't going to be any more servants at The Garrison. Whatever the reason—it may just have been apathy—he made no attempt to procure any.

To begin with he found it difficult enough to carry on. Black had to teach him how to light the range—and Marcus was very slow to get the hang of it. It would have been unlike him to be quick to pick up anything of that sort.

In the following weeks both the Blacks noticed that he seemed unwell. He got thinner and paler, and his expression began to alter. He looked not exactly desperate, but, as it were, doomed. He only came out occasionally. They didn't know how he spent his time, but all through the nights there would be a light in one of the windows of the tower.

Black heard very few of the rumours that were going through the countryside. Those that he did hear he dismissed rather contemptuously. He and his wife kept to themselves. As Protestants in an entirely Roman Catholic area they were to a great extent out of touch with the rest of the community.

Two months passed before anything happened to disturb Black's incredulity, but towards the end of March he did have a rather peculiar experience. He was coming up the back avenue in broad daylight when he saw someone coming towards him from the house. "That's very like the Master," he thought. "I'd swear it was the Master, if I didn't know he was dead and buried." Of course he immediately remembered Mrs. Mullan's experience, but he was not alarmed. He and Mr. Burnaby had always been on the best of terms. He had been a loyal and faithful servant and he almost welcomed the opportunity of talking to Mr. Burnaby's ghost. As the figure approached he touched his cap and was about to speak. It was Mr. Burnaby's walk, but the face which looked at him and smiled at him with Mr. Burnaby's smile was the face of Marcus. Black didn't speak. He had been prepared to encounter a ghost. He didn't know what to make of a living man inhabited by a ghost. He walked on for a little, and then turned round. The figure was still walking down the drive. Again it looked like Mr. Burnaby. Black saw it reach the gate, open it, and disappear behind the hedge which bordered the road. He was deeply puzzled, but he had work to do and he saw no reason for neglecting it. He went to the garage, backed out the car, and began to wash it. As he was hosing the wheels he decided to keep his experience to himself. If he told his wife it would only make her nervous, and Black was convinced that there was really nothing to be nervous about. He didn't believe that a ghost could do either of them any harm.

Mrs. Black saw Mr. Burnaby in the distance on the twelfth of April. He was walking along the shore with Marcus. She noticed that he looked much more vigorous than he had been during the last few years of his life. She was very much upset. Black was unable to convince her that it must be someone else, or alternatively that if it *were* Mr. Burnaby's ghost, there was no need to be alarmed. During the next few weeks several people declared they had seen Mr. Burnaby, either with Marcus or alone. Mrs. Black saw him again in the distance on the first of May. By this time, of course, she had heard some at least of the rumours. She became hysterical and made Black drive her to Portmallagh where she caught the afternoon train to Belfast. She had a married sister in Belfast with whom she intended to stay till Black could join her.

Black returned to The Garrison. All that evening he hung about in the hope of seeing Marcus; but Marcus did not appear. Eventually Black went into his own house, which adjoined The Garrison, though it did not actually communicate with the main building. He decided to give his notice in writing. He wrote the letter in the morning and went into the house through the kitchen door which was never closed. Marcus was in the kitchen eating his breakfast. Black noticed that he had tea, a boiled egg, and bread and butter. The kitchen fire was lit. Mr. Burnaby was sitting at the table with Marcus. His appearance was exactly as it had been before his illness. Black was embarrassed. He felt it more difficult to give his notice to Mr. Burnaby, whom he had known for so long, than to Marcus.

"I'm sorry for coming in like this, Sir," he said to Mr. Burnaby.

Mr. Burnaby did not speak but he smiled very pleasantly.

Marcus looked a little uncomfortable, almost ashamed, Black thought. "That's all right," he answered, though it was not really to him Black had spoken.

"I'm very sorry to have to give a week's notice," Black went on. "I'm sorry after all this time. It's not that I've not been treated well, but it's on account of the wife. I've no complaints."

He held out his letter and Marcus took it. "I quite understand," Marcus said. "It just can't be helped." He looked very sad—"Sort of hopeless," is Black's description.

Black withdrew. He worked faithfully up to the last. Before he went he arranged for provisions to be delivered regularly at The Garrison. The best he was able to do was to have them put at the gate for Marcus to collect. On his last day he brought down a large meat safe from the house and placed it just outside the gate. Milk and eggs were to be put in this every other day, groceries twice a week.

Most of the appearances of Mr. Burnaby may be explained away. The people who saw him, or imagined they saw him, were uneducated and many of them superstitious. Even if one is to admit that he did appear at all, some of the reports have to be dismissed as false. To this day any unidentified figure seen in the distance, or in the dusk, in the neighbourhood of The Garrison is described as "Owld Burnaby's ghost"—and one or two people claim to have seen Marcus's ghost also. It is generally believed that for years the two of them had been trafficking with the Devil.

As I have said however there is corroborative evidence, though it is only circumstantial. There are a considerable number of entries in Mr. Burnaby's journal after Mr. Burnaby's death. They extend from the date of Marcus's return to The Garrison to within ten days or so of the presumed date of Marcus's death.

Though the handwriting and style are Mr. Burnaby's I have no doubt whatever that physically they were made by Marcus. At the same time I do not think they are forgeries. Marcus was not sufficiently clever to have forged them. I imagine that their only purpose was that the style and the handwriting *should* be noticed. They are concerned chiefly with Marcus. There is no description of any sort of other-worldly existence. I will give a few examples.

Sept. 10, 1935. Marcus of course is unhappy. He is divided, and he knows that neither of the courses before him can give him any feeling of contentment. He has a sense of futility in all that he does. He cannot have any illusion of acting under the direction of his own will. The gratification produced by personal achievement is impossible for him.

This afternoon he bathed—a very listless performance. The bathe, however, produced hunger and he enjoyed his tea. His youthfulness still emerges in moments of forgetfulness. Afterwards he was as morose as ever. Writing his book in the evening helped him a little.

Dec. 25, 1936. To all lonely people, to all except children and those surrounded by children or young people, this is the most melancholy day of the year. Marcus is counting the days till the summer. It is only the consciousness that he cannot go outside his pattern which prevents him from killing himself now;—that and his physical fear of violence.

No human being will ever spend Christmas in this house again, but it will have other inhabitants—first insects, crumbling the boards, then birds flying in and out through the windows; for boys, too terrified to enter, will have broken the glass with stones. Rain will get in, and damp will rot. Rust will eat into the hinges and the wind will break down the doors—and in fifty years there will be rabbit burrows in the hall.

April 2nd, 1937. Only Black is imperturbable. He is too unimaginative to be frightened: yet there is a great deal of value in him. What a pity that Marcus has not his strength of character. If he had, so much might have been accomplished. Both he and Mr. Burnaby have been failures. Yet they will have served their purpose in showing a little of what success will be *almi patri De Laura Lee moter poter vobiscum.*

The last seven words are in an unknown hand. I can't explain them, except as the work of a mischievous spirit. There are several similar insertions in this post-mortem part of Mr. Burnaby's journal.

May 12th, 1937. Poor Marcus. It is nearly over now. I shall be glad when it is finished.

Leaving out the gibberish passages, which I believe are unimportant, what strikes me about these entries is a quality in the personality of Mr. Burnaby. Sometimes he is just Mr. Burnaby; sometimes he is someone more, someone who is Burnaby and yet contains him and looks at him from the outside.

It may be wondered that during this period of almost two years from his last departure from home, Mr. and Mrs. Brownlow never came to see Marcus. They ought to have done so and ever since they have regretted not having intervened. All the same anyone who has read Marcus's letters to his mother will understand why they did not come. They are cold, unkind, and hostile. Yet with an after-knowledge of the facts they are pardonable and rather tragic. With one part of him Marcus would have liked them to come: at the same time he was afraid of them—and he knew they were not going to come. The letters he wrote seem in a way to have been dictated to him. Three times he invited them—for Christmas 1935, for September 1936 and again for Christmas 1936. He had never any intention of allowing these visits to take place. They were always put off by a telegram at the last moment, announcing that Marcus had been called away, once to London, once to Dublin and the third time, by a flight of fancy, to Paris. Of course he didn't go away at all. Mr. and Mrs. Brownlow were hurt. They could not help feeling that Marcus had become a very unpleasant person. Yet they both had a strong sense of duty. They were uneasy and they decided that they *must* see him.

Mr. Brownlow was in serious trouble with his business. He was getting old and he had come out of the slump badly. Otherwise no doubt he would have acted earlier and more vigorously. In February 1937 he and Mrs. Brownlow fixed a definite date for an unannounced visit. It was to be on the second Saturday of the month. On the Friday they received a letter from Marcus. "I am off again," he wrote. "I don't know how long I shall be away, but I want you to come and stay at the end of May. I shall be back then and this time I promise there will be no putting off."

So of course they didn't go. They looked forward to May hopefully, but not very confidently. They didn't expect to enjoy their visit, but surely he wouldn't put them off again. He didn't, but this letter written with a complete foreknowledge of the facts was surely the most cruel.

Black had left with the intention of getting in touch with the Brownlows as soon as he arrived in Belfast. For all his stolidity he had worried about Marcus. Unfortunately when he arrived at the Great Northern terminus he was met by his sister-in-law with the news that his wife was seriously ill. For the next ten days he was too occupied with his own troubles to think about Marcus. On the eighteenth of May he read in a newspaper that Marcus had disappeared and was believed to have been drowned. Two months later Marcus's body was found on a lonely little beach near the point. How long it had been there nobody could say for certain.

CHAPTER XXXV

I DO not know if it can be said that Marcus drowned himself. I think it is certain that he foresaw his death and the manner of it and that he met it deliberately. Why he had to die is perhaps not quite clear. All I can offer are the conjectures I have made from the evidence available.

In the first place I think Marcus knew, before Mr. Burnaby died, the rough outline of the rest of his own life. I don't suppose he knew every detail; he may have seen every detail in advance, but probably he only remembered certain incidents and in particular the incident of his own death. I don't know why he went home or why he returned to The Garrison when he did. Probably it was one of the things which he knew he would do: it was part of the plan, which he could not alter in any way.

I accept the theory that we are all parts of a whole, that this whole has a consciousness of the whole of itself. I believe too that when we die our own individual consciousness may not be immediately absorbed into the total consciousness. In the case of Mr. Burnaby this absorption was very slow. He remained, though in touch with the whole, sufficiently himself to direct Marcus, to govern him. Indeed he inserted himself into Marcus, not ousting Marcus's own individuality completely, but leaving him a resentful junior partner in himself. Sometimes he was no more than an unwanted companion, visibly present, not only to Marcus, but to others: sometimes when it suited his purpose better he entered into Marcus and took complete control. It was then that he made the entries in Marcus's journal: then that he was seen by Kate, by Mrs. Mullan, and by Black, when he encountered what was half Marcus, half Mr. Burnaby on the drive.

While Mr. Burnaby was alive there had always been times when Marcus could escape from him into his own individuality. If my assumptions are to be accepted, there can have been no such escapes after Mr. Burnaby died. If Marcus were to live on it could only be as a continuation of Mr. Burnaby. He had no hope of ever again being entirely himself.

Marcus's interest in the work he did with Mr. Burnaby had been partly curious, partly a reflection of Mr. Burnaby's own interest. By the time Mr. Burnaby died his curiosity was satisfied. He knew all he could ever know; and he had not Mr. Burnaby's sense of Mission. He was haunted and oppressed, and would be so, wherever he went, whatever he did, for as long as he remained alive. By dying he must have hoped to merge himself completely in the whole. Perhaps however this may not have been so easy. Perhaps he lingered on, an unwilling ghost on that barren, haunted shore.

I think we have to assume that the whole is God. That the whole is God, is to say that everything, every one of us, every beast, every bird, every flower, every stone, is God too. We might go further and suppose that there is a purpose in all that is done. That purpose may be to make every part conscious of its identity with the whole, to make every part share continually in the consciousness of God and of being God.

The fulfillment of such a purpose must seem so remote as to be almost without interest. It seemed so to Marcus. He had neither the will nor the desire to increase the importance of his contribution to its accomplishment. Death was before him in any case: for him death must be better than life. So he died—not sooner or later, but when he knew he had to die.